PRAISE F(

CU01510864

A Thousanc

"Readers will enjoy the rich lore."

—*Publishers Weekly*

"Cato's latest is an intriguing story filled with gods, magic, and enough culinary references to please any fan of epicurean magic."

—*Library Journal*

"The characters and action of *A Thousand Recipes for Revenge* are exciting and compelling. Cato has a gift for plot twists and suspense that bring the cast of characters and their world to vivid life and make it difficult to put her book down. The ending will have readers craving a sequel."

—*Booklist*

"*A Thousand Recipes for Revenge* takes the reader on a thrilling journey to a place where every alley has surprises and every character has secrets. Beth Cato has created a wondrous feast of delights, astonishing and yet, somehow, utterly believable. Every sentence made me smile, or gasp, or fall a little more in love with Ada and Solenn and their world."

—Kate Heartfield, author of *The Embroidered Book*

"Both deliciously political and politically delicious, Beth Cato's *A Thousand Recipes for Revenge* will have you tasting magic!"

—Juliette Wade, author of *Mazes of Power*

"Food magic! *A Thousand Recipes for Revenge* brings epic fantasy tropes to the table and serves them up with zesty new magic in the form of magical foods. It gives you the gods of food you never knew you wanted along with fast-paced adventure, intriguing characters, and the black market in epicurea. Beth's love of baking and of cheese shine through on almost every page. By turns delightful and serious, the novel will both make you hungry and fill you up. Chef's kiss!"

—Lisbeth Campbell, author of *The Vanished Queen*

A Feast for Starving Stone

"Fantasy readers will enjoy Cato's characters and her original, sensuous world."

—*Booklist*

"The sequel to *A Thousand Recipes for Revenge* is an intriguing intersection of culinary magic and political machinations."

—*Library Journal*

A
HOUSE
BETWEEN
SEA AND
SKY

ALSO BY BETH CATO

The Clockwork Dagger Series

The Clockwork Dagger

The Clockwork Crown

Deep Roots

The Blood of Earth Trilogy

Breath of Earth

Call of Fire

Roar of Sky

The Chefs of the Five Gods Series

A Thousand Recipes for Revenge

A Feast for Starving Stone

A
HOUSE
BETWEEN
SEA AND
SKY

A NOVEL

BETH CATO

Published by 47North, Seattle

www.apub.com

Amazon, the Amazon logo, and 47North are trademarks of Amazon.com, Inc., or its affiliates.

EU product safety contact:
Amazon Media EU S. à r.l.
38, avenue John F. Kennedy, L-1855 Luxembourg
amazonpublishing-gpsr@amazon.com

ISBN-13: 9781662527760 (paperback)
ISBN-13: 9781662527777 (digital)

Cover design by Philip Pascuzzo
Cover illustration © Pepco Studio
Cover image: © piola666, RLT_Images, Ryan Rad / Getty; © ma_rish / Shutterstock

Printed in the United States of America

To the librarians. Keep fighting the good fight.

A NOTE FROM THE AUTHOR

This is a tale of found family and hope. Through darkness shines light. You are not alone. If you or a loved one are in need of help, please reach out to one of these organizations:

- The Trevor Project (Suicide Prevention for LGBTQ+ Young People)
  Visit https://thetrevorproject.org/, call 1-866-488-7386, or text *START* to 678-678.
- The 988 Suicide and Crisis Lifeline
  Visit https://988lifeline.org/ or dial 988 to speak with someone today.

Chapter 1

Fayette Wynne unpacked deuced Mother. Mother was not to be confused with Ma, who had now been dead about a week and rested in a grave alongside two of her children. No, much to Fayette's intense vexation, Mother was alive and bubbling. Ripe for use.

She vigorously shook the tall, wide glass free from its swaddling, a pilling green cardigan. The clear curves showed the jar to be about a third full of viscous sourdough starter. Setting it on the battered kitchen table, she popped open the lid. She grimaced, and not because it stank—no, the contents had the distinct moist, clean smell of rye and other flours.

"There. Your home is open again, Mother," growled Fayette. "I figure I should thank you for not exploding through the lid and overflowing into my belongings. That's the least you could do."

Bread starters had long been called "mothers" because of the way they could be divided to perpetuate new starters and create bready goods, but this was no common starter. No, this was *Mother*. Fayette's skin prickled as though the temperature had shifted; that meant Mother was focusing on her. She shook her head as she turned away.

She'd had half a mind to leave the jar behind in Hollywood, but her vindictive urge had been squelched by the knowledge that Ma would've been horrified that Fayette had even considered such a thing. "Mother is our responsibility, our blessing," Ma had said, time and again.

Mother was also their burden, their obligation, their inefficient handful of manna from heaven.

Because of Mother's ethereal inadequacies, the rest of Fayette's family was dead. She was alone.

With stomping steps, she carried her suitcase into the cottage's singular bedroom and returned to the entry to unpack her more pleasant priority: her Corona 3 typewriter.

She set it up on a rectangular table in the parlor, below a window; a peek through the blinds confirmed a view of the darkened garden, with deep-gray clouds above. Maybe, if she was lucky, she would have a glimpse of the ocean in daylight. In any case, she was pleased. This was a fine workspace. If muses existed, this was where she would trap them.

For the first time in weeks—no, months—she was excited to write. This trip to Carmel-by-the-Sea meant a fresh start. A new phase of her life. She'd get her overdue continuity done. She'd enjoy the pretty views, enjoy time away from the house she loved, which persisted in stinking of slow, stale death.

But she wasn't going to think about that right now, oh no, she would not. She'd shove those thoughts away like the thick wad of doctors' bills with their circled due dates.

Fayette made a fuss of arranging her compact Corona just so. Some of the most-used keys featured faint letters, but she could've typed with confidence even if blindfolded. She knew the distinct click-clack sound each one made, how the hinges bounced beneath her fingertips. On the left side, she placed a stack of clean pages; to the right, her completed set. The blank sheets far outnumbered the typed ones. That would change. It must. Her job depended on it.

Someone knocked at the door.

She turned and paused, the hot prickles of Mother's attention reminding her that she was not alone in the house.

She approached to lightly drop the customary red-checkered cloth over the top. That'd allow the starter space to breathe while keeping out bugs. After a second of hesitation, she also moved the jar to rest against the glass of a shaded kitchen window. The coolness would discourage growth.

"I'm coming!" she called, hurrying to the door.

On the other side, she found a woman more bone than flesh, her skin a sallow brown. A careworn drop-waisted frock draped from her shoulders like clothes on a hanger. By the weary intensity in her gaze, the woman could be anywhere from thirty-five to sixty, but Fayette guessed her to be nearer the low end of that spectrum. Younger than her, most likely.

Almost hidden behind her was another woman. She was scarcely over five feet tall. A modest lace kerchief held her blond-brown hair away from her face. She looked to be in her mid-twenties, her pale cheeks rosily glowing as she smiled.

The woman in front didn't smile. The lines in her face had all the rigidness of oak bark. She wore her thin black hair pinned atop her head, the late Victorian style reminiscent of a limp pillow.

"You're Fayette Wynne?" she asked in a brusque tone. At Fayette's nod, she continued: "I am Mrs. Fitz. I apologize that we were occupied and couldn't answer your knock. I trust the house meets your needs?"

"It does." The place was austere, but she couldn't afford fancy. The coins in her pocket weren't making much music these days. "Thank you for leaving the note by the door."

The slip of paper had encouraged her to make herself comfortable in Grangeville Cottage, while reminding her of the rules Mrs. Fitz had laid out in their phone call days before: No male guests. No parties. No illegal enterprises.

The latter point had made Fayette desperately curious whether someone had actually tried to rent the place to set up a distillery in violation of Prohibition, but Mrs. Fitz's glower didn't make her appear receptive to nosy questions.

"If any violations occur, I'll know," Mrs. Fitz said with grave menace. "I'm ten feet away." She gestured to the nearby back door.

"The only noises you'll hear are my typewriter and me grumbling to myself as I work." Fayette's light words garnered no smile from Mrs. Fitz, but the woman behind her quietly giggled with a hand to her mouth. As young and as ready for levity as the woman appeared, Fayette recognized an intensity to her gaze that indicated both intelligence and years hard lived.

Mrs. Fitz followed Fayette's line of sight and nodded to the woman in her shadow. "This is Heidi. She's my hired helper. She cannot speak, but she can write when she's so inclined."

"Nice to meet you, Heidi," Fayette said. "I don't always want to write, either, but it's my job, so I must muddle through."

Again, Heidi's round cheeks seemed to glow with amusement, while Mrs. Fitz looked impossibly more sour. "That's right—you're a movie writer. I expect you to be on good behavior."

"You'll find I'm a delightfully boring individual, Mrs. Fitz." She paused, hearing a distant rumble of thunder. "I don't suppose you have some candles in the house in case the electricity goes? The power back home seems to fail if anyone yawns in the proximity of a live wire." She smiled to cover up her twinge of anxiety.

"Yes, there are candles and matches." Mrs. Fitz turned, frowning up at the clouds. "I must go home. Heidi?"

The younger woman stepped forward with an enthusiastic nod. She made a shooing motion at Mrs. Fitz, causing the older woman's expression to soften for the first time.

"Thank you both. I'd hoped to get here while it was still daylight, but my bus decided to get a flat tire about every two hours." Fayette had scarcely spoken over the course of the day, and now the words kept rolling like a boulder down a steep slope. "The flats kept a far more consistent schedule than the bus itself. I'm glad I brought some Cream of Wheat packets for meals. Any grocers are bound to be shut by now since it's Sunday. I'll need to shop tomorrow."

She'd packed two peanut butter sandwiches for the trip and polished off the second one hours ago, as her stomach cruelly reminded her at that very moment. She was actually surprised to find herself feeling hungry. Sadness had filled Fayette's gut to the brim, dense as gravel. There hadn't been room for much else.

"I don't think we have any grocers open on Sunday. This isn't Los Angeles." The words were chiding, but Mrs. Fitz's tone was gentler. "Heidi will make certain you're ready for the weather tonight." At that, she whirled away.

Fayette stood back to let Heidi through the door. She stepped across the threshold and stopped dead in her tracks. Fayette had started to swing the door shut and blocked it with her shoulder. Heidi didn't seem to notice the door's loud thud as she stared ahead with pale-faced dread.

"Are you all right? What, did you see a ghost?" She'd never encountered such entities herself, but they weren't uncommon. Besides, as a person raised in the company of a preternatural sourdough starter, she retained an open mind when it came to encounters with the unusual.

Heidi shook her head as she emerged from her reverie, but the smile that fell into place was rigid, like that of her employer. She motioned for Fayette to follow her.

What had that been about? The woman had looked like she'd met Medusa's stony gaze, and all Heidi had done was step inside a house she probably knew as well as her own.

Heidi stopped at a hallway closet. The bulbs from the nearby rooms didn't cast light in that direction, causing Heidi to fumble beneath shelves of linens to pull out a crate with a peeling label for an orange company out of Tulare. Inside were candles of various sizes and other supplies. Fayette tested a flashlight. The beam arced over the distant dining room table and glanced upon Mother's jar with its red-checkered hat. Fayette promptly shut the light off and turned to face Heidi, only to see her still staring toward the kitchen.

"I feel better with these items handy. I'm not fond of storms," Fayette said with a shrug.

When she was little, her brother, Thayer, used to act as her refuge when storms blew through. He'd create a cave with a quilt flung over his head and beckon her beneath. She'd crouch in darkness that didn't feel so dark with his presence, his body warmth a comfort even if it was a hot summer day. Thayer would then talk to her about most anything to distract her. Often he'd retell a book he'd read—he had Jules Verne's and Edgar Allan Poe's works practically memorized by the time he was ten. Or he'd elaborate on a baseball game he'd played in, or describe how machinery worked in ways that were almost understandable.

When she was too big to hunker under a quilt with him, he'd come check on her, especially when a storm passed in the night. He'd continued that practice through his final months of life, even though their red heads were starting to lighten to silver. To her mind, her big brother's shuffling steps and the ever-so-quiet way he leaned over her to ask "Fayette, how're you doing?" made him her guardian angel.

But Thayer was dead and gone, along with Briar and Ma. Fayette was forty-five, with no kin left in this world, every ounce of her an orphan.

She had been holding up well today, she thought. Hadn't cried once, even though the bus ride had provided her thoughts an unpleasant amount of time and space to rove. But now grief had sneaked up behind her and smacked her in the skull like a Louisville Slugger.

A fast rat-a-tat knock shuddered through the front door. Fayette blinked to form a dam against her tears as she moved forward. "Who can that be?" she asked, profoundly relieved by the interruption. Heidi padded behind her.

She found Mrs. Fitz at the door, a cloth-covered plate in her hand. "Here." She thrust the plate at Fayette with all the menace of a robber with a gun. "We had spinach quiche tonight. There's bread, too. I heated them, as the cottage you're in only has a hot plate. Heidi made the full supper, but bread is her particular specialty." Pride came through her words.

There was no refusing this meal. Fayette hurriedly set the flashlight down on a nearby side table and took the dish, the tears in her eyes now from gratitude. "Why, thank you. You didn't have to do this."

Thunder growled, louder than before, accompanied by small flashes that reminded Fayette of the fireflies of her Arkansas youth.

Mrs. Fitz continued as if Fayette hadn't said a thing. "Put the plate and cloth in the cupboard when you're done. They won't match anything else. We'll fetch them later. Come along, Heidi."

Heidi's expression was pensive as she passed by. Whatever had shaken her hadn't let go.

The wind whistled through the gap between the small houses, threatening to dash away with the cloth over her meal. Fayette ducked inside.

She sat down to eat at a round table marked with heavy gouges as if it'd been used as a shield in a medieval battle. The single chair faced Mother. She adjusted the angle, but Mother continued to loom over her shoulder. To radiate.

Ma had always regarded Mother as divine. Fayette thought of the sourdough starter as magical, because that's how her brain churned. When she saw motes of light, after all, she first thought of fairies, not God's glory. Oh, how she and Ma used to argue on this topic! Magic wasn't everywhere, Ma would fuss, but God was. Fayette didn't think the two should necessarily be separate. There was no debating, however, that an extra sparkle to the world was a special thing. A normal person might see a unicorn or encounter a genuine witch perhaps a time or two in life, if they were lucky—or unlucky, depending on how those meetings went.

Mother was special, all right. And especially frustrating.

With spiteful delight, Fayette bit into the wedge of bread round. The crust crunched with a small shower of crumbs. Butter had been freshly melted into the pale, hole-flecked center. The rich yellow fat gilded her tongue. Her moan wasn't simply a performance to exaggerate her joy before Mother—this bread was *good*. Heidi had the knack, which was a delightful surprise. More and more people bought bland bread from the store these days.

Mother's heat and power remained at a consistent hum, stoic in the face of Fayette's bold flaunt. Not like Mother had ever shown jealousy at other bread in the past, though, but it was hard to know how the sourdough starter felt about anything. She was simply there, a palpable presence, even as people lived and loved around her. Even as they died.

Fayette took another massive chomp, not caring about the crumbs. She'd clean them up later, or she wouldn't. There was no Ma to chastise her as if she were a small child making a big mess.

There was no Ma, and that was Mother's fault.

Fayette ate on, her meal flavored by salty tears.

Her cheeks dried and her gut unusually full, Fayette got to work.

Her hands shaking as thunder growled, she finished typing a line and expelled the page from the platen roller, setting the sheet atop her slender stack. She'd lit one candle as a precaution against power failure and set it on the sill above her workstation. Funny how she'd gone without electricity for most of her life, and now she could scarcely function without it. That candle provided some comfort, but it didn't change the fact that the weather illuminated her loneliness and worries like an arc light focused upon a set.

The greater comfort came through absorption in her story.

In her script for *The Mystery of the Shattered Book*, intrepid lead Dorothy "Dot" Baker was employed as a nurse for an ill rich aunt, utilizing skills she'd learned in service during the war. The old woman has just been found dead. The butler and doctor think she met a natural end. Dot is the only one who finds the circumstances suspicious, and persists in her belief even after she's laughed out of the police station when she attempts to report the crime.

Fayette started the fresh page with a close-up.

C.U. of Dot's determined face, her jaw set. She adjusts her cloche hat to rest at a jaunty angle atop her head.

SP: "I KNOW WHAT I'M TALKING ABOUT. IF THEY WON'T INVESTIGATE, I WILL!" (Fade out.)

Fayette was working off an initial draft called a one-line continuity, which in actuality broke scenes into one or two sentences. She'd fortunately finished it back in September, before Ma's health took a worse turn. She was slogging through the second continuity now, staging each scene and adding capital-letter dialogue and descriptions for the title cards. It usually took about three weeks to complete a five-reeler like this.

That meant, with steady progress, Fayette's stay in Carmel *should* enable her to finish her overdue continuity and also complete a one-liner for a movie coming up in spring 1927. She'd be caught up and, upon her return to in-studio work, stay caught up.

That thought was both comforting and horrible. She wanted to be back in her familiar domain—but was it truly home anymore?

No, no. She had to focus on work, not think about her Gower Street house and how everything there and everywhere around would feel strange and empty. She was making good progress tonight, more than she'd done in weeks.

A quick reread of what she'd just typed immersed her in the narrative again. The keys resumed a mechanical symphony.

Two pages later, having gotten Dot through a suspenseful snooping foray in a law office, Fayette's work came to a screeching halt.

Her notes told her what to do, but her fingers didn't want to budge. Exhaustion wasn't the reason, either, though by all logic, she should've been tired by this hour. She'd only dozed a few times on the bus. Instead, her brain sparked as if she'd guzzled down a pot of coffee.

That's when she realized the weather outside had gone absolutely quiet.

Beth Cato

She stood to better peer out the window. She saw only blackness through the slats.

If the storm had stopped, that meant she could take a walk. But was that a wise thing to do, in the dark, on slick surfaces in a strange place? No, it was not. Even so, increasing restlessness seemed to swim through her, demanding movement, and she knew why.

For the past month, this had been the one time of day when Ma had usually managed brief, genuine sleep and Fayette had been free to walk outside after endless hours at her bedside. One of her neighbors—usually Luis—would come sit on the porch by Ma's open window to listen and beckon Fayette to hustle faster down the block if she awakened early.

The reason the neighbors had stayed outside was simple: Ma hadn't wanted anyone other than Fayette and the doctors to see her wasted condition near the end. She had her pride. She had no idea, though, how much of a burden that restriction would place on Fayette alone.

Fayette had felt like she could truly breathe on those walks. Her world had become small, a box of a room, and that limited time outside reminded her that other people still existed and stars continued to sparkle in the heavens.

She could use some sparkle about now, even if it was playing peekaboo with the clouds.

She threw on her wool coat and, grabbing the flashlight still sitting by the door, headed out.

Her flashlight cast a broad beam on the packed-mud street. The Fitz property formed the very end of the neighborhood. Gramophone strains of "Yes! We Have No Bananas" carried from one of the nearby houses. To the south, darkness found new depths, the clouds a turbulent swirl of black, gray, and purple. She headed that way. The paper map her pal April had given her had shown beach access in this direction.

The ocean hissed to her right, invisible yet close. She dodged a few downed branches in her way, then stopped. She experienced the sudden, intense sense that she was being watched. Even more, her skin prickled as it did when Mother focused upon her.

Fayette faced west, bringing up her flashlight to find a wall of bushes. Wax myrtles, she guessed, the evergreen branches like long bottle brushes arcing up from the base. The hot prickles intensified, reverberating through her body just as the thunder had a short time ago.

She had the rationale to realize she should be scared, being in the presence of something mighty. More than anything, though, she was curious. Fayette had never encountered anything of the same ilk as Mother.

She couldn't walk away from something that could very well be mythological-made-real. As a storyteller, she needed to know what tale she was in.

She found a gap in the bushes and pushed through, blinking away a spray of water droplets shed by the leaves.

A building loomed ahead in silhouette. No lights shone from it. She drew closer, intrigued. Knee-high vegetation batted at her skirt, and then she felt dense rock underfoot. Her light showed the slick, rounded dark rocks rising in a gentle slope to seemingly fuse with the different-colored pale rocks of the small log house's foundation. There couldn't have been much more than a single room inside. While it could be termed a cottage, it lacked the British-inspired feel that was the current fashion in the rest of Carmel. Was it Bavarian, perhaps? Polish? Whatever the style, she hadn't seen the like elsewhere in California, and she doubted her childhood had presented anything similar, either.

She spanned the light around. The ocean sounded very close, almost as if it was below her. She could see the door up ahead, but there were no stairs, no evident path. Reaching that door could be a dangerous trek on a wet night like this.

Something clattered on the rocks farther south. Fayette froze. Was there an animal out there? Better an animal than a person, she figured. Men were the worst creatures to unexpectedly meet in the dark. After a moment of thought, she turned off the flashlight. The heavy metal tube rested against her hip, a ready cudgel as she waited in place, listening.

Waves shushed and hushed with urgency, lightning flashing over the sea. That clattering sound carried from out on the rocks again, softer, more distant. If a person *was* out there on these slick rocks without a flashlight near the cliff, they were as zany as some barnstormer pilot. Maybe they were drunk, too. The illegal stuff people distilled these days could blind a person or addle their brains.

Someone might need her help.

In defiance of all common sense, she trod closer. She had walked some distance, the presence of the house no longer prickling at her back, when a flash of lightning revealed a tall human silhouette.

"Hello!" Fayette practically yodeled. "Who's out there?"

The wind brought a sudden lash of rain. She moved a little faster. Her left foot slid to lodge in a crevice for a smattering of seconds, but she regained her footing and continued.

"Hello!" she yelled into the wind. Her skirt rippled against her knees. "Do you need help?"

"No, I don't. Go back! It's dangerous out here." The voice was deep, and projected well against the rising storm. A distant flash showed a straight-edged male figure standing about fifteen feet away, looking downward. With a jolt, Fayette realized he stood at the precipice.

"You're one to talk! What do you think you're doing?" Even as she asked the question, she knew the answer.

He was here to kill himself.

"Please go back." His voice cracked. He faced her as another bolt zigzagged overhead. His illuminated face was ghost-pale and streaked wet. Short-cropped blond hair was plastered to his head. He lacked an overcoat. His dark suit had adhered to his body and gleamed with wetness.

"I'm not going anywhere without you." She stepped closer.

"I'm going to jump." He faced the water again.

"I'd rather you didn't."

He twisted in place to stare at her. The rapid-fire lightning made it easy to read the surprise in his face. Fayette imagined she looked pretty bedraggled, but she'd appear a lot worse fried by a bolt from the heavens. They really needed to get off this exposed cliff.

"Why do you say that?" he asked. "Why do you care?"

She thought of her brother, Thayer, and how she'd wished a thousand times over that she'd walked with him to the bus stop the day he died, as she had on so many other days when he'd lived, and that she'd seen the truck with its careening load and shoved him to safety.

And here was this stranger, ready to die. She didn't know him, but he just might have a sister who loved him, too.

Fayette didn't waste time with words. She jumped him.

She had a brief, dizzying view of thrashing white-capped waves below, and then she grappled him with both arms and jerked him backward. Her soles lost traction. Instead of dragging him off in a deft move, she hit the rocks hard, him atop her. Pain jarred her left shoulder. An agonized cry tore from her throat. The man grunted as well. He promptly pushed himself off her, rolling to one side, but she kept her right arm around him. The precipice, at least, was not behind him. He wasn't going to get away that easily.

"That didn't go as planned," she said, gasping. "Did you break anything?" She eased up onto her left elbow.

"No. But you—you're hurt—"

"I'm fine. Don't you dare go back toward—"

"You shouldn't have stopped me; you could have—"

"Maybe you should've thought of how other people could be hurt by your actions before you decided to teeter at the top of a cliff." Fayette spat rain from her mouth as it began to fall in torrents. "Do you have any family? Parents? Siblings?"

At those words, he slumped against her. "Yes. Both parents, and six younger brothers and sisters. But they—they don't understand . . ."

He *did* have a sister. *Sisters.* "Do they love you?" Grunting, she pushed herself up the rest of the way. Gravity was determined to keep her down, but it hadn't met her brand of stubborn.

Once standing upright, she wiped her hands on her coat. Both of her palms stung. She felt a different sort of discomfort, too—the loose waistband of her skirt was tenaciously hooked onto her hip bones. If she took more than a few steps, her skirt would likely fall off. Trying to be subtle, she tucked a hand into her coat to roll the waistband over twice, thickening it to make it stay put.

The man remained a lump at her feet. He looked up at her, his expression pained. She didn't know why his sodden figure looked so familiar.

"Yes. I'm loved." His murmur was almost lost against the din.

"Then cling to that love and be grateful. My only brother and sister are dead, and my mother joined them last week."

He jerked as if she'd kicked him. "I'm sorry."

Fayette extended a hand to him. "Then show proper gratitude by getting out of this storm with me. I feel like a wet dog."

His hand was broad, potentially strong, yet flaccid, and she held on to it as if he were a toddler prone to running toward traffic. His entire body seemed to be as pliable as an overcooked noodle. If she were of a mind to nudge him toward the cliff, he'd just flop over. Instead, she led him north. Her flashlight was gone, probably dashed to pieces on the cliff, but the just-visible gleams of Carmel's lights provided guidance. Not that they needed to make it that far. They needed only to escape the rain and cold. Needlelike water stung her exposed face and tortured her throbbing shoulder.

The man stumbled, but her strong grip kept him from falling. "Stay with me," she shouted. There before them was the peculiar cottage. That'd have to do.

Chapter 2

I am a house, but I am more than a house, and so I can smell, taste, hear, see, and feel. Oh, I can feel.

I smell blood against the tang of the ocean and the freshness of water from the sky. Blood is a liquid long familiar to me, one I have sipped and guzzled as circumstances required. Sometimes one drinks what one is given. It's polite. Also, blood is messy, and I cannot bear for it to linger upon my surfaces. I will *not* be stained.

Bolder than the blood, however, is the sweetness of desperation and need, especially from the woman. Her presence is strangely bright— really, her soul is brighter than that of most humans. She's known magic, this woman, and known it her entire life. I let her approach me earlier because I was curious in my grogginess. I've had little need to pay attention to the world these recent years, though I do maintain a distant awareness of my new witch. She remains tantalizingly close, but never close enough.

For a time, I feared she would run far away from me—people *do* often flee when they resist their life quest. Back in days of old, my witch would order me to intercept wayfarers, to force a confrontation, but I cannot move now.

I miss my witch. She welcomed me from the roost, replaced my head and body, granted me all-seeing eyes. She shaped my walls and first stoked my fire. She took care of me, and I of her. My witch was wonderful and brilliant. Oh, so brilliant! Those who came to my door—most always royalty of some sort, as my witch was vain about who she helped—could only survive and leave by utilizing their wits. They had no idea how much she admired them when she was defeated, how proud she was! Why, more than once she even feigned death so that they would truly feel as though they had vanquished her.

But my witch would not die so easily, no, no, no. But she *did* eventually die. I feel the weight of her bones even now, and they grieve me because I cannot dispose of them as I do wandering mice or spiders. They are *her* and should be treated with respect, but they still make me feel *dirty*.

She is dead, dead, dead, and my fire is also dead, and I am cold. I've known snow piled to my eaves, but even then I was warm inside. Cozy. I was *proud* of being cozy.

Those princes and princesses, they dared to cross my threshold as part of their valiant quests, but my own quest was simple.

To be a home.

I was a good home, I think. I hope.

The woman seasoned by magic is coming to my door. She is injured. There is a man with her. I have never been fond of men, as they so often sought to hurt my witch by swords, guns, and torches. Why, princes even dared to attack me in such ways a few times, but that never ended well for them, no.

Yet this man . . . he is no threat. He has fallen astray of his quest. Misery drenches his soul, as sure as rain soaks his body.

If my old witch were here, she wouldn't like these people. They are not of the motherland—and oh, she could smell from hundreds of yards if someone was of Rus. Nor are they royal. Those of such lineage carry a flavor all their own.

Actually, that was a major reason why my witch favored royalty. They tended to eat well, indulging in more meat and fat than common folk, and were delicious after a stint in my oven.

My witch would have ordered me to hide completely from this woman's sight. The whiff of ancient magic around her carries nothing of

Rus, and to my witch, that would have meant it was inherently inferior and to be regarded with disdain.

The ways of Rus are often superior, yes—and yet . . . and yet. My witch is dead. I am alone. Roosting. Immobile. This woman and man are on a quest. My witch is not here to deny them.

I am not their home, but I can be a refuge. I can, maybe, know the warmth of bodies and voices again, my hollowness less hollow.

I open my entry to them in invitation.

Chapter 3

Ahead of them, the front door of the strange cottage opened wide. The interior remained dark. No person was visible. Fayette balked. The man with her, blindly stumbling along as he was, staggered another step before she arrested his movement.

"Is someone there?" she called. Lightning boomed overhead.

"What is it?" the man asked, his head lifting.

"The door. It seemed to open on its own." Her hand squirmed against his, the friction stinging her cuts. This could be a trap. A dangerous place. An isolated, abandoned property like this could host a hooch brewery and people not inclined toward friendliness.

And yet this building was imbued with . . . something powerful. She couldn't ignore that. She counted haunted-house stories, fictional and nonfictional, among her favorites in books and magazines. If a door could open, it could also shut and stay shut, and God alone knew who or what might be there for company.

The prospects of this place were both terrifying and titillating.

Lightning cracked overhead, the flash and the rumble instantaneous. That motivated a fast decision.

"Okay," she said to herself. "Okay." She extracted her hand from that of the strange man. "We're going in. Be ready for anything."

Fayette formed two fists and approached the door. Her heartbeat pounded as intensely as the rain.

Absolute darkness lurked within. She leaned to look inside. There was a kind of foyer, about five feet long, and she saw another door beyond that. Against one wall was a bench, a series of hooks above. "Come inside." She beckoned to the man behind her. His hesitant footsteps echoed in the small space.

"It's like a foyer," he said, to which she nodded.

"Take a seat." She positioned him on the wooden bench as if he were a large doll. He was about the same height and weight as her, she estimated. If she'd been any less than six feet and not stout of build, she would've had a much harder time dragging him this far.

Fayette eyed the interior door. If someone else *was* in the building . . .

"Actually, get up again," she said to the man. When he only gazed at her blankly, she drew him to his feet with a tug at his armpit. *He* certainly wasn't a threat as her lone company in this foyer. She could knock him over with a breath, scatter him like dandelion seeds.

She hauled up the bench and moved it to block the door. Now it couldn't swing out. If a moonshiner decided they didn't want two strangers sheltering in the building after all, the blockade would slow them down and give Fayette and her companion adequate time to skedaddle.

"Let's sit on the floor." She let herself slide down the wall facing the open entrance, her bottom finding the wood-paneled floor with a somewhat squishy thump. She patted the spot beside her, farther from the door. After a second, the man joined her.

The view out the door showed wavering thick lines of rain brightened by near-constant flashes. No water seemed to be blowing inside, which was surprising. As much as she hated feeling exposed to the storm's energy, its power, she decided to keep the door open. For one, they needed the light. This chamber had no windows. Two, her actions of the past few minutes—this man in peril, the view of the violent waves, the frightening trek across the rocks—all seemed to catch up with her at once, leaving her as quivery as party aspic.

"Why'd you stop me?" The man's voice held a raw rasp. "You don't know me from Adam."

She eyed him. "I like you more than Adam. I hold no respect for a man who puts all the blame for his poor choices upon the woman, as if he isn't an adult in possession of his own mind." She stopped herself there, knowing well how she tended to ramble when she was anxious. "Your deep sadness is a familiar thing to me."

The house was listening to them. She knew it the way she used to sense Ma checking on her during the night, a presence leaning over her, breaths and feet silent but still obviously *there*.

Maybe no one else was in the house at all. Maybe the place itself had invited them in.

Maybe she would prefer to meet a moody bootlegger after all.

"If you understand, then why do you want me to continue suffering?" the man asked.

"I don't want you to keep on suffering, though I'm well aware life delivers that in plenty. But I do know that as much as *I'm* hurting right now, things will eventually get better. Wounds turn to scars."

"'Wounds turn to scars,'" he echoed with soft thoughtfulness.

A prolonged flash of lightning made his face glow as if he stood beneath an arc light. In that instant, she recognized him.

"You're Rex Hallstrom," Fayette said, her voice level. His recent role had been in an elaborate Russian historical piece, one of the last movies she'd seen back in the summertime.

He released a long sigh. "I'm in no mood to pretend otherwise. Yes. I'm Rex Hallstrom."

"Don't worry, I'm not going to ask for your autograph. I'm in the business, too—I'm a scenarist at Astrophel Studios. You won't have heard of it. It's over on Poverty Row." She kept her voice light to indicate she'd take no offense at his ignorance.

The two worked in the same town, but they might as well have been on opposite sides of the planet. Rex Hallstrom knew the studios farther west in Hollywood. She sometimes walked down that way, too, just to ogle alongside the other tourists, to pass by Warner Bros. with its white pillars and expansive lawns, and United Artists, ruled by married Tinsel Town royalty Mary Pickford and Douglas Fairbanks.

In stark contrast, her familiar habitat was found amid a cluster of pseudo-Spanish-style baroque buildings east of Gower Street. Fayette had a deep fondness and nostalgia for the area, even though she knew established actors regarded it with horror—going from the big time to Poverty Row was like a plummet from heaven into an outer ring of hell.

Rex, to his credit, didn't recoil from her as if she were a leper. "You're right, I don't know about Astrophel. What kind of pictures do they put out?" He sounded not only friendly but also genuinely interested.

"Dramas and serial comedies, mostly. I've been there nine years now." Her work felt like an inane topic, but she welcomed the distraction. He probably did as well. "An older fellow named Peacock bought Astrophel this summer. He sells automobiles back in Pennsylvania. His whole family's now learning the moviemaking business."

"Ugh. I'm sorry. That sounds decidedly unpleasant."

"Like getting a painful tooth extracted every day, and the bad tooth keeps growing back," she said perkily.

He laughed. "That's worse than anything Sisyphus went through."

That was the truth. The new owner's son, Mr. Peacock the Younger, had come on as a producer; his talents included smoking cigars most every waking minute and leering at the younger women on set. Fayette hadn't suffered from the latter attention. He had instead dubbed her "the Spinster" and even addressed notes to her using that moniker. He thought it was a travesty for any woman over twenty to be unmarried and employed. The "fairer sex"—in his words—"should be devoted mothers and homemakers, as God intended."

When she'd started out at Astrophel, there'd been many women on staff, and half the crew had consisted of fresh immigrants with thick accents and bright dreams. There'd been ogling and blather around them, sure, but the overall mood was positive. They were all involved in an industry in its infancy. It was *exciting*.

Things were different now. Movies were clearly here to stay. There was money to be made, and certain people were there to make it.

"My bosses gave me leave to take care of my mother as she died. I promised I'd continue to work from home. That didn't happen." Fayette shook her head, guffawing at the ridiculousness of her vow, at how she was spilling her woes out to this stranger who made more in a week than she made in months, maybe even a year. "My continuity is now way overdue. I'm here in Carmel to finish that up, away from all distractions. Yet here I am." She limply gestured around them.

"Ah, the lengths a writer will go to in order to procrastinate. I suppose I'm not so different in doing things I ought not, though." His head cocked to one side. "I'm supposed to be getting married right now."

"Ah." Fayette paused to take that in. "I take it that this relationship's not going so well."

"Nope." Rex closed his eyes as he leaned against the wall. She tried to summon to mind any fresh Hollywood gossip about him, but she'd barely seen the California sun, much less taken in the studio jabber. All she knew was his face, a few of his films, and that his reputation as an actor rightly built him up as the next Douglas Fairbanks or Rudolph Valentino. She hoped he fared better than the latter. Even as isolated as Fayette had been of late, she knew about Valentino's horrible death and the mourning that surrounded him still.

Fayette studied the gouges and cuts on her hands. The bleeding had stopped. Her shoulder continued to throb. If it pained her tomorrow, she may need to bake bread from Mother after all. That dependence on Mother irritated her, though she knew she should be grateful. She'd never had to buy treatments for minor aches and pains—not with Mother around.

When she glanced at Rex next, she found he was studying her, his expression unreadable. "Are you of sound mind to stay away from the cliff or other points of peril tonight?" she asked.

"All my gumption went into walking up to the cliff. I think I'll have a hard time doing much of anything tonight."

His slumped shoulders indicated exhaustion, but she didn't trust him any more than she would a sleepy cat at a fishmonger's stall. "Do you have a gun or access to one?"

"If I had, I wouldn't be sitting here now." That carried a ring of truth. "Carmel seemed like a fine place to do the deed, you know? There's a history of suicides among the Bohemians here." That famed group of artists had begun to congregate in Carmel after the 1906 San Francisco earthquake and fire. There couldn't be many of them left by now.

"Suicide is nothing to glorify," she snapped.

"I'm sorry." Rex seemed to be apologizing for upsetting her.

"You should be." She paused, flinching as lightning cracked overhead. "Death is horrible to endure, and it's horrible for those who've lost someone they love. Think beyond yourself."

His laugh was as sharp and bitter as a spoonful of lemon zest. "I never stop doing that. I often wonder if wanting to be who I am is asking too much of the world. No matter what I do, I can't win."

"Fie on the world and what it wants," Fayette said with blatant scorn, then sighed. "I'm sorry. My grief is muddled with rage, and I shouldn't take that out on you. I can't imagine it helps you one bit to be called selfish or anything else. It's not right for me to define you or how you feel. Or for the world to do so." Her tone was soft.

His smile was thin. "I'm an actor. What the world wants defines who I am."

She shook her head, loose tendrils of her drying hair slapping her cheeks. "Maybe you should define yourself for a change."

"I don't know how," he said in a bare whisper.

"I have a dictionary you can borrow. A thesaurus, too."

He stared at her a moment before snorting. Fayette had the odd sense that she'd just grappled him from a cliff a second time. "You're a bear cat of a gal, aren't you? I don't even know your name."

"Fayette Wynne." She stuck out her right hand.

"Allow me to introduce myself properly. I'm Rex Hallstrom." They shook hands. Unlike before, this time his grip was firm and strong.

⊷❈⊱

The rain ceased with a hush as the wind continued a stubborn howl. Fayette used the log wall at her back to help her stand. Keeping her body rigid seemed to reduce the agony in her shoulder. "We'd best hustle into town during this break in the storm."

Rex began to rise, but then squatted down again to pat at the floor. "That's odd."

"What?" With the lightning absent, it was even harder to see. She took advantage of the poor light, and his distraction, to adjust her skirt once more. She probably needed to take in the waist again. Good thing she had her sewing kit in her luggage. Never in her life had she tried to be stylish, but if she didn't stop losing weight, her clothes would soon be unacceptably frumpy.

"There should be a puddle here. We were sopping wet." His fingers palpated the wall. "There's no moisture at all. The floor feels even, too. I don't think the water drained away."

Fayette had that sense again that they weren't alone. "Did you . . . notice anything peculiar about this house?"

"What, beyond that it's dark and vacant? Perhaps haunted, as it was so nice as to let us in all on its own?" His tone was light, but thoughtful rather than mocking. "To look at the matter rationally, most any dark place will seem creepy in such weather. I can't help but wonder if this is a magical sort of house, though. I never thought I'd encounter such a thing myself. I saw a wolfman from a distance once when I was in my teens, out visiting cousins near Milwaukee. I thought I'd met my lifelong quota for encountering the extraordinary."

"Finding special creatures or items *is* supposed to be incredibly rare." She hoped her purposefully vague statement didn't come across as fishy, but he showed no outward reaction. Good. She didn't want to invite questions about her own personal experiences. She'd been raised from an early age to keep Mother's abilities secret.

As soon as they stepped outside, the door quietly closed behind them. Fayette and Rex looked back, then at each other.

"Do you suppose there's a trigger buried in the ground here, to open and close the door hands-free?" Rex asked.

"I don't think even Harold Lloyd's gagmen could contrive that kind of trick in solid rock like this." She tapped the surface with the toe of a shoe.

"This house . . . it really is something special, isn't it?" He sounded wistful. Yearning, even.

"I think so, yes." She tried to reassure him with a smile. "A good kind of special."

"No argument there. This place was a true refuge in a storm. Maybe we should come back in daylight and have a better look around," Rex mused as they started walking. "We wouldn't go inside, of course. Just take in the appearance of the property."

"I'd be game for that." The peril of this mysterious house didn't seem so terrible if someone was willing to investigate with her.

They passed by the Fitzes' property. Rex was leading the way, lost in thought, and she let him. The streets were dark, lacking any light but for that cast from porches and windows. Were his thoughts dark to match? She couldn't help but worry about him.

"Listen here, Rex. I'm going to ask you something without a single ounce of innuendo. Do you need company tonight, someone to talk to and make sure you're not a harm to yourself?" Puddles sloshed underfoot.

He gazed at her in surprise. His drying blond hair wavered in the wind. He truly was the epitome of an ideal man by Hollywood standards. Chiseled features, pale skin, blue eyes, thick brows. Pretty lips, just the right thickness. She knew she was a stark contrast to him in many ways. Tall for a woman, thickset, pasty in the way of redheads.

Even as a child, she'd been jeered at for looking "manly" because of her square jaw and big build. They made for an odd couple.

"'Without a single ounce of innuendo,'" he mused. "If some people said that, I wouldn't believe them, but you're a funny duck, Fayette Wynne. You would do that for me, would you?"

"Quack, quack," she said, deadpan. "Yes, I would. Now, answer me truthfully."

"I think I'll be okay now. I won't . . . try that again. Not tonight. Not in any way. Now, where are you staying? I should make sure you get back safely."

She pointed over her good shoulder with her thumb. "Way back that way."

"What? You should've said something!"

"Are we about to reach your place?"

"Well, yes, but you're injured because of me, and it's only—"

"Rex!" A woman flanked by two men emerged from the manicured shrubberies along the street. The men carried flashlights. Fayette grimaced as both beams spanned over her, dazzling her sight.

"Where've you been, Rex?" asked the woman. Through the spots, Fayette saw her advance with hands on her hips. Her short, blond hair curled over her ears and up from her jawline, a popular shingle bob, the top of her head crowned by a lacy white cloche. A white skirt swayed beneath the hem of a sleek black peacoat. Even though her expression was twisted in anger, she had to be among the prettiest women Fayette had ever encountered, and she'd encountered a lot of prettiness in her line of work. "We've looked all over for you!"

"I'm sorry, Margaret. I needed to get away," Rex said in a contrite tone.

This Margaret had to be Rex's jilted bride.

Margaret whirled around to confront Fayette. "And you! Who're you?"

"Is ol' Rex providing you business tonight?" asked the man in the tweed cap, chortling.

Fayette hesitated a moment to absorb the accusation, then burst out laughing. The three faces across from her went wide eyed in surprise. "I'm in the film industry as a scenarist. I should be plying *that* trade right now, actually, but I went for a walk and ended up sheltering from the storm with Rex here. He slipped a while ago and banged his head, so I needed to make sure he made it back to his place okay." Fayette didn't count herself as much of a liar—stories, to her way of thinking, held essential truths and weren't deceitful—so she was pleasantly surprised by how the falsehoods rolled off her tongue.

Both flashlights spanned over Rex's face and body. "My mug is fine," Rex snapped, flapping his hand as if to swat away the beams like flies.

"You shouldn't have gone out in that weather," said Margaret, wringing her hands. "You were so distraught. I was worried."

"Distraught!" The other man in the party, attired in a dark-blue pin-striped suit and black homburg, outright sneered. "He got no reason to be distraught, running out on a gal like you, all dolled up and ready to get hitched." He faced Fayette. "Yeah, yeah, Rex here was supposed to get married tonight, did you know that?"

"I'm not marrying. I can't go through with this deal," Rex said. *Deal?* He made it sound like a hooch-smuggling operation.

Margaret's blue eyes glistened with tears. "But, Rex, we both need— You oughta listen to reason!"

"No." Rex added weight to the word.

"Hey, now," said Tweed Hat. "She's trying to help you out."

"Maybe I don't need *your* sort of help." Rex had his dander up. "You had the audacity to accuse this woman with me, who has been nothing but genuinely kind and helpful, of being a ladybird, and you haven't even apologized to her."

Tweed Hat's mouth opened and closed. "Sorry," he muttered. Fayette had seen better acting from a cup of Ovaltine.

Margaret's painted lips pursed. Her face was without blemish, all rosiness and cream. "I'll apologize on my associate's behalf, Miss

Wynne. His insult was crude and wrong. You didn't deserve that, and neither did Rex." She came across as a good egg.

Homburg Man shook his head. "There still needs to be a wedding."

"'Needs'?" echoed Rex. His big fists were balled up and ready. He paced beside Fayette with the springy movements of an athlete. Anger had poured new life into him. "I told you before and I'll tell you again: The deal is off. I'm going into my cottage." He pointed to the other side of the bushes. "I'm going in alone. You all go get some shut-eye yourselves."

"There's always tomorrow," said Homburg Man, the threat of the words clear.

"No. No. There will be no wedding tomorrow, or the next day. You tell the papers I got cold feet. You'll probably get more press out of that than the actual wedding, you know?" The two hatted men shared a look as they seemed to consider that possibility. "You let Fayette here get home without issue, too. I won't have you dragging her into this morass. And, Margaret . . ." His brows curved in pain. "I'm sorry."

"Oh, Rex," Margaret wailed against her hands. Her grief rang as both real and contrived at the same time.

Fayette tabulated the hints and subtext. This whole affair reeked of the studio morality police.

The past few years, Hollywood had been pestered by an embarrassing series of scandals that made the industry out to be a newfangled Sodom and Gomorrah. The accusations of rape and manslaughter against Fatty Arbuckle had headed up the parade; William Desmond Taylor's murder had been another sensation. Smaller dramas had emerged, too, from paternity demands to public drunkenness to not-so-secret lavish orgies.

Studios needed to peddle their wares to the religious farmers of middle America. To ensure decency in their medium—or, at minimum, the appearance of it—the major studios had brought on a former US Postmaster General, one William Hays. The "Formula" that Hays had provided established moral guidelines for films going forward.

For over a year now, Fayette's continuities had to be read and approved by Hays's subordinates, a process she found annoying and, frankly, insulting. Actors were under worse scrutiny, though, because their very lives needed to meet an increasingly rising moral standard. That meant bodies needed to be buried deep, out-of-wedlock babies put up for adoption, and marriages made among near strangers.

The latter had to be what was happening here. Rex and Margaret were supposed to get hitched for publicity purposes, but Fayette was so out of touch, she couldn't guess why.

"We're going to tell the bosses," said Homburg Man, another threat as obvious as a bared knife.

"You do that." Rex sounded confident and chipper. "Good night, Margaret, Fayette." At that, he went through the nearby open white picket gate, closed it behind him, and vanished behind the wall of shrubberies.

At the click and thud of a door closing, the two hatted men shared a grim look. Afraid they'd try to drag Rex out again, Fayette sidestepped to stand between them and the gate. She folded her arms over her broad chest and considered them levelly. "Let me guess: You all work at the same studio?"

Tweed Hat took a step closer to her. The guy had to be half her age, but by the scars on his face, he'd lived a lot in that short span of time. Fayette raised her chin as she glared him down. She would not be cowed. Truth was, she felt more alive than she had in months. She hadn't been able to save Ma, but she had rescued someone else tonight, and that profound sense of usefulness seemed to have roused her soul.

"You need to keep your trap shut about all this. No going to the papers or nothing like that. Got it?" He sounded like a stock character in a gangster film. The stereotype had to come from somewhere, she supposed.

"I'm not on your studio's pay; you can't order me around."

They continued to glare each other down.

Homburg Man stepped closer. "We're asking for your discretion, that's all."

Fayette didn't budge. Tension lingered. Margaret looked between them, her expression puzzled. Finally, Tweed Hat stepped back with a sigh as he scratched his ear.

"Stubborn dame," he muttered.

Fayette chose to ignore that comment as she faced Homburg Man. "I'm so discreet, I won't even tell my own mother," she said, in absolute truth. After all, Ma was dead.

He grunted. "Good. Let's go back to the hotel. Come along, Miss Margaret." His tone turned kinder as he addressed her.

"I suppose there's nothing else to be done, is there?" Margaret sniffled.

When Fayette glanced over, she expected accusation or anger in her eyes, but instead, she recognized utter hopelessness. The same bleakness she'd seen on Rex's face not long ago.

Fayette opened her lips, wondering if she could do something to help Margaret, too, but the two men herded her away as if they were sheepdogs, Margaret the lamb.

Fayette shook her head to herself as she walked back toward Grangeville Cottage. What had she gotten herself into? She much preferred to keep the drama in her life confined to paper and screen.

Chapter 4

The warmth of people—living people—lingers inside me! It has been too long since I've heard voices echoed within my chambers, known the weight of footsteps, the cadence of voices. My new witch, she comes close to me sometimes, and whenever she does, I cannot help but stir awake as I wonder if this is it, if this is when she'll embrace her quest, when she'll accept *me*.

But she hasn't. I don't know if she ever will.

The woman and man, though, they were appreciative of my help! They even noticed that I siphoned the rain away from their bodies. They didn't observe that I pulled away the blood they shed, too, but it wasn't that much, really. Human bodies hold a lot, and you don't realize how much until it's spilled all over the floor!

They spoke as if they would visit me again. I want them to, even as I feel guilty for my yearning, because my witch would say I was tainted. I'm not, though! I was clean when I welcomed them, and I'm clean now—but I can be cleaner, I think. Humans love a pristine house, especially if they do not need to do the work. I made sure to keep myself tidy for my witch, but if some duke or duchess or other royal arrived on a quest, she would have me refrain from work or even purposefully soil myself so that they could engage in cleaning instead.

I never told her this because she was my witch, but I *hated* making myself dirty. My floorboards would *itch*. Even more, I would sometimes need to stay like that for hours and hours as the person did whatever test she'd arranged, like separating grains of wheat by color or making a broom of all-straight straws. Even if someone did a decent job on a cleaning task, I do better because I understand my nooks and crannies. I can feel a single grain in a crevice or the cat hair that fell from their clothes.

Sometimes, if the people created a huge mess, I'd tip my body to pour their filth from my windows and doors.

I cannot do that now, though. My witch's last order was that I roost here until my new witch comes to stay, so that is what I must do.

And really, without a witch to share in power, I must stay put to pull in magic from the node beneath me. This isn't the safest of spots, though. I've known that from the start, when I landed here in desperation, but now that I'm awake, I can feel how the cliff beneath me is growing weaker. I'm not worried, really. I can keep the cliff stable, and more.

Maybe the humans will stay longer on their next visit? Perhaps they'll admire my carved eaves! I *love* when people admire my ornamented wood! Oh, oh, my logs shiver at the thought!

I never, ever told my witch how I feel about humans. She never asked. She would never have thought to. I was her house. My duty was to be her home and do as she bade. Sometimes—often—that meant people met their end within my walls or just outside.

That bothers me. It's never stopped bothering me. And not simply because of the mess, though that truly does vex me, but because I feel the *loss*. I can see the sprawling promise of their life, and that all just . . . *ends.*

I wasn't supposed to feel that way, though. From my earliest memories after hatching, I was told that I think too much, that I'm too emotional, that I am to exist to serve my witch, and only that.

But I can't snuff out who I am. I tried. I tried to be the best house I could, and *only* that.

But always, always, I experienced giddiness about the people who came to my door. Always, always, I hoped their wits would help them survive my witch. Always, always, I did what I was told to do and hid my sadness inside me, like a ruble beneath a floorboard.

I liked having an opportunity tonight to help this woman and man—both of them with such amazing quests before them! Quests can shift from minute to minute, and it's ever so exciting to discover what happens.

I hope I'm still part of their quests, I really do. After all, I opened my door to make them welcome! I did not try to drain extra blood from their bodies, no; I only took what little dripped away.

Oh! Oh! Maybe they'll return and light my oven! I cannot form that spark on my own. Oh, to be filled with warmth again!

I won't even try to coax them inside the oven. That's what my witch liked to do to guests sometimes. She'd say, *Oh, save a piece of jewelry that is snagged on a log back there*, or *Oh, I hid an enchanted sword way in the back of the oven, and if you survive the fire, it's yours.* People act rather silly when it comes to enchanted swords.

But if the woman and man went inside my oven with the fire lit, why, they'd be dead, and they can't return a third time. Their flesh would be all wasted, too, because there's no one here to enjoy it. I sure wouldn't. And their quests would be over. Done. What a loss that would be—not just for me, but for so many others!

I like having people here. I like *these* people, especially the woman. The magic upon her is so old and interesting! It's even older than I am!

Yes, yes, my fence must stand tall! My locks must gleam! My logs must be smooth to the touch, not sending a single splinter into their sensitive skin! I must be ready if they return.

Chapter 5

"I don't want to bake bread," Fayette snapped at Mother. The attention of the starter prickled at her consciousness. Yes, yes, bread leavened with Mother would alleviate the throbbing pain in Fayette's shoulder, but it never did enough. It hadn't stopped Briar from bleeding out in childbirth, even though she'd eaten Mother's bread her entire life, including the day before the birthing process began. The bread hadn't stopped a truck from crushing Thayer, but it had sustained Ma to a point.

In hindsight, Fayette realized that the blessed bread had probably dragged out Ma's suffering. Mother couldn't save Ma.

"I don't want to bake bread!" she said again, smacking the table for emphasis. Even though she'd used her good arm, the motion hurt.

She turned from the box of Cream of Wheat still sealed on the table. She knew she should eat to start the day right, but she just . . . couldn't. Well, skipping another meal would conserve more money. At this rate, she'd gradually save enough to get rich!

She couldn't resume her continuity now, either. The pain was too much, in her shoulder and in her mind. She needed to get out and about.

As she passed the Fitz household, she noted the heavy weathering on the building's white paint, large sections devoid of color. An eave drooped overhead. A few shingles were gone. The entire place was in need of urgent repair, in stark contrast to her rental cottage, which was newer and in much better shape. The surrounding garden was consistently gorgeous, however, abounding in greenery. Even though December was days away, unidentifiable flowers were blooming. The very sight of the place coaxed a smile onto her face as some of her strain began to ease.

She followed the natural downward slope of the next cross street to where it ended at a shallow cliff over the ocean. A strangely blue sky with sparse cotton-puff clouds spanned over a seemingly endless stretch of the Pacific. About ten feet below, waves crashed amid the rocks without the violence of the previous night. Seagulls swirled and screeched overhead.

A road undulated parallel to the ocean. As Fayette walked northward, most houses stood to her left. Colors beamed brighter in the storm's aftermath, the air both salty and fresh. An old-fashioned milk wagon plodded by, a strawberry roan in the shafts. She watched as the driver paused alongside a raised cubby set along the street. He took empty bottles from the cabinet and placed full ones in their stead. Gazing ahead, she saw more boxes like that spaced out every block or so.

Fayette shook her head in awe. Folks here must be imbued with a trustworthiness she'd never encountered in her decades in Southern California. She'd had milk stolen off her doorstep more than once.

Traffic increased by foot and automobile as she neared the main beach. Towering, gnarled Monterey cypresses along the way were like gigantic versions of the bonsai trees one of her neighbors cultivated. Up ahead, a cluster of people congregated as if watching a performance.

She welcomed the chance to pause. Her steps had started to drag, her muscles feeling rubbery and weak, likely because she hadn't eaten. She still didn't feel hungry, though—not really. Later, she'd need to force down some food. Wouldn't do to have shaky fingers on her typewriter keys when she finally sat down to work. A headache might creep in, too, and that wouldn't help her productivity.

Fayette peered around the idling people, expecting to see something like a small breed of dragon doing tricks or maybe a fellow juggling on a unicycle. Instead, she saw what appeared to be a cop or a soldier. The man wore a khaki military suit, his bearing regal as he faced down a tall, reedy man in a plaid tweed suit, a hat clutched at his torso.

"How long do you intend to stay in Carmel?" the man in khaki asked. His vowels dragged out in a particular way; she'd bet her best coat he hailed from Sweden.

The younger man's fingers twitched on the brim of his hat. "A few days, maybe a week. People need time to see my notice on the board or in a newspaper."

A black horse a few feet behind the cop released a whuff of breath, as if incredulous.

A woman beside Fayette in a red-striped dress leaned closer. "New here?" she whispered. Fayette nodded. "That there is the Marshal, August Englund. He's our sole policeman, our taxman, our general helper. He's sober as a pilgrim, but the nicest fellow you'll ever—"

"I am skeptical of spiritualism. Too many mediums are fraudulent. That said, I won't deny people the ability to practice here," the Marshal continued, his expression severe. "However, if I hear that your rates are exorbitant or you are engaged in blatant skulduggery—"

"I would never!"

"Then I will hold you accountable. That may include detainment before transportation to the jail in Monterey. You should keep this in mind as you engage in your . . . trade here."

"There's no jail in Carmel?" Fayette whispered.

The woman leaned close again. "The Marshal's garage works in a pinch if someone needs to be locked up overnight."

The medium stood tall. "You won't have any troubles with me, sir, not at all! But I'm glad that you're alert for mediums who do not act to benefit people. That's important."

The Marshal blinked, blatantly surprised by the gratitude. "Yes, well, your paper may stay on the board here and elsewhere, but know I'm watching."

"Yes, sir. Thank you, sir." The young man bowed several times as he backed away. The small circle of onlookers parted to let him through, then dispersed. Fayette was left shaking her head, disappointed that the man had been given the opportunity to do business at all.

Though elements magical and spiritual were undeniable aspects of the world, the current fad of spiritualism had grown to prominence in the wake of the tremendous worldwide grief arising from the war and the flu. Faith alone hadn't provided enough of a balm; the bereft craved an immediate connection to those they'd lost. Of course, other people sought to profit off those sentiments. A year or two ago, for script research, she'd even read Houdini's fascinating exposé on the schemes of mediums. She'd found it educational as well as depressing. Life was already so difficult—why did other people have to make it worse?

"You there. You're a visitor here." The Marshal strode toward Fayette, his tone brusque. His horse clip-clopped behind him.

"I am, sir." She normally thought it prudent to avoid cops whenever possible. A person couldn't readily tell the good from the bad with a single whiff, as with milk, but her thoughts toward the Marshal already tilted toward favorable. "My name's Fayette Wynne. I'm here for a few weeks, staying at Grangeville Cottage."

"Ah, the Fitz place." He nodded with instant recognition. "How do you find it?"

"It suited my needs nicely last night. A solid shelter through the storm."

"Good." He considered her. "How do you regard spiritualism?"

She hesitated. Even though she knew his sentiments, she wanted to be tactful with a person of such power in town. "I don't hold with people practicing parlor tricks and pretending to engage with ghosts in order to bleed victims dry of their savings, and that's what most of spiritualism is these days."

"A sensible outlook. If you see that man around the house where you stay"—he jerked a thumb in the direction in which the medium had fled—"do monitor proceedings and inform me of overt chicanery."

"I will. I can. Of course," she stammered, taken off guard by the request. As he tipped his hat and turned away, she had to blurt out, "Your mare is beautiful. What's her name?"

It turned out that complimenting the man's horse was the trick to get his severe face to soften into a smile. "Beauty." He tipped his hat again and moved on.

Beauty. Of course. Fayette was buffeted by memory.

Her sister, Briar, had loved horses as a child. Actually, *loved* was too gentle a term—the girl had been obsessed. Briar had known the name of every horse that stayed more than a day in town, and if the beast didn't have a name, she endowed one. Fayette had stood in fear and awe as her big sister, at the whopping age of eight, faced down a drunk mule skinner who was beating a jack in his mule train. As was only right, one of Briar's favorite books had been *Black Beauty*.

Briar had been dead eight years now, but Fayette still had the sudden urge to write her a letter about how she'd met a black Beauty of her own today. She could still imagine how Briar would've reacted to the news, too. Even at about age fifty, Briar would've clapped her hands and squealed as if she'd been presented with a delicious birthday cake she hadn't had to make herself.

There'd be no need to compose such a letter, though. Fayette needed to engage in other word-making instead.

She propelled herself forward to the message board. The shadow cast by the gangly pine might've made it hard to read the notices, if more had been present. The storm had waterlogged and shredded what few sheets tenaciously remained, making the medium's fresh page stand out all the more. There was one other curiosity, though—a small painted sign that read Looking for a Mate with a leather shoe dangling beside it, tied by the laces to a nail. In warped ink, a small slip beneath the sign responded Take Mine, Please. She guffawed.

"A fine morning for a constitutional!" announced an older man with a thick accent as he strolled past with swinging arms. He wore a long garish red velvet jacket with oddly mismatched plus fours that

A House Between Sea and Sky

would've been better suited for golfing at nearby Pebble Beach. A woman in a flowing formal drop-waisted gown hung off his arm.

"Yes, um, a fine morning," Fayette replied, trying not to grin too broadly. She expected such strange sights in Hollywood—where people cast as scenery earned more money if they wore their own fine garb or costumery for a shoot—but not here.

Every time she felt as low as a garter snake in a ditch, Carmel managed to brighten her spirits again somehow.

"How far do you think we can walk before the bus arrives, Count?" the woman cooed as they passed.

Count. Fayette almost burst out laughing. Unless she missed her guess, the woman had made a point of stating that title while Fayette was in hearing range. Cats will spray on furniture and trees to mark their territory; possessive people will just happen to mention royal rank as they claim what's theirs.

"I don't know, my dear, but a promenade before the long ride will do us both good," said the man. His accent was all over the place. He was trying to be Russian, she reckoned, but he might've only succeeded if his words had been in subtitles.

Quite a few White Russian émigrés had come to Hollywood since the Revolution. The Whites had been part of a diverse group—really diverse—that included monarchists, capitalists, rival socialist movements, and other groups that had fought in opposition to Red Russians, the socialist Bolsheviks. While select few Whites were indeed nobility or high-ranking officers beneath the Romanovs, as royalty and clergy had been the Revolution's primary targets, the public and the film industry tended to romanticize all refugees as being cast down from privileged ranks. Fayette had heard tales of a taxi driver in town who was a duke, and a dishwasher who was a general's daughter. From overseas, there'd been stories that the czar's slaughtered children were actually alive and in Berlin, Australia, or London, somewhere safe where they could, at some point, raise a flag and lead the political refugees back to their homeland.

But in the meantime, proclaimed connections to the old regime could earn a person sympathy and, perhaps, access to the shadowed realms beneath a skirt.

Several motion pictures, like Rex's *Dance After Midnight*, had avoided controversial contemporary realities, instead giving life to the centuries-past court of Catherine the Great. That was a safer era and setting to utilize while still capitalizing on public interest in Russia.

Ah, Rex. Maybe it was late enough in the day to check on him without being as pesky as birds chirping at dawn. She might've saved him the previous night, but people didn't stay saved. She needed to keep an eye on him—no, more than that, she *wanted* to keep an eye on him.

On the way to his place, she was glad to find a small grocery store. Having a selection of food at the cottage would encourage her to eat. She continued on her way, a laden canvas bag swaying from her good shoulder.

As she raised her fist to knock on Rex's door, it swung back. Her hand hovered a few inches from his forehead.

Fayette and Rex stared at each other a long moment before they both burst out laughing.

"Well, good morning to you. I was in the area buying some groceries, and I thought I'd check in." She pivoted to motion to her bag. Its presence made her appearance more casual, she hoped. Not that she'd walked into town just for him. "Did you sleep well?"

"Surprisingly, yes. I've been up about an hour now." He rubbed his smooth jaw. A few faint nicks on his pale skin revealed that he'd just shaved. He looked even more handsome by daylight, a flush of wellness to his cheeks. Not that she trusted rosy cheeks to indicate his full health. She knew from her long years in Hollywood that sometimes folks wore their most convincing masks when under direct light.

"That's good," she said. "The weather's pleasant and the day bright. Are you up to—"

"Surveilling that house from last night? I can't stop thinking about that place, so yes! I don't suppose you witnessed anyone lurking around

The danger isn't imminent, though. I have things under control. I do. Big earthquakes don't happen that often, and I know to keep my body very still while my legs and wings cannot function.

Can I keep the woman and the man safe if the cliff fails while they are here? I can, I think. Long enough for them to evacuate. That's how you take good care of people—by not killing them. And also by being clean.

Chapter 7

The highly peaked roof of the house was visible past the line of California wax myrtles that lined the road for some twenty feet. Just beyond that, the rocky promontory formed the southern boundary of this section of cliffs. Rex pointed out that there was a nice beach just south, at the mouth of the Carmel River—the place Fayette hadn't reached on her late-night walk—and that the Carmel Mission wasn't far away, either, just to the east. It'd fallen into ruin in the last century and had only recently been restored.

"You seem to know a lot about the area," Fayette said, shifting her shoulders. Though she'd carried the grocery bag on her good side, the strain lingered with her even after she'd dropped off her goods at Grangeville Cottage. She'd quickly eaten an apple, too, and felt steadier as a result. Logically, though, she knew a person needed more food than that to get through a day. The way things were going, she'd soon be able to see her ribs. That perturbed her. She *liked* having a stout figure. She liked feeling strong. Ma used to say that the women in their family had been built to strap a child on each hip and push a plow at the same time, and Fayette had relished in that imagery.

Well, she'd eat more when she returned to the cottage. She'd make herself.

They stopped walking at the line of wax myrtles. Rex gazed around, expression bright with curiosity. "I've come up here every few months for the past couple years. Carmel is probably one of my favorite places in the state. In all the times I've been here, though, I've never noticed a cottage all by itself down here on the cliff."

"The myrtles do block most of the view," Fayette said. The thick shrubs stretched to just above their head level.

"I can't even say I noticed the myrtles. I think back on my walks along here, and I remember passing the last of the houses." He pointed to the trees up the way that marked the edge of the Fitz property. "But then, I feel like I came upon the beach right away. I don't get it. That roof is right there! It doesn't look like anything else in town—and I *like* looking at houses. Give me a free Saturday, and I'll read through house plans for fun. If I'm invited to someone's house, I'd rather tour the rooms and hear the history of the property than gab about inane topics in the parlor."

"I could think of worse ways to spend a Saturday." She shouldered her way between two of the myrtles. "There's no path or drive to approach the place. I'd say it was abandoned, but it looked well kept when we were inside." Before them, the knobby, heavily eroded rock sloped upward to the cottage. The house stood maybe twenty feet by fifteen, the high-angled roof about twenty feet up. The thick beam that formed the roof's ridge jutted out with a slight hook to it.

"Huh. That's a house made for snow," said Rex. At her arched brow, he continued, "The roof's slope—it's so the snow doesn't pile up or weigh it down."

"You're familiar with that kind of weather?" Fayette had one faint childhood memory of a winter with snow, of throwing snowballs at her siblings and how cold her teeth were when she took a blow to the mouth.

"Born and raised in Minnesota, so yes." He laughed at her gaped-mouth surprise. "I did some stage work in New York before I ever came to California, and I quickly learned to adapt my accent. As soon as I step off the train into Saint Paul Union Depot, though, I blend right in."

"I couldn't lose my drawl if I tried, and I've been in this state since I was twelve."

"I was wondering where you're from. Texas?"

"Lord, no. Never. I'm from Arkansas, up near the Missouri border. My pa liked to call it God's country, but considering how near we came to starvation time and again, I'm fine with regarding it as a pretty waystation on my family's gradual westward trek."

"I apologize deeply for my mistake." A smile quirked at a corner of his mouth. "I wasn't aware that being called a Texan was such a grave insult."

"It is if the person hails from Oklahoma or Arkansas. Now you know to be more cautious in your assumptions." She affected a lofty tone. The tingling presence of magic brushed her skin as the tall grasses rustled against her skirt. She paused. A fence stood at the boundary between the grass and the rocks, a gate already open as if in wait for them.

"Is that driftwood?" Rex asked as he studied the posts. He touched the top of a stick and then recoiled. "That's— It looks like a leg bone!"

He was right. The fence resembled a row of femurs, bound in a neat line by two parallel lines of thick rope.

"The rope looks like it's made of hair, too. Maybe horse hair?" she asked, her sense of ill ease increasing. The house was watching them.

She stepped through the open gateway, then looked around. "I didn't see any fence or gate last night. It's like it sprang up overnight. What do you think? Am I imagining the wrong approach in the dark?"

Rex continued to stare at the fence, and after a prolonged silence, he shook his head. "Sorry, I'm still rather distracted by the fence made out of bones."

By all logic, she should've been hightailing it for town without looking back, but instead, she walked forward. This place was creepy— and yet, like the house itself, she was curious. A necessary thing in her line of work. She needed to understand the story behind places, things, and people, and here before her was a mystery that seemed even more peculiar than the divine sourdough starter she'd known her whole life.

Her gaze went to the elaborate carving on the closed wooden shutters and the eaves of the roof. Some of the etchings were of recognizable phases of the moon, the sun, and birds, but other symbols, such as a heart with a divot in the center, were less clear.

As they reached the top, Rex trod with caution toward the cliff's edge. "That foundation looks like it's melted into the rock, and the placement of the house doesn't make sense at all. Look here, Fayette."

She gasped. The log structure's western wall arose from the very edge of the cliff. As if that weren't dramatic enough, from where they stood, they could see the rock beneath the house was only about five feet thick. They walked around, past the door, to check the north-facing side. It, too, arose from the very edge of the rocks.

"How's the weight being supported?" Fayette posed the question not to Rex, but to the house and the heavens above. "The very construction of this place should've brought it down."

"And look, there's a water pump near the entrance. Where could the water possibly come from? This place gives me the willies."

Fayette approached the east-facing door, hoping, dreading that the passage would open for them again.

It did. The door quietly swung inward.

Rex took in a sharp breath. "There's no trigger to cause that. This is all rock, real rock." His right shoe tapped the ground for emphasis.

"Yes," Fayette said simply. She hunkered over to squint at the doorknob, then rose to glance at the hinges and the locking mechanism in the frame.

"What is it?" he asked.

"More bone, I think." She affected a casual tone. The doorknob, which they had yet to even touch, seemed to be a smooth yellow knob of bone—from where and what, she didn't know, but the texture and look were familiar enough. The hinges were definitely fingers, and the locking mechanism was constructed of teeth arranged in a kind of frame.

"Well," Rex said, somewhat faint, "I was taught that every bit of a butchered animal should be used, but this type of repurposing is something more. The teeth look human, don't they?"

"They could be."

"Do you really want to go inside? Would that be trespassing?"

She stepped forward. "Yes, I want to go inside. It's not trespassing if the door opens for us."

A big part of her was sure that she was a fool, but she couldn't forget that the house had provided them shelter and let them leave the night before. That had to mean something.

She entered.

Right away, she saw the bench had been moved back from the interior door—which also opened at her approach. She regretted that she hadn't thought of buying a new flashlight somewhere, but then the next, much larger room brightened as she passed through the doorway. The wooden shutters folded outward as she watched. The two long walls to the north and south each had five windows, and all of them now cast light inward.

"No one did that," Rex murmured from a step behind her.

"The *house* did that," she corrected.

The large room, with its high-spanning ceiling, was furnished with several tables and benches, but the most dominant aspect loomed before them: an oven of white bricks that took up about a third of the space. It alone was as big as her bedroom back home! A large alcove for fire stood blackened and empty, a nook above an obvious place for things such as bread to be baked by the heat below. On the other side of the oven were empty inset shelves—were they for food storage, perhaps? Many other built-in nooks contained pots and pans, with more hanging from the nearby log wall. A series of built-in steps led to the top of the oven, which was flat and spacious. A brick chimney on one side rose to meet the ceiling.

Rex released a cry of delight. "I've seen ovens like this! They were in Russian reference books kept on set for *Dance After Midnight*. I talked about them with a friend of mine. He never lived in such a house—he described them as countryside peasant huts—and he mentioned that people actually sleep on top of the oven through the long winter."

Sleep on top of the oven? That sounded like something a cat would do, and in her experience, cats tended to be smarter than humans most of the time. "How many people could sleep up there, you think?"

"Depends on the house and oven, I suppose, but most definitely the children and elderly, those more vulnerable to the cold. This oven has such a big opening for wood, too—a person could fit in there, but that would be a bit too warm and toasty! I wonder what Art would think, seeing something like this in California, of all places."

"Maybe a White Russian had this place built," she said, even as she held doubts. Something about the house felt ancient, though it lacked the mustiness one might expect in an old building.

Rex didn't answer. He was too busy climbing the steps to study the top of the stove. "It's clean as a whistle up here. I could go around with a white glove and not find a speck of dirt. Who's keeping up this place?" He sounded increasingly excited. "You know, European castles and manors have been hauled over the Atlantic to be rebuilt in America. I don't see why someone couldn't do the same thing with a log cabin. The size would make it easier to rebuild—but why do so on such a precarious cliff?" His shoes clapped on the floor as he came down, but her gaze stayed on the oven as she thought of bread.

How incredible would bread taste, made in a wood-fire oven like this? She'd used gas or electric ovens through her adult life, though she'd made basic flatbreads on campfires when her family traveled. Mother had never shown a preference for how her bread or other food items were baked. A place like this, imbued with power similar to that of Mother—what would that do to the inherent magic of a loaf? Would it be more effective?

Her stomach rumbled, hungry at last.

Fayette realized that Rex was waiting for her to say something. "I don't know. Everything about this house seems odd. If this place is

Russian, well . . . Russians have been in California for centuries. Fur traders used to go up and down this coast, hunting otters and other critters. I thought they mostly lived in a fort up north, though. This sure doesn't seem like something the native residents would've made."

"I agree." He shook his head. "I can't help but think about a slab found in Minnesota a few years back that has Viking runes on it. Some people think it's proof that explorers from Europe came over a thousand years ago. Others say it's a fraud."

"What do you say?" She made herself look away from the oven to face him.

"I say I haven't a clue what to make of that Viking slab, but when it comes to *this* property, we can use common sense and check the records at town hall." He grinned. "I don't have faith in much these days, but I fully believe the government will want tax money from whoever owns this ground."

"That's a good idea. I can look into it. I like digging around in dusty old bins for bits of paper. I can get us a name."

"A name." His voice went hollow. She recognized the abrupt shift in his mood the way she sensed the approach of a lightning storm. "Maybe a name will help, or maybe it'll be a lie."

"Rex? What's going on in that head of yours?"

"I don't even know anymore." He sighed. "Sometimes my thoughts flicker like someone hit a switch. It just occurred to me that Margaret wasn't going to change her surname to mine—which was fine by me. I understand the importance of keeping a name the same once you have a reputation. I changed my own name early on, when I'd only had bit parts."

Fayette realized she needed to tread carefully. His flickering thoughts could guide him toward the cliff outside. "That's not an uncommon thing in Hollywood. What was your name?"

"I was born 'Helmer Hallstrom.' A producer a few years ago told me that Helmer wasn't an American name, that I needed a name to match my looks." His laugh was brittle. "My parents came over as children. I was born here. We're all Americans."

"I can see why you went with Rex instead. Nothing says *America* quite like Latin." She'd hoped for a laugh and she earned one. She hesitated a moment before continuing. "Would you like for me to call you Helmer when no one else is around?"

Fayette's question jolted him. "What? No, no. You'd best not. I'm Rex Hallstrom unless I'm back home." He started toward the door.

"Are we leaving?" she asked.

He stopped, gazing back in surprise as if only just realizing what he was doing. "We should. At least, I should. I need to do more Rex Hallstrom kinds of things today out in public. Word will be getting out about what happened last night—or what didn't happen—and I need to show I'm getting by."

"Are you getting by? Really?" she asked quietly.

His eyes squeezed shut. "I'm not suicidal, if that's what you're asking. I just— The hopelessness stays with me like a shadow. And I'm worried about Margaret, that my selfishness will hurt her."

"You were both being pressured into marriage. That's not right. Even someone in an arranged marriage ought to agree to that and everything that comes after. No one should be forced to hold a wedding. No one."

The hardness in her voice seemed to make him open his eyes. "You sound like you're speaking from experience."

"I'm forty-five years old. I've never been married—never *wanted* to be married. I can write fine romances, mind you, but enduring one myself?" Fayette blew a raspberry. "I want my own bed, with books and crossword puzzles strewn on the mattress beside me, and my own schedule."

"I rather fancy the idea of marriage," Rex said softly. "But not with Margaret."

"Then you have true reason to celebrate your freedom! Go out and golf. Look at houses! It's a beautiful day. Enjoy it."

His nod started slowly, then repeated a few times with growing conviction. "I will. I'll try. Golf sounds good. I have clubs at my place."

She hadn't proposed the sport on a whim. She'd seen the clubs leaning in a corner by his front door. "I'm going to stay here a bit longer, and then I'll see what I can discover about this land we're on. I'll drop by your place to let you know if I find anything interesting."

"I'll see you later, I suppose." He hesitated, looking toward the door and then back at her. "Fayette, why do you want to find out more about this house?"

She gazed around. "Because it's extraordinary. It let us inside! Twice! And I've never seen a structure quite like it. I want . . . Oh, this will sound silly."

"Go on." The gravity in his voice wasn't depressive now, but somber in respect.

"I loved Lang's Fairy Books as a child. Still do, really. I reread them into adulthood. Those illustrations!" She grinned at the memory. "I've forgotten many of the specific stories by now, but I remember how they made me *feel*. The magic. The possibility. The morbidness, at times. This place makes me feel like I'm part of those stories, and as a writer now myself, I want to understand my place in the narrative."

"That's not so silly. Not compared to my reason."

"Oh?"

"I've never encountered anything like this house before, either. My curiosity makes me feel alive," Rex said softly. "To borrow some of your wording, I can't stop my story partway. I need more answers first."

"There's nothing silly about that."

Rex tilted his head, his smile wistful. "Maybe not. My reason didn't sound so bad, said out loud." He walked on. The doors quietly opened and closed in sequence.

She and the house were alone.

Fayette spun in a slow circle, taking in the grand yet small space. "What are you, house? Mind you, I'm much obliged for your kindness last night, but you're a thing of magic, and I just . . . I don't put much faith in magic these days, even though I've always known its presence in my life. I guess faith isn't always about believing if something is genuine. It goes deeper than that."

She walked a lap around the place, her skin tingling all the while. She ended up near the door, which opened at her approach. A glance back at the oven showed that nothing had changed. Everything was quiet. Still, but for the doors.

She shook her head, disgusted at her own sense of disappointment. What, had she expected the house to wait until after Rex was gone to speak to her? It was a *building*.

A building that was keeping both her and Rex going—Rex in particular. If he needed morsels to motivate him to live, she'd feed him the information she uncovered, one pinch at a time.

As soon as she was outside, the windows closed themselves with a series of dense, wooden thuds.

Another sound caught her attention, something rattling in the bushes near the road. Fayette blinked as she recognized a short figure with a dark-blond braid just as they vanished into the leaves: Heidi, Mrs. Fitz's help.

Chapter 8

Fayette considered Heidi's presence there. Did she visit the cottage, too? Was she the reason why it was so spick and span? Or had she simply followed Fayette after she'd dropped off her groceries?

Heidi couldn't have eavesdropped beneath the windows, could she? And heard about Rex's suicidal inclinations? Climbing the rocks wasn't a quiet task, though.

Well, Fayette could ask Heidi questions later. For now, she needed to pursue another line of query—actually, three.

She walked north again and asked for guidance from a fellow pedestrian, soon finding herself outside the small redwood building that housed the Carmel Library.

Inside, the librarian's desk was vacant. The place was eerily quiet, even by library standards. Good. While help could be fine sometimes, there was no freedom like that of wandering among full bookshelves. She turned toward the juvenile section. It was so small, she had no problem at all finding the fairy-tale books. None focused on Russia alone. To her delight, the shelf contained one of her old favorites, Lang's *Blue Fairy Book*, but the table of contents didn't label the stories by country of origin, and none stood out to her as possibly Russian. She flipped through, hoping one of the ink illustrations might show a familiar house, but no.

She blew a raspberry in frustration. Well, that was a dead end. She ran a hand through her short hair, twirling the strands.

A tuft came off between her fingers.

She brought it closer to her face to blink in disbelief. She'd been losing more hair in her brush the past week or so, but losing a clump was something new. She knew why this must be happening, too.

A survivors-stranded-on-a-deserted-isle flicker years ago had featured people shedding hair as they wasted away from starvation. Though it was obvious the actors had worn wigs, the effect in the film had been disturbing.

Fayette wasn't *trying* to starve herself, but that had to be what was happening. Her body might start showing other signs, too. Would her teeth loosen? Or was that specifically caused by scurvy? She pressed her tongue to each tooth in turn to test its solidity. No issues with that yet, in any case.

Fayette rubbed the hair strands between her fingers, causing them to separate as they drifted to the floor.

Well, on to the next line of investigation.

A small faced-out shelf of magazines sat not far from the entrance. Recent issues of *Photoplay* and *Picture-Play Magazine* leaned near the very top, the paper covers already creased by loving attention.

Perfect. These fan magazines, populated with cheery gossip and press from studio publicity departments, were bound to assist in one of her investigations.

In the third issue, she struck gold. Rex's portrait filled a full page, his charismatic glow not so much dimmed as it was channeled through gray-toned wood pulp. His pale-blue eyes came across as light gray, his blond hair white. The popular mode of thin mustache, reminiscent of Douglas Fairbanks in *The Mark of Zorro* and the recent *Don Q*, seemed to somehow emphasize the fullness of his lips. Fayette hadn't the itch to kiss him or anyone else, but readily understood his were the very definition of *kissable*.

She skimmed the accompanying text. This issue had come out right after the release of *Dance After Midnight*, his Russian historical piece, but it was more about Rex than the movie. He came across as friendly and approachable as he discussed growing up riding horses on his family farm ("I do all of my own stunts, including galloping and sword-fighting," he says, drawing a comparison to Francis X. Bushman, setting up Rex as the next handsome athlete to grace pictures), how he got seasick and therefore avoided boats ("I'm happiest on land, but I love a view of the water. As a child, I loved watching paddleboats and barges on the Mississippi. I could do that for hours!"), and how his mother shipped him a beloved elderly neighbor's Norwegian lefse the past few Christmases because he couldn't travel back home ("Lefse is like a thin flatbread made from potatoes. If people are familiar with Mexican tortillas, lefse looks similar, but the flavor is different.").

If he had been any more squeaky clean, he'd be covered in bubbles.

Fayette flipped the page to find a full portrait of another familiar blonde: Margaret Proudlock, Rex's jilted bride and costar in *Dance After Midnight*.

Just as Rex had been promoted as a fit, handsome leading man, Margaret was marketed as a feminine ideal. She loved shopping ("I'm glad Santa Barbara is recovering from the earthquake, as I missed those shops and sea breezes") and children ("I could happily have a dozen!"), and how she had learned embroidery from her late grandmother ("Every time I use her needles, I think of her and what she taught me about sewing, God, and cooking").

A final paragraph was about Rex and Margaret as a couple, mentioning the two movies they'd starred in together and how they'd been seen on Catalina (Rex endured the brief, turbulent sea to enjoy a sojourn with his ladylove) and had an outing to buy dates from an operation out near Palm Springs. The accompanying picture, with Rex on a ladder to pick fruit off a short date palm, was so obviously posed that it struck Fayette as ludicrous.

She shut the magazine and pondered. Both stars had sugary-perfect reputations that they must have somehow violated, according to their bosses. After all, it was one thing for studios to pair their stars to create press and interest, quite something more to force them both into marriage, with the vows witnessed by heavies who'd look natural in a mobster picture.

"Oh, hello!" a high-pitched voice rang from behind Fayette, causing her to twist around. A young woman approached, her brown hair pulled back into a black mesh snood. "I hope you haven't been waiting long.

I was just in the next room, but I didn't hear a thing!" She set down a stack of thin children's books.

"That's fine. I've only been here a couple minutes." Fayette put her magazines back on the rack. "I could use your help. I'd like to look through local history and property books, please."

"Oh? I've lived here my whole life. I might know what you need off the top of my head. I'm Cecilia Rogers, by the way, but everyone calls me Miss Cecilia."

"I'm Fayette Wynne."

"Are you a new resident? In order to check out books, you'll need to pay a dollar for the next year." She moved toward the desk as if ready to whip out the cards and the cashbox.

Fayette dryly gulped at the sum. "I-I'm just a visitor, here for the next few weeks."

"Oh, I see. A tourist." The welcoming smile withered into something brittle. "Well, maybe I can help you with your query so that you don't need to check out anything."

Fayette sure hoped so. She'd need to skimp on her already meager meals if she doled out a whole dollar to access books. "I'm looking for information about the unique-looking cottage on the cliff all by itself, down on the road toward the Carmel River? The place might be Russian in design."

"A Russian house? There?" Miss Cecilia wrinkled her nose. "Oh! The one with the tall, peaked roof?"

"Yes, that one!"

"An odd thing about that place. I'm a photographer, you see. The pictures on the walls here are mine." She gestured around with obvious pride. Fayette murmured praise, though she hadn't taken a gander at a single one. "I take photographs of Abalone League games, the outdoor theater, most any activity in town. I've tried to take pictures of that roofline more than once—it looks so pretty with clouds behind it!—but the images never turn out. I've tried at different times of day and taken special care in processing, and yet . . ."

"Why don't you get closer?" Fayette asked.

"Get closer?" Miss Cecilia's brow furrowed, tone softening.

"Yes. If you cross to the other side of the bushes, you have a clear view of the house, and you're not trespassing terribly." Not as she and Rex had.

"What house?" She sounded confused.

Fayette blinked. "The Russian cottage we're talking about. The one with the peaked roof visible from the road?"

"Oh, yes, I know the one you're talking about. I've tried to photograph it more than once. They never turn out."

Miss Cecilia's focus had gone as fizzy as a soda pop.

"That's why you should get closer to the house to get a better angle," said Fayette, with labored patience.

"What?" Her tone had gone dreamy again. "Better angle of what?"

Fayette suddenly recalled that Rex had said he hadn't noticed the property at all, even though he'd gone that way many times. Miss Cecilia, at least, could see the roof. The way her voice trailed off, though, it was as if a thick tule fog prevented the woman from talking about the cottage or truly seeing it.

Fayette recalled a game she'd played with her siblings when they were young, one of their own invention that they'd dubbed Ghost. One of them would pretend to be invisible and haunt the others, and the goal was for the two "living" children to successfully ignore the ghost for a stint of time, usually something like ten minutes.

Fayette had been the grand champion, both at being the ghost and playing stoic as a living participant. Briar and Thayer burst out in hysterical giggles over her antics, nor could they get a reaction out of Fayette when she decided to ignore a haunting.

What if the house could play its own game of Ghost? A game at which it won, because it stayed hidden, and most people won, as they were oblivious to the oddity on the cliff? But Fayette had been treated differently, for some reason.

How was she going to get the answers she needed under these circumstances? Fayette resolved to act like her character Dot. Play the detective. Ask about the building without asking about the building.

"Miss Cecilia, who owns the land along the cliff, right before Carmel River? And if you don't know, can you direct me to where I might find the information, here or at city hall?"

A spark of clarity returned to Miss Cecilia's brown eyes. "Oh, Mr. Fitz owns the land at that end of town. Well, he owns it, but Mrs. Fitz is the caretaker, as her husband is . . . indisposed."

"Mrs. Fitz?" Fayette echoed. "Really? I'm staying at her Grangeville Cottage. I haven't met Mr. Fitz yet."

Miss Cecilia leaned forward, apparently more eager to dispense gossip than library books. "Few people see him these days. The Fitz family settled here early on, you see. Mr. Fitz owned quite a bit of property at the southern end of Carmel. He was gravely injured during the war. He's alive, but only that. Mrs. Fitz has been selling off parcels over the past few years. At this point, I think they only have left the lots where they live, your rental house, and the property just south."

"What a terrible situation!" Fayette said, aghast.

"Oh, yes." Miss Cecilia nodded with what could only be described as pleasure. "She's squandering the money, too. She's certain there's a way to cure him. Meanwhile, she's wasting away herself because she's watching him day and night. If her health fails, well . . . I don't know what would happen then."

Fayette remembered how the Marshal had asked her to look out for Mrs. Fitz. Was she spending her money on mediums? "They do have Heidi there to help."

"Oh, that girl?" She waved away Heidi like a gnat. "She should be useful, after all that Mrs. Fitz has done for her. She's practically adopted the girl. Heidi isn't much better about managing funds, though. She's downright *wasteful*."

"Wasteful? How?"

"She cooks for the other servant families around, making large batches of bread and biscuits, and she gives it all out for *free*. The Fitzes are barely getting by as it is!"

Fayette blinked. "That sounds like . . . kindness." The sort of kindness Mrs. Fitz had extended toward her as well, with Heidi's cooking. Fayette couldn't recall when she'd last baked bread of any sort to help neighbors, and that was bothersome. "Does Mrs. Fitz object to her household supplies being used in this way?"

Miss Cecilia's mouth opened and closed. She looked as though she'd expected ready agreement to her gossip, not a challenge. "I . . . I haven't heard anything of that sort."

"How long have you known the Fitz family?" Fayette made an effort to keep her tone friendly.

"Oh, I've known Gerald Fitz my whole life, but his wife isn't from here. She looks and acts white, as I'm sure you noticed, but she's *Portuguese*. Came over as a young child. A lot of people don't realize what she is because she blends in."

Mrs. Fitz had offered Fayette comfort at a moment when she was tired and hungry, and like a stray dog thrown a bone, Fayette now regarded her landlady with absolute loyalty. She'd had about enough of this mean-spirited jabber.

"Is that so?" Fayette asked through gritted teeth. "And what could she do that would possibly cause you to accept her? If she 'acted' Portuguese, you'd hate her for that, too, wouldn't you?" Miss Cecilia flushed. Fayette didn't give her time to respond. She didn't want to hear another word out of this woman's foul mouth. "Much obliged for your assistance."

Fayette exited, her steps powered by flowing rage. The nerve of that woman! Her judgmental attitude probably shooed away many prospective readers. What a tragedy. Fayette could only hope the other staff here were more accommodating. Truly, a bad librarian was much like a bad cook. Both could feed a person something essential that could settle deep into the gut, and make a person ill for a very long time.

Fayette's trip to the library hadn't been in vain, though. She left with a greater understanding of the peculiar house—and would know even more after a chat with her landlady.

Chapter 9

Mrs. Fitz was sweeping debris from her front stoop. She stopped to watch Fayette approach, one hand planted on her hip.

"You were out and about late last night," she said by way of greeting.

Mrs. Fitz's brusque mannerisms did nothing to dissuade Fayette's fierce affection. "I was. During a gap in the storm, I went on a walk to clear my head, but the gap ended up being a wee bit short. I ended up taking shelter until the violent weather eased off again."

"You're fortunate you weren't electrocuted. There was a lot of lightning in those clouds."

"I took shelter in that cottage to the south of here, the one by itself on the rocks."

Mrs. Fitz stared at her a moment before bursting out in laughter. Fayette hadn't heard her make the sound yet, and it rang out wild and *alive*, a contrast to the state of perpetual exhaustion that weighed down her features. "The house let you find it? Well, well."

So, Mrs. Fitz recognized the existence of the house and that not everyone had the capability. "Whatever do you mean?"

"The house is cursed. Its origin is Hell itself." She placed capital-letter emphasis on the place-name.

"Hell?" Fayette hadn't expected *that* pronouncement.

"It appeared in the span of a night, with no need for construction. One day it was suddenly there—and I was the only one who could fully see it or approach it." Her lips bared in a grimace. "Some people in town can see the roof, and a few reach the other side of the trees, but if I squeeze that much detail out of them, I can get no more."

"I found that out already," Fayette said. "People lose all train of thought."

Mrs. Fitz nodded as she set her broom to lean against the house. "It's like trying to hold an intelligent conversation with someone more pickled than any cucumber. I've tried to enlist every real estate agent in the area to market that property. You can imagine how that went. What makes *you* different?" she asked with a glower.

Rex really had been like everyone else, Fayette realized. He must have been able to take shelter in the house—and truly see it today—because he'd been with her. "How close have you gotten to the building?"

"To the doorstep, but I will not go inside. I dare not. You must not, either. It's not safe."

"Do you know when exactly the house appeared on the cliff?" Fayette asked.

"Yes. July of 1918. That month, I first put out red, white, and blue ribbons to support my husband and the other men away fighting. I've kept doing it every year since. That year, I remember the ribbons being there when I tried to tell Gus Englund—he's our policeman—what I'd found. Him and so many other people. I thought I'd forever be the only one to know the confounded building was there." Sadness seeped into her voice.

Mrs. Fitz thought only the two of them had access. She didn't know about Heidi, but then, Fayette wasn't sure how close Heidi could get to the house. She could be one of those people who could cross the bush line, and only that.

"I found one real estate agent—*one*—out of Monterey," Mrs. Fitz continued, "who could see the roof and almost describe the house. But when he went through the bushes, he came out a moment later yelling that he'd been lost for hours, and he had chicken feathers stuck to him by static! Black feathers with white speckles, the things as long as my forearm!" Mrs. Fitz released her hold on Fayette to hold up her arm as an example. "I had to swat them off of him, and by the time I got him back to the house to give him some tea, he couldn't recall what had happened."

"Beg your pardon, but covered in massive chicken feathers?" Fayette didn't know how to take that revelation.

"I tell the truth," Mrs. Fitz said bluntly. "I walked back to the house a short time later, determined to get a feather as proof that something was there, but I couldn't find any of them. They were gone—gone back to Hell. You believe me, don't you?" Desperation crackled in her voice.

Fayette felt another twist of sympathy. "Yes, I believe you." It sounded mad, sure, but many things about the house came across that way.

"Satan's henhouse, on my property." Mrs. Fitz wrung her hands together. "I wish it'd fall into the sea and be gone, or magic itself away again."

That statement bothered Fayette. While she found the cottage creepy in many ways, it'd also provided her and Rex shelter when they were in desperate need. If she'd tried to haul him a longer distance from the cliff, they could have very well been struck by lightning or had a bad fall. If they'd made it into town, well . . . their conversation would have been brief, and then they would have parted ways. Rex might have found other means and places where he could've ended himself last night.

The house had acted to save his life.

"That must be possible," Fayette said, feeling the need to say something. "The house arrived there. Surely it can leave as well. 'Magic itself away.'"

"Yes, yes." Mrs. Fitz studied Fayette with a critical eye. "Not all magic in the world is bad, however. You understand this, correct?"

"Yes?" Where was this going?

"You seem to be of open mind and heart. I'm inviting you to my house for a séance tomorrow evening."

Even though the Marshal had implied such a thing may happen, even though she'd wondered already about Mrs. Fitz's search for a cure for her husband, the invitation jolted her.

"There are other worlds that overlap with ours," Mrs. Fitz continued with confidence. "We'll bridge that gap."

Labeling the house as the property of Satan and yet fully embracing séances seemed contradictory, but it fit a pattern Fayette had seen before. If Mrs. Fitz had been raised Catholic, as many Portuguese were, her background had simply been melded into whatever she'd accepted now. Fayette had known a Mormon and a Baptist who'd acted similarly when they'd engaged in spiritualism after losing family.

"You've . . . taken part in séances before?" Fayette asked.

"Oh, yes." She said this with pride. "I have some mediumship skill myself, but I will not be conducting this event. I've hired a new young man to do so. You must understand, these gatherings enable me to gain insights into my husband's condition. We have already gone to doctors. So many doctors. The best in America, up in San Francisco." She practically spat in bitterness. "They think I should institutionalize my husband and keep on living my life. What kind of life is that?"

Fayette made a noise of sympathy.

"I'm careful about whom I invite. Some people treat séances as if they are some . . . frolic. They should be as serious as church. Séances are a chance to contemplate our places in this world, the places of our souls. The mysterious is everywhere. That peculiar house on the cliff is proof of that." Mrs. Fitz's expression tightened.

That house. Could a real medium help them discover more truths about the place? Finding someone with authentic abilities would be the issue, though. If the medium Mrs. Fitz had booked was the same man the Marshal had confronted earlier—which seemed likely—Fayette had little confidence he was the real deal.

What she was certain of, however, was that she needed to be in attendance at this séance. Mrs. Fitz could use more support.

And also, if there was a slim possibility that this medium could indeed channel spirits, Fayette needed a partner present to provide perspective. Sometimes it was hard to spot sleight of hand even when looking for it.

Fayette spoke slowly to give herself time to think. "Oddly enough, I spoke to another fellow in town about séances just this morning. Neither of us has attended one before. If I see this man again, could he come as well? I beg your pardon for my boldness."

A deep black cloud seemed to pass over Mrs. Fitz's face. "This man . . . you don't intend to carry on with him, do you?"

"Absolutely not."

"He was sober? Modest?"

Fayette resisted the urge to press a hand to her face and sigh. Ma had never even questioned Fayette like this in regard to her interactions with men, probably because she'd known that the only males Fayette would ever bring home had a tail, whiskers, and meowed.

"He was sober at that moment, and quite well dressed. He said he'd been in town a few weeks already."

"Well, if you happen upon him again, I suppose you may invite him, but I need confirmation by the end of today. Just know that I allow no ill energy in my home. If his behavior is inappropriate, I will evict him."

"I understand completely."

Mrs. Fitz stepped into the open doorway behind her. "My medium will be here soon to conduct a preliminary photography session. I must prepare. Mind you, the séance is set for tomorrow night at eight o'clock sharp. Hors d'oeuvres will be served. Goodbye, Miss Wynne."

With that, she closed the door in Fayette's face.

Chapter 10

Fayette continued on to Grangeville Cottage, to be greeted with a wave of prickles across her skin. Mother.

"I placed you by a cold window for a reason." Fayette stalked across the small house to glare at Mother. Her glass-jar housing was two-thirds full, myriad bubbles visible against the curved surface. Mother wanted to be divvied up and used. That was as clear as a neon movie marquee in the dark. "I fed you so you'd get by for the trip, and then you were supposed to hibernate like a bear in winter. I don't want . . . I don't want to deal with you." She couldn't say that she didn't want Mother at all—not directly to her. That felt like telling a family member that you hated them.

Fayette understood from rudimentary science that any sourdough starter was alive, to a degree, because all flour contained some natural yeast. The addition of water and a warm temperature encouraged vibrant growth. Adding concentrated yeast to flour and water did the same thing, but a lot faster—a person didn't need a microscope to see how the mixture bloomed and expanded. Sourdough starters, because they used inherent yeast, tended to mosey rather than race.

Mother, however, was something more than alive.

Fayette once asked Granny if it hurt Mother to be divided on a regular basis and for some portion of her to be baked into bread and, essentially, killed.

"What Mother feels is known only to her and God, I reckon," Granny said. "But she does want to be baked. She asks for it. Bread dough has a life cycle. I think Mother understands that better than any of us."

With that in mind, savagery in her motions, Fayette divided Mother.

She used a large spoon from a drawer to scoop up the vast majority of Mother, which she dumped into the rose bed just outside the kitchen door. Its magical presence promptly diminished. Fayette's skin broke out in goose bumps, colder in its absence. She poured a cup of water over the mass, diluting its beige upon the rich brown earth, then used a twig to mix it into the soil. The contents of any starter, even the nonmagical variety, could nourish plants. She regarded it as akin to the new vitamin fad for people.

What remained of Mother was a still-vibrant smear at the bottom of her jar.

"I'm going to feed you and you're going to be satisfied, hear?" Fayette said, thumping ingredients onto the counter for emphasis. The small bags, hauled all the way from Hollywood, emitted gasps of powder. She eyeballed the amounts of rye flour and white flour she added to Mother, as if to smother her, and added water from the tap—cold water. That ought to discourage growth; Mother had more of an appetite than she did, for certain. Fayette stirred everything together, blending Mother with the new, and immediately felt a swell of power.

"Oh, no you don't." She covered Mother's jar with the red-checkered cloth and put her back by the chilly window. "My shoulder hurts, but I'll get by the way most folks do. I'd need to beg Mrs. Fitz or someone else for access to an oven anyway, unless—" Her eyes widened. "You can't possibly know about the oven I saw in that hut."

Mother hummed with power. Potential.

"I'm here to work," Fayette snapped. "Not to baby you for a day or two as your bread rises. You take up too much time as it is. If you keep rising like you just did—I'll keep discarding you. I will."

In the hands of someone who wasn't family, a portion of Mother would produce bread that was delicious and nothing more. Mother's magic didn't work for just anyone. Fayette's Grandpop used to relate a cautionary tale from when he was a boy. The town scoundrel had heard rumors about the family's magical bread and had actually stolen Mother. The family never quite knew what had happened, but the man fled town. Grandpop and his family had set off in pursuit. Out in the woods, they'd recognized the prickles of her power. That had led them to a scant amount of Mother, sitting atop a log in a pond, as if she'd survived an attempted drowning. They'd salvaged her, leaving the dirty bits behind. Repeated feedings had brought Mother back to her vigorous self.

The thief's body was found floating in the same pond days later, bloated with water, but with no other apparent injuries.

Fayette didn't think the story implied that Mother had acted in an evil way. No, sometimes a person or bread starter had to defend themself. Mother was a smidgen of heaven, truly. And as a smidgen, inadequate.

"I thought I might type again, but I can't—not with you being a pest," Fayette said to Mother. Part of her recognized she was being petty, blaming the starter for her procrastination, and that only made her crankier. Fact was, though, if she stayed in the house, she'd obsess over the jar and its amount of rise. Best thing was to get away.

She threw together a peanut butter sandwich and left with that in hand. Passing by the Fitzes' cottage, she was surprised to recognize the strains of the old hymn "Nearer, My God, to Thee" wafting out the open windows. Two voices were raised in song: a quavering feminine pitch she assumed to be Mrs. Fitz, with a deep baritone in accompaniment. From everything she'd been told, that couldn't be her husband. Was the medium singing? Hadn't he been coming over to take photographs?

Fayette shook her head, frustrated by those questions and a pile of others.

She took a hearty bite of her sandwich. *There.* She was eating. Her body could stop thinking it was starving. She walked on, her next bites small. The food was falling heavily into her stomach, like boulders tossed down a mine shaft. But she *needed* to finish this sandwich; she knew she did.

She kept eating, her footsteps taking her northward. Maybe Rex would be home. She could tell him what little she'd learned.

⤞❧⤝

Rex was not home. Grumbling beneath her breath, she jotted down a note on the pad by his door, taking care not to leave any details that might arouse the curiosity of the studio goons if they returned.

She turned to leave and found Margaret Proudlock standing just within the yard, one hand on the gate to swing it closed. She gazed at Fayette with wide-eyed surprise.

Today Margaret appeared much as she had in her magazine feature: perfect. Blond hair smoothed to follow the shape of her head, curving to frame her jaw. She had a heart-shaped face, her light touch with cosmetics enough to soften her skin and add brightness to her eyes. A green cloche with a rosette topped her head, a matching green-striped frock draping to the knee in a way that made her look as straight as a column.

"Margaret," Fayette said with a nod. "I'm looking for Rex, but I vow to you, I'm not pursuing a romantic or physical relationship with him." Belatedly, she realized the defensive start probably made her look all the more guilty.

"I believe you," Margaret said, much to Fayette's surprise. "I came by to talk to him, too. I'm worried about him."

"He told me he might go golfing."

Margaret took a few mincing steps forward, her hands clutching a purse against the box plaits at the front of her skirt. "Please tell me . . ."

Her voice was a murmur. "When you were with him last night, did he come across as . . . profoundly unwell?"

"You'd best talk to him about such a private matter. I will say this, though: No one should be forced to marry."

"You're right." Margaret sagged, and Fayette felt like she was glimpsing beneath a mask. "Being married carries benefits, though. Benefits we both need."

Fayette didn't hold back her grimace. "This is 1926, for heaven's sake, not medieval France. You don't need to bind two families to prevent war."

"No, but we need to keep our contracts and encourage the lettuce to keep growing." *Lettuce*, a newfangled term for money. "See, I couldn't rub two pennies together when I was a kid. Back then, I thought a bank account would make everything better. It doesn't. The money doesn't stay put. You make one movie, you need to make another, and with good—"

A click rang out behind Fayette, causing her to turn. Rex swung the door wide, leaning on the frame. "What's this confab?"

"Have you been listening all the while?" Fayette asked.

"Nope, I just arrived. I came in the back door. I spied your movements through the curtains." He waved them both to come inside. "Margaret, I thought you were gone already?"

Fayette's and Margaret's footsteps echoed on the Mediterranean-style tile of the foyer. "I refused to ride back with them," Margaret said. After a second of thought, Fayette realized she had to be referring to the two studio louts. "They wouldn't let off. I called up Mikey and told him that the wedding was as dead as Harding, that the guys needed to back down."

An array of emotions flicked over Rex's face in a span of seconds. Surprise. Relief. Worry. "I see. How're you going to get back to the city, then? Do you need—"

"I bought a bus ticket. It leaves in, oh, fifteen minutes. I'll wear my sunglasses. No one will recognize me." Fayette arched an eyebrow in disbelief, causing Margaret to laugh. "I *am* an actress, you know." Her proud demeanor dissolved. She stood hunched, her arms wrapping around her torso as if she was shielding herself. Her expression shifted, her jowls softening, eyes casting downward. In all of two seconds, she'd transitioned from a bold flapper to a meek young woman, off to take the bus for the first time. All without saying a word.

"Well, then." Fayette looked between them, well aware of the ticking clock. "What's going to happen to you both now that you're refusing this studio arrangement?" She hated feeling like a parent and mediator, but she was very aware that Margaret was of an age to be her daughter. Rex, at least, was a bit older.

"An announcement of our nuptials is likely being published in major papers today, to be followed by a retraction," said Rex.

"There was already quite a bit in the way of buildup, you know," Margaret said.

"Ah, yes. The date-picking," said Fayette.

Margaret rolled her eyes. "You know what still bothers me about that whole outing? They wouldn't let us have any! I'd rather have California dates than just about any fruit, and here we were, surrounded, and utterly denied. 'Dates will rot your teeth,' they said. 'You need to keep your girlish figure,' they said."

"I know what to send you for Christmas, then," Fayette noted. "How will this all impact your picture deals?"

"I still have two years on my contract, but they can always take me off top billing or loan me out to lesser studios," Rex said. He lifted his newsboy cap to run a hand through his pale-blond hair. He wore the perfect attire for a golf outing: a white collared shirt, wool vest, and brown plus fours.

"My contract's about the same. I'm sure someone will waggle a finger in my face this week and tell me I oughta be a good girl. I'll nod and say yessir, and everything will be jake for a while." Margaret shrugged.

Fayette had to wonder what Margaret had done—and would do again—that was so *bad*. Same with Rex. She could imagine Margaret could be quite the vamp, but Rex still came across as a devout choirboy.

Rex sighed. "Sometimes I wonder if I just should go back home, take up my uncle's farm. Get away from all this . . . fuss. But being back home means a different kind of misery."

"I don't know you well, brother, but I do know you love acting." Margaret gave him a shrewd look. "You wouldn't be happy in some small-town theater, either—not after you've been under the big lights. In any case, time for me to vamoose. I'll see you on Thursday?"

"Yes." He grimaced, then glanced at Fayette. "We're meeting with the studio heads in San Francisco on the second. It was arranged weeks ago."

"Oughta be especially fun now," said Margaret, her tone chipper.

"You're leaving Carmel, then?" Fayette asked with a sudden twist of sadness. December second was three days away.

"Only for the day. I'm not due on set until after Christmas. I don't have any desire to see Southern California anytime soon. Other people love it there in the winter—but me, I hate it. The palms and pepper trees. That sunlight, day after day. It never fits with Santa Clauses and carols about snow. Here in Carmel, at least, there are more gray days, and the feel of the light is different. I can still get some work done as needed, too."

"Ah, work, work, work. You're supposed to be on vacation—on your honeymoon, for cryin' out loud." Margaret planted a quick kiss on Rex's cheek. "Fayette, can you be a dear and walk with me out to the gate?"

"Don't you need to hustle? Get your bags before the bus arrives?" Fayette asked.

"I dropped them at the station already." Margaret hooked her arm around Fayette's. Margaret was a few dimes over five feet, not uncommon for the lead actresses of the day, and Fayette felt like a giantess next to her. "Come on."

Once they were out the door, Margaret slowed as if she trudged through cement, bringing Fayette into stride with her. "How much longer are you staying here?" she whispered.

"I've booked about three weeks."

"You're going to stick to Rex like a bur, right? Oh, I don't mean that in a romantic way. You two have chemistry, no doubt, but not that sort. You're friends, and that's what he needs right now. I have a hunch that you did more than just talk last night. You kept him from walking off a plank, didn't you?"

"Something like that." Margaret had rightly guessed the truth, but it was still up for Rex to disclose specifics.

"I was told time and again when I was a girl that suicide was a ticket straight to hell. A faster route there than most anything else," Margaret said softly. "I may be a wimp in a lotta ways, but I'll scold anyone who says Rex Hallstrom oughta go to hell. I don't know him as well as I'd like to, but he's one of the gentlest, kindest souls in Hollywood, which is exactly why that place is going to do its utmost to break him. You keep doing what you're doing."

"You don't even need to ask that of me."

"Oh, I know." Margaret released her to rest both hands on top of the white gate. "But if I say it, I feel like I'm doing something for once, too."

"If you see a pattern in yourself you don't like, fight to change it," Fayette said. "You're not without power. If the studio sliced up your contract tomorrow, you'd still get by."

Margaret gazed down at her hands. "I more wonder if I'll live until my contract is supposed to end. That's what makes the bosses shiver, too. But no, I'm not . . . not in a dark place like Rex is," she added, seeming to realize how she'd come across.

Fayette thought of the people she'd worked with in recent years, the things she'd heard of and seen. "Is it alcohol or drugs that've got you snared by the ankle? No, no, I shouldn't have even asked; it's none of my beeswax—"

"Cocaine." The word was a raw breath.

"Oh." Fayette considered that a long moment, then sighed. "A lot of people have stepped into that snare."

"Yeah. Well. It's not always awful, is it? And that's the problem. You should've been a priest. Look at me, confessing here." Margaret shrugged and, in that motion, slipped back into the carefree version of herself. "Time to skedaddle. You're an absolute doll, Fayette Wynne." To Fayette's surprise, she garnered a kiss on the cheek. "You take care of our farm boy in there, you hear me?"

Margaret departed with a wave. Fayette closed the gate behind her.

She slowly walked back to the door, her mind swirling. The studio thought Margaret's marriage to Rex would . . . do what, exactly? Was he supposed to babysit her, keep drugs out of the house? Or was their wedlock supposed to simply add to her wholesome image so that when word of her addiction—or worse—went public, she could better weather the publicity nightmare?

It wasn't fair to put Rex in that place, nor was it fair for the higher-ups to expect Margaret to save Rex in some similar fashion. By Rex's and Margaret's own admissions, they barely knew each other.

Fayette had a hunch that Margaret probably didn't even know Rex's real name was Helmer.

She found Rex idling in a cozy little parlor. A steaming mug awaited her on a mat. "It's tea. Earl Grey," he said, gesturing for her to sit across from him in a leather chair. "I wasn't sure if I'd see you again today, but I'm glad you came by." For her, his grin was tired but sincere. She realized with a jolt that he'd been acting when Margaret was here, playing like everything was fine.

She was touched that he revealed the truth to her, but at the same time, she was perturbed that she'd believed his initial portrayal. Those dark thoughts must still be dogging him.

"I had to come by," she said airily. "I found out all kinds of things about that mystery house."

"Oh?" He genuinely perked up. She had him hooked.

With the warm mug between her palms, she told him what she'd learned about how the house hid from people—including him, until the previous day—and of Mrs. Fitz's role and the invitation extended their way.

"I've been treated as a celebrity in a lot of ways," Rex said, setting down his empty cup. "But I'm truly honored that I'm among the select few to gain entrance to Satan's henhouse."

"Is entry into Satan's henhouse more special than an invite to Hearst Castle?"

"Sure. Randolph invites scads of people. This nearby cliff house of ours, it's *exclusive*," he said. She laughed. She liked that he referred to the house as theirs. "Of course, I'll gladly attend the séance with you. I've been to a few already, and each one has made me less of a believer. Too many medium tricks remind me of film gags. Those special cabinets, the sleight of hand, the knocking. I haven't seen anyone oozing ectoplasm yet, and I'm not sure if I should be sad or glad about that."

"Well, pretend this is your first séance. Mrs. Fitz expects us to have *positive energy.*"

"Positive energy. I hate to think that she's being taken advantage of by a series of crooks."

"Seems to me that the Marshal is already trying to look out for her, but he can only do so much," she said, to which Rex nodded. He'd been coming to Carmel for years, so of course he knew who the Marshal was. "I've read that a lot of these mediums actually share information that they've gathered about their clients. That way, they can act like the spirits are passing along a person's intimate information, when in reality the details were collected by previous mediums."

"Scoundrels." He scowled. "Trying to protect your landlady puts you in an odd spot, though. If your energy is too negative, she might toss you out of your rental."

"I can handle any consequences. I'll stay in Satan's henhouse if I must." She sipped the last of her tea.

"Well, it'd provide shelter, but it'd be cold." He paused in thought. "If almost no one can see the house, that means we can light the oven without worry, make the temperature more tolerable. Why don't we go back and do that very thing later? I'd like to see the place in the dark when there's no storm. I have a golf game in just a bit, but I should be done by seven."

"Sure. That's a good time to get together."

Seven o'clock. That'd been the designated hour for her and Ma to sit together these past few years. They'd often reminisce about Briar, Thayer, and Pa. Ma would do her lacework or mending while Fayette tended to little house chores, but never work. That stretch from seven to about nine was a precious period when they were more than mother and daughter. They were best friends. Any stress that clung like static finally released its hold, leaving them relaxed and ready for bedtime.

They'd often eat Mother's bread then, too. There was something comforting about any good, wholesome bread in those kinds of moments, but of course, Mother offered something more.

Rex needed something more right about now.

"I'll bring firewood and meet you at the hut—if I can find it," he said.

"You're able to talk about the house. I reckon that means the enchantment doesn't have a hold on you anymore." Fayette stood.

"That makes a lot of sense. As much as anything does." He laughed, the sound bright and carefree. "*That* enchantment may not have a hold on me, but I'm enchanted nevertheless. I love that house. I love encountering some magic in the world."

Fayette had always known that the world had magic in it, but now she was considering that power from a fresh perspective.

So, Mother wanted to be made into bread? Fine. Fayette would divide her and do just that. Fayette would bake the loaf in the cottage, too.

The divine nature of the bread would act as a much-needed balm for Rex's aching spirit.

Chapter 11

"Much obliged for the help with the doors," Fayette said to the house as she entered that evening, the shutters folding open as part of her welcome. Her laden canvas bag swung from her shoulder, Mother's discard in a cup within her hand. As she'd expected, Mother had stubbornly grown with vigor during the day. Fayette had removed a portion—which still sparkled with vivacity, seemingly aware of its fate—and refreshed Mother's main body with a new dose of flour and water.

When in the vicinity of Grangeville Cottage, she'd attended to another important task: She left a note at Mrs. Fitz's door to inform her that her acquaintance, Rex Hallstrom, would be joining them at the séance tomorrow. She'd hoped to talk to Heidi about her experience with the house, but unfortunately, she was nowhere to be found.

Starlight shone down through the open windows, giving Fayette a smidgen of light without ruining her night vision. She considered removing her coat, as was proper when going indoors, but living in the south had apparently ruined her tolerance for the cold. The night air had a particular bite tonight.

She set down her burdens on the rectangular table. "Please be so kind as to let Rex in when he arrives, too," she said to the house. "He'll also be carrying a heavy load. He's bringing wood."

The house buzzed with power. Fayette laughed to herself and shook her head. Just two days ago, she'd described herself as boring. Maybe she still was, compared to the fashionable party set, but the company of a magical house surely offset her wears-cardigans-and-flat-shoes dullness to some degree.

She arrayed her supplies and fetched some tools from the built-in shelves around the grand oven. One of the pots was the perfect size for mixing the dough and housing it through the first rise. Mother's remnant, its paleness almost aglow in the meager light, already seemed to be growing despite the cold. It'd normally be a shriveled, sticky mass at the bottom of a basin at this point.

Rex should have been there by now.

The realization caused slow dread to slide along her spine. Maybe he'd been held up by his golf game. Maybe some person had recognized him on the street and proceeded to gab. Or maybe . . .

The two doors to outside opened in quick succession as she dashed out. Her view looking southward showed darkness, except for a light bobbing along somewhere out on the cliff. Anyone could be out there—anyone fool enough to brave that little promontory in the dark—but her gut instinct told her it was Rex.

He was on the cliff again.

Fayette's heart threatened to outpace her as she picked her way down the slope. At the base, off to one side, a pale bundle caught her eye. Was it cloth? A body? Had someone fallen as they tried to climb the slope? She sidetracked to investigate, discovering that the pale object was a large blanket wrapped around a bundle of stout sticks.

This was the firewood he'd said he would bring. He'd set it here and gone on to the cliff. It *was* Rex out there, it was.

She moved faster on the more-even ground, but she couldn't run—not on the rocks, not in the dark. "Rex!" she yelled. "Rex!"

The light moved up ahead. "Fayette?" His deep voice carried over the nearby roar of crashing waves.

"Rex! Don't do it! Don't jump!" She heaved for breath. The light arced and swung as he approached. That meant he was away from the edge. He couldn't jump now, he wouldn't jump, she wouldn't let him.

"I'm not going to. I'm here." His figure was a shadow behind the light. She grappled for him and found his free hand, lurching him off-balance as she gripped him. They rocked together but, unlike the first time they met, both stayed upright.

"You didn't— You weren't—" Fayette couldn't manage speech.

"I didn't go out there to . . . Really. I didn't." His voice was soft. "I wanted to revisit the place. I wanted to see how it felt, how it looked. Last night I couldn't take that in."

"You shouldn't have gone on the cliff by yourself, not this soon." She squeezed his hand. She didn't let go. Rex just might be a balloon as well as a man, and if she let go, he could fly away forever.

"You're crying," he said softly, in awe. "I'm sorry. I didn't mean to scare you. I brought wood. I left it closer to the house."

"I saw." She raised her empty hand to her cheek. He was right; she was crying. "You were depressed earlier. You—you really weren't going to—"

He seemed to understand that he needed to be blunt to be believable. "I didn't go out there to kill myself tonight, no. But I won't deny that I still feel sad. That I *am* still sad. I think I wanted to see if being in that same spot again made me feel better. More powerful."

"And if you hadn't?" She let go of him but remained wary.

Freshly freed, however, Rex didn't soar away. He stood there, flashlight angled downward, the faint illumination revealing his stillness as he studied her. "I guess I didn't think through that part of the challenge."

Fayette shook her head, unable to muster words. Her heartbeat continued to gallop. She was glad, too. Not only that he hadn't been fully on the verge of suicide tonight, but that she'd already started making bread for him. Mother's bread would help him as nothing else could.

"Fayette." His touch to her sleeve was like the brush of a wing. "I'm sorry I scared you; I truly am. I won't do that again."

"You'd better not," she rasped. The excitement must have quickly burned off the sliced apple she'd had with peanut butter a short while ago, as she suddenly felt quivery and weak again. "Now, how about you get that wood and we go inside?" She didn't even like standing this close to the cliff where he'd made his attempt.

She took the flashlight while he hoisted the load again using the blanket. The doors of the house softly whooshed open to admit them.

"I see our house here is as friendly as ever." Rex panted as he set down the wood by the oven. "What do you have on the table over there?" He began to place logs into a nook inset beside the fireplace segment.

"The makings for bread, but don't get too excited. It's not for tonight. This old-fashioned sort of bread needs a day or two to develop, usually."

"That's still something to look forward to tomorrow," Rex said. He sounded forcefully upbeat, as if he was trying to prove to her that he was optimistic. "I've had bread baked in brick ovens back home. There's nothing quite like it." He worked to get the fire going.

"I'm going to fetch some water from the pump outside. Or try to." Even if salt water came through the pump, that'd be an extraordinary thing, but she certainly hoped for something potable. No normal pipe could safely work through the ledge they were on. As a last resort, she could haul a water pail to and from Grangeville Cottage, but the very thought of that effort made her shoulder hurt.

"I'm curious as to what'll come out of the pump, too. Can you bring extra? I'd like to wash my hands off."

"Of course."

Fayette hesitated a moment. Were they really going to pretend like nothing had happened on the cliff just now? But then, what *had* happened? He'd said he hadn't been suicidal, but his mood could've changed in an instant, and that's all he would have needed to take action. One second of impetuousness and despair.

Even though she'd left the flashlight on the table, leaving them in gray starlight, he must've detected something of her mood. "Fayette,

I'm fine right now. I'll tell you when I'm not." There was a soft gravity to his voice that convinced her that he meant it. "You don't need to keep an eye on me."

"If you ever need company, just know that we can talk if you want, but I can also be there, quiet as a raisin. Just . . . with you. I have a whole book of crossword puzzles I've barely started on."

He laughed, the sound bright. "I think every other person is doing crosswords these past few years. I might be one of the last holdouts."

"Maybe I can convert you, then." She flashed him a grin before heading out.

Stars softened the harsh blackness outside. Even so, she trailed a hand along the house wall to help her maintain her balance along the uneven rocks. The ocean roared and thrummed below and around her. She gripped the cold metal of the pump and began to pull it up and down, glad she was feeling steadier again. Liquid emerged at her first effort. She paused and brought the sloshing pail near to her face. The contents didn't smell like salt water, or oil, or blood, or whatever else might emerge from a building with a fence made of femurs. She sipped the liquid from her palm.

"Huh," she said, then returned the pail to the ground to pump more. She thanked the house as it opened the doors for her return inside.

"You need to taste this," Fayette said, approaching Rex. He had the fire going. She grabbed a ladle from the hanging tools and brought up a dripping scoopful.

Rex sniffed at the ladle, then took a tentative slurp. His blue eyes widened. "I don't like the flavor of Carmel water much, so this . . . is quite the contrast. It tastes like melted snow. Should we still boil it before having more?"

"I don't know if there's a point. If this cottage wanted to do something to us, I reckon it would." She ladled water into a smaller pot and set it on the shelf high above the fire. "I need to warm this up a touch before I add it to the other ingredients. The pail's going to sit here. Use whatever you need."

"Thank you. I'm going to light the candles around the room."

"Here, give me a lit stick," she said. "I'll help."

Together they made the rounds to light the candles already set out on the table, on the far side of the massive oven, and in multiple wall sconces.

She checked on the pot afterward to find the water had warmed to a level she'd term room temperature.

She could now make bread, and she wanted to. She *needed* to help Rex. Mother's small presence radiated eagerness that stood out above the normal miasma of the house. Fayette used her fingertips to whisk the goop into the water. As she finished combining the dry ingredients, she paused, her hands hovering.

Three weeks ago, she had last used Mother for bread. Three weeks ago, she had been fully aware that Ma was dying. Fayette had shoved her emotions into the bread, weeping, raging, pleading. As the loaf had risen over the next day, she had shot it different looks depending on her mood. Sometimes desperate. Sometimes angry. Sometimes empty and exhausted. All the while, Mother's magic had been steady. Present.

In the end, Ma had only been able to eat a few bites from the baked loaf. For that, Fayette had been grateful, even in her bitterness. She'd kept the rest of the loaf near Ma's bedside because there was power found in merely being in its proximity—and she'd hoped that maybe, just maybe, Ma would gain an appetite as she had before.

This time, she didn't. Mother's power helped, but it was never enough. Never enough.

"Are you all right?" Rex asked quietly.

"Not particularly, no," she said, as honest with him as she wanted him to be with her. She resumed work, eyeballing the right amount of water to pour in. Fayette had made bread from Mother since she was about five. She knew by smell, feel, and sight if the portions were right. She delved into the dough with both hands.

"Do you want to talk about it?" Rex asked. He sat across the table from her, the candle between them casting a spooky glow into the refined lines of his face.

"I can, yes." She'd explain things to a limited degree, anyway. "I'm making this bread from a starter that's been in my family at least a hundred years, as far as I can figure. Before my paternal grandfather received it, the starter had been with a great-aunt, who'd used it for some forty years."

"Wow." He looked genuinely impressed. "Starters take some work to keep alive, don't they?"

"Yes. They need to be fed regularly, divided on occasion, and kept in an environment that's not too hot or too cold. They are living beings. Finicky beings, at that. We call ours Mother, with a capital *M*."

"Mother," he repeated with a smile. He had no idea how the dough quivered under her fingertips in response to his call. The dough liked him, approved of him. Fayette was pleased, and yet also mystified. Mother, even when she was called upon to help non–family members in need, didn't usually respond in such an obvious way. Her magic simply worked if she approved of someone—and if she didn't approve, well . . . the bread was simply bread, still a fine thing.

As Fayette continued to knead, though, she had to acknowledge that Mother wasn't just responding to Rex but also to the house itself. She knew that because the house's aura had intensified, too. Fayette felt warm, and not simply because the oven's fire continued to steadily burn.

"Bread made from a starter that old must have a particular flavor to it." Rex rose as she did, following her over to the oven. She scanned over the various available nooks.

"It does. You won't have better-tasting bread in your life." That was a fact, no matter how her emotions were mixed when it came to Mother. Fayette draped one of the house's woven towels over the pot and set it on a shelf on the far side from the warmth of the oven. "I'll check on the rise in a bit, and depending on how things go, I'll likely shape the loaf tomorrow morning or later in the day." If it rose so fast that she needed to shape it tonight—well, that'd be peculiar, but she figured she should, perhaps, expect peculiar here.

"Are you going to use a pan for that, or . . . ?"

"More often than not, I just do a basic bread round, but with my recipe, I could do pancakes or dinner rolls or—"

"Fayette." Her name emerged from Rex, strangled. She turned. He was looking past her. "There's a door. A new door. Over there."

She looked. There, at the side of the house nearest the ocean, was a rectangular wooden door where none had been before.

"That can't— Where can it lead?" she asked, taking a step closer.

"Fayette. No. Don't. It— The cliff is there—"

"I'm very aware of what's on the other side of that wall," she said breathily. This was a different sort of magic than she had ever known before. The true stuff of old stories. "The door has to be there for a reason, doesn't it?"

She stepped closer, closer.

Chapter 12

No, no, I feel I must do this. *She* has been there far too long. I cleaned up the messy bits years ago, a task made much easier by the lack of flesh, but it bothers me that she lingers as she does. After all, my witch lifted me from the nest. She fed me, stroked me, grafted me, made me what I am. Her hands were first upon my doors. She started my first fire!

I know she would not want to be buried here in this foreign land, but surely *something* could be done. After all, I cannot take her home, not while I am forced to roost here.

I've never conversed with bread dough before, and you're an incredible listener. And you're part of a greater entity called Mother? How interesting! I usually avoid using names because of the power that act accords, but I already sense the rightness of Mother through you. My use of her name is a minor thing that will not enhance her inherent might. And I am amazed that you're thriving now even as you're well aware of your imminent doom! I understand that you are old, yes, older than I am, but we are very different, the two of us. We see and experience the world in different ways. Why, I once knew an enchanted sword that thrummed with power, but it couldn't be trusted to do anything but *cut*! What a sad, limiting life it had, slicing through bone yet never comprehending poetry!

I'm glad that tale amuses you. I'm glad you're here. I've talked to myself for a long time, a very long time. If my new witch would come closer, would step inside, I could speak to her, too, but will she ever? Will she ever? I don't know!

But it feels good to have company within me. I like this woman, flavored by your magic. Your Mother's magic. She is the sort who scarcely needs help on her quest. She makes her own path. I'm glad you like her, too. That endorsement means much. The man, I like as well. He made fire within me! Fire! That is such a powerful, kind act—he has no idea how good I feel, warmed from within. Like I'm waking up in even more ways. I am still moored here, of course, but by the fire's light and energy, I see more of the world. That is a wonderful thing, even if I can't get up and dance. Oh, I wouldn't do that right here where I am, of course. I know better than *anyone* the weakness of the cliff beneath me. I wish I'd found someplace better to rest, but at that moment, I knew only my last order to fly across the sea, to save *her*, and the fog was so terrible that day—not simply an ocean fog, but the fog caused by war, terror, grief. I was scared. I won't deny that. I'm not so foolish as to try. My witch was dying amid her great exertion, and her last words echoed within me, fainter by the second. My greatest power faded with her, too. I didn't have long to find a landing place, no, but I knew there was a well here that could help sustain me as I idled. That would warm me in some ways, even as my innards cooled.

You feel the earth's power flow beneath us, too, don't you? Of course you do.

I won't scare off the woman and man by creating this door. Not the woman, certainly. Do you doubt her, even as you have fed each other for so long? Why?

I don't think that's fair. You see one aspect of her potential, but I see another. You nourish and heal; I am a house. I used to be very good at being a home, and I can be a home again. I can! Why, I'm among the last survivors of my brood, and that must be for a reason, right?

I want to provide shelter to those who need it, and help people along their way. Sometimes, to my dismay, that way was within my oven. Sometimes the people ended up on a throne or in other places of power. Quests are fickle things, and that's what makes them fun. And frustrating.

My witch's quest ended in a way we never expected, that is for sure.

And she's still here within me. Not rotting—oh, goodness no! But here, nevertheless. That's why I need help. I don't mind evicting the bodies of the mice that try to force their way into my seni, but I can't treat *her* like that. No.

Maybe this woman will understand what to do.

I won't scare her away. Will I? I don't think so.

I suppose we'll find out.

Chapter 13

Rex had the sense to grab his flashlight as he came up behind Fayette. As the beam glanced over the wall, the door opened.

Fayette had worked with some fine film cutters. There was art involved in slicing and splicing film to create a cohesive flow that, in an action scene, could make an audience's tension zoom higher than any geyser of black gold. Whoever was piecing together this bizarre reality before her had their timing down right if they wanted to scare the willies out of her.

"There's a room?" Fayette almost squealed.

"There's a room," Rex verified, his voice faint. Neither of them need say a room couldn't—shouldn't—exist there. It was free-floating over the turbulent ocean.

They walked closer. Rex's light, directed inside the room, traced a lump on the floor and paused on the gleaming white of a skull. Fayette screeched. Rex fell backward with a shocked, guttural cry, casting the room again into darkness—briefly. He regained his bearings and focused the beam forward once more.

"Move the light around," Fayette said, her mouth dry. She came to a standstill to one side of the open door, allowed him to illuminate what was within.

The skeleton wore brightly colored layers of skirts, embroidery extending along the hem and up the bodice. A red scarf curved around the back of the skull and tied beneath the jaw. Any hair seemed to be gone. The body lay somewhat on its side, facing the door, arms extended outward. No trace of flesh remained. The bones were as pristine as a specimen in a science laboratory.

"By the clothes, that looks like a woman?" Fayette asked, needing validation for what she saw.

"Yes. She's dressed like the village mobs in my movie." He aimed the beam past the corpse. The chamber that held the body was small, sparsely furnished. There were barrels in the background, along with heaped bags. It looked like a storeroom. A storeroom existing where it should not.

"Fayette, don't go forward. Please don't go forward." His deep voice trembled.

She didn't want to step into that room—she truly didn't. What if it ceased to be? What would happen if the door closed behind her? But there was something to this appearance, something magical that was unlike magic as she'd known it her entire life. Something she needed to understand.

"Rex, listen here. We can place something in the doorway—one of the large pots hanging from the rafter, maybe—and that way it won't close—"

"How do you know that? The house made a room that shouldn't exist! You think a pot is going to block the door?" His voice had a high, hysterical edge as he rose to his feet. "Fayette. Please. No." She let him pull her back a step, then two.

"But what are we—"

"No. Outside. Please. We shouldn't be in this place at all."

"Rex—"

"Please."

For his sake, she retreated. As they backed up toward the table, the strange door ahead of them slowly, tentatively closed. An instant later, it vanished completely.

Fayette's temptation gone, she joined Rex in a sprint. The interior doors barely opened in time to let them out. Once outside, they stopped on the flat rocks just beyond the entrance. They both turned to face the house. Fayette wondered if the entry door would vanish the way the other door had, but no, it remained—and stayed open. An invitation to return.

"What was that?" Rex asked, gasping for breath.

"We were shown something," Fayette said.

"A dead body! We were shown a corpse!"

"Briefly, yes, but it did stay dead and immobile."

"*That's* the positive you're taking away from this?"

"It's a significant perk, don't you think? The house . . . it displayed the skeleton for us."

Rex rubbed his face with his free hand. "If you visit a house, someone might show off a nice piece of furniture or some flowers. Not a dead body on the floor."

"We're not dealing with a human being. This is a house. It can't speak. We have to try to view things from its perspective." Fayette was amazed at how calm and rational she sounded, even as she trembled like a leaf in a hurricane. "The house has welcomed us, as it greets few others. It's opened windows so that we can see when we're inside. It's been accommodating."

"It showed us a dead body. And don't forget, there's a fence of femurs just over there." He waved the flashlight's beam farther down the slope.

"The house let us go just now, Rex. It didn't *have* to."

"You're doing a lousy job of comforting me, you should know."

"I'm scared, too. I didn't expect to be shown such a sight. But . . . I wonder at the timing."

"What do you mean?"

"This is our third visit here. I just made bread dough. You made a fire. The place is starting to feel warm and homey."

Rex snorted as he seemed to get her point. "When my folks taught me hospitality, that didn't include showing off a corpse on the third visit—but then, I've been told Swedes do things differently."

Fayette smiled. "I assure you, we weren't taught to show off corpses in Arkansas, either. Not even on the fifth visit."

"You want to go back inside, don't you?"

"Yes. I'm not letting my fear get the best of me."

"Well, you're not going in alone." He had a determined grimace.

Within the cottage, the fire continued to burn bright, the house's sparkling consciousness likewise bright. The new door didn't reappear as they entered the room, for which she was grateful. She walked up to that far wall against the cliff.

"You scared us, house," she said, craning her neck to look around. "I'd like to think you showed us that body for some purpose other than terrifying us, though. It's part of my job to understand what motivates people to act as they do. I confess, I've never had to consider what motivates a house before, especially one as extraordinary as you."

She touched the wall in the tentative way one tests a pot to see if it's cool enough for contact. The logs were smooth, bark sheared away, the surface oddly clean. Patting the area where the door had stood, she found no vertical seam, no deviation from the pattern of the logs. It was as if the door hadn't been there at all.

"Do you feel anything odd?" Rex had turned off the flashlight but continued to hold it like a cudgel, which was rather endearing. What, would he pound at the nonsensical door if it dared reappear? Or batter at these walls, which looked as stout as an American frontier fort?

"No. It feels like a log house." To her fingertips, at least.

"Do you really think the house understands English?"

She considered that, facing him. "If it doesn't, a lot comes through in tone. I only know a few words in Russian. A former Cossack works at the livery stable near my studio, and sometimes when I see him, he's in a mood to bolster my vocabulary."

"I only know a few words, too. I wish . . ." His voice trailed away.

"You wish what?"

"My friend Art can speak Russian. And English, German, French, maybe some other languages I don't know about. I wonder if he could be more . . . conversational with the house. Not like this place is speaking Russian to us, anyway. But maybe it could." He shook his head. "I wish I could get his take on this house, that's all."

"Why can't you invite him here? Is he out of the country? Committed to work?" She brought down the towel-covered pot. The iron was cool but not cold—perfect for encouraging a prolonged, gradual rise. The dough inside looked fine, too, still low. Things were developing at a fairly normal pace. She was glad for that. She needed another surprise tonight like a cat needed its tail stomped on.

"No. I'm just . . . We can't." Frustration punctuated that sentence. When she looked toward him, he glanced away, his jaw at a stubborn set.

"Well, I'm curious what a Russian would say about this kind of house. There *are* some Russians around here, or people who claim those origins," she said, thinking of the pompous so-called count near the beach. "But I wouldn't trust them to hold a nickel for me, much less come onto these grounds. A trustworthy friend is something else."

"He is that," Rex said in a murmur that didn't encourage the line of discussion.

"Okay." She wouldn't press him. Maybe he and his pal had had a tiff. "I'm going to leave the dough here overnight. We'll need to come back tomorrow so I can bake."

"You really want to come back here, even after . . . that?" He waved toward the wall.

"Especially after that! There's a mystery here we need to solve."

"A mystery. That makes it sound so . . . benign."

"You don't have to come back," she said softly. She hated the idea of coming here alone, of not sharing in this experience with someone, but she also didn't want him to feel uncomfortable or coerced.

Fayette seemed to have nicked his pride. His chin lifted with a new defiant tilt. "If you're returning, so am I. I can't meet early in the day, though. I had a thick envelope of fan mail arrive, and if I don't make progress on my replies, I'll soon be buried in an avalanche of paper like someone in a Chaplin gag."

"I'm amazed you don't have someone reply for you. I thought that's what all the big stars did."

"Some do. I don't. My name is already not my own. I'm not having someone else use it to sign letters, saying Lord-knows-what. I like to personalize every reply, even if it's just a line. These letters mean a lot to people. I respect that."

She smiled. "I respect you for it, too. I'll come by in the morning to shape the bread, then. What if we meet here again at . . . what, four? Will that work? The bread can be part of a supper here." She regarded her breadmaking supplies and shifted them to the end of the table rather than packing the flour and salt to go back to Grangeville Cottage. She'd already left enough flour there to feed Mother in the coming days.

"Four will do. I'll leave my fire-starting kit here. You'll need to rekindle the oven."

"That's fine. You brought plenty of wood. Let's go ahead and snuff the candles." They did that and met by the entrance. Rex turned on his light and, with some sheepishness, handed her a second one that'd been in his pocket all the while.

The doors opened to let them out. Rex released an audible sigh of relief.

"See you tomorrow, house," Fayette called. "Take good care of my dough. It's special."

"You're getting me excited about this bread of yours," Rex said.

"Good."

As she fell into stride with him, she realized that her trip to Carmel had introduced her to something that was, in a way, more extraordinary than a magical house that could hide itself: a new friendship.

Chapter 14

SP: "I must lose them somehow!"

Dot dashes through the dark mansion, looking over her shoulder every few seconds.

INSERT-Close-up view of two-tone men's shoes moving across the wood and rug-adorned floor, the feet stepping faster, faster.

Dot enters a parlor, spinning around, and then dives behind a large upholstered chair. She grabs a Chinese vase from a low wall shelf behind her and positions herself right near the entrance to the room.

C.U. of Dot's pale but determined face under dim illumination, her arms bringing the vase overhead.

Oh, this was good, this was very good. Fayette was caught up in her own manufactured tension, the fast clicking of her keys creating a more beautiful song than any bird. She'd awakened that morning with a stubborn determination to make solid progress on her continuity, and today the muses had agreed.

To think, all she'd needed to do to make such progress was escape Hollywood, begin a repeated sequence of breaking and entering in a hell-sent enchanted house, and encounter a corpse secured within a vanishing room. Why, if she could repeat this cycle again, she'd be as cozy in her career as a purebred Persian cat on a sunny velvet pillow!

She ended the scene with an irised-in view of a gloved hand covering Dot's mouth as the woman wiggled in need of escape. After that, the screen would go black in transition.

That meant Fayette had reached a good resting point for herself as well. She stood, stretching. Her left side was still stiff, the skin across the knob of her shoulder as black and purple as a cloudy nighttime sky. The joint felt better than it looked, at least. Eating some of Mother's bread later would complete the healing process.

The bread. Any pauses in her work had brought her thoughts to the events of the previous night. As vivid as her imagination was, Fayette had no idea how the house might surprise them next. Things had been normal enough—well, as normal as could be—when she'd jaunted down there first thing in the morning to check on the dough. Rex must have made a trip there after all, as the fire continued its steady burn and had no need of new wood.

She'd shaped the loaf into a round and placed it on a baker's peel that'd been hanging on the wall—an accessory she hadn't observed on previous visits, and she would've definitely made note of a handy tool such as that. The incredible house on the cliff seemed to possess the means to acquire or create certain goods.

Fayette gasped when she saw the time. It was almost the hour for her to meet Rex! The whole day had passed in a blur, but it was a good sort of blur—not the sort where you restlessly dozed the hours away at the bedside of someone who constantly thrashed and moaned in agony.

She'd even had adequate appetite across the day to down two peanut butter sandwiches along with the last of her apples, plus a big chunk of Dry Monterey Jack cheese. As a result, her fingers had been steady and her brain free of headaches, but she'd still shed far too much hair when she brushed it that morning.

Glancing out the front window, she could see through the parted curtains into the Fitz household. Heidi loomed in the window, bobbing in movement. Good, Fayette had been wanting to pin her down. She hurriedly attired herself for an outing and crossed directly to the back door. Heidi answered her knock.

Heidi's dark-blond hair was snugly pulled back into a snood, the white cap on her head leaving no ambiguity about her profession. She wore a plain white apron over a light-blue dress that fell to knee level, white stockings underneath. She had a small, stocky build, the stuff of a farm family or ancient warrior clan, or both.

Her smile for Fayette was tight. Was she upset about the interruption to her work, or was she still leery around Fayette because of whatever had made her balk at the door Sunday night?

Heidi motioned over her shoulder and mouthed words that, after a second, Fayette realized were "I'll get her."

Fayette shook her head. "I'm not here to talk to Mrs. Fitz. I hoped to chat with you. Could you perhaps grab some means to write?"

Heidi's expression was impassive. Her head tilted against the half-open door, her feet making no effort to move.

Well, this wasn't going to make things easy, and she gathered that that was the point. "You greeted me with such pleasantness, and then when you took me to get the candles, something changed. Did I offend you somehow? If I did, I'm sorry."

Heidi's eyes turned downcast, troubled, and she shook her head.

"I can't say I'm relieved by that answer, because even if I didn't offend you, something is still bothering you. Could you help me out, please?" Fayette was no people pleaser—not anymore. Nevertheless, she was perturbed to be disliked for no discernible reason. If someone wanted to hate her, by gum and by golly, she could surely give them proper motivation.

Without meeting her eye, Heidi shook her head again.

Fayette released a long, frustrated exhalation. "I saw you in the bushes at that house down on the cliff yesterday, and I was wondering if—"

That garnered a reaction—a swift one. Heidi's face uplifted, her expression a mix of fear and anger as she stepped back through the door, which then slammed in Fayette's face.

"Well, then," she said to the door. That encounter hadn't clarified the situation between her and Heidi, not one bit.

Frustrated, she walked on past the house and to the ocean a block away. Gulls swirled and griped, the insistent barks of seals carrying from the distance. The cliff here was some twenty feet high, and not a steep drop—more like a jagged, gradual decline to meet the thrashing waves below. Patchy gray clouds adorned the blue sky as the sun neared its nightly departure from this side of the planet.

To the south, she could see the magical house by itself on the cliff. It was maybe a third of a mile away, all by its lonesome against the dramatic backdrop of sky. It was gorgeous, a true spectacle. If people could see it, surely they'd snap pictures galore, just as they did of other local landmarks such as Tor House or the Lone Cypress.

She couldn't let the view distract her from the greater issue, though. She needed answers from Heidi, and since Heidi wasn't going to cooperate, that made her wonder more about Heidi herself. Where was she from? Who was she, really?

What would Fayette's character Dot do to investigate under similar circumstances?

Why, she'd seek out people who knew what was going on in town.

Like the Marshal. He had to be around here somewhere. Carmel wasn't that big of a place—just six hundred people or so, plus tourists.

Fayette set off on a walk. She asked a woman working in her yard if she'd seen the Marshal recently, and was told he'd passed by not long before. When she came across a still-hot pile of horse manure in the street, she knew she was likely on the right track.

Around the corner, she found him standing cross-armed as he supervised a grimy blond boy adding fist-size rocks to a flower bed already filled with porous stones. Beauty idled to one side, long tail swishing.

"Miss Wynne." The Marshal greeted her with a brisk nod, even as his gaze stayed on his young charge.

"Marshal. Pardon, I hoped to talk to you for a few, but you seem busy."

"I need a moment more here. This young man thought Mrs. Golden's rocks were for throwing at other boys, not for the flower bed. He's now had to gather, oh, how many pails of new rocks for the garden?" The question was pointed.

"Five, sir." No wonder the boy looked exhausted.

"Will you throw rocks again?" the Marshal asked with severity.

"No, sir."

"Can I trust you to finish this task on your own and then inform Mrs. Golden that you are done?"

"Yes, sir."

With a satisfied nod, the Marshal turned his attention to her. "Let us speak, hmm?"

They walked to a nearby vista of the ocean, Beauty following with an easy gait. "First of all, Marshal, I wanted to let you know that Mrs. Fitz is hosting a séance tonight. She invited me to attend."

He heavily sighed. "Mrs. Fitz. She is a noble woman. Any of us could hope to be loved the way she loves."

"She is an incredibly kind person in her own way. I would've wanted to look out for her interests even if you hadn't asked me to. If anything sketchy happens tonight, I'll let you know."

Fayette gazed south and saw the house on the cliff. She recalled what Mrs. Fitz had said about trying to inform the Marshal about it years ago. Was the fog of enchantment still draped over him?

She pointed to the house. "I've been told the Fitzes own the land south of here. Does that include that building there?"

The Marshal blinked quickly, brow furrowed beneath the brim of his hat. "They own the land between here and the beach, yes, and used to own much more."

"But what of the house there?"

Again, he blinked as if he had something in his eye and couldn't get it out. "A house, Miss Wynne?"

Fayette sighed. No point in continuing that particular exercise. "Never you mind. On the subject of the Fitz household, however, I've tried to speak with their hired woman, Heidi. She didn't want to talk to me, and I'm not sure why."

"Ah, Miss Heidi. She keeps to herself, but she is a good worker and one of the kindest people around."

"I heard she gives away bread."

"Yes, and it is excellent bread. She says a great deal through her actions, without the need to ever speak. You must understand, Heidi works for Mrs. Fitz, but they are a family. They look out for each other, which is good and right. I do not think Heidi will ever fully recover from her near drowning. Many people don't." Sadness sagged his features.

"Wait. Near drowning?"

"Yes. She was found in the water, floating, unconscious. We, everyone in town, feared she was already dead or would soon die, but she pulled through, though she had days of delirium after she first awoke. She is strong." Admiration came through his tone.

"Delirium? She could speak, then?"

"She spoke many languages during her illness, but after she fully awoke, she said nothing. The brain . . . sometimes it is damaged by such things as drowning." He tapped the crown of his hat for emphasis.

"When did this happen?"

The Marshal tilted up his head in thought. "Near ten years ago. Before the war ended."

"How did she come to stay with Mrs. Fitz?"

"Her house was closest when Heidi was found on the beach." That meant Heidi had been recovered near the river's mouth, not at the beach adjacent to downtown. "Doctors tended her there. As Heidi recovered, she stayed and began to contribute. Her help became even more important after Mr. Fitz returned."

"She's never made to leave town?"

The Marshal swayed when he shook his head. "No, no. I do not think she has a safe place to go. I suspect, you see, that a husband or other man attacked her and threw her overboard." He spoke as if he'd witnessed many such altercations. "She is safe here. She and Mrs. Fitz, they take care of each other, and the mister."

"Yes, I can see that," Fayette said, though she actually hadn't seen "the mister" herself yet. She supposed that would happen tonight. As the Marshal pulled himself back into the saddle, she asked, "Does Heidi have a last name? It's never been mentioned."

"There is none. She never even gave the name Heidi." He used his heel to bring Beauty around to face north. "Mrs. Fitz named her out of love for the book character. Her hope was that the beauty of Carmel would heal Heidi, much as the book characters were helped by the glory of the Alps."

Fayette nodded, thoughtful. "That does seem like a suitable name for that reason."

The Marshal looked down at her, his frown severe. "Now that you know the story, do not pester Heidi. If she does not wish to communicate with you, respect her wishes."

"No, no, of course not. Thank you for looking out for Heidi in this way." Truly, her respect for the Marshal couldn't get higher at this point.

As the Marshal and Beauty departed, Fayette faced the darkening sea. Heidi was a mystery, right along with the house. A house that Heidi could also access to some degree. What did that mean? Why was she among the chosen few?

"Fayette!" a deep voice called. She looked back to see Rex on the nearby road. With both hands, he carried a large burlap bag that swayed as if it was heavy. "Could you lend a hand?"

"Of course!" She hurried over to meet him. His face was flushed with exertion. "What are you carrying, an anvil?"

"Something a bit more enjoyable, but also useful for crushing our enemies—a stack of hardbound architecture books, courtesy of my neighbor." He set down his load to pull out two tacket-bound books about as long as her arm and passed them to her. "I got to jabbering with him on the subject of Russian architecture—I told him I was trying to identify something I saw on set—and he said he'd lend me any books he had that might help me in my search."

"You could've left these massive tomes in your place and invited me over to look!" she chastised as they began to walk.

"They didn't seem so heavy at first." He gave his head a rueful shake.

"Well, we now have something to read as the bread bakes." Fayette shifted her burden more to her right side. She couldn't let him know how the books strained her injured shoulder.

"On the subject of bread, how do you like other fixings like cheese, butter, and dry sausage?"

Fayette stopped in her tracks. "What, do you have the contents of a picnic basket in your pack there?" She nodded toward the strap over his shoulder.

"I do. I brought root beer bottles, too."

Hot tears stung her eyes. If she discounted her fellow captives on the endless bus ride up to Carmel, the last person she'd eaten with had been Ma.

Actually, now that she thought about it, she'd almost always had company during meals. At work, she'd be with April and the other women, and at home, Ma had usually been within talking distance in their small house.

Was her . . . newfound loneliness part of why it was so hard to eat? Was that why Rex's offer had almost induced her to bawling out of a strange sense of *relief*?

Rex glanced back, clearly puzzled by her pause. She started walking again with a huff of effort.

"Well, I like how you think, Rex Hallstrom. At least when it comes to food. You sure misjudged the weight of these books." She forced levity into her voice as she followed him through the wax myrtles.

"I can't be perfect," he said with a laugh.

"I'm not fool enough to expect perfection, but you gave thought to pairing cheese and butter with bread, and that's certainly the way angels must think." She said that with absolute sincerity.

When they reached the rocks beneath the house, a thought occurred to her, and she turned around.

"We just walked straight through the grass," she said.

"Yes." Understanding dawned on his face. "The fence is gone?"

"So it seems. Look."

Rex paced the area where it once stood. "I can't even feel postholes underfoot. What do you think happened to the fence?"

"I haven't the foggiest."

"Do you think the house will offer up any additional marvels today?" he asked, breaths huffing as they climbed the rise.

"We should be ready for most anything, I think," Fayette said, considering the house that loomed in silhouette above.

"That's not exactly a comfort."

"I like to think of myself as pragmatic."

He cast her a smile. "I like that about you, especially after being in Hollywood for years."

"Whatever happens inside the house, just keep in mind that it has shocked us in major ways but it's never acted maliciously toward us. Not yet, anyway."

Rex's laugh portrayed a high note of anxiety. "Yet here we are, about to go inside again."

The door swung open.

"Yes, here we are," Fayette said, wondering how a building that was in so many ways frightening could also feel so cozy and right.

Chapter 15

"The oven fire's still burning!" Rex said as soon as they entered the house.

"It was lit and enthusiastic when I visited to shape the bread. I didn't need to add any wood. Did you come by early in the morning?"

"No." Rex grunted as he set his load of books on the table, then went back to study the doorframe. "The fixtures on the door don't look like bone anymore, but metal." He went to the oven.

"The house . . . kept the fire going? And removed the scary bits around the property?" Fayette wondered aloud as she set down her books. She went to the water bucket she'd kept near the stove. As she washed her hands, she noted Rex had a funny look on his face. "What're you thinking?"

"It really does seem like the house removed specific things that alarmed us before—and having said that, I just noticed something new and peculiar. The wood is the exact same." At her puzzled look, he continued, "The branches I put in the fire yesterday are still there. See that stick?" He stooped to point. "It has wicked knobs that practically gutted me as I toted the load here. I put it in the fireplace first thing, and it's still burning a day later. That's both magical and creepy as all get-out."

"This *is* Satan's henhouse, remember."

A smile softened his face. "We haven't seen demonic chickens yet, or feathers. We've been spared that oddity so far."

"So far. Now, shuffle back a step. My loaf must be ready to go in."

The sourdough boule had spread upward and out, creating a beautiful round loaf. She poked a finger into the side and nodded in pleasure when the impression slowly filled in. The dough was indeed ready. She used a nearby knife to score shallow lines across the top; the loaf would expand at those spots rather than explode out the sides. She'd learned that lesson the hard way when she'd made bread in haste. Not even Mother's bread was immune to a baker's mistakes.

She used the long wooden peel to shove the loaf far back within the baking cavity set above the fireplace.

"I'll need to watch the bread carefully, as this isn't my normal manner of baking. But hopefully, in a short while we'll have edible bread."

"Great. Let's light the candles again now. Actually . . ." Rex paused, head tilted in thought. "Fayette, why do you think the oven fire stayed lit but the candles haven't come back on their own?"

"We did snuff out the candles before we left yesterday. If we'd killed the oven fire, maybe it would have stayed out, too? We can try leaving the candles burning today, see what happens." The idea made her a little nervous. Rex frowned as he nodded, apparently feeling the same.

Using two sticks of lit kindling, they visited the candles. That done, they returned to the table and the books. She opened the top volume.

"Oh, the paper is nice in this one. Full-color illustrations, too." She petted a glossy frontispiece.

"Richard—that's my architect neighbor—said he thought that volume was the most likely one to have information on Russian peasant houses." Rex shook his head as he pulled one of the large books closer to his seat. "Richard has seven dogs, and I don't know how he can deal with them all. They take *him* for walks."

Fayette laughed. "I can imagine." Her finger trailed down the table of contents. Sections were organized by regions of the world. She flipped to the part on Russia.

"Eh, this book is all about palaces around the world. That's not what we want. I wish I'd noticed that before I hauled it all the way here."

Rex set that book aside. The glorious smell of baking bread began to fill the room.

"Oh! I think I found something." Fayette tapped the page with a forefinger. "Right at the very start of this section, here's our house! This style is found across Russia, Ukraine, Romania—that's a wide area."

The illustration showed a square log hut just like the one they sat in, the high-peaked roof featuring carved designs along the eaves. She flipped the page and gasped. There was a series of images depicting the interior.

"So, this style is called an izba," Rex muttered, displaying an ability to read upside down. "Some such houses are two stories. Some have basements." He shuddered. "I hope this one doesn't have a basement door appear. In a way, that'd be more unnerving than the door against the cliff."

Fayette nodded as she kept reading. "This says the massive oven is the main feature in an izba, but not all of these other details match." She motioned to the various black-and-white photographs across the page.

"No." Rex looked around the room. "The book says there should be a red corner there, filled with religious iconography. But there's nothing Christian here at all, not even a cross by the door. It's as if the Bolsheviks came through." The new Communist rule in Russia disapproved of religion. People weren't even allowed to celebrate Christmas anymore, observing a generic winter holiday instead.

"I have a hunch that this place is a lot older than the Bolsheviks and the Revolution," Fayette said.

"No argument with that." Rex tilted his head in thought. "This paragraph says that masonry ovens only began in the sixteenth century. Maybe the oven is the newest thing about this house. There's something here that feels older than Christianity, Judaism, Islam—any of that stuff. More pagan, primeval." He frowned toward the oven. "As good as that baking bread smells . . . is it really safe to eat something that was made here? The nature of this place could . . . change things."

"I know my bread. It's fine."

"How can you say that with any confidence?" Rex asked.

Because she knew the bread was *right*. Mother's power radiated outward with gentle tendrils. Even if there *had* been some taint from the house, Mother's intensity would nullify or overpower it. Especially at this moment. This bread, its presence, felt more potent than it'd been in a long time. As if Mother felt like she had something to prove.

"I know my bread," she repeated. "I literally cut my teeth on bread from this starter—my family fed me dried and toasted pieces as my first teeth came in. It probably formed my initial solid meals, too."

"But that has no bearing on if it's contaminated now. Flour can spoil, after all. The water you add could have typhoid." He grimaced. "Of course, I drank some of the water from the pump here yesterday and used it to wash up, too."

"That's it. You're already doomed. You may as well enjoy the bread since poison is already coursing through your veins." Fayette gave an exaggerated sigh.

"If I'm kaput, well . . . this delicious-smelling bread will make for a fine final meal." Rex laughed. "I know, it's a bit late to worry about things like the water quality. You're in bold contrast to me, though. You have full faith that the bread is good. I just wish I could understand why."

She wished she could provide a logical justification for what she sensed. "I'll eat it alone if you won't touch it." He'd still get some of the effects by being nearby, at least. She rose and walked toward the oven. By the fragrance, by the zing in the air, she knew the loaf had to be about done.

"As good as that bread smells, I'd be tortured if I didn't try a piece. Here, I'll move the books over so I can get the other food out— Ouch!"

"What happened?" She twisted around.

"A paper cut. A sizable one, courtesy of a long sheet of paper. It stings, but it's not bleeding."

She heard him rustling things around as she used a long iron tool to slide the bread toward her along the bricks. The smell became more powerful, more glorious, as it reached the front. A lovely golden crust crowned the top. She could already envision how it would crunch between her teeth.

"I brought . . . let's see here," said Rex. "Butter. Strawberry jam. Cheddar cheese. Sausage. Ah, good, the root beer is still cold. In all, a lovely picnic, I think."

A memory flooded her mind.

Her family, crowded around the table. She'd just gotten her job at Astrophel, and they had decided to celebrate by splurging. Briar had bought Fayette's favorite jam, apricot. Butter rested in a luscious log. Thayer had bought cold sausages made by a coworker's brother.

And then, of course, there was bread derived from Mother. It sat on the cutting board, its inherent power filling the room with warmth.

They'd all laughed and talked over each other, happy to be together, blissfully ignorant of how their numbers would soon dwindle until only Fayette remained.

Back in those days, their decades-old dining table always felt too small. More than once, Ma had vowed to replace it when they had more funds. That never happened.

It now felt as large as a royal banquet table when Fayette sat there alone.

She blinked back tears as she brought over the bread. "What, did you bring enough for eight people?" she asked in a forced joking tone, playing as if everything were fine.

"I'm hungry, and I'm sure you are, too."

"I wish we had more people to share this bounty with," she said, thinking again of her family.

"I'm fine with sharing with more people, but I don't know who else to trust in this place." He looked around with a wistful expression. "I feel honored that I was allowed to see it and come inside, thanks to you. I was a lost soul. Now I'm . . . a little less lost."

She thought again of her family and her lonesome table. "This bread is meant for lost souls like us. Now, you put down that knife. If you cut into the loaf right away, the whole thing will deflate. Let it cool a bit longer."

"I'm sorry. I honestly don't think I've ever smelled bread this good." She could hear the saliva in his words.

"This bread is unlike any other you've had in your life. It'll make you feel right as rain," she said softly, already feeling the ache in her shoulder begin to fade.

Chapter 16

I understand the ways of lost souls. Not that I have ever been lost myself, of course, but I do have a soul! I happen to always know exactly where I am. Birds have a good sense of direction, and I am in many ways a bird, even if I don't have a beak to speak aloud or eyes in the way most living beings have eyes.

Most every person on a quest becomes a lost soul at several points in their journey. That is the way of such things. These people know they have a place where they need to be and the path toward that point is muddled. That's where I come in! My witch would direct me where to go so that I may intercept them, and after that, she'd intercede.

But I can't move right now while I am forced to wait.

The woman and man want to feed other lost souls.

The bread would want to be used for that purpose, too. It said as much as its voice baked away, telling me of how Mother exists to help people who need aid the most. Also, that Mother doesn't think she has done enough of that. She has regrets, as fresh as stormwater.

I understand regrets, just as I understand lost souls.

I want to make my current people happy. I haven't met Mother yet, but I want to help her help others, too.

With my oven and wits lit, I feel more like myself than I have since my witch died. I wouldn't have even been able to open the door to her private room a week ago when I sat here, cold inside and out. But I could open that door now, easily.

I can open other doors, too. I can actually help people *survive* their quests instead of being an end point.

I haven't done far-reaching doors in a very long time. My witch used to visit her sisters in that way, and she didn't simply do so because of speed. Some of my siblings like to fight, and some of the other witches enjoy such bouts, too. Feathers and shutters fly, log walls bleed, and everything inside is tossed into disarray. The very thought of such a mess makes me shudder in horror. I was fortunate in that my old witch was of the same sentiment.

If one of my witch's sisters happened to be nearby, she could hop in her flying mortar with pestle and fly there for a visit, but that usually was not the case. Rus was—and still is—large, and we were all certainly capable of wandering beyond its fluctuating borders if we so chose. Because of that, quite often the best way for the witches to visit each other was for us houses to create connecting doors.

I could identify wherever her sisters were in the world. I had a special knack for that, really. In that same way, I can find lost souls. I know their hollowness, their need. Their hunger, physical and spiritual. I can smell them, the way a hen smells coming rain. I can find someone who needs this bread.

That will please the woman, won't it? If I bring her a lost soul, surely she will bring more portions of Mother and bake more bread, right?

But my action might scare her even if it pleases her. The dough was right to advise caution when I created my previous door—its appearance did frighten the people away, briefly. I suppose one should heed the advice of bread dough when it deems to speak.

The people did come back, though. That was all because of the woman, who has now made bread that radiates heat, power, and promise. Bread that is ready to eat.

Now, to find someone who can partake in this feast . . .

Chapter 17

Rex's gasp rang out with a panicked hiss.

"The door. It's back!" He stood, braced against the table, ready to bolt.

Fayette whirled around to face the far wall, frowning. "That's not the same door."

The door the previous day had been timbered much like the two entrance doors to the house, of like-colored dense wood and iron. This door was rectangular and made of warped planks, the color pale white and mottled by wear. A tattered lavender curtain adorned a small inset window.

This was a door that led outside—a horrifying thought, with the ocean just beyond. But this door didn't match this house any more than a new-model Perfection Oil Cook Stove would. The passage couldn't lead out over the ocean, it couldn't.

The door opened.

A girl stumbled through. Stick-thin in a wasted way, she could've been anywhere between ten and fifteen. Her knee-length dress— her whole body—was brown with drying mud. Her skin color was impossible to gauge beneath the muck, her black hair twisted into two thick braids. Her widening eyes glowed white by candlelight. Behind her, Fayette had a glimpse of dark sky—which didn't fit with the fading sunset visible through the hut's open windows.

As the girl stood straight, the door behind her closed and vanished as if it'd never been there at all.

Fayette didn't remember standing up or running, but in the space of two ragged breaths, she was there before the girl. "How are you?"

"Can we help?" Rex was right beside her.

"What's this place? Where am I?" A quavering note of terror crept into the girl's words as she clutched her arms against her chest.

Seeing no way to duck around the scary truth, Fayette spoke up. "You've . . . arrived in a magical house. In California. Are you hurt?"

"California?" The breathy word held yearning and disbelief. "How can I be in California? It's . . . it's so far away!" Fayette tried to place her accent. Polish, maybe German, but still easy to understand.

"We don't fully understand, either," Rex said. "But—"

The girl looked past him. "Do I smell bread?"

Fayette and Rex shared a look. The house had brought this girl here right as they were ready to eat. That couldn't be an accident. "Yes. Let's get you some water to wash up—"

"No. I can't. I need to be able to hide from him, I need to—" Her fingers clutched at the broad collar of her dress as she turned, a slight scream escaping her throat. "It closed! The door, it closed; it is gone! How do I get back?"

Another shared look, of dread and fear. "We've never had someone arrive here like this before," Fayette said. "But this house . . . we will ask it nicely. It can open the way for you again." She portrayed more confidence than she felt, her thoughts tumbling into prayers she hadn't even bothered with in Ma's final days.

"If your . . . situation is that bad, do you want to go back?" Rex asked softly.

The girl whirled around to face him, chin tilting up. "I will not abandon my sisters."

Oh Lord, oh Lord. Fayette could imagine what was happening but didn't want to. "Come eat. Please."

The girl's dull-black shoes tentatively tapped across the floor until she came within five feet of the table. She rushed through those last steps, her hands raising to her mouth. "A feast," she said breathlessly. "Oh, there's so *much*."

A feast. Another pang right through Fayette's heart. She grabbed the knife. "I'll cut the bread. Rex—"

"I'll pour us all some water, and then I'll slice the sausage." From the pitcher, he tipped water into clay cups found on the oven shelves. "Would you like to have root beer, too?" he asked the girl.

"Oh, yes." When Fayette popped off the lid, the girl observed the soft drink's hiss and bubble the way someone might've watched an old-time miracle, like a hand reattaching to an arm.

"Make yourself drink and eat slowly. You can get sick if you down everything too fast," Fayette said to the girl as she tipped back the brown bottle.

The girl nodded as she set the bottle down again. "I know," she said simply. "Can I—"

"Eat as much as you want, of whatever you want. Just go slowly, like Fayette said." Tears swam in Rex's eyes.

The girl, with shaking hands, spread butter onto a thick end slice, topping it with a walnut-size dollop of jam. She used the back of a spoon to spread the strawberry jam into a chunky layer, then bit into it with her eyes half closed. Fayette didn't say a darn thing as flaked mud fell from the girl's arms and onto the table, or when it absorbed into the wood like water into a sponge.

She and Rex shared another look; then they each reached for their own pieces of bread and began to eat, though at a much slower pace than the girl. She needed to have first dibs. Goose bumps broke out across Fayette's skin as she felt Mother's full magic begin its work.

Foremost, Mother's presence in bread brought a sense of wellness. Hope. It was fleeting, as was everything in this world, but the feeling of contentedness was as solid as the bread itself. This, really, was why Fayette had wanted to bake on Rex's behalf. She wanted him to experience some levity of spirit. Nothing about Mother was a cure-all, of course, but if despair was a thick fog, Mother's magic was sunlight shining from high above.

And then there was Mother's healing power.

As Fayette finished her slice, the tenacious pain in her shoulder vanished at last. She shifted the joint, testing the movement, and released a long exhale of relief. As she reached for a coin of sausage, she noted her pointer finger, which had been scraped raw in her fall on the cliff, was now sheathed in fresh pink skin.

When had she last eaten meat? She had to wonder that as she thoughtfully chewed. Her body probably had been needing a meal like this for weeks—as had her spirit.

The girl guzzled down more root beer, eyes closed in bliss.

Gazing around, Fayette realized this was a true thanksgiving, almost a week after she had observed the American holiday alone, cocooned in her misery. Someone had knocked on her door—probably Luis, and likely to invite her over. She hadn't answered. She hadn't eaten anything at all that day. Ma had been buried the evening before, and Fayette had felt heavy and listless, as if she'd worn herself out by digging the deep grave herself.

She ate now, with slow, careful, grateful bites. She ate with a smile.

"This is the best bread I've ever had in my life." Tears cleansed trails down the girl's face. "Can I— Would it be okay if I—" A sob choked off her words.

"Yes?" asked Fayette in encouragement.

"Can I bring food back for my sisters?" she blurted out. "If I need to work for it, I can. I'm a hard worker—the best."

Oh. "You don't need to work for this, sweetheart," Rex said. "If you need more food than we have here, or anything else, we can get it, too."

The girl hefted the pitcher. "Is there more water? I have a canteen I need to fill."

"There's a pump outside. I can fill your canteen." Fayette stood. "Actually, would you like to see the California coast?"

Her eyes widened. "The ocean? It's right outside?"

For the first time, Fayette realized they couldn't hear the ocean in the house, even though it stood on the brink. Here she prided herself on her authorial skills of observation, and yet she'd missed such a glaring omission. "Yes. In a normal building, you'd be able to hear it from this close, but this house—"

"Is of God. Yes." The girl leaped to her feet. "Let me see, please."

This house was of God. That felt nearer to the truth than naming it Satan's henhouse.

The girl stopped at the threshold to outside.

"I've never seen a rock this dark and big," she said. "It looks slippery."

"It can be, even when it's not rainy. Would you like to hold my hand? We'll go slowly, together." The girl promptly accepted Fayette's offer. They walked around the side of the house to stare out at the endless sprawl of the Pacific.

There are sunsets, and then there are sunsets on the California coast. Shreds of deep purple clouds stretched out, royal and bold against a pink-and-gold sky. The small, glowing sun perched atop a cloud like a bird on the nest. The ocean below teemed in deep blue and purple, the breakers like long, jagged rows of lace. Far, far out on the horizon, a large boat resembled a mere toy.

The girl gasped and murmured something in another language. New tears traced lines down her cheeks.

"I have never seen anything so beautiful in all my life." The words in English rattled like coins in a can. To Fayette's surprise, the girl then faced the house feet away. They stood near the corner, where, inside, her transportive door had appeared. "You, house, you are part of this most beautiful scene." She took a step closer and spread her arms wide to hug the house, as best as a log wall can be hugged.

With a hand still on the wall for balance, the girl gazed outward again. "Is that a boat far out there?" She pointed.

"Yes, probably a steamer going from San Francisco down to Los Angeles, or maybe to the Hawaiian Islands."

"Hawaii!" Her face glowed even through the mud. "This is California. I am truly in California. Where is Hollywood?"

Fayette laughed. Of course the girl would ask about that fabled place. "Hours south. We're along the Central Coast right now, between the larger cities. San Francisco is much closer to us than Los Angeles." Fayette glanced back. Rex had come outside with them, but she couldn't see him now.

The girl nodded, staring at the horizon and far beyond. "We're going to come to California," she said with soft determination. "This is our land of promise." That sounded like an intertitle from a movie, the kind that came across as corny on the screen. It didn't ring that way when the girl said it. The words were a vow, hope twined into a thin string of syllables.

They went back inside. Rex was tying a knot in a bundle made from the blanket he'd used for wood the day before. It wasn't clean, but that hardly mattered right now. "I've packed up food for you. The rest of the butter is between the slices of bread. The jam jar and the other root beer are wrapped in some extra cloth. I hope they keep. Oh, there's a bottle opener, too."

"Thank you. I'll be careful." She took the bundle, and as she did, she stood on tiptoe to kiss his cheek. "Now I can say I kissed the movie actor Rex Hallstrom." There was a new lightness around her that Fayette knew had been partially inspired by the bread—but only partially.

"You *recognized* me?" To Fayette's surprise, Rex actually blushed.

"Oh, yes. As soon as we sat at the table. On another day, meeting you would be quite the thing, but this day, the house and the food are most important," she said with grave sincerity.

Rex smiled. "I am fine with being upstaged by this particular house. If there's anything else you need, I just need time to—"

"No. There is no more time. This, this is a godsend. With this food, we will make it farther tonight." She spun on a foot to face Fayette. She, too, was given a kiss on the cheek. "My thanks to you, for the food and the sunset."

"You are more than welcome." Fayette led the way to the blank log wall. "House," she said, "our guest needs the door back, leading right where it did before. Can you kindly open the way for her?"

In a blink, the battered door returned, the curtains on the inset window still limp and threadbare. Fayette released a rattling, relieved exhalation.

The girl smiled; she had demonstrated no doubt that the house would do as requested. "Yes, that is my door. Thank you, good house. I love you." She leaned in to kiss the log wall before gripping the doorknob. As she opened the door, cold night air drifted over Fayette, the smell of rain strong.

"Goodbye," the girl said to Fayette and Rex. "God keep you." With that, she passed through. The door quietly closed at her heels. An instant later, it was gone.

"Oh my. Oh my." Fayette pressed a hand to her lips. "That girl, what she and her sisters must be going through—" Her words stopped with a sob.

"That experience was . . . something different, and better, than the view of that corpse yesterday."

"Yes." Fayette wiped her eyes. She hated crying; it made her nose run. "Mrs. Fitz might think this house is demonic, but what it did right now—"

"There's divinity to it. The house worked to save that girl, and through that action, her sisters, too. And then there was the bread as well."

"What about the bread?" she asked in a bland tone. She'd rather hoped he hadn't noticed anything peculiar amid all else that was going on.

"It made me feel good. Not simply because of the company, either. That wicked paper cut that made me yelp aloud a short time ago? It's gone." He brandished the intact pointer finger as proof. "Having that bread was like . . . drinking a good cider. Not the kind sold in shops these days, but with full alcohol, though the buzz didn't make me feel inebriated or out of control, just . . . comfortable." The last word was a whisper.

"You haven't felt that way lately, have you?"

"No." He squinted at her. "You felt the same thing from the bread, didn't you? I'm not alone in this?"

The words of her grandparents, her parents, her siblings resonated through her. The power of the bread needed to be kept secret. Mother had been stolen before. A theft could happen again. That's why the bread they made needed to primarily stay within the family, and if it was gifted, it needed to be anonymous. There had been many nights, when she was a child, where she'd go out on Ma's order and quietly set a paper-wrapped loaf on the stoop of someone who had been kind to them or was otherwise in need. Along with the gift would be a note, simply stating that the bread was given in gratitude and would restore their spirits.

Fayette hadn't made any such deliveries in years.

She'd spent so many weeks and months immersed in bitterness because Mother hadn't done enough for her family, but had she done enough for Mother? Truly used her to the utmost? The answer to both questions was no, definitely not. She had taken for granted this blessing within her family. She'd always known Mother and assumed she always would—and that Mother was an onerous burden for her to bear alone, from here on.

As Rex regarded Fayette with worried eyes, she recognized how easy it would be for her to credit the house with the bread's power, but that would mean lying to him after they'd already shared so many moments of profound intimacy and vulnerability in recent days.

Fayette took a steadying breath. "The bread was . . . as it should be. As it's always been. As far as I can tell, by all my faculties, the bread wanted to be made and baked in this place."

His brows curved together. "How could it *want* to be made?"

"Let's sit so I can tell the tale."

As Fayette explained the nature of Mother and the bread to Rex, the magic of the house flared, too. Her skin warmed as if she stood near the fire. It was as though the house's presence was heightened as it listened in. The cozy fire-lit environment felt right for reciting stories tinged by the kind of old-world magic that one didn't commonly encounter during this current age of airplanes and radio. Rex asked a few questions, but most of all, he listened.

She realized that was one of the things she appreciated most about him. He listened with full attention. That was part of his power on the screen, too. His focus, his respect, for the actors around him came through, and his serious regard made everything more real.

"I think I understand now why you had more trust in the house from the start," Rex said. Before him, the butter crock sat empty but for a few stubborn smears. "You had familiarity with the magical, and that particular magical thing seemed keen on coming here, too."

"As far as I can tell, yes. I hope you understand why I dared not tell you any of this before now."

"Absolutely. I value your trust in me. There was no reason for you to offer me such a gift the first night we met." A flicker of dismay passed over his face. Was he recalling what had happened on the cliff? After a few seconds, he continued, "When do you think you'll make more bread?"

"That depends on Mother. Back in the day, when we fed a whole house, we kept Mother active and made two loaves a week. She needs time to recover between batches. If her rise continues to be enthusiastic, though . . ."

"You've talked a lot about intuition and gut instinct in how you perceive magic. I don't detect any of that, but to my ordinary observational skills, I feel as though the house brought that girl to us, to the bread." They both stared at the blank wall against the sea.

"Now that I think about it, I *asked* for that to happen," Fayette said, her thoughts spinning. "Remember? Just as we sat down to eat, we talked about lost souls, and I wished we could share what we had."

"The house listened and delivered. It just might do so again." Worry clouded his brow. "That girl and her sisters. I hope they escape from whatever they're in. Maybe she'll show up on one of my sets someday to say hello. I hope so." He paused, a flush coloring his cheeks. "I put all the single dollar bills I had in the bundle, too. I didn't do coins because of the noise, and I feared larger bills might seem suspicious. I didn't want people to think she was a thief. The dollars will be risky enough, but—"

"Oh, thank you for even thinking of that! I'm accustomed to being stingy." With her coins and with her bread. Again, Fayette was prickled by guilt.

"I don't know how wonderful it'll be if the money garners her attention and trouble, but maybe the funds will cover train fares for herself and her sisters so they can make it west." He cleared his throat as he stood. "And my watch tells me we should depart soon ourselves."

"That's right, the séance." Fayette had totally forgotten.

Whatever happened at the séance, genuine or contrived, would surely pale in comparison to what they had already seen that evening.

Chapter 18

She said I'm a good house.

I was *kissed.* And hugged. Such things have never happened to *me.* My timbers have never even known affection within their confines, not until the past few days. My witch, she was not so inclined. If she laid her arm upon someone's shoulders, she pushed them inside my oven.

I'm good. I'm good. I'm GOOD!

I didn't scare the woman and man as much with my second door. It was just a little scare, like a mosquito compared to a bear, and then they took care of things in the way that people on quests do. The bread, baked and voiceless, could not directly express its pleasure, but I think it would have approved—I really do.

I've had many young children enter my environs before. Not all of them left. That was the witch's way. If she could help them along on their quest, she was pleased; if she had meat fresh for days and packed away more for the cold months, she was pleased. Of course, I had no say in how things developed, but I always wanted any mess to be cleaned up promptly.

The woman and man actually try to clean up messes on their own. Why, the evening they first lit my candles, they snuffed them out of *concern for my safety!* My witch never worried about such things, though I know she cared for me. The fact that I still exist, that we escaped Rus, that I am still conscious and empowered even without a witch, says much about how she preserved me.

Lo those many years ago, when I was a chick with fresh grafts, I didn't understand much about the broader world I could sense, but I knew I was special—that my brood was special. That we'd been created as a cooperative effort by a sisterhood that did not often cooperate.

As I extend my senses now, out of curiosity, I can still detect three of my nest-mates, but they are quiet. Inert, as I recently was. We've all been alive for a long time. We've encountered war and watched how the nature of war has changed. This recent fighting, though—that was different. I speak not only of the Revolution in Rus, but elsewhere. These events changed the world in ways that even my witch, as powerful as she was, did not anticipate.

I had never seen her cry before, not in all our centuries together. Not even in her worst physical pain.

I had never before known her to be hopeless.

I had never thought that I'd be where her quest . . . ended, and that it would be her own choice. The magic she employed, why, it was greater than anything she had done before, and she in the past had changed men to pigs—though, really, for some men, this wasn't much of an alteration—and caused ribbons to become rainbow bridges across seas.

I had never thought I'd be left alone. That my new witch would shun her quest—would shun her inheritance.

I was to be her home. Her quest. She didn't simply deny her path. She denied *me*.

I wasn't a good house, a home, for her. But this girl today who came through the door that I summoned—*she kissed me.*

I'm so glad I wasn't asked to roast her in my oven! I would've disobeyed. Yes, I would have. I say that, though, knowing that statement is easy to profess with my witch gone. Defying her, in all her wrath and hunger, would've been hard, but as humans like to sing so often, sometimes one must stand up for love.

That girl loved me. And I loved her.

I also love how I feel with my candles lit, how shoes thud across my floor, how buttocks warm my benches. The heat of my oven seeps into my foundation, my attic, my shingles, even into the other rooms I keep private, such as where my witch's body is sprawled. I love helping people *survive* their quests.

I hope, I so very much hope, that the woman bakes bread here again. I want to talk to more aspects of Mother! Or Mother herself! I want to tell her what I did and what I'll do again.

I want her to approve. Yes, yes, I do.

I'm going to open more doors inside me, oh, yes, I will. Right when the bread is ready, when the woman and the man are ready. They won't even be scared these next times. They'll expect the company.

Oh, oh, I hope I can be a good house for whoever comes next!

I don't even care if anyone else kisses me. Not really.

That girl's kiss on my timbers? It was special.

There will never be another like that.

Chapter 19

"I'm medium Silas Pennington. Please feel free to call me Silas. A séance is an intimate event, and it's best to be familiar from the start. Welcome." He gestured Fayette and Rex inside the Fitz household.

Yes, this was the same man Fayette had witnessed in confrontation with the Marshal the day before. Silas had to be in his twenties, near Heidi's age. He towered over six feet tall with a slight stoop to his posture, as if he never quite trusted ceilings with his head, wariness that was probably wise in the claustrophobic Fitz cottage. His slicked-down brown hair would've brushed the front doorway if he stood on tiptoe. Milky-white skin bore a few acne scars on his cheeks. The black suit he wore was fitted but modest, not sleek or bespoke. But then, Fayette thought, when you likely made your living bilking the grieving out of their funds, it was probably best to not advertise one's evilly obtained fortune.

"I'm Rex Hallstrom," said Rex as the men shook hands.

"Rex Hallstrom!" Silas's eyebrows rose. "The actor? My oh my! Very nice to make your acquaintance."

"Likewise." Rex was, truly, a good actor. He affected nothing but genteel politeness.

"And I'm Fayette Wynne." Silas's hand cupped hers, his skin soft with a few calluses, as one would expect of a clerk. Or someone who practiced sleight of hand. Fayette endeavored to equal Rex's pleasant smile, even as she was ready to wrestle Silas face down into the carpet while Rex scampered off for the Marshal. "I'm boarding here on the Fitzes' property."

"I'm glad you could come. Please, come into the dining room. Mrs. Fitz has food ready."

Mrs. Fitz bustled over, new brightness in her face and movements. "Yes, I have some appetizer sandwiches, along with lemonade and tea. Heidi, do come over and say hello in your own way, please! You're an actor, Mr. Hallstrom? I'm sorry, I don't think I've seen a picture in . . . goodness, over eight years."

Fayette experienced a spike of worry. Would Mrs. Fitz's strict morality inspire her to give Rex the boot? After all, actors were peddlers of deception and sin. Rex, however, approached Mrs. Fitz with a sparkling smile as he clasped her shoulders with both hands.

"I am. Thank you kindly for extending an invitation."

"Oh. Well. I'm delighted to have you here. My place isn't large, but I do like to think of it as homey. Can I get you some lemonade, Mr. Hallstrom?"

"I'd love some, thank you. And please, feel free to call me Rex. All my friends do."

Fayette had to wonder if Rex's charm could get him away from gangsters with tommy guns in hand.

Mrs. Fitz appeared outright flustered in the face of handsome friendliness. "Well, then. Rex. Mr. Hallstrom. I do insist that people call me Mrs. Fitz. Not to be standoffish, but as an honor to my husband."

"I understand," he said, as smooth and sweet as butter creamed with honey. He followed her into the next room.

Silas matched Fayette's stride as they trailed their host. She felt the need to say something. "Have you been in Carmel for long?" She'd know if he lied in his reply.

"I arrived this past weekend. Such a lovely place. I haven't been here before. How about you, Fayette?"

Ah, he'd told the truth. "I arrived Sunday evening to stay for a few weeks. Oh, what nice sandwiches." What looked to be a savory cream cheese had been spread onto finger-size crustless cuts of brown graham bread, a single walnut meat crowning each piece.

Was she hungry enough to eat more? Should she? Additional food felt indulgent—but even as she thought that, she realized how absurd that idea was. This might seem indulgent in comparison to her meals of late, but her total for the day was still inadequate. She *needed* to eat more.

She picked up one of the gently toasted sandwiches and nibbled away, managing to keep up a properly polite conversation with Silas, Mrs. Fitz, and Rex. Heidi lurked in the background. She looked uncomfortable, attired in a basic frock that was quite distinct from her normal work dress. When she tidied things around the room, Mrs. Fitz quietly scolded her to act like a guest, that she wasn't there to work, which seemed to only make Heidi look more ill at ease. She clearly would've been happier if she was allowed to do something.

Mr. Fitz was so quiet, it took Fayette a minute to notice him.

He sat in a dining room chair against the wall, obscured by Silas and Rex as they stood chatting. Mr. Fitz rested slumped against the back of his chair. A simple button-up shirt and slacks adorned his reedy body. He looked young, likely not past his mid-thirties, his thinning red hair combed over his shiny pate. His face held a vacant expression. Every few minutes, Mrs. Fitz made a circuit of the room to check on her husband and discreetly wipe drool from the corners of his mouth. Her obvious affection for him was touching to witness.

"My last séance was back at Halloween," Mrs. Fitz was saying to Silas. Fayette listened as she ate another sandwich. "I was delighted to find a medium in town on such a night of auspicious energy. Madame Lilac was her name. Perhaps you know her?"

"There are many spiritualists traveling the country these days," he said in an apologetic tone.

"Well, she was most interesting—she exuded *ectoplasm*! I'd never seen the like! The stuff had such a glow."

"It does," Silas confirmed. "But I'm glad to say that my gifts aren't of that nature. I don't favor the mess that ectoplasm creates."

"I didn't need to clean it up, thank goodness, as Madame Lilac's assistant took care of that. I've had a few trumpet talkers here as well. They seem more common, as mediums go."

"You speak as if you have vast experience with them," said Rex before sipping his lemonade.

"Oh, I do." Mrs. Fitz's wrist flexed, her bracelets jangling. "Silas here is my twenty-first hire. I have also been taking correspondence lessons in an effort to improve my own psychic abilities. I was told that, as I'm so attuned to my husband's needs, our bond extends into the ethereal realms and I am therefore the most qualified person to make him whole."

Fayette stiffened, ready to speak up about an obvious effort to defraud her, only for Silas to talk first. "Mrs. Fitz, you must be wary of charlatans." His manicured brow furrowed in concern. "Very few people are attuned to the unseen, but there are so-called mediums out there who will sell the promise of such skills as readily as a shop peddles Wrigley's gum."

Rex didn't hold back his look of surprise. Fayette knew she had to be revealing some shock as well. Was Silas standing up against fraud because he was the real deal—or because the blatant charlatans were hurting his own business?

"I'm aware that there are swindlers," Mrs. Fitz said in a miffed tone. "I'm careful."

"As you must be. You're caring for your husband, after all." Silas motioned to the statue-like Mr. Fitz.

"Silas, you said you don't ooze ectoplasm or employ trumpets. How are your talents expressed?" Fayette asked.

"Psychic insights run in my family. My grandmother had premonitions that bothered her immensely, as she felt they came into conflict with her deep Christian faith. I don't think spiritualism is inherently evil, but it can be used for that purpose, just as any religion can be. My intent, my calling, is to help people find comfort amid their grief."

"A noble goal," Rex said blandly, covering his mouth as he finished chewing a sandwich. "Where all have you traveled?"

Silas's eyes gleamed with enthusiasm. "Most people are unaware that natural rivers of magic are hidden everywhere along physical boundaries in our world. I've been traveling down the Pacific coastline for a few months now." He set down his cup to gesture with both hands. His dress and mannerisms reminded Fayette of a preacher's. "Carmel, I think, is especially potent. The continent's landmass meets the ocean, and the Carmel River flows out here, too. They create a convergence of power. These sorts of invisible rivers are called *waylines*. Magic and spirits flow and pool in these areas."

Mrs. Fitz nodded. "Many authors who've come here have written about nearby Point Lobos as a place of old energy."

"Creative people are often attuned to the unseen. I would like some book recommendations from you later, Mrs. Fitz. I collect works on this subject, fiction and nonfiction. My trunk is the bane of porters everywhere! But look at the time. We should get started."

He turned off the electric lights. A lit candelabra in the center of the circular table cast everyone in a spectral glow.

Mrs. Fitz sat beside her husband, with Silas on the other side of Mr. Fitz. Fayette sat with her back to the bay window. The open curtains provided a view of the dark yard. She supposed it was a good thing she didn't need to lock her door here, as the pitch-black night would make it a challenge to put a key in a lock. Rex was to her right, across from Mr. and Mrs. Fitz. Heidi faced the window and had the greatest ease in moving about.

Silas began by discussing what spiritualism was, how most souls went to the Summerland after their earthly bodies died, and some of his personal experiences as a medium. He was a surprisingly engaging storyteller. Fayette could see many people being persuaded by his personable ways.

Silas reached for a portfolio case at his feet. "I took photographs yesterday using a camera that has been blessed by holy men of five faiths." Fayette didn't roll her eyes, which was good, because if she'd done so, the effort would've been so strong, she might've strained something. "As I photographed Mr. Fitz, we sang his favorite hymn in order to channel the right energy for this effort. I developed the film myself yesterday at a laboratory here in town. You can clearly see the detached presence of Mr. Fitz's soul in each image." He slid a short stack of photograph cards to Mrs. Fitz. She angled them so that her husband could also see, but neither his head nor his eyes moved.

"Here, we should have more light. Pardon, but what was your name again—Heidi? Yes, could you turn on that lamp behind you? Thank you," said Silas. Heidi did as he bade.

Fayette frowned. He'd turned off the lights two minutes before. Either he was disorganized, or he was up to something.

"Yes, yes, these are good photographs," Mrs. Fitz murmured. "We had similar images done before—but his spirit is closer to his body than it was previously. See?" She flashed the cards at Heidi, who acknowledged her with a tight smile. "That means our efforts are working! You can be whole again." She squeezed her husband's limp hand on the table as she slid the images to Heidi.

"I beg your pardon, Mrs. Fitz, but your understanding is that Mr. Fitz is . . . haunted by himself?" Rex asked, presenting the question in a more pleasant tone than Fayette could've mustered.

"Oh, yes." She nodded. "You'll see for yourself in the photographs."

Heidi, with her head ducked, gave the pictures a glance, then passed them to Rex. He spread them out so he and Fayette could see them together by candlelight. The series showed Mr. Fitz propped up in an upholstered chair. Above his left shoulder was a long, pale wisp, like the floating flame of a candle. The tail of it seemed to extend to his nearest shoulder, almost like the tether on a kite.

"Double exposure?" Rex asked beneath his breath. Across the table, Silas continued to murmur with Mrs. Fitz.

"Almost certainly," Fayette whispered back. They shared grim looks. Motion pictures had used similar double exposure tricks to portray ghosts and plot devices such as memories going back to the very start of the industry.

This right here was solid proof to present to the Marshal, but Fayette didn't rise. Not yet. The more evidence she could gather tonight, the better.

"The dilemma, of course, is how to meld his body and soul again," Silas was saying. "I'll admit, I haven't attempted anything like this before. I was reviewing my texts last night and found there are some rituals we could attempt, but nothing is without risk—"

"My husband's daily existence is a risk. Every time I feed him, he could choke. When we dress him"—Mrs. Fitz nodded to Heidi—"we risk dropping him and perhaps breaking bones. His doctor says bones become brittle when a person can't move on their own. We imperil ourselves when we move him, too. When I twisted my back this past spring—I don't know how I would've gotten by without Heidi!" She gestured to heaven. "I need my husband to fully come back to me, but most of all, I need to know his soul is at peace."

Fayette couldn't help but think that Mr. Fitz looked as peaceful as a person could be—but she also knew how easy it was for a person to hide a soul in turmoil. Her own grief, and Rex's recent despair, were proof of that. If she could be certain of anything, it was that Mr. Fitz showed no outward manifestation of pain.

"You have no other family nearby?" Fayette asked Mrs. Fitz gently, then realized she shouldn't have. However Mrs. Fitz replied, she would be feeding Silas more information.

"I left my family when I was young," she said with a shrug. "I made my way to San Francisco. That's where I met my husband. I just have Gerald and Heidi." She cast them both fond glances. Heidi managed a small smile in return.

"So much suffering and loss," murmured Silas. "I understand that kind of sorrow. I had a brother, you see, who died as a child. His brief life . . . it wasn't easy. I'll do whatever I can to help you."

An odd keening sound escaped Heidi's throat. She pointed toward the bay window.

Fayette turned around. A glowing white object danced around the garden. It stood several feet in length and about a foot wide. It swayed back and forth and jumped to one side, then the other.

"Mr. Fitz's luminous spirit is briefly visible to us! Your joy over the photographs gave him the power to briefly manifest here," Silas said, resting a hand on Mrs. Fitz's shoulder.

"He . . . we . . . we loved dancing," she managed to get out before heaving with sobs. Heidi stepped aside to pour a glass of water from a nearby pitcher.

Fayette studied the dancing spirit with fascination. Rex's hot breath met her cheek as he leaned close. "There are a few ways to create incandescence," he murmured. "One way is by removing the tips of a lot of matchsticks—and I mean *a lot*—to create an incandescent light. Not sure if that technique would work on cloth, though."

"Was that used in one of your movies?" she whispered back.

"Nah. I have brothers."

The glowing figure made a few more bounds and then was snuffed out in an instant. Fayette couldn't tolerate this charade anymore. She stood, and that's when a peculiar expression crept into Silas's face. He didn't look mad or upset, but his face focused away, puzzled. "Oh. Oh." He pressed both hands to his forehead. "Now? It has to happen now? I—I, oh Lord."

Fayette was not in the mood for another trick. "Rex, how about we—"

Silas's head lifted. The pensive frown stayed on his face. "Fayette Wynne. Your family cares for an entity ancient and holy. You have it with you in Carmel even now. Magic swirls around you, through you."

"What?" she asked, blinking in shock.

He rubbed his head. "I wish this sight didn't have to hurt so. I don't know how my grandmother endured these episodes. She had them all the time. It's been almost a year since I had one. Ugh." He looked at Fayette as if he saw through her. "Your magic nourishes the body and soul. Your shoulder—it's still glowing with a concentration of power." He tapped his left shoulder. The same shoulder she'd injured in her fall onto the rocks when saving Rex.

The séance had shifted from fraudulent to accurate in an instant.

Silas's deep-seeing gaze turned to Rex. "You've been touched by this power, too. Recently. For the first time. She glows like a coal because she's always known this magic, but you—it's fresh within you. Everywhere." He looked at Heidi, his frown deepening. "You . . . What are you? You're *dead*. You're rotting, even now, but you're also standing here alive. Your flesh isn't your own? How can that be? You lived when no one else did, and now you—" He clutched his head with both hands, moaning.

Heidi's chair squealed as she pushed it back. She ran away, the front door slamming behind her.

Rex's chair scooted back as he stood. "Silas? Can we—"

Silas's whole body went limp. His face smacked the table, nose-first.

Chapter 20

Fayette stared in disbelief. Silas wasn't moving. Rex rushed around the table to pull him upright. The medium's eyes were closed. Thick blood oozed from both nostrils, sliding toward his gaping mouth.

While Fayette knew that it wasn't hard to fake a bloody nose, she'd heard Silas's face crunch as it impacted on the table. His current strange condition resounded as genuine. She went around to help hold him up.

Mrs. Fitz clutched her husband. "Oh my goodness. Oh my goodness."

"We need to lay Silas down," Rex said to Mrs. Fitz. "Is there a sofa we can—"

"Yes, of course! In the front room!"

Fayette was glad she and Rex were near the same height; it wasn't hard for the two of them to work in concert to haul tall-and-reedy Silas into the next room and stretch him out on the divan. Fayette pressed a hand to Silas's chest. "His heartbeat seems normal. So is his breath."

"Do you have smelling salts? Maybe some ammonia?" Rex asked Mrs. Fitz, who trailed them to stand in the doorway, a hand pressed to her heart.

"I have some ammonia, yes, but—"

"No. We shouldn't rush to wake him." Fayette stood. "Whatever . . . induced this seemed to cause tremendous head pain before he even collapsed into the table. Let's give his body some natural time to work through."

"How long, do you think?" Rex asked.

Fayette gave an exaggerated shrug. "I haven't the foggiest, but if we don't see an improvement soon, we should fetch a doctor. Can you turn on the lights again, Mrs. Fitz? Thank you. Do you think your husband will be fine sitting on his own for a bit so you can keep Silas company? Rex, why don't we go into the kitchen and pull out more food and drink? Silas was talking a lot before he fell unconscious. I bet some refreshment will do him right once he's awake."

Under the bloom of electric lighting, she could see the instant that Rex picked up on her hint: They needed to chat in private. "Refreshment sounds good after that intense event. Mrs. Fitz? Can we get you something?"

"Oh. Lemonade, please. And maybe some sandwiches." Mrs. Fitz sat in a companion chair to the divan, bent over Silas with a worried expression.

Fayette and Rex hurried into the kitchen, which, thankfully, was on the far side of the dining room. The wooden floor squeaked ever so slightly when walked upon. Only a floating spirit could sneak up on them, and she doubted any had attended this séance.

"As real as Silas's swoon seems, it sure had convenient timing," Fayette muttered, accepting the sandwiches as Rex passed her the platter. She had no inclination to have more herself. She felt not only full but also oddly satisfied; those were separate sensations, she realized. "I was ready to fetch the Marshal."

"I agree. His act was getting intolerable. But that last bit . . . What happened when his head began to hurt? I expected him to try to convince us he was real by saying we had ghosts hovering about us and that their names began with either *S*, *M*, *R*, or *T*, that we'd known great suffering, et cetera. Instead, he seemed to describe your sourdough starter. He even got your hurt shoulder correct."

Fayette shook her head in awe. "The séance was bunkum, until the very end."

Rex poured lemonade into clean glasses. "What do you make of what he said about Heidi?"

"I don't know," she murmured. "Everything around Heidi is a mystery. This only adds to it. Silas had to be telling the truth about her, because he was right about the two of us. If so, Heidi has been sort-of dead since . . . well, maybe since she washed up in Carmel, whenever that was." Fayette had already told Rex about how Heidi had come to work with Mrs. Fitz.

"Let me do the research this time," Rex said. "A drowned, nameless woman would've been a big story. The mayor—well, he was mayor, but he's still a trustee—is a fellow named Perry Newberry. He publishes *The Carmel Pine Cone*. I've met him on a couple visits here. I can visit his office and—"

"Silas is stirring!" cried Mrs. Fitz.

Fayette carried in the platter while Rex brought drinks with both hands. As they set their items down on the nearby coffee table, Silas was moaning softly, a hand to his head. His eyes squinted open. "What happened?"

"You seemed to get a terrible headache along with a series of insights about us." Fayette wondered if he was going to claim amnesia. She'd used that plot element in more than one continuity and knew it to be a major rarity in reality.

"That's right. I remember," he said, surprising her. He sat up. "The full sight only strikes me when I'm close to something or someone that is profoundly magical. It takes a while for my body to react, though. I don't have any warning. Once, I shared a train car with a man for three hours, and only then did I babble and faint." His smile was wry. "Turned out that he was carrying a dagger that'd been in his family for centuries. I then almost babbled and fainted *again* from sheer terror as I desperately tried to convince him to not kill me."

"How did you make it out?" Fayette asked.

"The train came to his stop, and he concluded that I was harmless. I'm still more relieved than insulted. Oh, is that lemonade? I think I could chug down the whole pitcher."

As Silas drank, Rex prodded Fayette with a subtle elbow. "Since he's the real deal, he may be able to provide insights on that house of ours."

"That's an idea, if he can stay conscious and focus on the task at hand," she whispered back. Then, in a louder voice, she asked, "Silas, you said you noticed something unusual about us. Is it paining you to be in our presence right now?"

"Yes." He grimaced. "My head still feels like a lumberjack is attempting to crack open my skull from the inside, but it's always worst when the pain first starts. I can tolerate how things are now, as awful as it is. Has that other young woman come back? Heidi? I'm sorry if what I said alarmed her. In the moment, I don't always think about what I'm saying."

Mrs. Fitz's normally prim expression dimmed to chagrin. "Heidi is always upset when she hears such insights about herself," she said softly.

"Wait a second," said Rex. "She's heard that kind of thing before? About being dead, her body rotting and all?"

"Several times over now. In truth, a medium's awareness of her nature has become a means to verify a person's gift. Others have not experienced pain as Silas has, though."

"Lucky me," Silas said, cringing. "I imagine the other mediums needed to still be in her company awhile before they had a flash of her truth?"

"Yes. That remains the same."

Fayette considered all these clues. "You're not alarmed by this news," she said to Mrs. Fitz. "That means you already know she died."

Mrs. Fitz nodded. "Yes. After she drowned in the ocean, she was essentially reborn. Her skin was even pink like a newborn's! Her continued life is a miracle." A rare smile graced her face, and it was beautiful. Fayette felt herself frowning, though. That explanation only partially worked. What did Silas mean by saying she was rotting? He'd mentioned that, present tense. "Now, I didn't expect you both to garner mentions in Mr. Pennington's vision, but it doesn't sound like this . . . thing that you carry with you is harmful to me and mine?" Her gaze upon Fayette was shrewd.

"It is not," Fayette said with firmness.

"I certainly had no sense of a threat, either," said Silas.

Rex frowned. "It sounds like your profound reaction to magic could make it hard for you to do your job or travel. You never know when you might encounter something."

"That's true, but my sensitivity has no bearing on my regular work. Keep in mind, spirits aren't magical—we all have spirits! Ghosts, really, are as common as electric ovens these days, but they are only noticeable to living people when they behave at extremes. Actual magic is infrequent to come across, and it's usually old in origin."

Fayette considered his statement. "If you're warned in advance that you might be in the presence of something magical, is there any way you can prepare?"

Even though he still looked to be in profound pain, Silas perked up. "Why, are you going to share with me whatever this . . . entity of yours is? I'm always on the lookout for new items for my collection, especially books."

Fayette had not been implying that at all, and didn't contain her glower. "That doesn't answer my question."

"I take that as a no, then." He munched on one of the little walnut sandwiches. His complexion remained ghastly pale. "Yes. If I have warning, I do several rituals that . . . I suppose I could explain them as armoring my physical body's mental defenses." He paused, seeming to struggle with swallowing his last bite. His throat bulged as he finally got it down. "I beg your pardon, but I feel pretty lousy. I think I should return to my room."

He teetered as he stood. Rex stepped closer and offered him an arm for support, which was received with a grateful smile.

"Whereabouts are you staying?" Rex asked him.

"The Pine Inn."

"My place is nearby. I'll walk with you." Rex cast Fayette a slight nod. She interpreted that as a cue that he'd follow up with her later.

"I'll retire to my cottage, too," Fayette said to Mrs. Fitz. "Unless you need more help here?"

Mrs. Fitz's smile was tight. "I'm sure Heidi will be back in a minute."

"If she's not here soon, please come and knock at my door. You know I'm not far away."

Mrs. Fitz nodded, and Fayette understood that she would not be asked to help. "I'm sorry that your reaction ended up being so severe, Mr. Pennington," said Mrs. Fitz as she walked them to the door.

Silas gave her a limp wave. "So am I, but I have no regrets. Everything is a learning experience!" Amazing how the man could be perky yet blatantly agonized, all at once.

They made their farewells. Fayette's thoughts swirled like a whirlpool as she rounded the side of the house to see that a lamp was on within Grangeville Cottage.

She hadn't left any lights on after she and Rex had brought the architecture books there before the séance. He'd originally intended to haul them back now, but that'd need to wait. Silas was his priority.

And now this intruder was hers.

A glance around the garden confirmed that there were no shovels or posts within easy reach. Well, Fayette was no trained pugilist, but she could wield her fists if need be, and could kick like an ostrich.

Her boldness was squelched in an instant as she tripped over something in the dark. She staggered a few steps before catching herself in a crouch, hand on the grass. What on earth . . . ? Fayette pivoted to probe the ground. A long piece of cloth stuck out from underneath a bush. How had that come to be there? The heft reminded her of a gown or a child's blanket. Maybe the breeze had pulled it off someone's clothesline.

Cloth in her hand, heartbeat hammering, she continued forward.

She opened the front door slowly. Slight sounds carried from the kitchen. Leaving the door open so that it wouldn't click, she crept through the mostly dark space—and collided with an end table. There was a moment of silence, followed by a dense cracking sound, then the quick patter of feet.

Fayette gave chase in time to see the back door from the kitchen slamming shut—but then her gaze went to Mother's shattered jar upon the kitchen tiles. The freed scent of fermented flour filled the room.

"Mother! Oh no, oh no!" She turned on the overhead light and crouched down. Lifting away the checkered cloth that usually crowned the jar showed Mother in a bubble-flecked beige heap amid the wreckage of her container. Mother's magical presence was still strong—actually, quite strong. The intensity put Fayette in mind of a fervent heartbeat.

Her hands hovered in space for a moment, afraid to touch anything, as she might if a man had collapsed in a heart attack in front of her, and then she went to work.

"I'm here, Mother, I'm here. First of all, I need a new container for you." She scanned the counter and pantry, and there—her peanut butter jar, still mostly full. It was the one thing she had with a screw-on lid, a necessity for the return trip to Southern California. She didn't want to move Mother more than absolutely necessary. She used a knife to swirl the peanut butter into one of the ceramic bowls that came with the cottage. The food would need to be moved elsewhere later, but for now, she had to care for Mother. Oh, Mother.

Mother's mood stayed stable. Fayette wanted to think that this meant Mother trusted her to salvage her, and Fayette appreciated that level of faith, as she was in a total panic and only hoped she was doing the right thing.

"You survived being dumped in a swamp in Grandpop's day," Fayette said, her voice shaking. "Surely you'll survive being dropped on a floor in Carmel. Right?"

She scrubbed out the jar as fast as she could, making sure every last remnant of peanut butter was out—never an easy thing, and now more aggravating than ever before.

The new home for the starter clean and ready, she had to retrieve what she could of Mother.

This was the scary bit. If there were shards of glass everywhere, what could she do? She couldn't put starter through a strainer; it was goopy and adhesive by nature. She supposed she could pick through by hand, even if her fingers were cut in the process. Better her fingers than her mouth, throat, or innards when she ate bread later. Mother's healing powers would mitigate some of that danger, true, but that didn't mean the experience should be given an invitation.

A large spoon in hand, she probed through Mother's deflated mass. The spoon clinked on glass as Fayette lifted up a heap of Mother. Her fingertips explored and couldn't find any shards. She dropped the glop into the jar. The next spoonful scraped along the curved base that once formed the jar's bottom. Again, no shards. Enough of Mother was accumulated to form a low layer in the repurposed peanut butter jar.

This was good. Mother could be about this level after being divided to make bread.

"I reckon I can save a little more," Fayette said, lifting up another spoonful. No, this one had a long sliver that came close to slicing her forefinger. Fayette had to wipe some residue from her skin to ensure that she hadn't been sliced. The last thing she needed to do was contaminate Mother with blood!

The next spoonful seemed fine, but the rest . . . A large portion of Mother had overflowed the pieces and oozed along the floor. That amount looked like a lost cause, and Mother seemed to agree; when Fayette hovered a hand over it, she detected the faintest heat and prickles. The magic was dissipating. She could only guess that Mother had a good reason for giving up on that segment of herself, probably due to glass.

Fayette had salvaged the bare minimum to keep Mother going.

Mother seemed to read her despair, as Fayette felt a wave of reassuring warmth. She had to smile at the reminder that this was not a normal starter. She needed to have faith in Mother.

Faith, faith. Something that should be flexible, ebbing and growing, but instead had felt increasingly brittle.

But maybe less so, here and now.

She used the dustpan—which would need a thorough washing later—to scoop the rest of Mother into the trash.

That done, her hands washed, she set about healing Mother the only way she knew how—by food. Thank goodness Fayette hadn't taken all her flour to the house on the cliff! That would've meant a frantic, dangerous trip in the dark about now.

"Small mercies," she murmured. "Small, vital mercies."

The new mixture stirred into the old with a profound swell of power. Mother was hurt, not dead.

But Mother could die.

That thought left Fayette shaken as she made a circuit of the house to verify nothing else was broken or taken—and to finally close the front door, which she had left open when she made a poor attempt to sneak inside. She'd dropped the cloth that'd tripped her there, too, but she let that be. She had more important things to concern herself with now.

Just days before, embittered, Fayette had been half tempted to leave Mother behind so that she wouldn't have to face the onerous burden of caring for the starter. That spite had been all the more alluring because part of her hadn't acknowledged that Mother could die. The starter seemed immortal, reproducing itself on a regular basis. Why, Mother had been in her family for over a century—probably for much of the time her kin had been in America. Who could care for Mother next? Fayette sure was not going to have children—she had never, ever wanted them.

Really, she and Mother were the last survivors in her family. Fayette was stunned to consider that there'd be a point in the future when she needed to figure out who . . . inherited Mother. Maybe Rex could. He had accepted Mother's magical ways with incredible aplomb, and he might marry someone who was not Margaret and pass the starter along.

Fayette's mind pondered additional questions in a persistent parade. Who had been in her house? There was nothing that made her think the attack had been malicious—Mother hadn't been thrown, after all. Whoever it was, they'd been holding Mother when Fayette made her inept effort to creep inside.

That evoked more questions, too, however. Why would someone have been interested in the starter at all? Most people probably wouldn't have even recognized what was inside the jar. Home bakers tended to use either cake yeast or baking powder these days; anything else was very "old country."

After dithering for a bit, she brought Mother into her bedroom before making one final circuit of the house to lock the doors and windows. She also brought a rolling pin from the kitchen to set on her nightstand. Anyone else who tried to meddle with Mother tonight would, appropriately, get flattened like dough.

Chapter 21

Oh dear. Oh no.

When I extended my awareness into the world, when I opened that door, I sent out a flare of power. It was unavoidable. When my old witch was dying, she probably would have advised me that I shouldn't take such actions on my own—but then, she *was* rather busy with the dying. She also would've thought that I would be without a witch for mere minutes, not years. It would've been inconceivable to her that I would have been left vulnerable to her sisters in such a way.

But vulnerable I am, and now another witch has found me.

I can sense the weight of her gaze, even at this distance. Her palpable interest.

I myself feel deep, terrible dread.

In helping the woman and the man to help others, I fear I have made a terrible mistake.

Chapter 22

After Fayette finally fell asleep, she dreamed of bread, of Mother, of the strangeness of baking in the nearby hut. More than once, she fully awakened to check on Mother by lamplight. She logically knew that a visual check wasn't necessary—she could smell the starter's healthy presence even in her dreams—but she really wanted to ensure that all was well.

By the time she gave up on sleep soon after dawn, Mother had risen to half fill her jar. Fayette discarded a large portion of that new growth, as was usual procedure, and the particular dense, sticky texture made clear that Mother wasn't recovered enough to use in bread. But that was fine. That was normal. After feeding Mother anew, she set the jar on the sunny windowsill right by her typewriter.

Today, she'd get work done—and guard Mother. The rolling pin stayed within reach.

Fayette's character, Dot, was much better at sneaking around than Fayette was, which was good. After all, Dot had to deal with a murderer on the loose along with an assortment of other no-gooders.

Fayette measured the progress of the day not only by the accumulation of finished pages but also by the incremental growth in the former peanut butter jar.

A knock at the door interrupted her as she ate lunch: a thick peanut butter sandwich with added slices of Bartlett pear, a few coarse chunks of Dry Monterey Jack on the side. Her busy brainwork seemed to have stimulated her appetite.

As she approached the door, she nudged aside the cloth still in the entrance; it was black, dried leaves stuck in the weave. She opened the door to find a stick-thin boy of about ten. A white shirt was neatly tucked into a pair of patched navy-blue knickerbockers. He straightened when he saw her, running a hand through his bowl-cut black hair. His other hand held out an envelope.

"Hello, ma'am. I am Koichi Matsumoto. I run a courier service here in town. I have a letter for you from Rex Hallstrom!" His introduction had been said with practiced pride, but the last line portrayed absolute glee. He obviously knew who Rex was.

"You do? Why, thank you kindly, Mr. Matsumoto." She accepted the letter. "You're quite enterprising, running your own business like this." Back in her youth, she and her siblings had also missed some school days when there had been opportunities to pick fruit or do other chores to bring in money.

"Thank you, ma'am. *Oh.*" He emitted a soft squeak, his eyes widening as he stared past her.

"What is it?" she asked, looking behind her. Surely he wasn't reacting to the cottage as Heidi had?

"That gown on the floor. It's mine. Well, my boss's. It's not— It shouldn't be here." His expression had gone from happy to miserable in an instant.

Fayette set the letter on the table as she hoisted the cloth up from her floor. "Explain, please, Mr. Matsumoto."

He took a deep breath. "I had to wear that gown for work last night."

"Go on." She could guess where this was going.

"You see, I do all sorts of odd jobs around town." His words tumbled out, faster and faster. "Whenever I see a medium's here, I always ask if they need help. They most always need an assistant even if they brought one. Usually, the work means I'm in a dark cabinet for a couple hours or crouched under a table. For Mr. Pennington, though, I played a ghost!" A brief grin revealed a missing front tooth.

"How'd you play a ghost?" she asked, holding back a smile of her own. As much as Silas's confirmed deceit irked her, she could only imagine how much fun this job had been for Koichi.

"That costume glows in the dark. Well, the white layer underneath does, anyway." He nodded toward the cloth. "I had to wait for a signal lamp to turn on inside, and then I popped up and danced around. I didn't do the Charleston, though. I was told not to do anything too modern. At the end, I flipped up the black cloth to cover up the glowing layer, and I left. Mr. Pennington was supposed to fetch the costume later!" Koichi sounded indignant. Betrayed, even.

"Mr. Pennington came down quite ill. He was in no condition to retrieve this last night." She folded the cloth over, debating how to delicately word things. "You probably hear a lot about what people say around town, don't you?" He nodded. "Then you know something about the plight of the mister and the missus at the Fitz house?"

"I do," he said softly. "But I know Heidi best of all. She gives us bread. The best bread."

"She's a fine cook, for certain. I have a kindness to ask of you, Mr. Matsumoto. Please avoid engaging in ghost or cabinet acts at the Fitz household again. They are terribly vulnerable these days."

"You won't tell the Marshal about my work, then?" Koichi asked, his brows curved in worry. Ah, he'd already grasped the ethical issues at hand. "Or Heidi?"

"I won't tell either of them." Fayette set the cloth on the nearby table. She had no intention of returning that article of clothing to Silas. "Here, wait a moment."

It didn't matter that her bank account was about as hollow as a villain's heart. Koichi was getting a penny for his delivery to her house. As soon as that coin hit the boy's palm, a bright smile returned to his face.

"Oh. Thank you. I didn't think you'd still . . ." He ducked his head.

146

"You performed your job this morning as asked, and you were forthright about what you did last night, too. Now, scamper along. I'm sure you have other work to do."

"Yes, ma'am. Thank you, ma'am." He sprinted off as if he were running from the law. She guffawed and shook her head.

While still standing in the doorway, she tore open the envelope. Rex's letter said he'd arranged for them to consult with Silas Pennington. She was to meet Rex at his cottage at noon.

She spun around to regard the wall clock. It was almost noon now!

She inhaled her remaining sandwich. By some miracle, she didn't choke on the thick peanut butter. On the verge of heading out the door, she reconsidered Mother's placement. She went back to hide Mother on the high shelf of her wardrobe. Mother's jar didn't smell strongly; someone would need to make a real effort to find her in the bedroom.

Rex was waiting for her at his front gate.

"I'm sorry, I just got your note!" she said, huffing for breath.

"Drat it all, I should've told the boy to deliver my letter right away."

"I'm fine. I just need to catch my breath. Are we going to the Pine Inn?"

"Yes, it's not far."

"Well, I have a lot to tell you in a short walk, then."

She related what had befallen Mother, quite literally, and he remained troubled even after hearing about the starter's stalwart recovery. "How long will it take for her to be ready for breadmaking?"

Fayette kept her voice low, as there were other people about. "Normally, I'd wait two or three days between batches, and feed her night and day to reinvigorate her. I'll check on her texture when I return to the cottage. That's an even better indicator than her magical aura. The starter needs to be webby with bubbles." She paused. It sure felt weird to frankly discuss Mother with someone who wasn't family. "I wonder if I should take Mother to the cottage on the cliff. Few people can access it."

Rex tilted his head in consideration. "The house itself could meddle with Mother, but I'm inclined to think that the interference would be of a positive nature. You also said Heidi could access the grounds. I do wish I'd had the chance to speak with her last night. She looked pretty miserable."

"Heidi . . ." Fayette stopped moving on the sidewalk, causing a man behind them to grumble and go around. The hotel was just ahead. "She ran away from the séance after Silas said that I'd brought something magical with me."

Rex let out a low whistle. "You think she dropped Mother? How would she have even identified that jar as the thing Silas was talking about?"

Fayette gasped. "The night I arrived! Heidi came inside to pull out storm supplies. She'd been all smiles when we first met, and that withered away. Something spooked her. She was staring into the kitchen at one point. Right at Mother. I thought she was just following my flashlight beam as I tested it out, but . . ."

"Maybe she senses Mother, as you can?" he murmured.

"She'd have to, to react the way she did."

"I wonder how that connects to the other things Silas said about her." That was indeed a good point to ponder. "I have my own insights about Heidi to relate. I dropped by the *Pine Cone* office this morning."

"And?" Fayette demanded as Rex made a dramatic pause.

"Mr. Newberry remembered that she'd been found in July 1918, and with that in mind, he went through his files. The July twenty-sixth issue had a 'Girl Found Near Drowned!' headline squished between a piece on a performance of *Androcles and the Lion* and a visiting piano-tuner available for appointments. Heidi had been found on July eighteenth."

Fayette gasped. "Mrs. Fitz clearly recalled that the house appeared in July of 1918 while her husband was deployed. If we're thinking that Heidi and the house are somehow connected . . . and she's Russian like the house . . ."

"The Revolution had been underway for months by then," said Rex. "But wasn't the czar's family killed in July?"

"I think so—but I confess, I wasn't paying close attention to that kind of news at the time." Briar had died the month before. Fayette didn't recall many details about the rest of 1918. Even the armistice seemed to emerge from a blur of eat, sleep, work, grieve. "I remember hearing about a woman over in Germany who claims to be one of the czar's daughters, and that many people don't believe her."

Rex shook his head. "There's no way the Bolsheviks would've left any of the Romanov heirs alive for people to rally behind. They were ruthless. Nobles and clergy either escaped or died. Heidi's escape method was simply more . . . unconventional. How did the house get from Russia to Carmel, anyway? By tornado?"

"Oz doesn't seem so unbelievable at this point," said Fayette with a smile. Baum's books were among her favorites.

"I think I understand why Heidi dodges questions from you. If she made it out of the Revolution, running is a survival method," Rex murmured. "My friend Art . . . he also endured a lot."

"I don't even want to imagine." Life had been hard for her, for too many people, these past few years. She sighed. "Well, are we ready to talk to Silas, you think?"

Rex agreed, and they went inside. As he and the clerk spoke, Fayette noted two women in the adjacent parlor were stringing up garlands over a broad doorway. Fayette grimaced. It was only the first of December. Couldn't these people wait at least another week to start dolling up everything for Christmas? She had never had a Christmas without Ma. She didn't want to think of going through one now—Thanksgiving had been miserable enough. Maybe she needed to stockpile supplies like a Yukon miner ready to hold a claim through the winter, and she could emerge in January, when the calendar was less cruel.

Rex returned. "They've dispatched a boy to fetch Silas, but the clerk confirmed he's already been downstairs for breakfast. That's good. He was quite weak on our walk here yesterday." They went to a parlor off to one side, where they shared a view of the main stairs.

Fayette had considered staying at this inn, the first to open in Carmel-by-the-Sea, but a call had confirmed it was beyond her budget. It looked out of her budget, too, with gorgeous, gleaming wooden panels and a glamorous touch that made her feel like a dowdy interloper. No one seemed to be giving her a gimlet eye as a trespasser—but Rex was earning stares as people either recognized him or noted his incredible handsomeness. He was utterly oblivious, in a low voice relating to her some of the other curious newspaper headlines he'd seen in the *Pine Cone* office.

When her scalp began to prickle and the sensation traveled down her body, nauseating and strange, she knew Silas must be approaching. Sure enough, he came into view on the stairs.

"What on earth?" she muttered to herself.

"What is it?" Rex asked.

"He definitely did *something* magical." But she had no time to clarify, as Silas dodged around other people to approach them, a strong pep in his step. They made their greetings. Silas beckoned for them to follow him to the sunroom.

Midday light streamed through the broad windows. Chairs sat in clusters, potted plants arranged to give each setting some privacy. Silas took them to where three chairs awaited.

"I'm glad to speak with you both today. Last night didn't end in a way I preferred, for certain, but it was also exciting. You two are curiosities." Said the man whose presence made Fayette's skin hotly tingle as if she were in immediate danger of being struck by lightning. "What kind of job did you both wish to discuss today?"

"We've encountered a house here with a truly magical presence," Rex said. "It's alive. We'd like to see if you can find out more about it."

"Alive? This house is alive?" Silas looked giddy. She was suddenly glad that, if Silas proved to be useless in this job, he wouldn't be able to access the house on his own. "How do you mean? You're certain there aren't spirits?"

"Only in that the house itself is a kind of spirit," said Fayette. "I suppose it does do some things people expect of ghosts, like opening and closing doors, but . . . it's nothing like what you expect of a haunted house." She didn't want to give him too many details—certainly nothing about the doors that could reveal a dead body or create a gate across a distance—but he needed to understand enough to be prepared for the assault to his senses.

Silas eagerly nodded. "There are stories about houses like that. Old stories. I have some in my books. You say you encountered this house. How? You don't own it?"

"The house hides itself from almost everyone else in town. You can't reach it without us." She gave him a level look. There'd be no way for him to set up tricks, no excuse to hire Koichi to hide in a cabinet for hours. "Mr. and Mrs. Fitz own it."

Silas cocked his head, puzzled. "I asked her about her connections with the spiritual. She said nothing about a house."

"Mrs. Fitz is aware of the house but doesn't regard it as within the realm of spiritualism," Rex added. "To her, it's evil. She wants nothing to do with it. She's not paying for your work on the property. I am."

Silas didn't appear put-off that they weren't the owners. Instead, his enthusiasm remained boyishly high as Rex and Fayette discussed more observations about the house and additional details they'd discovered.

"Russia. Such a large area with many different peoples," Silas murmured, tapping his pencil. "But there are some common stories across the region. I left most of my books on the Asian continent in storage in San Francisco. I may need to send for them, or fetch them myself."

"You'll take the job, then?" asked Rex.

"Oh, a thousand times over, yes! I'm already fascinated. This sounds like nothing else I've encountered. I hope walking up to it doesn't make me fall over dead." He said that with a big grin, clearly not dissuaded. He jotted down a few numbers, then slid the page across the table to Rex. "That is the fee for my assessment. We can discuss more from there."

Fayette reached for the paper. Rex deftly slid it out of her reach. "Rex—" She hated having to speak on this subject.

"I've got this one," he said, as if there had been or would be another time for her to financially contribute. She stewed, self-conscious and embarrassed, even though Silas seemed too absorbed in this new project to pay her much note.

"What's your availability?" Rex asked Silas.

"How about seven tomorrow night? You can leave a check for half the total in my box at the front desk sometime today."

"Seven works for us," Rex said, to which Fayette nodded. "I'll get the check to the desk soon." Rex and Silas stood, shaking hands, and Fayette followed suit.

A minute later, the two of them were outside. Clouds had blown in, casting the world in gray. "Rex. That fee. How much was it?"

"I'm covering it. Please, it's fine."

She shifted in discomfort. "I dislike not contributing a share."

"I understand that. Can you accept this as a gift? You're making bread and aware of so much more about the house. I can do this. Please, let me."

She worked her jaw for a minute as she debated over what to say. "I don't want you to think I see you as a bank account. That I'm using you. Plenty of people would do that, I know, and I'm—"

"You have your pride, and I respect that. You know, I felt rather useless yesterday. I bought food and brought it. You . . . *did things*."

Her smile was wry as they walked down the block. "Again, you spent the money."

"I have it to spend, for the first time in my life," he said evenly. "Please, let me?" Fayette sighed and nodded, seeing no point in hashing it out more. He nodded up the street. "The post office isn't far away. I should see if I have more studio mail."

"I should ask if I've gotten anything, too."

There was a line, with reason; apparently, no houses had personal delivery in Carmel. When their turn came, Rex found he had several envelopes awaiting him. Fayette, to her surprise, had one, and she knew the sender by the handwriting alone—her friend and coworker, April. As they headed back outside, she tucked the envelope inside her coat so that it wouldn't be carried off by the breeze. In the same motion, she recognized a few pale strands of her hair on the lapel and brushed them away. How long would it take, she wondered, for her to stop shedding so aggressively once her diet had stabilized again?

"Rex, should we meet at— Wait, what's the matter?"

He had a peculiar expression on his face as he stared at one of his envelopes.

"Nothing." He stuffed his mail inside his coat. "You were asking something?"

"About when we were going to meet at the house later today. Would six or seven work?"

"Sure. Let's do six. I should work more on my fan mail this afternoon since I'll be out all day tomorrow." There was an emptiness in his voice that sent a chill through her.

"Rex, are you sure you're all right?" she asked quietly.

He looked away and then back. His eyes were the same color as the bright sky. "I'll let you know later," he said in a chipper tone.

He strolled away, his gait carefree. She stared after him, believing neither his tone nor the pep in his step.

Suddenly scared, she blurted out, "Promise me I'll see you later!"

Rex stopped about ten feet away and turned around. They were close enough that she could see how his eyes glistened.

"I promise. I'll bring picnic fare, too, and we'll talk."

"Okay," she said, her worry abating some. "Okay."

They stared at each other a moment more, a standoff, a judgment of mental soundness, and then Rex went on his way. Fayette continued to watch until he turned the corner at the next block.

What on earth had he gotten in the mail?

Chapter 23

Days before, Fayette had swaddled Mother's jar within her clothes for the travel day out of a sense of embittered obligation. Today, she took loving care of Mother for the short walk to the house on the cliff. In her canvas bag, she toted the rest of her breadmaking supplies, but Mother, she cuddled like a baby.

The cottage welcomed her, as ever, with a wide-open door. The oven fire burned bright, the exact same wood burning in the flames, the same wood stacked nearby. The warmth was especially welcome, as the night was already cold, a waft of distant rain in the air.

She set Mother on the table and removed the lid. The starter was viscous and riddled with holes—ready to ferment a loaf.

And Fayette, to her own surprise, was eager to make one.

The dough came together with ease, sticky as she first kneaded, then smoothing out as it developed. She placed it in the pot she'd used before and set it on a nook near the oven where it was warm but not too warm.

"I can come by tomorrow morning to shape you, or—" She frowned, staring at the dough. It was incrementally rising even as she watched. She was reminded of watching clouds and doing a double take to verify that yes, the cloud really was moving fast.

"Truly? You want to be baked . . . tonight?" she asked, shaking her head in awe. "Well, I suppose today's the better day to bake. Rex will be away much of tomorrow, and I don't think I want to have bread going when Silas is here. I don't need him asking questions about you, Mother, though the house's immense power should hide you for the most part, shouldn't it?"

Mother, of course, offered no reply beyond the bizarre rise in the jar, but that action said enough.

৵৵

Fayette fed Mother, then checked on the dough again. It had ballooned in minutes and was ready to shape. "I can't believe this," she muttered, forming the loaf by tightening and tucking. She wouldn't have expected a rise like this until tomorrow morning, even from Mother. The starter and the house were definitely in cahoots.

With the dough on the peel, Fayette realized she'd gotten flour on her coat. As she unbuttoned it to better brush away the white powder, she found the envelope from April still tucked in her interior pocket. She tore it open.

The first line stood out, bold and terrible.

You must know that the bosses are about to fire you.

Fayette paced beneath a candle sconce as she read onward, her heart pounding as if she were running from a barking dog.

"Hello!" Rex called as he entered. Fayette tried to put on her all-is-well mask, but it apparently didn't fit well, as he stopped in his tracks, a burlap bag swaying against his thigh. "What's wrong?"

"I'm about to be given the sack." She waved the pages in the air as she tried to affect a perky tone. "The new owner wants to bring on his nephew."

"Can the young man write?"

"I reckon he knows the alphabet. That's an important starting place. Beyond that, goodness, don't you know writing for movies is easy? Anyone can do it! Books say so."

No, the mask wasn't functioning right at all. Rex looked outright worried. "Come over and have a seat. If it wasn't for Volstead, I'd offer you a stiff drink somewhere."

"I've never been a drinker." That kind of habit was too expensive. If she were going to indulge, she'd get ice cream.

She took a seat. He placed his bag beside her.

How was she going to pay the mortgage? Buy food? Ma's medical bills—she'd promised the doctors she'd pay them by the new year, and her word was honor. Money would've been tight even *with* her job. What was she going to do now?

Numb, terrified, she pressed her fists to her heart as if to restrain its panic. Rex sat there, steady as a rock, and she realized he was doing what she said she'd do for him—just being there.

"How's the bread going?" Rex looked toward the oven. The fragrance of dough was detectable from their distance.

"In defiance of all science, the dough is probably fit to bake. Mother has never responded with this kind of speed before. And I appreciate that you're distracting me with a discussion of bread, but I still see the guillotine hovering over my neck."

"Don't look up, then," he quipped, then sobered. "What do you think you'll do?"

He began to set food out on the table. Cold cuts of turkey. Sliced Swiss cheese, with holes large enough for a finger. Apricot jam. A long loaf of store-bought bread—an obvious precaution in case none would be baked today.

Her loaf, however, was indeed rounded and ready to bake. A finger-poke confirmed it. After slashing the top of the round, she scooted it into the baking nook. She stayed there, staring at the fire. She certainly didn't want to look at the bounty of food on the table; it all looked about as edible as a rubber tire. Rex joined her, saying nothing as he gave her space to think.

Fayette finally spoke up. "I can look into freelance work, but it doesn't pay much. I'm coming from Astrophel, after all, not United

Artists. I'm not in Frances Marion's league. No studio is going to beg and plead for me to join up." She faced Rex with a frown. "I could do other writing, though. I love short-story magazines. I haven't had the time or the energy to pursue that angle."

"There you go!" His grin couldn't help but encourage her. "What magazines do you favor?"

"*Ghost Stories* and *Black Mask* are my favorites. I like detective stories, mysteries—tales that make my brain work. Oh, people sniff in disdain, say that it's all hack work, but what I've been doing is hack work, too. I pushed for a year to get Astrophel to do a detective film that could expand into a series. That's what I'm working on now."

"Tell me about it," he said, and to her surprise, she wanted to. She was proud of what she was creating, of her intrepid nurse Dot, of the suspense she'd built scene by scene. He listened attentively, and by the burn of magic, she had the strong sense that Mother and the house listened as well. The luscious scent of baking bread filled the small room.

"I was inspired by some recent books and stories. Have you read any Agatha Christie? She's a new mystery writer out of England." He shook his head. "She had this book out a few years ago, *The Secret Adversary*, with a couple, Tommy and Tuppence. Tuppence, the young woman, is the very mode of an impoverished flapper, and she has grit. She worked in hospitals during the war. That inspired the background I gave Dot."

"I hate to say it, but I haven't had much time for books as my career has picked up. Willa Cather's probably my favorite, though."

"Willa Cather! She writes the way that angels must speak. I study her sentences, her descriptions, to try to figure out what makes them work."

Rex laughed. "That's rather like listening to an orchestra and trying to identify the notes of each instrument, isn't it? I'd rather enjoy the full song."

"Well, you're not a writer," Fayette admonished. They stared at each other a moment and then both burst out laughing. "You should be proud of yourself for successfully distracting me yet again. I needed your company tonight."

"I won't lie to you," he said softly. "The promise you had me make earlier, to meet you here? That motivated me through today."

"What came in your mail? Can you tell me now?"

"Yes." He took a deep breath. "It was a mix of good and bad, really, but the good is bittersweet. My friend Art sent me a letter, you see. He really shouldn't have—but then, I shouldn't have sent him a note that I was coming to Carmel, so." Rex shrugged.

Fayette had to wonder about this Art that he kept mentioning. "Is there something suspicious about this letter?" she said with melodramatic concern. "Was it composed of cut-out words from a newspaper, like the one in *Hound of the Baskervilles*? It wasn't addressed from Yuma Territorial Prison, was it?"

As she'd hoped, that got a laugh out of him. "No, nothing like that. And I'm glad he mailed me." His voice didn't portray enthusiasm. "The other letter, though, came from my producer. I'm supposed to see him tomorrow in San Francisco, but what he wanted to say couldn't wait."

"Let me guess: You misbehaved terribly by not marrying Margaret, and he's going to make you sit in the corner of the schoolroom with a dunce cap."

"That, with more adult consequences." His blue eyes filled with tears. "He told me that if Margaret is found dead, it's my fault."

Rage burned through her in an instant. "He has no right to lay blame on you for her actions, now or later! As if being married to her would automatically save her, anyway! That man's brain is full of swamp mud and his soul is a cankerous—"

"Calm down the creative wordplay. I know he's wrong, by logic, but—"

"You still feel guilty."

His shrug was weary. "I can't help it. I *do* want to help Margaret, even though I barely know her. I don't want anyone to suffer."

"That's because you're a good person. Not-good people try to take advantage of that sometimes."

"I keep thinking that if I'm with her, maybe she won't go out, and maybe she won't take— Oh, please forget I said that." He paled. "It's not my place to reveal her struggles."

Especially as he hadn't confessed his own. "She already told me about the cocaine."

"What? She did?" His eyes rounded in astonishment.

"She did indeed. I've had a few neighbors die of drugs over the past year. Margaret's not the only one enduring such a struggle these days, for sure." Fayette sighed. "The studios are more interested in keeping things quiet than actually helping people. You'd think after the William Desmond Taylor hullabaloo, they'd change their approach, but no."

That fiasco had ruled the newspaper headlines starting back in 1922. Taylor had been a well-known director in his late forties. He was found dead, shot. Speculation named several actresses who might have done the deed—and one's mother might have killed him, too—and there were other vivid characters to round out the cast. Cocaine played into the drama as well.

"No," agreed Rex, the single word steeped with exhaustion. "That case, I think, made things worse in a lot of ways. I heard several studios paid off the cops to stop the investigation, but their efforts to silence the papers didn't take."

"There was too much money to be made. Here, the bread smells like it's done." Fayette pulled out the loaf and tapped it. Beneath the crisp crust, the interior rang as hollow. Perfect. She used the peel to bring it to the table.

Rex began to slice up the sausage. He'd brought even more food today, enough to feed six, maybe more. To her surprise, her stomach rumbled in anticipation. "Oh, before I forget, I realized that we didn't arrange a meeting place with Silas tomorrow. I included a note with the check to say we'll convene outside of the Fitz household. I should be back well in advance of that if all goes—"

A door appeared on the far wall. A screen door, its mesh patched, the frame's green paint crackled to show brown beneath. It swung open. Two women staggered through and stopped. Both were short, with deep-brown skin and black hair, their dresses thin and worn. They stared at Rex and Fayette with blatant fear.

Fayette and Rex stood, their hands up, smiles coaxing.

The women spoke quietly in a language Fayette didn't recognize. She knew a good bit of Spanish and some Japanese, courtesy of her longtime neighbors, but this was something different.

"Hello there!" Rex called with one of his grins. "We have food for you to enjoy." They hadn't even cut into the fresh loaf yet, but the house must have known that it was ready to be eaten.

The women had frozen in place like jackrabbits caught in the open. The door hadn't closed behind them.

The first time Fayette had seen a look like that on someone's face, the person had been Briar. They'd still lived in Coalinga then. It'd been a rough and ready California oil boom town in those days, with few families like theirs around. Thayer, Briar, and Fayette had been taught that there were some streets they were never, ever to go near. They heeded those strong words, but drunk men didn't stay corralled as they ought. Briar had been a block away from home when three sozzled men got hold of her. In the end, she wasn't physically harmed, but her dress was torn as she fought free.

She'd arrived home with the same panicked eyes as these women.

That expression of acute terror had returned often to Briar, especially in those next few weeks. When someone knocked at the door, Briar was afraid the men had found where she lived. She didn't go alone outside anywhere, not even to the outhouse. Groups of men—and there were so many more men than women in Coalinga in those days— caused her to be fearful and alert.

In the end, that attack on Briar influenced her family's move a few hours south to Los Angeles, where Pa stayed on as an oil worker as operations expanded in the area. Briar never lost her sense of vigilance, though, and Fayette picked up on it, too. That wariness had saved her from a scrape more than once.

These women needed saving, too.

"Rex," Fayette said softly, grabbing his arm to pull it down. "We need to leave."

"Leave?" He looked baffled. "What d'you mean?"

"We need to go outside. They're not going to come any closer if we're here."

"But surely we can—"

"No." The harshness of her tone made the women cower and edge toward the door behind them. What had they seen, what had they endured? "Your smile can't win them over. We need to go out. Now."

"But—"

"You're a *man*. A white man. Here I am, a varied shade of pale from you. We don't speak their language, and even if we did, maybe they have good reason not to believe us. *Go*."

Rex glanced at his right hand as if he'd never really seen it before. "Oh."

He let her pull him closer to the entrance. There, Fayette paused to gesture to the food again with a smile. "Yours," she projected, and then, in a low voice, to the house said, "Let me close the door. They need to see me close it."

Therefore, as they entered the foyer, she had her hand on the knob for the first time as she drew it closed. Rain pattered softly on the roof. Odd how that sound carried but not the nearby ocean.

They waited, their breaths the only sound for a minute, and then came a clatter. The women hadn't fled. Thank God, truly, thank God. Fayette wiped tears from her eyes. The fear on their faces—not just fear of having arrived in a strange place, but their fear of Rex. Of *her*. She never would've thought the sight of her could evoke such terror, but what did she know? Not much, that was for sure.

Objects thudded on the wooden floor. Soft feet pounded, going the other way. The clunk of the closing screen door echoed. Only then did Fayette open the interior door.

The table had been cleared of food and implements, the canvas bag gone. A few pieces of cheese lay on the floor as evidence of the women's haste. The bench had tipped, her coat pinned beneath. She lifted up the bench, and as she pulled up her coat, for a second it seemed to stick to the floor. She glanced at the fabric. There was nothing on it.

Oh. Had they tried to take her coat and the house . . . stopped them? She would have missed it greatly and had to deprive herself of food in order to replace it, but she still felt oddly selfish with the bundle in her arms.

"The bread will help those women," Fayette said, slipping on her coat again. She needed its well-worn comfort and warmth. Cold just seemed to linger in her bones these days. "All of the food will help them."

Another familiar thing brushed her skin—Mother's heat. Mother!

The repurposed jar remained where Fayette had left it in one of the oven's storage nooks far away from heat. Either the women hadn't taken time to explore the room, or the house had made certain that Mother stayed here.

But Fayette could've lost Mother again, and here she'd thought she'd brought the starter where it could be safer. Maybe she shouldn't have kept Mother, though, just as she perhaps shouldn't still have her coat.

Fayette choked out a sob, both hands to her face.

Rex lightly touched her shoulder. "Fayette?"

"I'm fine. I'm not— This isn't about me. Too much has been about me. It's just—my family has hoarded Mother for so long, and I've been angry at Mother for not doing enough. My family has had it good in many ways, though. There are many people in greater need." She waved toward the empty wall where the doors had appeared. "If they'd taken Mother, I would've understood. Maybe that would've been for the best."

He stayed quiet for a long moment. "Mother has stayed with you, with your whole family, for a reason. If she's a living, responsive being . . . is it far-fetched to think that she may love you and your other family members? You've been caring for each other for a century, right?"

"Yes." Her family had certainly loved Mother. Ma had never been ashamed to say so to Mother or to anyone else, but Fayette tended to be more reticent unless she was putting words on paper.

If Mother truly loved them in turn—oh. That would also mean that she, too, had known grief through these recent years. Briar, Thayer, Ma. How many others had Mother tended to over the years? How many had she also grieved in her quiet, fermented way?

And here Mother had also borne the brunt of Fayette's grief, her rage.

"I'm sorry," she said, walking up to the jar. Her tear-moistened fingers touched the glass. "I'm sorry that I never considered your feelings, too."

Mother's warmth resonated, and Fayette could have sworn that the warmth targeted her chest, right above her heart.

Chapter 24

Finding people is getting easier with practice, but there are so many people in the world who need help on their quests! So many!

Creating a doorway has become easier, too. That's probably the easiest thing of all. Usually, people are near some kind of doorway during the day. Really, any kind of passage will do. A gate, a branch curved into an arch, a cave, a large pipe beneath a road—anything that represents a border between realms.

Maybe this will surprise you, Mother, though I know you've seen a lot in your long life, but getting someone to come through my passage, that's the hard bit.

I can only crack the door for them or show a hint of light, in some way revealing that another world is on the far side. They have to look up at the right moment—that means they must be aware and awake! How amazing it is, the number of humans asleep at any one moment. So they must see the door, and then they must choose to open it wide and step through.

Many don't. This night, I made fifty-three doors. Fifteen people approached. But this pair of women, only these two, came through.

I hated that I scared them so much. I knew the door couldn't close behind them, or they'd have been even more terrified. The other girl yesterday, she was comforted by the man and the woman. That could not be repeated today, but the woman-flavored-by-Mother knew what to do, just as I knew she would.

I like making people feel welcome here, Mother. And it's strangely easy to do! You just pay attention to how they react and adjust things accordingly. But even if it *was* hard, I'd still do it. It's the kind of thing a home does.

But wait. Wait. Oh no.

The other witch has been watching me, I know. Once she knew where I was, that I was awake, that I was alone, of course she would watch me.

But this— Is she really? Right now?

She is. Oh no, she is.

What am I going to do? I can't—or can I? No, I must stop her. This isn't solely about me, about what she will do.

My people and Mother are here.

My friends.

Oh, this is about so much more than me.

Chapter 25

Fayette turned to Rex. "I'm dog-tired. Today has been too much and I'm ready to—"

A door formed of wood and metal opened on the far wall. Fayette and Rex stared at each other.

"But . . . we have no bread. There's nothing for us to—" Rex began.

A bench at the nearby table blinked away. A second later, a board appeared at a horizontal angle over the door, a sound like the thuds of hammers in accompaniment. An instant later, there was another long board at a diagonal across the top of the door.

Fayette took a step forward in disbelief. Hot prickles of magic pressed on her, more potent than she'd ever experienced before. "What, is the bench being reused to block the door? How can—"

Someone, something, knocked at the door. Thud, thud, thud—the noise loud, commanding. Like a policeman, she thought. Or someone angry after being unexpectedly locked out in the cold.

"That door . . . it looks like the first one that appeared. The one that led to the skeleton," Fayette said.

"That can't be whoever is knocking, can it?" Rex asked with blatant horror.

Fayette opened her lips to answer, but at that moment, the door bulged forward, as if the wood had warped to form a balloon. Another board smacked across it, then another, then another. Boom, boom,

boom, each board at a different angle. The bulge was knocked back. Everything went still.

"God help us," said Rex. "What is—"

The knocks returned, impossibly loud, clanging through Fayette's senses as if she stood with her head in a cathedral bell. The sound resounded and boomed around her, through her, the vibration painful even in her molars.

The other bench vanished.

The door ballooned again. Two boards popped free and were flung across the room, right toward Fayette and Rex, only to boomerang back to nail over the door again, joined in quick succession by other boards that flickered into existence so quickly she couldn't count them.

A high, frustrated scream rang out, muffled by distance. And piles of wood.

"Should we leave?" Rex shouted over the ruckus.

Fayette lunged to grab Mother, cushioning the glass jar against her chest. Mother's prickling presence remained as steady as ever. Fayette resolved to follow her stalwart example.

"No, we might need to help the house in some—"

The door shuddered and heaved. One board dropped off only to throw itself back into the fray. And that's what this was—a fray, a battle.

The entirety of the heavy wooden table pivoted around as it began to float in the air. Its legs detached from what had been the underside. They floated out to form three-board-thick shields that dropped down to hover in front of Fayette, Mother, and Rex.

That barricade almost obscured the view of the black mist that began to flow around the few bits of uncovered doorframe. Fayette's first panicked thought was of mustard gas attacks in the war, but she detected no smell. The only unpleasantness was that prickles of magic escalated to the point of pain, as if porcupines were pressed against Fayette's whole body, eyeballs included. She was, quite abruptly, reconsidering her decision to stay.

With movement so fast that Fayette's ears actually popped, the massive table soared across the room to clash against the wall, a ten-foot-by-three-foot barricade. A cascade of thumps echoed through the room, as if someone was hammering faster than any human being could possibly hammer.

The mist was gone. Everything was quiet but for the roar of Fayette's heart and both her and Rex's panicked gasps.

The incident probably hadn't even taken more than a minute.

"Well." Fayette swallowed dryly. "That was interesting." The heady sense of magic withdrew so quickly, her legs went wobbly in the sudden absence of pain.

"That's a cosmic understatement, Fayette." His voice shook.

Their shields flew back to where the table had been, and two seconds later, the table wrenched itself away from the wall and rotated back to its old spot. The planks blinked away next, revealing a blank, normal log wall. The benches returned, one set out as if in anticipation of Fayette's need. She plopped down while Rex stayed standing, eyeing the furniture as if it were a tarantula.

"I don't think you need to worry about if the house is on our side or not," Fayette said. "It looks to me like it just defended us from . . . something."

"I'm not concerned about its allegiance, more that the table might need to become a blockade again."

"If it does, well, our bottoms will hit the floor, but I'd rather have a sore backside than meet whatever tried to come through just now."

Rex nodded and ran a hand through his blond hair. "Our house didn't make that door, and that cloud wasn't smoke. Did you . . . sense anything about it?"

"Magic. It was all magic. The attack, the mist, everything."

"Okay, then. Okay." Rex looked around, seeming to need a minute to absorb this news. "Was that— Is there another house out there like this one? Maybe?"

"That's all I can think. We talked about this place being like a witch's house. If that . . . invader was another witch, in another door-making house . . . well, I don't think they are very nice. Not like this house." Fayette gave the bench a fond pat-pat.

"But . . . why?" Rex sounded hoarse as he sat beside her, leaning on his thighs. "That was an outright attack."

"I can't even guess at what fully happened there. The only thing that *is* clear is that the house was attacked and defended itself."

"I agree with that wholeheartedly," he murmured, lifting his head to meet her gaze. "What was it you were saying right before that happened?" Rex's smile was wry. He already knew the answer, but rattled as Fayette was, she had to think for a second.

"Oh. I was saying I was tired and that this day had been too much."

They both laughed at a high, hysterical pitch.

"On that note, we should go." Rex stood, the movement shaky. "I don't know if you have to deal with that kind of assault all the time, house, and we just happened to be here now, or what, but . . ." He exhaled, pausing. "Thank you for shielding us as you did."

Fayette looked down at the jar in her hands, dithering for a moment, then returned it to its nook near the oven. She backed away. The house's interior looked as spick and span as ever, with no signs of the conflict that had just occurred.

They both moved toward the door. Fayette lingered with a hand on the doorframe. "Thank you for taking care of us and Mother, and most of all, for taking care of yourself, house."

Fayette and Rex, both still unsteady from nerves, helped each other down the rocks.

"You know," Rex said as they pushed through the wax myrtles, "tomorrow's trip to San Francisco doesn't seem as daunting now. The studio execs can do a lot, but they aren't witches wielding black clouds of magic."

"I don't know, maybe they have a few secrets you'd best not uncover," she said, to which he laughed. She stopped moving, fists on her hips. "Be that as it may, I'll be terribly disappointed if you come back with a wedding ring."

"Other people might take that a certain way."

"I have no designs on you. If you haven't grasped that by now, then your head is filled with straw tick."

"Oh, I know you're not trying to pursue a romance." His smile was pensive. "That's what I like about being with you. I feel . . . safe. That sounds funny, after what we just went through, but . . ." He shrugged.

With that, he continued onward, leaving her staring after him with the strange realization that being with him felt oddly right, too. Even when the building they were in was enduring some kind of preternatural assault.

Chapter 26

I wish I could tell the man that I had never had to bar a door in such a way before, but maybe it's best that I cannot. He will probably feel more secure if he thinks that I know what I am doing.

He cannot know how terrified I am.

I erred, oh, I erred, and I cannot undo my actions, nor do I wish to. The woman and man have been so happy to share their meals! And that first girl—she loved me. She still does. I know her devotion as she works westward, inch by inch getting closer to this coastline, though hundreds of miles away yet. And I love her in return.

The other witch who sought entrance to me did not do so out of love. Her quest was as clear as a noon sun on a cloudless day.

Her house hasn't been kept in good care; the damage is too significant to be repaired by magic. To her eyes, I am a magic house abandoned, and my excellent condition is to her advantage. I am to be repurposed. My soul is to be slain, with each of my parts assessed in turn to be joined to and rejuvenate her house, or to be discarded. My logs pried away, my roof dissembled, each feather scrutinized. My meat eaten. My oven—my very heart—likely to replace that of my sibling, as her bricks are soiled and frail. My feet boiled to make glue to bind my scraps to their new body.

I daresay, the remains of my witch would not be regarded with respect, either. The sisterhood doesn't tend toward sentimentality.

The good news is, I suppose, that the other witch cannot try to force another door within me. She had one chance, and I thwarted her and sealed the way—and I was only able to do so because of the intense flow of power from my well below.

But this has made her angry. Angry enough that she and her house are now airborne over Rus. She is set to leave behind the motherland so that she may pillage my body.

Soon, she will be over the ocean.

Soon, she will be here.

She knows the verse that will open my front door. I cannot refuse her entrance if she comes that way.

If my new witch doesn't take occupancy of me soon, I will no longer be here in wait of her, for I will be dead.

Chapter 27

The next morning, Fayette regarded her typewriter the way she did a rattlesnake.

Rattlers had existed back in their old home of Sturkie, Arkansas, but she somehow didn't encounter one directly until they'd moved to the golden hills of Central California. That initial slithering visitor had awaited them on the front stoop one morning, right where they'd get milk delivered three times a week.

"Snakes like sunny spots, see?" Ma had said, making a lesson of the rattlesnake as they all craned their necks out of a nearby window. "He's probably got a den right nearby. That means I got to kill him." She'd sighed.

"Why you sad about that?" Thayer had asked as Ma grabbed a shovel from near the back door.

"Snakes eat vermin. That fellow out there will keep mice from coming inside the house, getting into our food. If you see a snake out far from the house, you leave him be. Respect him. He has a place in nature. But this fellow—he chose the wrong stoop."

Fayette didn't watch, but she heard the distinct metallic clink of the shovel slicing through flesh to stone. Ma had killed the snake with a single deft blow.

Fayette respected her typewriter. She did. She loved the thing, truly—the Corona 3 had been something of an indulgence soon after she was hired at Astrophel, but she knew it'd get a lot of use since she could take it between the studio and home. It'd needed a few repairs here and there, as any machine did, but the typewriter had been more reliable than she was, especially these past few months.

But right about now, she wondered whether she should haul the typewriter out back and take a shovel to it.

She knew, though, that her destructive urge was misdirected. Her typewriter wasn't the problem. The Peacocks of Pennsylvania were, and being a fairly law-abiding citizen, she couldn't take a shovel to them or use the tool again afterward to cover up the evidence.

Last night, as she'd readied for bed, she pondered walking the beach today or wandering shops to make the hours tick by without Rex. She could visit the cliff house again, of course, make sure it and Mother were still as fine as rosebuds after that peculiar assault, but she didn't need to be there all the day long.

To her surprise, though, the more she stared at her typewriter, the more strongly bloomed the desire to write and make her continuity the best it could be before she turned it in to Astrophel. That enraged, spiteful urge continued even after she reminded herself that she wouldn't be credited in the final picture. She'd seen other people fired in recent months have their existences erased. As she trusted that the Peacocks would destroy her work during production, however, she was okay with her heir owning the disaster that he created.

Fayette washed her hands, straightened her notes, and went to work with her lips frozen in a snarl.

The climax neared. Dot's peril increased by the page.

This truly was going to be her best-ever script. A shame that it'd be squandered in the end—but that was life, wasn't it?

That was life.

That thought didn't plummet her back into despair at this moment, but acted like a pushed-down gas pedal to rev up her stubborn determination.

She blinked at the pink light gleaming through the window and needed a moment to register that the sun was setting. It was almost five.

Shouldn't Rex be back by now?

She paced through the house for a few minutes, stretching her legs, then went outside. Heidi was kneeling on an old pillow to weed a garden bed in the fading light. She twisted around at the sound of the door closing and, upon seeing Fayette, pushed herself to rise.

"Please, please don't go. Give me a chance to speak with you a minute," said Fayette.

Heidi's rounded face took on a stubborn set, but she nodded for Fayette to continue.

"I figure you don't want me to ask you about what that medium said. I understand. I do want to point out that he said things about me and Rex, too, and his words were eerily right. That means I recognize that what he said about you carries some form of truth, too." Heidi looked wary, but she didn't bolt. "I'm not going to ask you questions without opening myself up to questions as well. I want you to know that. I have all intentions to be fair."

Heidi pulled off her gloves and dropped them to her feet as she yanked a notepad from her apron pocket. After writing a moment, she turned the paper for Fayette to read.

I wish to be left alone. Your affairs are your own.

Heidi's cursive handwriting was among the prettiest Fayette had ever seen. The young woman could make a living by writing calligraphy for people.

Fayette mulled over what to say next. "I respect your privacy, but at the same time, you need to understand that our lives have intersected in odd ways. That peculiar Russian house just south of here—" Heidi's eyes widened. She took a step back. "I can enter the place. Because of me, I think, Rex can go there, too, but for a long time, he didn't know the place existed. Almost no one else in town can—please, Heidi, don't go yet—but I saw you on the grounds a few days ago. I need to understand why you also can—" Heidi was five feet away now. "We're asking Silas Pennington to assess the place tonight, and I want you to feel free to—"

Heidi was gone, skirts a pale flash in the dim light as she sprinted around the corner.

Fayette wished she'd had a chance to ask Heidi about what had happened to Mother's jar, but an answer probably wouldn't have been forthcoming anyway.

As Fayette stacked the abandoned gloves with the other tools, an engine roared closer along the road. Few cars seemed to come this far, so she couldn't help but be curious about the sound. She took the path around to find a vivid-yellow top-down roadster shutting off in front of the Fitz homestead. A woman was in the driver's seat, her head swaddled in a scarf with goggles over her eyes. The driver saw Fayette, and her arm raised in a wave. "Darling! Here!"

With those two words, Fayette recognized Margaret.

Fayette advanced to stand at the driver's-side door as Margaret finished untwining her scarf. "I brought you a gift," she said, pulling her goggles off. She gave her short hair a flounce. "Check under the blanket on the back seat."

Unsure what to expect, Fayette did as she bade, uncovering a pair of black, glossy men's shoes.

"It's me. I'm the gift." Rex's muffled voice came from the other end as he pulled down the blanket to reveal his tousled blond hair. "I suppose you can try to return me at the store, but I don't know if you can get your money back. You may need to do a trade."

"Oh, you." Margaret laughed.

"I suppose the bus was too good for your return trip?" Fayette asked, casting a look back at the house. The curtains moved. Heidi stood there, watching, safe behind walls and glass. Fayette thought about what Rex had said about refugees running to survive. Heidi certainly had become a real pro.

"The bus would've been fine, really," said Rex. "Though on the way up this morning, I did have three ladies pin me in my seat as they quizzed me about life as an actor. It made the ride pass quickly, but Margaret's method was faster yet."

Margaret gave her hair another toss. "If a car can go eighty miles an hour, it should."

"Not on those curves, it shouldn't," Rex retorted.

"Were you under the blanket the whole time?" Fayette asked.

"Only when we went through towns. She wanted to go eighty there, too."

"God help me! The man would have me drive like a granny. This is a brand-spankin'-new Chrysler Imperial," Margaret said to Fayette. "One of these was the pace car for the Indianapolis 500 back in May. This beauty can go from a stop to sixty in twenty seconds!" She said that as if it should impress Fayette, who managed to make a suitable "Oh!" sound and smile, but really, she held about as much affection for automobiles as she did for hammers or wheelbarrows or other basic tools.

"Mind sharing the reason for this brand-spankin'-new lifeboat?" Fayette asked.

"The studio executives invited a priest along to lunch." Rex exited the car.

Fayette's stomach twisted in dread. "Oh no. What happened?"

"I told this man of the cloth that he'd been invited there under false pretenses, as me and Margaret scarcely knew each other and had no desire to be wed. He was justifiably angry, but not at us. He'd apparently been told that we'd been in love for months and that we wanted a simple religious ceremony in San Francisco—"

"The same sort of tale they've already spun in the papers and magazines," Margaret added.

Rex nodded. "The priest, God bless the man, knew right where to lay the blame. He embarrassed a whole handful of powerful men."

"They embarrassed themselves," Fayette said.

"Sadly, these sorts of men lack that kind of self-awareness," Rex said. "After the priest left, I was mobbed by angry fellows who kept telling me they had the best of intentions and that I needed to play along for my own good."

"I should point out that they applied no pressure to me at all," said Margaret with a feral grin. "They thought I was their good girl, ready to do exactly as they said. And you know what? A week ago, I would have. But then I met you." She nodded toward Fayette.

"Me?" Fayette blinked.

"Yes, you. You told me I oughta start standing up for myself, so I did, but they didn't even realize what a conniving little bitch I was until it was too late." She cackled.

Fayette felt a surge of pride at Margaret's ascendancy into agency and, well, bitchiness.

"Margaret's acting was at its finest," Rex said with fondness. "She stepped out, saying she needed to powder her nose. She went down the block and bought a car, came back, and idled at the entrance while a valet ran up with orders to whisper to me to make a run for the front entrance. When I did that, men chasing me to the elevator like in a Chaplin comedy, I ran across the lobby and jumped in her car. She sped off like she was *in* the Indianapolis 500!"

"Maybe I should start doing my own stunts in movies," Margaret mused. "That was too much fun."

"You'd better hope that they don't realize it was you dolled up in that scarf," added Rex. "Let me be the one in the stewpot of trouble."

She flipped a wrist to wave off the concern. "You don't need to take the blame alone, manly man that you are. That's a load of applesauce."

"Didn't you have to be rescued by Rex in *Dance After Midnight*?" Fayette asked. "You rescued him today in reality!"

"I did, didn't I?" Her grin was radiant as she settled into her seat again. She pulled on her goggles and began to secure her scarf. "Well, I'm going to drive onward. I might stop in Gilroy or another fine village tonight. Or maybe I'll go on to Hollywood! I don't know."

"You've already done a lot of driving today. You need to stop if you feel tired," said Fayette, not hiding her concern.

"Oh, I can go days without sleep sometimes, without even taking a thing, and then I can practically snooze for a week!" Margaret's laugh was carefree. "I'm a good driver. I haven't had an accident yet."

"Don't change that tonight. You take care of yourself." Rex tapped her car door as he looked on her with blatant worry.

"Oh, darling." She blew him a kiss. "I always do."

Rex stood by Fayette as the car engine revved up. Margaret waved a gloved hand as she took the car in a U-turn, and then off she went.

In the sudden silence, Rex sighed. "She'll take care of herself, one way or another."

Fayette waved Rex to follow. "Let's take a seat while we wait for Silas. This bench gives a good view of the street. I can bring you a pear or something, if you want." She sat on a stone bench underneath cypress trees at the southern edge of the yard. The seat was cold but, after a day of clear weather, mercifully dry.

"I'm good for now, thanks. I did manage to eat a hefty lunch, before . . ." He summed up the other events with a shrug. "I hope your day was better than mine."

"To my own shock, I worked on my continuity. The accursed thing is almost done."

He grinned. "I'm not shocked. You love the story, and you'll put your utmost into it."

How had he come to know her so well, so quickly? "I *do* love it. All the good that'll do. Like everything and everyone I love, it'll be destroyed, and all I can do is stand back and watch." The words were harsh, her tone light.

"We should be thankful, then, that there's no limit to what we can love," he said. "On that note, I have some news for you that will make you upset." They were far enough from the house that they could speak freely.

She didn't like the sound of that. "What, did you enjoy another sourdough bread while you were in the city? Don't worry, Mother doesn't get jealous."

Rex ignored the jest. "You're mentioned in the gossip pages as the cause of my delayed nuptials with Margaret."

Her jaw fell slack. "Please tell me you're joking."

"I wish I was. I can only guess that Horatio remembered your name from that confrontation after . . . the incident on the cliff." Horatio had to be one of the hatted goons. "I cannot express how sorry I am, Fayette. I never wanted you dragged into this mess." He looked, in all sincerity, like he was about to cry.

"Huh." She felt more bewildered than anything. "I've watched studio games from afar. I know how they go. I reckon it's a good thing I was already getting the sack, or I would've been gone for sure now." She tilted her head to one side, thoughtful, then burst out laughing. "It's funny, though. One of the producers at Astrophel has given me grief for *years* about being unmarried at my age. He'd sometimes ask me how I got by, having never brought children into the world. He acted like I was poisoned and refused the antidote. One time, I got fed up with him and said I got by just fine and that I slept through the night better than he did, for certain. He didn't appreciate that, having a brood of six. Mind you, he's probably not helping his wife as much as he could when a baby cries in the night—he'd be one to awaken just to gripe. That sainted woman does everything for him. She irons his *socks*." Fayette knew she was babbling, but needed to. "He'll probably fall over in a swoon when he reads that I snared someone like *you*."

Rex leaned toward her, a mischievous spark in his eye. "Seize that sentiment like it's a buoy saving you from drowning."

"I beg your pardon?"

"Flaunt that you, as you put it, 'snared' me." Oh, that grin of his. Those gals on the bus probably fought palpitations every time those teeth flashed. Not even Fayette was fully immune to their power. "I'm not ashamed to be seen with you. Not here in Carmel, not in Beverly Hills. If you want, I can dress you up in sparkles that'll make the heavens jealous and take you to Musso & Frank Grill for the best food you'll have in your life. You'll have photographers' bulbs flashing all around you and—"

"Be utterly miserable. That's no life for me. Get me tamales from the pushcart vendor with the green shirt who likes to lurk around Santa Monica and Gower."

"That's why I said I'd do it, if you wanted."

"You love the cameras on you, don't you?"

"I do. To me, it's another stage. I put on a suit like this, and I'm Rex Hallstrom." He tugged at his bespoke suit jacket. "I'm not some barefoot brat who escaped the farm."

"You're not Helmer," Fayette murmured.

"I'm a million miles from Helmer." His smile turned wan.

"I like both Rex and Helmer, but I'm biased toward Helmer, I think. I also wouldn't mind eating at Musso & Frank Grill sometime, if we sneak in the back. I've heard their Welsh rarebit is the bee's knees."

"What you heard is right. They don't skimp on the cheese, and the bread they use—well, it's the next best thing to magical. I suppose I *am* starting to get hungry, but it's too late for a snack because here comes our medium." He stood. Fayette joined him in watching Silas approach. By the light cast from nearby houses, she could see Silas carried a heavy bag that swayed with each step.

"I hope no more strange doors appear, friendly or otherwise. But most of all, I hope the sheer magic doesn't boil his brain," Fayette murmured as she stood.

"I hope not, too, even though we know where to stash a body where it'd never be found," he muttered, then spoke up with his booming, friendly Rex Hallstrom voice. "Hey there, Silas! How're you doing this evening?"

Chapter 28

This new man in my yard *reeks* like nothing I have known before. He is a stew into which everything has been dumped, over many years. Whole vessels of basil, cumin, and most every other herb known. The pepper and salt—oh, the salt! The foulness of the mixed magics upon *and* within him makes me want to sneeze, but I *can't*, as I must stay roosted. If he had only blended one or two magics, that would've been fine, even interesting—yes, yes, just as you are interesting, Mother.

But this? *This?*

He is *Stinky*.

Oh dear. I fear I have named him through my emphasis upon that adjective. I should not have done that, no, no, but now it is done and cannot be undone, just as how being distracted as meat roasts for even two minutes can result in foul char.

I don't want him near me. I don't. I dare not describe him further, dare not empower him with more names. There are so many words I could accord him, the worst of words. The woman and man, however, don't have the senses I do—they don't know the depths of his awfulness.

Mother, your senses are even more different than ours. Does he bother you? Would you retain the empowerment within your bread for him? Would you—

Oh. You want me to be quiet now so you can continue to think? You've been quiet all day, I suppose. Well, I'll try to be quiet soon, too, but for now—

Ah! Ah! He's inside me! Oh, he's even worse up close. Such foulness! I thought it'd be awful to have the other witch inside me, but this, this is a different sort of assault! This is *degradation*. But I couldn't keep him out, not without excluding the woman and the man. At least . . . I don't think so. I've never tried before to pry apart people in a group. I don't know what to do, I don't—but, oh, he's walking across my floor. *He's touching me! Ah!*

I must get Stinky out of here somehow, some way, somehow! Oh, what would my witch do were she here?!

Chapter 29

The house was quivering, and only Fayette noticed. Her skin flashed hot and cold in turns, the dramatic shifts worse than what she experienced in the hot flashes she'd gotten in recent years if she had something delicious and sugary near bedtime. Mother's presence was quiet in the background.

Rex was checking the fire, as he most always did upon entering, even though it burned as steadily as ever with its seemingly endless supply of fuel. Meanwhile, Silas hadn't stopped jabbering since they'd taken him by the arms and pulled him through the bushes.

Fayette had to open the doors for the first time, though. Once her hand was on the knob, the way had opened easily enough, but she had to wonder at the absence of their usual welcome and the house's quivering.

Silas craned his neck to look at the high peak of the ceiling. "The building here is quite solid, these logs thick! Do we know what kind of wood this is? You're right, the place looks old. There was a word you used for this style of home—"

"An izba," said Rex.

"Izba." Silas tested the syllables on his tongue. "That's a new word for me, and I can speak a smattering of Latin and German. Those are the major languages of magic, you know." Fayette had to look askance at that bold statement. The world was much larger than that small portion of Europe, but that small portion tended to think highly of itself. "Now, this oven!" Silas stood before it, opening his arms wide. "It's like a quaint version of an industrial oven! And yet so large for a small house!"

"People can sleep on top," Rex said, standing on the first step to demonstrate access.

"And heat comes through the bricks and flue . . . yes, yes, that's a clever way to stay warm through a cold winter." Silas dragged his fingers along the bricks.

The house's quiver intensified, and with it, a sense in the air almost like thick humidity. A form of resistance, yes, as if walking through the room took extra effort. Fayette's sense of ill ease increased.

"Silas, you don't need to touch everything," she called.

"Sorry, sorry." He released a giddy giggle. "I'm simply amazed by the place and I want to take it in through all of my senses! I should use my camera—" He let the satchel drop to the ground and began to reach inside.

"Nothing will turn out," Fayette interrupted. "The negative will be gray or smeared. When we said the house hid, we meant that it did so in every possible way. A pilot flying over likely wouldn't see a thing." Meanwhile, Silas seemed only partially affected by the house's enchantment; he had clearly seen the place from the road but couldn't cross the bush line without their help. He hadn't forgotten any of their preparatory conversation the previous day, either.

Silas nodded repeatedly. "That's incredibly powerful magic, to affect so many people—and objects—in such a way." He continued his circuit, moving toward the far wall that had hosted coming-and-going doors.

Rex sidled close to her. "An observation," he murmured low enough that Silas couldn't hear.

"Yes?" Was he going to say he noticed the house felt different as well? She didn't want to mention it first and taint his perspective.

"*We* haven't tried taking a photograph. The hut likes us. We may actually be able to preserve images of this place."

Fayette considered that statement. "Even if we can, I don't think we should." At his curious expression, she continued, "The house is hiding for a reason. Exposing it in such a way . . . well, it seems like a violation. What we're doing right now is increasingly feeling that way, too."

By his widening eyes, she'd surprised him. "What, really? But we came inside!"

"The doors didn't open to welcome us. Even more—" She gasped, feeling an especially violent quiver. "Silas, what are you doing?"

"This wall." He stood right where the doors had appeared. "My headache is worse when I stand here, despite my layered efforts to safeguard myself." Their approach to the house had strained him, too, a vicious headache rendering him weak-kneed. He hadn't passed out, though, proof that the proactive magic he'd conducted had obviously worked.

Fayette and Rex glanced at each other sidelong. "How peculiar," she said.

"You said the house appeared here, when?" Silas asked, moving back toward the oven.

"Near the end of the war," Fayette said, being purposefully vague.

"And this land is owned by Mr. and Mrs. Fitz. I wonder if this connects to Mr. Fitz's condition?" Silas asked.

Fayette recoiled. "That seems like a stretch."

"I don't know. It would make things tidy if these details were tied together. Selfishly so, for me, but Mr. Fitz's situation has lingered with me. I still want to help him, even if the job I was paid to do is done. I don't forget about the people I haven't been able to aid." His voice softened.

"You can't help everyone, no matter how you try," Fayette said, thinking of Mother's bread.

"True, and yet . . ." Silas paced in front of the fire. "This location is a prime example of a wayline. Land meets water meets river, and there may be a fault line as well. The 1906 San Francisco earthquake and the more recent one in Santa Barbara are proof of the energy being released along this coastline! That means spiritual energy, too. If this house was . . . elsewhere, I can see why it might be drawn here. Why, it may very well feed on the inherent magic of the area. That wall where my headache was worse—that's against the ocean. Yes, yes, I imagine that's why it emits more power than, say, the wall over there." He motioned to the opposite side that, outside, faced east and the interior of the country.

"That sounds like a possibility," Fayette said, and meant it.

"There's a lot of power here, too." Silas waved his hands to encompass the oven. "It's centrally located in the room. Creates heat, which is a different kind of power."

Mother also rested in a nook right in front of him, blending in with other tools.

"You've made a lot of interesting points," said Rex, ever tactful. "But what do you make of the house? What *is* it?"

"An izba?" Silas joked, then sobered when he saw they weren't laughing. "I vaguely remember there being a flying house in Russian mythology—"

"Flying? How?" asked Fayette, remembering what Mrs. Fitz had said about feathers.

"It was part bird. I want to say it was a chicken, because I vaguely remember a folk illustration along with a story. But as I said, it's been years since I've read some of my books, and when trying to read hundreds a year . . . well, the brain can only keep so much." Fayette had to nod to that. "In any case, after we spoke yesterday, I sent for my Russian books. I'm including that in my fee." He motioned to Rex.

"Thank you for that." Rex grimaced. "I feel like a fool for not stopping at a bookshop myself when I was in San Francisco earlier today."

"You were focused on other things," she said, making a purposeful understatement before Silas.

"Right now, I'd like to try connecting with the house's energies to see what I can gauge," said Silas, grinning. "This is exciting!"

"Exciting, perhaps, but is that kind of connection wise?" asked Fayette, well aware of the house's continued tremors. They really needed to get this over and done. "This house is . . . a potent power, and you theorized it might even be drawing energy from this area."

"That's why I'll start with rudimentary cantrips. I want to see if the magic has a particular . . . feel to it."

"Wait," Fayette said. "What do you sense right now, other than the headache?"

"I also have some weakness and vertigo, though I don't feel anywhere near losing consciousness."

"I mean, what do you feel from the house itself?"

"My pain is worse depending on where I am in the room."

He didn't sense the tremors. Did that mean something, or was it simply evidence of their individual approaches to magic?

Silas positioned himself before the oven fire. Half closing his eyes, he raised his arms like a conductor. His mouth moved without a sound as his hands traced symbols in the air.

The house *spasmed*. Fayette was knocked to the ground, catching herself in a crouch, one hand on the floor for balance. The ground felt strangely warm, considering her distance from the oven.

"Fayette?" Rex stared at her. He'd crouched to balance on the floor—he'd finally felt movement, too.

"Silas has to stop," she gasped. "The house doesn't like whatever he's doing." The thickness worsened, bringing with it palpable warmth. A sickening humidity.

Silas, eyes closed and mouth working, remained oblivious.

Rex grabbed Silas around the chest, and just in time, as an arm of flame roared from the oven and swiped at the medium. Fayette thought it'd missed by an inch—and then she saw smoke rising from his suit coat.

"Out, out, out!" she yelled.

"Wait, what?" Silas blinked and looked around as if he were awakening from slumber. He was utterly limp as Rex hauled him toward the door. "What happened?"

"You're on fire!" she snapped, catching up with them as they reached the interior door, which flew open with such force that it banged against the wall. Rex hesitated a second, letting her get in a few fast swats to snuff out a just-visible flame near a large button. "Fire's out! Now, haul him outside!"

As they entered the foyer, the door to outside was already gaping wide. The hint was not subtle. "He needs off the cliff completely," Fayette said. "And I don't mean a dunk in the sea."

"I can walk—" Silas began to say in a panic, squirming.

"I plan to get him to the street." Rex showed no indication that he was releasing Silas.

Fayette stopped in the doorway, pressing both hands to the wooden frame. "I'm sorry. Why our presence—why *his* presence—bothered you today, I have no idea. I should have made him leave as soon as we entered and I felt things were different, but I . . ." She sighed. "I selfishly wanted to see what happened. I hoped he might enlighten us. I suppose he did, really, but not the way we expected or wanted. I'm sorry. I want to keep saying that. Forgive us, please."

She felt the house's tension release like a sigh—an actual sigh, the breeze rustling her hair as if the house were expelling air. She glanced down the slope. As dark as it was, she could just make out that Rex had Silas off the lot. Fayette released a relieved exhalation of her own.

Fayette blinked. "Wait. Huh. House, did you smell Silas's stinky magic, too? If not, I reckon you detected him in some other way. Like how a dog can hear things most people can't. I really wish we had some way to communicate. I don't suppose you know any interpreters, do you?" Her laugh was shaky. "I'm going to join them now. I hope that when I come back here—and when Rex comes back—we're able to go inside again. I hope we can . . . still be friends, of a sort."

Friends, with a house that just tried to grab a man and burn him alive. She reckoned the cottage had a good reason, though. The idea of losing access to this place rattled her. She wasn't simply bothered by the idea that she'd never understand the mysteries the house offered up, or know its story, or that she'd worry about how to sustain Rex's sense of curiosity and hope. Somehow, even though this house had initially had a femur fence and teeth for locks, it'd become homey. What that said about her, she wasn't sure, but she was a writer and accepted that her mind worked in dark and mysterious ways.

Something thudded within the house, rhythmic, heavy. She glanced into the foyer and gasped. Silas's satchel came her way, heaved by the floorboards lifting up in sequence to propel it along. As the satchel reached the door outside, the board beneath it dipped down—like a baseball batter winding up for a ball—and then sprang up.

The satchel catapulted in a great arc to come down somewhere beyond the silhouetted trees that lined the road.

"House, you should play for the St. Louis Browns." She gave the doorframe an affectionate pat, then pulled her flashlight from her pocket to make her way down the slope. Halfway down, she chanced upon a shoe wedged in a crevasse. By the brown color, she knew it to be Silas's.

Rex and Silas were arguing at the side of the road.

"You had no business dragging me from there! I had only just begun the ritual!"

"You also nearly died," Rex snapped.

"No. Everything was fine. I was initiating contact—"

"The house didn't want to be touched," Fayette interrupted. "It didn't want you there at all. I recognized that from the start, and I should've heeded my intuition."

Silas scoffed. "I felt nothing of the sort. And I'm a medium and magician! A professional!"

"Says the man who conducts arcane arts with his eyes closed, oblivious to his near immolation," retorted Fayette.

Rex let his contempt show. "The vast majority of your act at the Fitz household was just that: an act. You're ninety-nine percent fraud. I work in movies. So does Fayette. We know the kinds of tricks you pulled."

Silas bristled. "I've been quite open with you that I'm . . . limited by my inability to predict when I might encounter magic. My work, nevertheless, is therapeutic in nature."

"I've seen your fee. You're not running a charity operation." Rex reached into his suit pocket and thrust a wad of bills into Silas's hands. "On that note, here's the remainder of what you're owed, because I'm a man of honor even to a scoundrel. Your real payday, though, is that you're still alive."

Silas shook his head. "My work isn't done. I *can* find out what the house is, I know I can. Once I discover that, why—I can figure out so much more! This place is like a node, a shrine, a place where magic bubbles up like a volcano. Do you realize what can be done with that kind of power?" Fayette braced herself for an argument about social and political clout, but he continued, "It can be used to help people! Why, there's Mr. Fitz—"

"That photograph you took of his hovering soul is as done up as Lon Chaney as the Hunchback of Notre Dame," Fayette snapped.

"Be that as it may"—Silas gave a flippant wave—"the man isn't whole, that's clear to anyone. Whether his soul is in the Summerland or heaven or France, that house offers a place where he might be healed."

"Or you get yourself fried, and perhaps him as well." Rex shook his head. "Our work with you is done, Silas. We aren't going to stand back and watch you kill yourself as you meddle with things you don't understand."

"Ignorance is a temporary condition." Silas whirled around to leave, his legs tottering.

"Silas," Fayette called. He turned. She tossed him his shoe, which he caught against the scorch mark on his brown coat. "The house ejected your satchel. I think it landed somewhere that way." She waved farther up the road.

"Oh," he said, wide eyed, then staggered onward without bothering to don his shoe. He faded into the darkness.

"I wondered what I'd heard hit the ground up that way," said Rex, pulling out his flashlight and switching it on. "I'm worried we haven't seen the last of him, though."

"He's a hound for money. He won't get more from you."

"This is about more than money for him. Silas is curious. People joke about the curiosity of cats, but human beings are the worst." They had just started up the slope when Rex paused to grab something near his foot.

As he stood, he illuminated the forearm-long feather in his hand.

"That's a chicken feather. A massive chicken feather." Fayette stared. It was black with white freckles, the quill almost the width of one of her fingers.

"Have you ever had chickens?" Rex asked, rotating the feather in his fingertips. She shook her head. "Stress can cause them to molt out of season."

"What would be *in season* for a house that is part chicken?" She looked up at the house, watching as his flashlight traced its contours. "Nothing about it looks chicken-like. No—wait." Black tufts had emerged from the boards that acted as long shingles along the steep roof. "The feathers are . . . layered there?"

Rex's laugh was a bit higher in pitch than usual. "Well, a layer of gigantic feathers could insulate like tar paper, I suppose."

"It's impossible to know how many feathers came loose. They'll blend in with the night and the rocks. We should take a look tomorrow and gather what we can so they don't blow where people might find them."

"*If* they can," Rex added, beginning the climb again. "People might not be able to see the feathers, but it's a sensible precaution. We may want to check the nearby beaches, too. I can look downtown in the morning."

"I'll do the same at the beach southward."

The door opened to greet them as it had prior to Silas's arrival. Fayette again stroked the doorway in apology, and she was heartened when Rex strolled up to the oven to voice his own words of remorse. The energy in the house was calm, as was Mother's presence.

"I think our plot to use mediums here is over," Fayette said. "And here I thought finding a legitimate one would be the biggest issue. I'm not sure what we can do now."

Rex's brow was drawn together in contemplation as he stared at the fire. After a moment, he twisted around to face her. "I can ask my friend Art to come."

"The friend you've repeatedly mentioned and always muttered that you're not supposed to talk to him, but you won't say why?"

Rex looked chagrined. "Yes. He knows about this kind of house. He'd know old Russian stories. He's trustworthy, too. I can call his apartment building this evening, see if I can get hold of him."

"If you're comfortable with that." Fayette tried to word that delicately. She wished he'd just say what was going on and stop hedging around the issue.

Rex hollowly laughed. "I'm not going to be comfortable with it, no, but . . ." He absently tapped his chest, right over his heart. With a start, she realized the letter he'd received from Art yesterday must still be tucked inside his coat.

Oh. *Oh.*

His friend Art might well be more than a friend, and if that was the case, Rex's suicide attempt and the studio pressure upon him suddenly made a lot more sense, if anything in this cruel world could make sense.

"I hope you can talk to him," she said, offering a smile that she could only pray brought some comfort.

"So do I." The tentative smile he returned wasn't entirely that of rising star Rex Hallstrom, but was also Helmer Hallstrom, a man in love with another man in a world that had no tolerance for such affections. Fayette had a small understanding of the kind of grief that went along with hiding those kinds of feelings from the greater world. She'd learned something about that experience from one of the men she'd loved best: her brother, Thayer.

Chapter 30

An interpreter, to help me to speak with the woman? That is an idea, a curious one. I *do* need a way to tell the woman and man about the other witch who is on the way here, and the cliff that's now even more fragile after my trembling, and that I need my new witch right away!

I imprinted on my old witch the moment I hatched, and therefore we always understood each other. I had no need to communicate with other humans beyond moving my body or withholding my services, as my witch bade.

For a mere moment, I experienced the same connection with my new witch as well, but not since. Our connection is too new, too tenuous. She needs to enter my walls.

She will enter my walls again soon, won't she? Proving myself to be a good home *must* help! I know she's not at all like my first witch, who had particular appetites. I don't believe the world makes women-who-become-witches quite like her these days.

I cannot speak aloud in any language. You understand that, Mother, as you are much the same in that regard.

Many people of Rus would rightly be too scared to approach my door, even though they'd know the words to open the way. If someone with knowledge recognized me and warned the woman and man—they could very well do the prudent thing and never return.

I was quite proud of the fear I once generated—proud because my witch told me I should be. She made me to be as I am.

Or, a person of Rus could use the words to invade my sanctum and violate me. I still feel the stain of Stinky upon my floors, his breath in my wood; I must continue to purify myself for hours yet. I don't want someone else to intrude here, someone whose quest is perverse and selfish. Oddly enough, for all his offensiveness, Stinky was not of that ilk . . . but I still don't want him to return.

What I do need is my new witch, right away, because the other witch is days away. She, at least, will kill me before desecrating my body.

But I don't want to die, I really don't. I don't want to suffer, either.

Therefore, I need the woman and man to know a little about me but not too much. We need an interpreter, an intermediary, who is ignorant but innovative, who will not be too scared.

I know, I know, my requirements for an interpreter will make it even more challenging for me to find the right someone who sees my door at just the right moment and is then imbued with the braveness to step through. I will try to time things, however, as I have before. Someone will be more willing to help us if they can dine on your fresh bread, Mother!

The words of the woman and man are lingering with me, too. They said names that may prove useful. They *evoked* people. There is power in names.

I will be vigilant, even as I am very scared.

Chapter 31

Fayette awoke thinking about Thayer.

Her brother had been one of the gentlest, kindest souls she'd ever known. He'd been a scrappy stick of a kid who'd grown into a burly bear of a man with a big beard and a bigger laugh. He was one of the most active young men in the family church, there if anyone in the congregation needed to have some new furniture carried upstairs, or to be a pallbearer, or to dare scale the roof to fix tiles. She knew he carried his kindness into his work in the oil fields, too, quietly bringing an extra lunch for someone who needed it but had too much pride to ask, or working extra shifts to cover for someone with a sick child.

She'd opened the back door one day to take trash out and spied Thayer in the shadows, kissing another fellow from work: Luis. One of their neighbors. She ducked back inside before the men saw her.

No denying that she was shocked—she'd never considered that either Thayer or Luis were "temperamental," as people around town liked to discreetly describe men who liked men. Thayer had had a few girlfriends over the years but never put his heart into the relationships. In hindsight, she recognized that he went on dates with women because he was expected to do so, and he was such a nice guy, he wouldn't want to hurt a woman's feelings with a no. Fayette had known a number of temperamental fellows at work, of course. Many people in film had come there through big-city theater companies where there was tolerance, if not acceptance, of people who defied traditional norms.

While the morality brigade of middle America liked to paint all of Hollywood as a new Babylon of constant excess, opulence, and orgies, the reality was that most people tended to keep their heads down and their inclinations quiet. They needed to. Even ten years ago, before Prohibition, Hays, and the crusades against so-called "lewd" movies, there were plenty of people around who would violently combat what they personally considered to be "sin."

She'd heard chilling stories about what happened to people whose proclivities were revealed, too. The attacks. The torment. The deaths. People who were different weren't safe. Lord knew, she'd put up with plenty of verbal abuse in her life—and survived a few terrifying incidents that'd almost turned physical—because of her own disinterest in men.

Other people had it a lot worse. The thought of someone attacking Thayer—of a lynch mob going after him—scared her more than any book or movie ever had.

By the time that Fayette became privy to Thayer's secret, their sister, Briar, was already dead. Fayette had to wonder if she had already known about Thayer. Briar had been the sort of person who kept confidences locked up like a bank vault. Not like Fayette was the sort to blab, really, but she might get excited and reveal a Christmas gift weeks early or let something slip in a moment of anger. Not so with Briar, whose quiet and tact were attributes Fayette had wistfully envied.

Months later, Thayer pulled Fayette aside, saying they needed to talk in private. He wept with relief when she said she'd known for ages.

It went without saying that they'd never tell Ma. She would've fretted for his soul to the point of making herself physically ill, as if the sheer force of her self-torture would save her child from the fires of damnation.

To Fayette's mind, if the Almighty regarded the full measure of someone's soul and sprinkled in some grace, then Thayer was just fine.

Like Thayer, Rex had to hide his truth. He was advertised as the All-American Man; he couldn't favor *men*. Nor could he go back home to his Minnesota farm and be himself. Rex had to play his role without ceasing and face being miserable one way or another, no matter where he was.

Or he could die. If the studio knew his secret, they could kill his career, and him, with a few words. It didn't take much to get an adoring crowd to turn as feral as hungry wolves.

No wonder his despair had propelled him to the brink of a cliff the night he was supposed to marry Margaret.

Her mood contemplative, Fayette returned to her typewriter. Her fingers knew what to do.

In a couple of hours, she finished her continuity.

To think, she'd been worried if three weeks in Carmel would be enough time to get it done. She'd completed it in five days.

If she hadn't gotten that letter from April, Fayette would've been game to delve into the other Astrophel work she'd ambitiously hoped to make progress on while here, but now that she was getting the sack, there was no point.

She could, however, work on something that established her new independence. The more she considered that option, the more she liked it.

After a moment to shake out her body, she resumed typing with defiant zeal, this time pounding out a sheet of notes for a story outline based on what she'd hoped would be another movie about Dot. She hadn't shared this concept with her bosses yet. Fayette would change names and circumstances, make it something that was her own that would stay her own.

In a way, moving forward with this new idea felt even more satisfying than finishing her continuity. She was going to do this for herself, her own survival, and when it was published—please, God, let it be published—it'd bear her byline.

Those notes done, she declared herself finished for the day. She had other tasks to attend to.

Beneath a gray blanket of clouds, she walked to the road's dead end at a sandy slope where the river met the almighty sea. No other human beings marred the beach at midmorning. Slipping off her shoes, she walked in ankle-deep white sand toward the water. Recent storms had deposited driftwood and logs, but she didn't see any unusually large feathers.

She kept walking around, struck by the idea that it'd been years since she had visited a beach—she was pretty sure she'd gone with Briar the last time! Briar died in 1918. It was 1926! Something seemed wrong about that. Los Angeles had many nice beaches not far away from her house, but they were also often crowded and Fayette was constantly busy, plus she had a dozen other excuses that varied by the day.

Nearby waves hushed and shushed, the gulls screeched, and the seals engaged in what had to be either romantic squabbles or political debates, but the plush sand underfoot and the green and gray views made her teary eyed at the sheer perfect-imperfection of the moment. She'd finished her continuity. She'd started work on a story. She'd made a new and dear friend. She was losing her job. Ma was dead and buried. She wanted to go home, but wondered if it was truly home anymore.

But Carmel was beautiful. Magical, even if not considering the incredible hut on the cliff. She was glad she'd come.

Fayette used an abandoned towel to wipe off her feet before donning her shoes again for a walk to the cliff house.

She entered with a sense of trepidation, hoping the house hadn't changed its mind about her in the wake of the séance. The welcome was as pleasant as ever.

Fayette made dough using Mother and debated on what to do next. Walking around downtown didn't appeal. She had no money to spend. She was considering a return to Grangeville Cottage when the door opened to admit Rex.

She couldn't help but grin. Every time she saw him, she experienced a swell of relief. He was still alive. He was well. He was here. She could never take those things for granted—not for him, not for anyone she cared about.

"I had a funny feeling you'd be here," he said by way of greeting.

"Did you try my rental?"

"Nah. I remembered what you said about Mrs. Fitz's rules for visitors. I don't imagine that, having met me, she would soften her views, though I should get those architecture books from you soon. How long have you been here?"

Rex seemed to be gazing everywhere but her face. Her thoughts went back to Thayer. He'd acted similarly as he worked up the nerve to tell her his secret. Was Rex about to do the same?

"Not too long. I started bread."

"Good, good." He peered into the pot in its warming nook. "I'm no baker, but that looks like a good rise already. Is this the first or second proof?"

"The first, but I may be able to shape it now—why, yes I can." She began to do that.

"While that's rising, can I take you out to lunch in town? I'd like to discuss something important with you."

"We can't speak here?" If he was going to say what she thought he was going to say, they couldn't risk someone overhearing.

"No. Not today. I'm hungry. I want to chat. Let's go out."

Curious. "I suppose," she said, wondering with dread what he was up to.

Chapter 32

On the walk into town, Rex giddily related that he'd talked to Art the previous night.

"I didn't even ask Art to come here," Rex said. "But when I told him I'd come across a Russian artifact that I couldn't make heads or tails of, he volunteered right away to visit and investigate, saying he'd missed our talks."

"When might he arrive?"

"He wasn't sure. He had to make certain his work was squared away first. I'm not sure if I've mentioned to you that he's a tailor. That fine suit I wore yesterday is his work, and he made or oversaw everything we wore in *Dance After Midnight*."

Fayette's jaw dropped. "Truly? The gorgeous clothes in every scene almost stole the show."

"They were all his," Rex said with pride.

"Well, I hope to meet such an artisan."

"He said he'd call the market's line when he knows more about his arrival time. I really hope his effort to come here isn't a wasted one. What if the house reacts to him like it did for Silas? What if Art can't help us with the house at all?"

Fayette resisted rolling her eyes. Whether or not Art could help them learn more about the house, this visit would be worthwhile for both men. Rex just couldn't admit why, not to her. Maybe not to himself.

She wouldn't be surprised if the letter Art had mailed was still secreted inside Rex's coat.

"So long as Art doesn't pull any stunts like Silas, he'll be fine. And if he can't give us insights to the house? Well, I'll make him some delicious bread, we'll show him the town, and a good time will still be had by all. Right?"

"Right," Rex said, but he still sounded nervous, like he'd volunteered to go wing-walking on a biplane.

Fayette would've been fine with eating a hot dog from a cart, so she balked when he guided her to the Court of the Golden Bough, a collection of artistic shops and food purveyors. The buildings were a curious blend of quaint Olde Britain and Mediterranean stucco. Like much of the architecture around here, it ended up being both historically confusing and beautiful.

"Are you sure about this place? It has to be expensive," she said, standing before a restaurant.

"Yes, I'm sure, but it's not that high-priced, really. Come on, Fayette."

The hostess recognized Rex, and with fawning glances at him, she guided them into a small private room with a central table for two. An arch-shaped window offered a view of green trees and light-gray skies.

"You booked an entire room?" Fayette asked as soon as the woman departed. The room didn't have a door, only an arched entry, but their seats were ten feet inside. As long as they kept their voices low and had an eye out for approaching staff, they'd have privacy. "This seems excessive."

"I think it's perfect." He pulled out a chair for her, something he had never done before. She didn't hide a perplexed look as she took the seat and scooted it in. "I asked another of my neighbors, a retired academic, for recommendations for the finest lunch in town. This was the only one that could offer a room like this."

A silver-haired woman entered and introduced herself as the owner. She recommended fried abalone as the first course, which sounded good to them both. Fayette had a good appetite today—still nowhere near normal, of course, but better. She reckoned a struggle like hers wasn't the kind of thing that'd go away after a major revelation and a few pleasant days. Returning home to that empty, lonely house seemed likely to exacerbate everything, too. Nothing about reality was ever as tidy as it was in the movies.

Rex and Fayette stayed quiet as they studied the menu as if for a test, not saying a word until the owner returned with their requested tea. After they'd placed their entrée orders, Rex leaned back in his chair, fingers pressed together as if in prayer.

"You're probably wondering what this is all about."

"You'd better believe I'm wondering. I hope that you don't have plans to drag this out like *Dr. Mabuse the Gambler*." She'd never seen the over-four-hour-long movie, and didn't plan to.

"I won't." His smile was shy and tense. "The past day got me thinking."

"A dangerous thing, thinking." Fayette sipped her tea, the steam thawing her cold nose.

"Very." Rex paused. "I'd be honored if you'd marry me, Fayette."

To her credit, she didn't choke, but it was a near thing. She swallowed and set down her cup. "I beg your pardon?"

"I'd be honored if you'd marry me." He leaned forward. "I think the arrangement would suit us both. We've become fast friends, after all, and that's what I'd like us to stay. Friends. I know you have no inclinations toward romance or marriage, and along those lines, I'm not asking for any of the usual . . . societal expectations. No consummation. No need for physical affection—"

"Rex, you don't want to do this."

He shook his head, stubborn. "In an ideal world? No. But this world is far from ideal, and we get along swell. We can make the relationship work."

Another little smile. She imagined he was terrified she was about to up and walk out, but she wouldn't do that to him. She respected Rex. Even more, she loved him. That made things all the messier.

"Does Art know about this proposal?" she asked quietly.

His little smile struggled to stay on his face, like an ambitious kitten clinging to a window screen that was starting to bow outward. "What? Why would I consult Art about this?"

"We both know why," she murmured. "You're the best actor I know, most of the time, but when it comes to Art, your feelings are about as subtle as a ball-peen hammer on stained glass."

His already pale face drained of color. "But I tried to— I didn't ever say . . . How—"

"My brother, Thayer, tried to hide how he felt about men, too. In hindsight, there were a lot of clues over the years that whizzed over my head like a baseball. Eventually, the truth had to smack me in the face."

"And you . . . How did you—"

"I loved my brother. I still do. What I learned didn't change how I felt about him. He was the same person he'd always been. I hated that he had to keep part of himself secret so he didn't lose his job, his place in church. His very life." She paused to add gravity to that statement. By the grimness on Rex's face, he well understood that risk already. "The lie of omission ate away at him, I know it did, especially when Ma would try to set him up with young ladies in the neighborhood. She didn't constantly nag him on the subject as some mothers do, mind you, but Thayer always had the pressure on him to carry on the family name and give her grandchildren." She sighed. "He was wonderful with kids, too. He would've been a great father if he'd had the chance to adopt."

Rex parted his lips to speak, but a new young woman entered, carrying a platter of golden-crisped fried abalone. "Abalone for you both," she said, but her eyes were only on Rex. She almost tripped over herself as she bowed while she backed away.

Rex ate two morsels before he spoke again, in a whisper. "I'm enduring the same pressure, even though my siblings have already supplied my parents with five grandchildren. They believe everyone needs marriage to be complete and happy. I don't deny I want marriage and that kind of stable, supportive relationship, and yet . . ." He sighed. "Children never factor into my fantasies, but I like them well enough."

Fayette ate her first piece of abalone. It was good, chewy. Not that different from fried clam, but sweeter. "I struggled to get along with children back when I was a child. I never even played with dolls. I preferred books and toy animals."

They stayed quiet as they picked at the rest of the abalone. That gave Fayette time to think.

"Margaret knows your secret, doesn't she?"

"She does. We had to reveal our . . . sins to each other when we were matched."

Sins. As if the people who judged them weren't heading off to meet their mistresses and bookies later that night. Fools and hypocrites.

"You're not alone in town, you know," Fayette said quietly.

"Oh, I know, but I feel like some of the other men are . . . not much like me in major ways. The only bordellos I've stepped into have been on Western sets, and I like my parties to end by ten o'clock, and the clothes stay on. I don't even like stripping down to a swimming suit!"

"You're my kind of boring," Fayette said, which earned her a tiny smile.

She had heard a rumor that brand-new full-fledged star Billy Haines and established heartthrob Ramón Novarro had been caught at a male bordello and that MGM had paid police and press to keeps things quiet. The two men had continued to concern their bosses, as she understood it—Haines now openly lived with another man and still had quite the wild night life, while Novarro was regarded as outrageously effeminate on-screen and off.

Rex's choirboy innocence and do-good sincerity were probably to his disadvantage. The expectations upon him were all the higher—and his bosses knew he was easy to manipulate.

They'd almost manipulated him right off an ocean cliff.

"You haven't had many relationships, have you?" she asked gently.

She wasn't surprised when he blushed, his gaze lowering. "No. I suppose I'm old-fashioned, in my own way. I have no interest in chasing a good time every night. I've wanted something that will last—that can be a good time for decades." The yearning in his voice about broke her heart. He raised his head. "I need to ask something personal, if that's all right."

"Only seems fair." Fayette shrugged.

"Have you . . . ever exchanged violets?"

"Really, Rex? You booked the private room for a reason. So long as we don't shout, we don't need euphemisms. You want to know if I favor women over men?" The modern use of violets among lesbians took inspiration from the poet Sappho. Rex blushed again; he actually seemed embarrassed by her bluntness. Good. No need to be coy. "The answer is no. I've never had romantic or physical inclinations of any sort. I did have a gal offer me violets once, but fortunately I'd already read about the symbolism. We kept in touch after I left the stenography pool to work at Astrophel, too." At least, until Ma's health had failed. Fayette's connections with most everyone had frayed since then. Thayer's companion, Luis, had remained one of her family's most stalwart supports, though, and her gratitude to him knew no limit. He was even watering the rosebushes while she was away.

"I'm glad you were able to stay friends," he said quietly.

"The two of us are still going to be friends, too," she said, picking up on his subtext. "Your proposed lavender marriage isn't changing that. *Lavender.*" She shook her head. "So many purple flowers. So many euphemisms. There are times for delicate speech and times when you say things as they are. Sometimes you need to slice a tomato, and sometimes you need to throw one."

"Fayette, when it comes to words, you're a regular Babe Ruth," Rex said. She had to laugh.

The rattle of dishes warned them of approaching servers. The empty platter was removed, their entrées set before them. The elder server said refills of tea would come next, providing them an excuse to start on their lunches without promptly resuming their discussion. Fayette slowly chewed on her cheese-and-mushroom omelet. As soon as their drinks arrived and the server departed, she spoke up.

"I now understand why you went out on the cliff," she said quietly. He regarded her as he ate his ham omelet. "You're in an even more difficult place than my brother was, and that's a horrible thing."

"I'm almost afraid to ask, but what happened to Thayer?" Rex asked.

"He didn't kill himself." She didn't want to mess with polite euphemisms—not now. "He was walking to the omnibus stop when a heavy truck took a turn too sharply. Its load dumped atop him."

"What about your sister?"

It felt right to reveal these details to Rex now. "Briar died while giving birth in 1918. I was with her, holding her hand at the time. The baby was stillborn. Her husband was away in the war. He came back. He's married again now—has three children, last I heard. He's a good man, kind. I'm glad he found happiness again, because for a while after he returned, we were all worried about him. No one needs to come home to find their family is gone. No one."

"Your mother?"

"Cancer. A slow death over months and weeks and the longest minutes a person can know."

Rex regarded her, his empty fork bobbing in his grip. "I now understand what drove you to risk your life to grab a stranger from a cliff's edge."

At a loss of what else to say, she resumed eating, and after a moment, he did the same.

Only after their forks were down did she speak again.

"I'm saying no to your proposal, though I see the benefits a union would offer the both of us. I'd appear to fill my womanly life achievement of being a wife." She couldn't contain the contemptuous curl of her lip. "You'd look safer to your studio and get some positive press. Marrying a commoner such as myself would get you quite a bit of attention."

He scoffed. "A commoner."

"You know I'm telling the truth. When you're a movie star in America, you become royalty. If this restaurant puts out that 'Rex Hallstrom ate the fried abalone and the ham omelet here,' you'd better believe they'd have people lining up out the door to eat what you ate, to sit where you sat. You're increasing the value of that chair with your buttocks even as we speak."

His eyes widened in surprise at the anatomical reference, and then he laughed. "People are strange."

"They are. And here I am, a working woman of fair to middling appearance, living paycheck to paycheck. Marrying you would be the fantasy of a lot of gals. Not only would they get to hang off your rather sculptured arm, but they'd get the easy life."

"Yet you're saying no," he said levelly.

"I am, because I hate that society is forcing us into something neither of us wants just so that we can survive. That rings of wrongness like a belfry full of bells. There's the financial aspect, too. I want to earn the easy life by working for it myself. I have no desire to be hired on as a wife and take over domestic duties in some big house. I don't want parties and *mingling*." She shuddered. "I cheer for flapper independence, but I'm not up for all-night dances and hoopla. I want to read a book or do crossword puzzles while I try to listen in on my neighbor's radio, and then hit bed by ten o'clock."

"I don't do late nights, either, not unless I'm on set. At parties, I'm first to arrive, first to leave. I'm renting an apartment these days. My paychecks are piling up at the bank. I've thought about buying a place in the next while. The area's building up. I would never want someplace palatial, though. I'll feel indulgent if I have a library with wheeled ladders." A wistful smile teased at his lips. "As for chores, I've always done my own dishes and laundry, and I can cook a mean minute steak. Beyond that, someone could be hired to clean."

"Someone hired to clean," she paraphrased slowly, as if trying to speak in a foreign language. "I find that concept hard to parse. One of my first jobs was cleaning houses."

"Here's pineapple upside-down cake for you both! Our treat," announced a young male server, coming in with a bright smile. Come to think of it, every dish had been brought out by someone new. The staff must have drawn lots to decide who would serve the famous actor.

"Pineapple upside-down cake was one of Briar's favorites," Fayette said softly as the server left. "But she hated the cherries. She always gave them to me." She pried the cherry from the caramelized crust and plunked it in her mouth.

"I didn't have pineapple upside-down cake until I came out to California," Rex said. "It then became one of my favorites. I feel like it's starting to show up everywhere now."

"Ma started making it for Christmas about a decade ago. Someone gave her the recipe. It immediately became the family favorite. More important than ham or turkey or anything else." Fayette considered the morsel on her fork. "It's December. I reckon this can count as my holiday pineapple upside-down cake."

She popped the piece in her mouth and closed her eyes to savor it. As far as she was concerned, the Christmas season was done after this meal, and it was only the third of the month. The trees and ribbons and music could go away now.

As they exited, Rex assumed his full Rex Hallstrom persona as the staff gathered to see him off with aplomb, as if he were making a grand bon voyage to France. A few of the staff shyly asked him to sign slips of paper. His tip must have been generous, too, as the owner was all smiles and tears as she thanked them for coming. The diners at the edge of the main hall gawked at the hullabaloo.

Fayette remembered how she'd told Rex to ignore the guilt that his boss had tried to lay on him about Margaret's drug use, but now she felt guilty for not doing more to support him as he moved forward in life—as he tried to survive a hostile world that demanded he be paired with a woman, or he may well be better off dead.

Was there a way for her to provide aid to him without condemning herself to live a lie right along with him?

Or was it her pride that stood in the way? The idea of living the easy life struck her as almost offensive. Maybe she was so accustomed to struggle that it'd become a form of martyrdom.

Could a middle path be found? Did one exist at all?

Chapter 33

The loaf had risen beautifully and was ready for the oven. As it baked, Fayette and Rex set more food on the table. They'd stopped by a grocer after their luncheon.

"So far, everyone who has been welcomed in this house has been a girl or woman, and I include myself in that, as a person who came through the front door," Fayette said. "Of course, we haven't had a large sample of the population, so that could change, but my gut instinct says it won't. Women seem to be subject to extra suffering in this world, often as property of the father or husband."

Rex nodded with a pensive expression.

"I wish I'd thought of this earlier, but now I'm wondering if we should get clothing in various sizes along with other things a woman in desperate straits may need." Period belts and rags came to mind.

"That's a great idea," he said, speaking louder as she crossed the room.

Fayette pulled out the baked bread and gave it a tap, tap, tap. Yes, it sounded hollow. The bread was done. Fayette leaned in to check on Mother. The bubbly starter had risen to half fill the former peanut butter jar. "Mother looks to be growing quickly again, but I don't know if we should try baking tomorrow. She may be magical, but no one should be pushed—"

A door appeared on the far wall, the bright light through the house's windows revealing it to be unlike the previous ones.

"It's a car door!" Rex declared just as it opened.

A stout figure in a skirt set came through, bent to fit through the door. Mud spattered her stockings up both calves. The newcomer gasped as she straightened. Stray strands of reddish-dun hair lashed her pale cheeks as she looked all around. "Where am I?" A cultured British accent came through clearly in those three words.

"This may be hard to believe, but California," Fayette said, standing. "Please don't go, not yet. Your door will be able to return later."

"Later?" She shook her head, bewildered, then pressed a hand to her forehead. "Oh. I fear the crash gave me a solid knock."

"I can help you sit down, if that's okay." Fayette would make no further effort to approach unless she had permission. Their last guests had taught her that.

"Yes, I would appreciate the aid, thank you. It smells like bread in here. Have I arrived at a magical bakery?"

"A bakery that specializes in only one product for now," Fayette said, hurrying over.

The newcomer grimaced as Fayette wrapped an arm around her waist. "Sorry. I'm a bit battered."

"No need to apologize." They were of similar thick builds, but Fayette towered over the woman by a good four inches. She had no problem helping her along. "Rex, can you pour water and pull the bench out?"

"Of course!" He set about those tasks.

Fayette had to wonder if the house was responding to the woman's need at the exact moment that the door appeared. The bread was still too warm to be sliced.

"Here you go, ma'am," Rex said, offering a hand to help her sit. The stranger hesitated for a second and then accepted his support. She set her small green velour hat and her purse on the bench beside her. Rex stood to one side, hands up to catch her if she tilted too far. "If you feel wobbly, try to let us know. I wish we had a chair with a back to give you more—"

A blink later, the bench on the other side of the table became two wooden chairs with high backs and armrests. They all gasped.

"Oh my. Did that really happen?" asked the woman.

"Yes," said Fayette. "Are you up to moving to that side or we can—"

"If you help me, I can walk over there," said the woman. Fayette guided her with a hand on her shoulder. As soon as she sat, she screeched, "The door! It's gone!"

"Like I said, don't worry. It'll come back." Fayette took the chair next to her. "We've had guests like you come here before. What's your name?"

"My name?" Her blue eyes blinked rapidly. "My name . . . I have a name. Me . . . her . . . Archie . . . I can't even think." She rubbed her head again, eyes squinted in pain. "Mrs. Neele?"

Fayette looked at Rex in concern. They might need to get this woman to a doctor. By his little nod and tight expression, he shared her concern. "Well, Mrs. Neele, I'm Fayette, and this here is Rex. Have some water, nice and slow. You seem to be concussed."

"Concussed. Yes. That diagnosis sounds right." Mrs. Neele's hands shook as she raised the mug, but she drank on her own.

"Where are you from?" Rex asked. The British accent could mean she was from anywhere in the world these days, Hollywood included.

"England. Devon. At least, that's where I was born. Yes." She sounded more certain by the end. "What *is* this place?"

Fayette tried to describe the house and its ways in the simplest of terms. Mrs. Neele accepted the tale with a furrowed brow, then pushed herself to stand, causing Fayette and Rex to rise as well. "If I'm in California, at the ocean, I should like to see it. I traveled the Pacific a few years ago, but we docked in British Columbia. I never thought I'd see California!" She said the name with an awe that reminded Fayette of their first arrival through a door.

"We're not near Hollywood, just so you know," Fayette said, anticipating that question next. "This is the Central coast, where it's colder and more rugged. If you've seen photographs of Big Sur and 17-Mile Drive, we're right between those places." The doors ahead opened on their own. Fayette encouraged Mrs. Neele forward with a wave.

A person could argue that Carmel maintained a high level of beauty, but that particular late afternoon was the sort that makes poets strain to find adequate words and photographers growl at the futility of their art. The sun posed at a perfect angle to send clean, bright light down over creation as it rested upon thin strands of cloud. The surrounding sky was colored pink, orange, and about a dozen shades of blue and purple. A rainbow without a prism.

"It's still daylight here!" Mrs. Neele said, shaking her head. "That makes sense, however, if my crossing was indeed instantaneous." Her attention turned to the house. "My, what an extraordinary structure, perched at the cliff's edge like a cat upon a shelf. I can believe that it's magical. It looks like something straight out of a storybook. Houses can hold surprises, can't they? They can comfort. They can betray." She took a step closer to the log wall, losing her footing on a crevasse. Fayette helped her to stay upright.

"Come along inside," Fayette said. "Food will do you good."

They sat again at the table. Rex sliced the warm bread and offered to serve, enabling Fayette to stay close to Mrs. Neele, who swayed even as she sat.

"This is wonderful bread," Mrs. Neele said, her eyes blissfully shut after her first bite. "I've hardly eaten today. I couldn't. I wouldn't have been able to keep anything down if I tried."

Fayette related to that all too well. "Do you remember much of your car crash?" Though something had apparently been going on before that, too.

"The car crash. Yes." Mrs. Neele sounded dreamy. "I had driven by the quarry earlier in the day, but Rosalind was with me. I thought about . . . what I could do—but not with her. And then later, after dark, I went back. The moment felt right. He was gone, away, and I was alone, quite alone. I made the effort, but trees caught my car right before the edge. I got out. I fell. Then when I tried to go back inside the car, the door didn't lead to the interior of my automobile, but here."

Fayette and Rex stared at each other across the table. Mrs. Neele had attempted suicide. The house's intervention became clearer.

"Who's Rosalind?" asked Fayette.

"Hmm." Mrs. Neele grimaced, pressing a hand to her head as she ate more bread. Fayette took the hint and stayed quiet. The healing powers of the bread were not always gentle—sometimes, as bones and flesh bound together again, the pain could be worse than the initial injury. Briar had fallen from a tree and broken her arm back when they lived in Coalinga, and when she ate bread later, the audible *snap* of the bone binding anew had been the stuff of nightmares for Fayette. A blessing and a relief, but horrible, too.

As the conversation entered a lull, Fayette nibbled on a thin piece of bread. She still felt fairly full from lunch. The bread crust had a pleasant crunch, softened by an overflow of butter. Luscious yellow lakes dappled the hole-flecked interior. Each bite was sweet, chewy, and the slightest bit tart from the ancient starter.

Fayette had no particular aches and pains today in need of healing, but from lifelong experience, she recognized Mother's gentle touch upon her mind. Mother was helping her to feel *good*. Days ago, Fayette would have fought back against this intrusion—because that's what it was. Hope and positivity could be beautiful or obnoxious, dependent on the moment. She was reminded of early in the previous month, when a chipper neighbor forced her into a hug as she told Fayette that God was good, that she should count her blessings. At the time, Ma was literally rotting away while still alive, and Fayette hadn't touched her manuscript in a week and had scarcely slept, too. But there was her neighbor, bright and smiling, and Fayette had come close to socking her right between the eyes.

Mother could be like that sometimes. Or she could intercede as she did right now—respectful of Fayette's space, her presence reassuring in closeness, within reach if Fayette tottered.

Rex ate his own bread, his expression pensive. She could only imagine he experienced similar thoughts to hers. Hope could be like bread, and difficult to ingest and digest at times.

Mrs. Neele ate the majority of the small loaf on her own but didn't seem fully aware of her own movements. Her eyes were partially closed, her fingers fumbling to add other food to her plate. Twice, Fayette saved the woman's water before it tipped and spilled.

When Mrs. Neele finally sat back with a contented sigh, she seemed somewhat less pained, though Fayette still had to wonder at the damage to her mind, physical and mental.

"If I wrote a story about how I came to be here and the deliciousness of this repast, it would need to be within the realm of fiction." Mrs. Neele stood, gathering her belongings. Fayette followed her up a second later. "I believe I should return home now. I think I can walk on my own, thank you." She primly set off by herself, her stride wobbling. Fayette and Rex followed a step behind.

"I don't know if she's in an appropriate condition to return," Rex whispered to Fayette. "I don't simply say that because she can't walk in a straight line."

"You think she may try to kill herself again," Fayette whispered back. He nodded.

Mrs. Neele stopped before the far wall. "I believe you said that the door would come back." Her imperious tone held a quiver of worry.

"It should. It always has before." But Fayette could see for herself that there was no door of any kind.

Mrs. Neele was stuck here.

Chapter 34

Why hadn't the door returned? Did the house share their concern about Mrs. Neele's well-being? Or did the bread simply need more time to help heal Mrs. Neele throughout?

Leaving Rex by Mrs. Neele, Fayette walked up to the oven.

"Why aren't you returning her door?" Fayette whispered to the house. The oven really felt like the face of the room and the best place to directly address the building. "Is she about to make another attempt at suicide? Or is there something else?" The magic remained consistent and warm.

"I'll get some more water," Rex was saying to Mrs. Neele. The woman was crying, more rattled now than when she first came through. As Rex passed Fayette, he shook his head. "If she truly *is* stuck here, I can get her back home," he murmured. "It's about a ten-day trip. I wouldn't trust her to manage it alone, though." He continued forward.

Fayette returned to Mrs. Neele, taking her hat and purse to set them on the table. "Let's sit again. We'll figure out what's going on."

"Fayette." Rex's voice hit an unusually high note. He was at the door to the foyer, his hand on the knob. He pulled on it. Metal jingled. The door didn't open.

The house wasn't letting them out.

"Is he stuck inside? *Are we stuck inside?*" asked Mrs. Neele.

In an even larger act of confirmation, the shutters closed all at once with a loud wooden clank. Greater darkness descended on the room, even as the candles seemed to loom brighter.

"For the time being, it seems so." Fayette kept her voice level, the way she'd talk to a growling dog or a drunken man. "This is a mystery we need to solve together, that's all."

"A mystery." That word seemed to calm Mrs. Neele, her chin lifting. "A mystery with people locked within a magical house. Yes. I can solve mysteries."

If that approach helped Mrs. Neele to stay composed, Fayette would use it to the utmost. "I've been working on a mystery of my own," she said. "I write scripts for a small studio that makes movies you've never heard of. I just finished a project featuring a woman who was a nurse during the war, and she must solve her great-aunt's murder. The police don't think it's murder, though—"

"Of course," Mrs. Neele murmured, a glint in her eye. "She will be disbelieved. She will fight to prove herself to them, to herself, and likely to a man in her life."

Fayette had to laugh. "That's the formula, yes." Mrs. Neele smiled. "Almost everything takes place in a grand old mansion. A far different place from this."

"Your protagonist was a nurse during the war? She uses those skills to solve the mystery?"

"Yes. I was inspired by a wonderful book I read called *The Secret Adversary* that has—" Fayette lurched forward to grip Mrs. Neele as her legs buckled.

"You've read *The Secret Adversary*? Here in California? That's . . . that's mine. *Mine!*" She sounded hysterical.

"What do you mean, it's yours? Do you need to sit?"

"No, no." She pushed herself to stand on her own. "But that name, that book title. It's mine. I know it, but I don't understand. There's madness in me tonight. Madness has always been within my family, but I thought—I prayed—that it would skip over me. Maybe it hasn't. Oh

God. Rosalind. I hope Rosalind doesn't have it." Both hands pressed to her cheeks.

Fayette kept herself placid to try to get Mrs. Neele calm. "Have you read the book? It's about Tommy and Tuppence. The author has other mysteries, too."

"Hercule Poirot." The name rattled.

"Yes! I haven't read the newest book, but I've been told it's incredible, with a shocking twist of an ending. One of my studio producers' wives is British. She gets a box of books sent over a few times a year. She promised to lend it to me once she's done." Fayette paused. She supposed that wouldn't happen now. "I hope I can read it before the next book comes out."

"*The Mystery of the Blue Train*," murmured Mrs. Neele, rubbing her head again. "It's *The Mystery of the Blue Train*. But it's not going well, is it? No. I've been distracted. Terribly distracted. My mother. She died this April and since then . . . everything has gotten worse." She trembled.

"I am so sorry for your loss," Fayette said, tears stinging her eyes. "My own mother died last week after a long, terrible illness. That's why I came here to Carmel. I needed to get away. I couldn't be in that house anymore."

Mrs. Neele gripped her arm with new strength. "I understand. When I returned to my childhood home, I felt like I was visiting a ghost. Every nook and cranny was familiar, and yet everything was wrong."

"Yes," Fayette whispered.

"When I returned to Styles afterward," Mrs. Neele continued, "I thought I would find comfort with my family there, but I didn't. I thought I'd find comfort in my book, but writing is like trying to shove a boulder through a small pipe." Her laugh was hollow.

Fayette scrutinized the woman beside her. Not all her words made sense, but it sounded more and more like this person had to be Agatha Christie, the author of *The Secret Adversary*—or was that a pen name? Was Mrs. Neele her real name? Fayette knew nothing about the author beyond that she was a British woman. Whatever the case, this person was dangerously addled and didn't seem like she fully understood who she was at the moment. Fayette had a terrible suspicion that pushing her for more personal information would cause further unraveling.

"What do we need to solve our current mystery and escape this house?" Fayette asked, determined to regain Mrs. Neele's focus.

"Clues," Mrs. Neele said with confidence. She looked between Rex and Fayette as they reunited. "Tell me everything you can about the nature of this house. You must have withheld details before."

Fayette and Rex did so, telling her things they had not told Silas, such as the shocking reveal of the skeleton in the concealed room, the invasive door that the house had fought against, and the feathers they'd found after the house became agitated. Fayette did, however, omit anything about Mother.

Mrs. Neele absorbed the information. "I wish I knew anything about Russian folklore. European or Egyptian, I know well. Hmm. I want to observe the house's response to certain stimuli." She returned to the table. "These plates are as clean as if they were washed in a sink, just as you said they would be, but I didn't witness how it happened."

She reached for the food items that had been brought for those in need, opening a box of saltine crackers. As Fayette drew closer in curiosity, Mrs. Neele clenched her fist over a handful of crackers. Crumbs fell to the wood in a shower. As soon as they struck the table, they seeped within the wood, absorbed.

"Fascinating." She bent to table-level to gaze in admiration. "Gone in an instant! It didn't happen that way as I ate."

"I reckon that the house sometimes holds back from doing things that might scare us. You weren't in much condition to see your crumbs vanish then, were you?"

"No. The sight of the bench becoming chairs almost undid me." Mrs. Neele looked around. "There are no books in here?"

"No writing of any kind. That would've made the identification of the house's origins much easier," said Rex.

"Curious, curious. Do you have some blank paper?" Mrs. Neele asked.

"Always," Fayette said, reaching into her coat for her notepad. "You want just one sheet?"

"Yes, thank you," Mrs. Neele said, setting the sheet on the table. "I am considering what I know about magical rituals around the world." Mrs. Neele frowned at the table, then reached for the knife used for the bread. Before Fayette and Rex could cry out in alarm, she brought the blade to her fingertip. She promptly pressed it to the paper, wincing as she smeared blood in a swath.

"House!" she called. "If you are able to write in a language known to the world, please do so using my blood as your medium."

Fayette didn't know whether this action was brilliant or another display of the madness that Mrs. Neele professed, but seconds later, the blood siphoned away from the yellow paper, revealing clean white lines. Letters.

"It's Cyrillic!" Fayette said with a gasp, gazing at Mrs. Neele in blatant admiration. "How did it even occur to you to attempt such a thing?"

Mrs. Neele made a small painful grunt as she finished coating the paper with blood. She motioned to Fayette for patience as she stuck her sliced fingertip in her mouth. As they watched, letters continued to appear, filling the paper almost top to bottom.

Mrs. Neele pulled out her finger, squinting at it, then smiled. "In this case, I wondered at how the house could pull things inward in a selective fashion. That adorned skeleton that you saw is preserved, which designates it as special somehow. And the house clearly recognizes when food is still being eaten and doesn't remove anything until the end, unlike some zealous restaurant servers."

"But realizing that the house could know a language . . . ?" Rex began.

Mrs. Neele shrugged. "I put myself in the house's place. It is likely centuries old, perhaps far older. Most older *humans* are rather set in their ways and believe their homeland to be superior to all others. The house seems to understand English to some degree, but that doesn't mean it can write it." On the sheet, the fresh blood was already drying to permanence.

"Think like the house," Fayette muttered. "I've tried to do that to a degree, but not in this way. Blood—that's a common thing of power in magic."

"Yes, since time immemorial. It seemed a more appropriate medium than common ink."

"I'm glad I already asked Art to try to come," Rex said to Fayette. Then to Mrs. Neele: "Art is a friend of mine, a Russian émigré."

"The house knew you were going to ask Art to come here, too," Fayette pointed out. "You talked about that here."

"I did." He grinned. "I hope that he can— The door's back!" Sure enough, that distinct metal car door was again inset in the log wall.

"Well, then! I passed the test. I'm now allowed to leave," murmured Mrs. Neele. She grabbed her hat from the bench, cringing as she settled it on her head, then clutched her purse.

"Would you like to take some food?" Fayette asked, trailing after Mrs. Neele as she made her slow approach to the door.

"I believe I'll be fine. I have . . . what *do* I have?" She opened the clasp of her purse. "Oh. Sixty pounds. Yes. Grandmother always said a woman should have that amount just in case . . . just in case . . ." She couldn't finish that sentence.

"Sixty pounds is a lot of money," Rex muttered to Fayette. She would have to take his word on that, as her experience with British currency came down to finding a three-pence coin on the floor of the studio once.

"Oh! Oh! Look at this!" Mrs. Neele smiled brightly as she held up a small photograph that depicted a dark-headed child with severe bangs.

"Is that . . . Rosalind?" Fayette asked. The mystery around Mrs. Neele hadn't been solved yet, even if the house regarded the immediate puzzle done.

Mrs. Neele only gave a thoughtful hum and smiled as she put the photograph away. She stopped before the car door as it opened toward her. Through the doorway, Fayette could see the leather and metal interior of a vehicle tipped at an angle—just as the door was angled, she now realized.

"I don't want to go there," Mrs. Neele said quietly, her fists tightening on her handbag. "If I go there . . . if I see that pit . . ."

"Is there somewhere else you would like to go?" Fayette asked, glancing at Rex. He looked pensive. She wondered if he was thinking of his own foolhardy return to the cliff. "Somewhere safe?"

Mrs. Neele blinked rapidly. "Somewhere safe? I was going to go to Yorkshire, to the Hydro, but now I don't know. I don't know." She looked down at her handbag again. With a start, Fayette realized her focus wasn't on her bag, but on her glistening wedding ring.

"You can always stay here for the night," Rex said. "I'm sure the house could conjure up bedding to make you comfortable."

"No. I should go back but—I could go to London. I can get anywhere from London, and that will give me time to think. Can I go to King's Cross station?" Mrs. Neele asked, craning her neck around.

The magic of the place flared. The shiny gray car door closed, then, an instant later, changed to become a tall rectangular door, the red paint glossy with rain. It again opened, this time to a view of a brick column a few feet away. A high light shone from somewhere to the right. There came a distant shrill whistle and rumbles of traffic. The scent of dank wetness drifted into the house. Fayette would've known at a glance—at a whiff—that this was nowhere in California. Those bricks looked older than America.

"You should reach out to people who may be missing you. To Rosalind," Fayette said. The change of venue wasn't enough. Mrs. Neele needed people to support her, just as Fayette had supported Rex. "Rosalind isn't alone, is she?"

Mrs. Neele startled. "Alone? No, of course not. Never. She's with Carlo."

Someone like Mrs. Neele probably had staff. "Rosalind needs you as well, though. You're her mother." Fayette hoped she was right in that assumption, and by Mrs. Neele's small nod, she was.

"Yes. But . . . I just need . . . I need to get away."

"I understand. I came to Carmel for a similar reason, remember?"

"I also came to Carmel to get away," Rex said. "But I did so on my own, and I couldn't be trusted by myself. You need to be careful, Mrs. Neele, especially with your head wound."

Mrs. Neele nodded, casting a brief smile to Fayette and Rex. "Thank you kindly for your hospitality. And thank you, house, for your intervention." At that, she stepped through the door. With a moist creak, it closed and vanished.

"Well." Rex rocked on his heels. "She was different from the others."

"She has more going on than that knock on her head, that's for certain. I think I've read some of her books." Fayette shook her head. "Eventually, she's going to need a good explanation for how she made it from some quarry to King's Cross."

"She's a storyteller. That should help her." Rex continued to regard the wall. "I just realized that this house could give us a shortcut anywhere in the world in an instant. It never occurred to me before that we could ask."

"I figure that Mrs. Neele is upper crust. She's used to asking for what she wants, and getting it. You're right, though. The house probably would do that for us, and yet . . ." Fayette frowned.

"And yet?" he echoed.

"It seems like a waste. The house is acting the way it is with some purpose." Fayette waved toward the table. "Doing anything else feels frivolous."

"Unless the travel wasn't for frivolous reasons." He spoke faster in excitement. "That starter of yours could help a lot of people in need, people who might be smart enough to avoid a door that opens to another world."

"That's a fine idea, but it makes me exhausted to even consider it. You'd never be able to bake enough to help everyone. And what was baked and eaten *couldn't* help everyone. What Mother does is never enough." That frustration stayed with her like a bur in tweed.

"I'm sorry," Rex said, abashed. "I wasn't trying to volunteer you for the job."

"Well, Mother *is* in my care. Who else would do it?" She sighed as she began to pack the unopened food back into the bag. They'd only cut into the butter that Rex had brought—well, and then there were the crackers, but they would keep well in their tin—which meant there was plenty of food in wait for their next guests.

"I'm sorry," Rex repeated, joining her in the tidying. At some point while they were distracted by the far wall, the high-backed chairs had transformed back into a bench.

Fayette paused to consider Mother. The jar was half full, and a peek inside showed the starter yet again with advanced development. That meant Fayette should divide and feed Mother before leaving, or . . . something Silas said came to mind. He'd continued to be concerned about Mr. Fitz, to his credit, and Fayette realized she should show more care for the Fitz family as well.

"I'm leaving Mother here tonight for safekeeping, but I'm going to bring some discard back to my cottage. I want to see about baking bread in the Fitz kitchen tomorrow."

Fayette found a lidded clay crock on a nearby shelf—an item that most definitely had not been there before. The house had supplied her with what she needed. She divided and fed Mother, setting the old peanut butter jar on a cool shelf on the far side of the oven.

"That portion you're taking away with you tonight—it still has power to it?" he asked.

"Yes." She sensed its unique strain of power like a warm pulse. "Mother makes a choice in that regard. If I gave that to someone else or had it stolen from me, it'd likely become a normal starter. It'd make good bread, if the baker knows what they're doing, but carry no magic.

But if, say, my sister, Briar, came for a visit, she could take a crock like this back to her house and make potent bread."

"Mother really does favor your family," he said.

"Yes, for some reason, she does," Fayette said softly, cradling the discard against her chest. "I'm grateful that I haven't lost her affection even while I've been so angry with her of late."

"That's the way mothers are, isn't it?" he asked.

Fayette could only nod.

Chapter 35

We did it, we did it, we did it! I worked with the humans, and with their help, I made *words*!

My witch once told me that any decent house should have a sense of pride as it stands up tall against whatever weather and wars offer, but I have never felt prouder of myself than in the moment I wrote for the first time. And I found help and set up everything without any help from a witch. *All on my own.*

Finding that guest yesterday made all the difference. Tracking her down wasn't hard because the woman-empowered-by-Mother provided me with a name. Names are power. That's why I shouldn't have named Stinky, but I couldn't help it. Sometimes a person is so terrible that they must be named so that they can be dealt with.

As for you, Mother—you're powerful unto yourself, so my acknowledgment of your name is a minor thing indeed.

This guest who came here has a long, fascinating quest ahead if she survives these next days. She has braveness to her.

I'm glad you agree with me, Mother. That means a lot, as you are far older than me. Older than my witch, too.

In any case, the guest did what she needed to do. I hated that I had to scare the people by locking them inside, but it was necessary. I couldn't let the guest go too early. There aren't many people in the world with her kind of mind—a shame that hers was damaged, but I'm glad you were able to help with her healing, Mother.

And soon the man's man will come, I hope, and he can read my words. I wonder if he'll arrive today? Tomorrow? Oh, I hope it's not a week! I won't last that long! I was very careful with my choice of words so that I will not scare the man's man as he translates, but I worry. I have no practice with such things. If I scare him, and he alerts the woman and man . . . if they were permanently scared away . . . if I lose my friends . . .

Yes, I think they are friends, Mother. The first human friends I have ever had. Neither one is a witch, or has the potential to be one, but I like them just the same. You chose a good family, Mother, you did. I think you're a friend, too! But if they were fully scared away, I would lose your company, too—

No, no, no, don't remind me that the woman and man must eventually go from this place and that this would mean that you leave, too. No. I cannot be left utterly alone again, I can't, I can't. I don't know if there's a point in fighting against the other witch if it means I'm all by myself again.

I've been a *GOOD HOUSE*. I'm hospitable, when I'm not locking my doors and windows to force people to solve puzzles! I made doors that go other places far away so the woman and man could help them and feel better by helping them! I didn't kill Stinky, though I really wanted to, but I knew that his death would scare away the woman and man forever.

I'd be a good home for my new witch, too, if she'll only come closer to recognize how helpful I am.

I'm good, aren't I? Oh, thank you, Mother! I really don't want you to go, but it's not like I can lock the people out and keep you for myself. I can regenerate wood for months once it's brought inside me and duplicate many tools once they've been here long enough to soak in my magic, but you're not something I can control like that. You're special. You need people to feed and divide you.

I think I need people, too. I just never realized that until I had no one.

Chapter 36

Fayette was already dressed and puttering around the cottage when Rex knocked on the door soon after eight o'clock. Rain was pounding down, the kind of violent, cold downpour that aspired to be hail.

"I didn't expect you by, and certainly not this early," she said, staring at him in surprise.

"I wanted to talk with you, and I didn't want to send anyone with a note, not in this weather. I don't need to come inside." He stood hunched, his black umbrella like a turtle shell over his back.

"Even sopping wet, you look as giddy as a child about to choose a kitten. You heard from Art, didn't you? Is he coming?"

His grin was broader and toothier than usual. "Yes. Not just him, though. I also heard from Margaret. The grocer's boy brought notes from them both. Margaret said that she arrived in Beverly Hills and that she was as right as rain and sends her love." Fayette nodded, relieved that Margaret hadn't wrecked her new race car somewhere along the Santa Lucia Range. "As for Art, he was heading out before dawn today. The bus should be here midafternoon."

He took a deep breath before continuing. "This is what I was thinking. I'm going to prepare my cottage for him. Since your continuity is done, I was hoping you'd come up and spend the day with me."

"That sounds lovely, but I'm working on a short story, and I feel like I can knock out the first draft quickly."

His expression went crestfallen but was replaced with a brilliant grin as she kept talking. "Really? That's wonderful!"

"I didn't expect to wake up at five today with words running around in my head like Man O' War circling a racetrack, but yes, it is wonderful. I still hope to make that bread for the Fitzes, too."

"I'm sorry, I was so excited to tell you the news, I didn't even remember that you'd brought discard here last night."

"I hate that you came all this way for me to say no."

"Don't feel badly, please. We'll still see each other later. Please, keep working for now. And make that bread!"

If this scene had been in a movie, Fayette knew, a woman in her place would've been dragged out and convinced to have a "good time" by society's standards. The fact that Rex respected her need to write and gave her space and time to do so made her feel a surge of emotion that English felt inadequate to describe. She felt loved, yes, but more than that, respected on a level as deep as the Grand Canyon. Rex understood her.

"Thank you. Try not to pace furrows in your floor as you wait for Art to arrive."

He departed, and Fayette returned to her typewriter. She skimmed over her last page to rediscover her flow, then resumed typing. Time blurred, her mind delving deep into a medical murder mystery that only her heroine could resolve.

Finally, she sat back, flexing her cramped hands. The draft was done. Additional blue-pencil labor could wait until later.

She'd had a lot of miracles to ponder recently, but the fact that she had churned out a story draft that fast—and felt so good about it— seemed like another touch of divine grace.

Time for a break. Time to see about making bread.

Even braced for the weather, the force of the rain knocked a gasp from her. Heidi's head was visible in the back window, her head angled downward. Fayette rapped loudly on the back door to get her attention over the drumming downpour. To her relief, Heidi answered in an instant and beckoned her inside, her brows curved in concern. Fayette found that heartening. However Heidi felt about her, the woman hadn't been so cruel as to leave her in the storm.

"Thank you. That rain packs a wallop. Is it okay if I . . . ?" She motioned to the nearby row of hooks on the wall. At Heidi's nod, she shed her hat and coat, scuffing her shoes on the mat to get as much water off as she could. "Are you making soup? That smells incredible!"

Heidi nodded as she returned to the stove set below the window. A large silver pot sat steaming on a burner.

"What's all this noise in here?" Mrs. Fitz entered. "Oh, Fayette Wynne! You shouldn't be out in this weather. I saw Mr. Hallstrom pass by some time ago. He looked like a drowned rat."

"He probably felt like one by the time he got back to his cottage. As brief as my walk was, I feel as if I was threshed with the wheat. I hope you don't mind my coming over."

"I don't. I worry about him, though. He shouldn't have gone out. I hope he had good cause." By the way Mrs. Fitz said it, she *was* genuinely concerned, not simply fishing for more information.

"He did. A dear friend of his is coming up on the bus today. He was asking if it'd be all right for the two of them to come over later, if the weather's agreeable." Fayette figured it was best to broach the topic now.

"Two men? That should be fine," said Mrs. Fitz, moving to hover over Heidi. There was almost a foot of height difference between them. She glanced over at Fayette with pursed lips. "You should all come here for supper tonight. We'll have plenty."

The surprise invitation caused her to blink in surprise. "I don't know what our plans may be, but I can extend the invitation. I will say, the incredible smell of this chicken soup has my mouth watering."

"This is actually cock-a-leekie, a particularly Scottish take on chicken soup," Mrs. Fitz corrected her with a note of peevishness, as if Fayette should have known the difference by scent alone. "It is the perfect food for this weather! We'll make bannocks alongside. They are rather like a biscuit."

"Oh. I actually came over to ask about baking something in your oven later," Fayette said. "You see, my family has kept a sourdough starter for years, and I brought it along with me. I have some discard to use." She didn't miss how the already pale Heidi blanched at the mention of the starter.

"Ah, and you have no oven in the cottage," Mrs. Fitz said, nodding in understanding.

"Exactly. I had hoped to bake a sourdough round here to share with you all. I understand if you say no, of course, especially as you already have plans."

"Sourdough actually sounds nice for a change. We can do that tonight." Mrs. Fitz turned back toward the hallway, missing the pensive expression on Heidi's face.

"Much obliged, Mrs. Fitz," said Fayette. "I'll go start the dough, then, and bring it over later when—"

"No." Mrs. Fitz was out of sight, but she had the strident commanding tone of a soldier. "You don't need to go back and forth all day in that rain. You'll catch pneumonia. Although . . ." She returned to the doorway. "The sourdough my aunt made when I was a girl needed a day or two for risings. Will it be ready by suppertime?"

"Hopefully," said Fayette. "If it's not ready until tomorrow, though, I can help Heidi make those bannocks. I've never had them before."

"Oh!" Mrs. Fitz brightened. "I'd never had them prior to meeting my husband, either. If we don't make them today, we will be certain to do so before you leave."

"I appreciate the offer," said Fayette.

Mrs. Fitz firmly nodded. "That is the plan, then." She whirled away without another word. A distant door closed.

Heidi's reaction raised a new issue, and due to the weather, this time the younger woman couldn't readily scamper away from a conversation. Fayette faced her. "Before I bring my ingredients over, I must ask you—will they be safe here?"

Heidi was still for a moment, then nodded.

"You were in my cottage and dropped my mother starter, didn't you?" Fayette kept her voice light.

Heidi stared at the pot as she nodded.

"Was it an accident because I surprised you?"

At that, Heidi looked up, her nod vigorous.

"Good. Thank you for being honest with me." She reckoned she wouldn't believe most people who answered that fast, but Heidi's selective answers carried more weight. "I've wondered why you picked up that jar, though, of all the things. I can only settle on one good reason." She waited until Heidi's reluctant gaze met hers again. "You're like me, aren't you? You can sense things that are magical." Fayette took a step closer to Heidi and gasped.

The young woman buzzed with such power that Fayette's scalp tingled.

Heidi inhaled sharply and took a small step back. The prickles immediately dissipated. No wonder Fayette hadn't sensed anything from her on the first day she arrived in Carmel. They had to practically touch to sense the magic of each other.

"You feel it come off me like a glow, don't you?" Fayette asked. When Heidi offered no confirmation, Fayette continued, "Silas's comment made you keen to investigate exactly what you'd sensed in my cottage earlier, didn't it? And then I returned and startled you."

Heidi mouthed, "I'm sorry."

"Thank you for that. Now, kindly let me tell you about how special this sourdough starter is."

With slow care, she explained who Mother was and what foods made with her could do to heal people. "I'm hoping Mother might help Mr. Fitz, in particular," she said in conclusion.

Heidi looked thoughtful as she nodded.

"Good." Fayette stepped back, relieved and anxious at the same time. "I'll be back in a jiffy."

The rain was no less brutal on the next back-and-forth. Fayette unloaded her supplies onto the dining table, the prime workspace in the small kitchen. As she did, the preferment's magic bloomed as if a gasoline can had been tossed onto a bonfire.

Heidi gasped as she took in the sensation, while Fayette stepped back, a hand to her mouth.

Mother used to greet Briar like that when she came for a visit. To be clear, Mother would say hello to Fayette, Thayer, and Ma when they returned from work or errands, too, but Briar had lived in her own place for the last few years of her life. Only made sense that Mother gave her a bolder welcome. A visit almost always meant that Briar would either make bread there or take a portion of Mother back to her own apartment.

How had Fayette never attributed that act to love before Rex had said something? How had she never considered that Mother also knew a surge of happiness during a reunion, and grief at death?

And why was Heidi being greeted like a member of the Wynne family? Fayette hadn't thought Mother would hold a grudge over the destruction of her jar, but this acceptance was something different altogether.

Heidi held up her hands in a shrug, quietly pleading for an explanation.

"You've been . . . chosen, I think. I've never seen a stranger invited to help make bread before. It's an honor." Fayette became more confident as she spoke.

Heidi looked scared rather than honored.

"Sourdough is slower to make, but in a lot of ways it's not that different than the yeast breads you're used to. We'll do it together and take turns keeping an eye on that pot, too."

For those first few minutes, Fayette was uncomfortable working by Heidi's side, their magical charges creating something akin to a shock when they brushed against each other. But as Heidi began to knead the dough, the motion was obviously familiar to her, and she began to relax. That calmed Fayette in turn, even as she kept wondering what Mother's reaction to Heidi meant. Maybe Mother would allow herself to be divided, for another Mother to be established here with Heidi. After all, that's what people did with normal starters, and Heidi already made bread often to feed others in town.

That idea made Fayette feel uneasy. Not oppositional, but just overall unsure of what to make of things.

She sensed a small flare of magic from the empty crock on the table. She looked over in time to see it vanish. When she patted the area, not even dust remained.

Heidi stared with questioning eyes. Fayette began, "That crock came from the house on the cliff, which is where—"

Heidi dropped the dough on the table and backed away, her floured hands raised as if she'd been confronted by robbers with tommy guns.

"After Mother's jar was shattered by an intruder, I had to think of where I could keep her safe," Fayette said in a rush. Heidi was quivering in terror. "The house is scary in some ways, but . . . it's not malicious. I'd even say it's kind—"

Heidi fervently shook her head.

"You've been kneading that bread for ten minutes. Was there anything that made you think it was tainted before you knew where the ingredients had been stored?"

Heidi shook her head, the motion small.

"I had to keep my starter someplace safe," Fayette repeated. "I didn't want to leave it with Rex. His cottage is farther away, and he wouldn't know what to do if I wasn't there. The bread that we've made in that cliff house is fine, and the starter is still fine, too."

Heidi looked to be on the verge of illness.

Fayette sighed. "You're not going to touch the dough again, are you?"

Heidi shook her head.

"I reckon you won't eat the bread, then, either. What about Mr. and Mrs. Fitz? Are you worried for them?"

She nodded.

What had her so terrified about anything and everything from that house? "Heidi, I've eaten all kinds of bready goods derived of this starter throughout my life. Mother is . . . probably one of the purest, most holy things I've come across in this world. Everything she does has been to help people, lousy and obstinate as humanity can be at times. I count myself in that number. For me, Mother's acceptance of the house allayed a lot of my initial fears." She took a deep breath. "If you don't want to eat the bread, that's your choice, but I'd like the Fitzes to know its healing powers. Will you allow that to happen at least?"

Heidi held up a hand, a motion to wait, and she washed off in the sink. As soon as her skin was dry, she pulled her notepad from a pocket.

Mrs. Fitz won't want anything from that place. She won't want Mr. Fitz to eat anything from there, either.

Fayette made a thoughtful sound. She knew Heidi was right. Fayette could make blessed bread at the cliff house sometime soon and bring it back here, but there'd be a ring of deceit in that action. Fayette already knew that offering the bread to Rex, when he was ignorant of its power, was morally ambiguous, like sneaking medicine into a child's food. But even more, Mother's divine nature would surely mean she'd be aware of Mrs. Fitz's strong opinions about the house, so the bread would likely lack power anyway. Mother wouldn't want to be forced on anyone.

"Well, then. I'm sorry," Fayette said, shifting her attention to the dough, which must have understood the subtext in her statement, as the magic withered away as she swiped her arm across the table. The dough flew off the surface to tumble on the floor once, twice, thrice, stopping on the bristled edge of the doormat as Heidi screeched in alarm.

A door flung open with a bang. "What's wrong? Are you burned?" Mrs. Fitz rushed in, her focus entirely on Heidi. As she took in that the pot was still on the stove and Heidi looked well, she studied Fayette as she rounded the table to find the dough on the floor.

"Oh." Mrs. Fitz deflated, a fist pressed to her flat chest. "The dough . . . ?"

"Met with a tragic kneading accident," Fayette said. Heidi's brow furrowed, and then she slightly inclined her head. Fayette interpreted that as a show of respect and an agreement in conspiracy. She stooped to pick up the dough. "I hate throwing out food, but this has some extra seasoning I doubt we want." She rotated it in her hands to display the grass and leaf bits she'd tracked in that now coated the exterior.

Into the garbage bin it went.

"That's a sad loss. I'm sorry," Mrs. Fitz said. "I suppose this is the day for bannocks after all." Heidi nodded and smiled, her relief obvious.

"How's Mr. Fitz doing today, by the way?" Fayette asked.

"Quite well, quite well. I think he'd like company. Do come in!" Mrs. Fitz waved her to follow.

Heidi snagged Fayette's coat sleeve as she passed. "Thank you," she mouthed.

At the end of the hallway was a small bedroom with a window that faced the street. The curtains were open to show a view of wavering torrential rain. Mr. Fitz lay propped up with a pillow on his bed. He stared outward, the same blank expression as ever. Mrs. Fitz took a seat in an upholstered chair at his bedside, her frail body ramrod straight. A book sat on the bedside table, a red lace bookmark dangling from the halfway point like a stubby tongue. Fayette couldn't see enough of the binding to make out the title.

"I can still smell that soup in here." Fayette took a deep, contented breath. The door had stayed open, and the luscious scent seemed to have followed them in to join them at the bedside. She couldn't help but be reminded of the soups Ma used to make. The recollection didn't promptly douse her in sadness, either, only sprinkling her with melancholy. "Heidi is taking great care with the stove. She showed me she can knead bread, too. She wasn't the one who dropped the dough." Fayette wanted to make it clear that Heidi wasn't to blame. She didn't figure Mrs. Fitz would try to punish Heidi over the waste, but she wasn't going to take any risk.

"Heidi has a wonderful knack for bread, and for cooking in general. Her household skills were, shall we say, uneven when she arrived here, but she was a quick learner."

"The Marshal told me the circumstances around her arrival in Carmel. She's lucky that she found a place with you."

"Luck had nothing to do with it. Her situation was terrible, but I felt blessed by her presence from the day she came. My husband was deployed, you see. This town . . . I did not readily find a place here," she said with tact. Fayette grimaced, thinking of the snobbish librarian. "She's not simply a maid in this household, but a true friend. I tell her often that I don't expect her to stay forever. She should find a young man and get married! Go see more of the world than Carmel! She laughs when I tell her that, but really, she doesn't need to be bound to this house like I am."

She said that softly, without a trace of bitterness. She stroked her husband's freckled forearm. His button sleeves were rolled up to the elbow.

"I stayed with my mother almost every minute of the day through her last months," Fayette said in a like tone. "We knew from the start that she wouldn't be improving, that her end was a matter of time. I think it would've been harder for me if I'd had a hope of recovery from the start. Instead . . ." She stopped herself, realizing that her words could be taken with offense.

Mrs. Fitz continued to pet her husband's arm, though, her expression placid. "Yes. Hope can be a terrible thing in that way, a fire that you think will warm you, save you, but instead leaves you cold." She faced Fayette. "I know you will not agree with my choice, but nevertheless: Silas Pennington will return here after lunch." Fayette recoiled in surprise. "He reached out to me with word that he's done more research into ways that he can help."

Soft footsteps outside the room revealed Heidi's approach. "Mrs. Fitz," Fayette said, thinking how best to delicately word things, "I don't believe Silas is without genuine talent, but much of what he presents is fraudulent because he has no true control over his inherent abilities. That makes him dangerous not only to himself, but to others."

Heidi leaned in the doorway, her mouth a hard line as she listened.

"I will see what Mr. Pennington says. I have not agreed to pay him money, and if I do, that's my affair."

"You're right," Fayette said. "I just worry that he may be leading you on with false hope that will—"

"Did you not hear me just admit that hope is a terrible thing?" Mrs. Fitz's voice rose, her fists balling up on her lap. "Prayer alone is nothing. Prayer needs action! I am trying to find the ways and means to make my husband whole. Doctors say nothing can be done, but if I do nothing, that means giving up, and I can't. I can't." A sob acted as punctuation as she looked to her husband. Oblivious to the tumult around him, he seemed to have fallen asleep.

Mrs. Fitz's hope and grief were in a constant tug-of-war, that much was clear. "I'm sorry," Fayette said, not knowing what else to say.

Heidi moved up beside Mrs. Fitz's chair. Mrs. Fitz leaned against her, tears coursing down her cheeks.

"You think I don't know the vanity of my effort? You think I don't realize that most everyone in town sees me as a figure of pity? I'm aware. I'm aware of much. But I must know that Gerald is at peace. If his soul . . . if it is adrift over him or in France or suffering elsewhere, I must help him."

Heidi and Fayette shared looks of sadness and despair.

"I don't want to be here during Mr. Pennington's visit," Fayette said. She knew just where she needed to go, too. "With the dough a loss, there's no reason for me to linger, especially as the storm seems to be easing up." She nodded toward the window. Rain still fell, but at a relaxed pace. The house across the way was now visible.

Heidi held up a hand. Moving away from Mrs. Fitz, she pulled out the notepad and pencil again.

I don't want to be in his company, either. I will do the shopping.

Mrs. Fitz sighed. "Neither of you needs to run for the hills yet. Please stay here, Miss Wynne, and have lunch with us. Mr. Pennington won't be here for another hour and a half yet. You're still invited for supper as well."

"Much obliged," Fayette said. "You do have me curious about those bannocks."

After a simple, delicious lunch of sandwiches and salads, the conversation awkward yet pleasant, Fayette set off for a walk across town.

She wondered, for an instant, if Rex might think she was Art arriving early and be disappointed when he saw her, but his expression of sheer delight stayed as he swung the door wide.

"You made it!" he said. "How did the writing go?"

"The first draft is done, and I made some inroads with Mrs. Fitz and Heidi, but I have a longer tale to tell about that."

"Come on in so you can play the raconteur. I'll make us tea. As far as I know, Art's bus is making steady progress this way." His grin couldn't possibly have been wider. "Really, I'm glad to see you," he added softly.

She was glad to see him, too.

Chapter 37

"What if Art doesn't believe me? Believe us? What if he thinks we're being taken in by a fraud like Silas, or simply batty?" Rex asked as they walked toward the bus stop. "There's actually a French term for a madness shared by two: *folie à deux*. One of my early movies used the concept."

"Rex." She'd reached an exasperation point. He'd brought up this worry constantly in the past few hours. "Like I said before, if he isn't willing to listen to you, to respect your experience, then you should question his presence in your life. I mean that. No matter what, I have your back, understand?"

"I do. You're right. Thank you."

She understood his terror. This was a modern world. Magic was largely gone, only encountered by sheer luck or relentless searching. She really hoped Art was open-minded, but more than that, she hoped he didn't turn out to be an odious person. She was more concerned with Rex's heart than his career, but if he was going to risk everything to be with Art, by God, this man needed to be worthwhile.

The bus rolled up just as they approached the stop.

Cries of greeting rang out in the waiting throng as riders began to disgorge. Rex leaned one way and then another, straining to see, then finally gasped. "There he is!"

Fayette saw a thickset brown-haired man with a fedora and a bearded neck who looked like a few other Russians she'd known, but this fellow stared toward Rex without recognition. From behind him emerged a tall man with a tanned glow to his skin, his thick brown hair parted in the middle. He held a black homburg hat against a suit tailored to fit his lean body, the fabric superior to anything she'd ever worn. As his strides sped up, a grin lit his face, bright as the sun above as it shoved away storm clouds so it could rule the sky again.

"Rex!" he called. He planted his hat atop his head so he could use that hand to shake with Rex. A leather duffel bag swayed from his other arm. "That trip seemed to take forever and a day." With a deft move, he faced Fayette, doffing his hat as he bowed. "You must be Fayette. I am Artem Jaroff, but you may call me Art. I'm honored to make your acquaintance. From what little I have heard thus far, you have become good friends in the past week, and I'm glad. This man, he needs more friends. He should collect them like my aunt used to accumulate cats!"

Fayette laughed, dazzled and delighted by his defiance of her expectations. "I assume she had a great many."

He shook his head dramatically. "Mathematicians are still counting them. It's why you no longer see abacuses used these days—they are all being devoted to that one cause!"

"Let's go by my cottage so you can clean up." Rex extended a hand to take Art's bag. Art tsked and held on to it.

"A stop by your place sounds good, but permit me to carry my bag. Moving my muscles feels good!"

Rex surrendered, both hands up. "I won't fight you for it." They began walking.

"Good. You'd lose most egregiously, and might risk damage to that million-dollar face of yours. That would be a tragedy!"

The man was pure effervescent friendliness, soda pop in human form. And Fayette didn't need to worry about Rex's affections being unrequited. Art's thickly lashed hazel eyes seemed to eat Rex up like candy.

"I already made deviled egg salad for you to throw into a sandwich or two," Rex said as they entered his cottage. "And then we can go down to Fayette's place, where—"

"I get ravenous after travel, and deviled egg sandwiches are my favorites," Art said to Fayette as she shut the door. "This man, he knows how to make them to perfection." He pinched his fingers to his lips in a kiss. Rex blushed.

"No wonder you couldn't hide anything from the studio, if you both were carrying on like this," Fayette said.

Art stopped in his tracks. "You know? About *us*?" he said quietly.

"She figured it out. I suppose I was about as subtle as an anvil," Rex said, sighing. "I'm sorry, Art. Sorry about all the fuss I've brought into your life. I hope that your coming here doesn't harm you even more."

"Harm. If the studio fires me, so what? I survived the army." He made a moue of distaste. He had to be referring to the Russian military. She had to wonder if he'd served willingly, but she wasn't about to pry for intimate details from a person she'd just met. "I survived the Revolution. I made it to America. I've had many jobs. What's one more? I know clothes. I will find other work as easy as pie, as Americans like to say. And as I told you, Rex—you can also find other work. I want him to go into theater. Have you heard him sing?" he asked Fayette, recognizing, rightly, that she would be his ally. "Dear God! You'd think an angel came down. We could go live in Greenwich Village, where we would be more accepted, and work for a different kind of stage. We'd get by just fine."

"I want to stay in movies, and that means Hollywood," Rex said softly, moving away. "This is about more than my job, though, and you know it." He faced Fayette. "My producer threatened to give leave for the papers to publish . . . gossip about me and Art."

"What? No other men have been purposefully exposed for being temperamental! Your studio has to be bluffing," she said, even as she considered that studio strong-arm tactics could only get worse as the government and religious organizations applied more censorship pressure. Revealing his relationship wouldn't simply damage his job prospects here and elsewhere, though—he could be seriously hurt or killed.

Rex sighed. "I couldn't risk our studio carrying through with the threat. I couldn't let Art be hurt because of me."

That was it. That was the biggest reason of all. As bad as everything could be for Rex personally, he couldn't bear to have Art dragged down with him. Fayette simultaneously wanted to weep and punch some stuffed-shirt executive in the face.

"That's why I had to break things off with Art," said Rex.

"He told me we could never speak again. Ever." Art shook his head. "It turns out, 'never' was twenty-two days. Who knew?"

"Our relationship should be private. If we were in the papers, why . . ." Rex couldn't even finish the sentence. He had that look on his face again, his despair as stark as fresh blood on a limed wall.

His family wouldn't approve; Fayette comprehended that with grim certainty. To lose the career he loved along with his family would . . . No, Fayette couldn't finish *that* sentence. She already knew how the *possibility* of those losses had carried Rex to the brink of suicide.

"Your studio hasn't turned on you yet, and I truly doubt that they would take such a drastic move. After all, they'd be hurt by the scandal, too." More than likely, his bosses would engage in the tactic that Rex had mentioned a few days before—they'd squander the rest of his contract by giving him low billing or lending him out to other studios, and then after that, he'd be blacklisted everywhere. If he wanted to keep acting in flickers, he'd probably only get shows on Poverty Row. As familiar and cozy as her particular section of town was to her, she didn't want that fate for him. "Doom isn't imminent, and some things in life are outright dandy. After all, look who came all the way to Carmel to see you! Look who counted the days you were apart!"

A wobbly smile returned to Rex's face. "You actually counted the days?" he asked Art.

"Give my tired brain a few moments, and I can calculate the hours and minutes. Of course I counted our time apart!" Art rolled his eyes with what could only be described as fond exasperation. "I missed you!"

"I missed you, too." Rex shuddered, as if physically shaking off the dark mood. "We shouldn't dilly-dally here. You must be exhausted and famished, and we need to get to that translation pronto. I'll go make your sandwiches while you freshen up, Art. How many do you want?"

"Two, please." After Rex stepped into the kitchen, Art turned to Fayette, his voice lowering. "That man worries me. Have his moods been shifting like that often?"

"I've seen it happen several times this week, yes."

Art released a huff of breath. "That is not like him. Has he—has he worried you as well?"

"From the moment I first met him, but that's his tale to tell. He's in a bad way, Art. I'm glad you're here to support him."

"So am I." His soft smile radiated gratitude. "Now, tell me: How dire is this matter of a Russian translation? At first, it sounded as though you both found an artifact, but as he spoke more, I was left confused and concerned. Is he being threatened by someone? Is that part of the terrible pressure upon him?"

"The matter is . . . complicated, but I can say that Rex is not being threatened. Please don't ask for any additional details right now, though. We'll reveal more about the letter at my rental."

"A letter, you say? Meaning, I may soon be reading aloud someone's translated grocery list?" His smile was wry as he shook his head. "That's fine. I don't mind if that's all it is. This matter gave Rex an excuse to reach out to me. I'll be thankful for that, even if I discover the list outlines someone's terrible taste in pickles."

Art stepped aside to shave and freshen up, and by the time he returned, the sandwiches were ready. He inhaled those along with a bottle of Coca-Cola, and minutes later, they walked back through Carmel.

Fayette felt more nervous with every stride, and judging by Rex's tense silence, his anxiety was escalating again, too. How *would* Art accept their tale? Would he even be willing to handle a sheet of paper warped with blood? Should she have tried to copy the Cyrillic to a fresh sheet? Why was it that this conversation felt as terrifying as—if not more so than—the other perturbing events of this week?

Once they were in Grangeville Cottage, their coats and hats on hooks by the door, Fayette offered the men seats at the small dining room table, but Art wanted to stand after being captive on a bus. Therefore, out of politeness, they all ended up standing, leaning against the sparse counters. Rex's arms crossed his chest, his posture defensive.

"I need to start by explaining how I met Fayette," he said in a quiet, trembling voice.

To her relief, Rex didn't hold back the reason for his walk to the cliff. As Art listened with tears in his eyes, Rex revealed the increased pressure to marry Margaret and the depth of his despair—and how Fayette had imperiled her own life to save his.

"It wasn't *that* risky," she muttered.

Art tapped her on the shoulder. "Thank you for acting to help a stranger. I wish . . . I wish you could've reached out to me, Helmer, but I know why you didn't." He said Rex's true name with gravitas. "My job is nice, I won't deny it, but there are other jobs. There's only one of you."

"Art. You can't call me by that name." Rex sounded pained.

Art sighed. "You're allowed to be yourself sometimes."

"I'm not . . . *completely* someone else. My name is something special, though. Something that needs to kept back home, packed away with my duck-cloth overalls and Red Wing boots. I'm sorry."

"You, always so quick to apologize when there's no need." Art sounded exasperated. "The error is mine. I'm the one who brings it up on occasion, and I should stop. I'm sorry, Rex."

It struck Fayette as sad that Rex couldn't allow for this one particular intimacy, and yet she understood. He was trying to maintain a boundary between his two selves. She and Art were probably in a select club that knew his true name.

Rex remained silent, his thoughts kept penned in his brain. "I can pick up the story now, if you'd like," Fayette murmured. At his nod, she did so.

She described the odd things she'd noticed that first night in the house on the cliff, and then her impressions during the daylight trip. By that time, Rex was able to speak again, and related his discovery of the fence and the interior layout of the hut.

Art looked more tense and pale as they continued. He finally raised a hand to speak. "I must ask you to pause and tell me: How many times have you been to this house now? That it has let you inside?"

"At least once each day for about the past week." Fayette found it incredible she had only been in Carmel six days.

"My God," Art muttered. "My God."

"You believe what we've seen?" Rex asked, his voice cracking.

"Of course! I'm well aware of the magical in the world, especially that of my homeland. I was dear friends with my household domovoy when I was a child—that would be akin to what the English call a brownie, I believe. I haven't encountered anything of the . . . magnitude of this house, though," Art said with reverence, shivering.

"Wait. You recognize our house from stories?" Fayette asked.

"Oh, yes." Art's smile was faint. "But do go on. Continue to amaze me."

Fayette and Rex took turns relating how the house seemed to reveal new facets of its nature each time they visited. Rex told of the skeleton they saw in the hidden room; Art trailed a hand along his face and asked for every detail about the clothing. He said nothing at all as Fayette described the different, living visitors through the appearing doors. His eyes widened when Rex recalled the discovery of the massive chicken feather, and their recounting of the invasive door incident made him moan in dismay.

When they reached the present, the only tidbit they had omitted was in regard to Mother's full nature.

The room was silent for a long moment. "Well, then," Art finally said. "I'm glad that you called me. If you had done so last weekend, after that initial night when you took shelter in the house, I would've boxed your ears as if you were small children and bade you to never, ever go back to that hut. And yet here you both are, still alive. And some kinds of chosen ones, at that. You're not even *Russian*." He shook his head, blatant awe in his voice.

"Good grief! Tell us already," Fayette snapped.

Art nodded. "Indeed I will. You've been blithely visiting Baba Yaga's house. Or the hut of *one* Baba Yaga, I should say. In some tales, many are visited in a row, as a Baba Yaga is part of a sisterhood, or used to be. The lot of them are witches, and all of them live in huts that rove about on massive chicken legs. Dear God!" Art's eyes rolled toward heaven. "We lost so much in the Revolution. I didn't think we had lost Baba Yaga as well."

Art was momentarily overcome, a fist pressed to his lips. Rex planted a hand on his shoulder, and he leaned in to the touch.

"I've never heard of this 'Baba Yaga,'" Rex said. "How does her story go?"

"There are many tales about her. I would say anywhere Russia has ruled or tried to rule over the past five centuries, Baba Yaga is said to have visited. I was obsessed with tales about her, Koschei, and the like when I was young, but that was a long time ago. Pardon me." Art closed his eyes, the very picture of deep thought. "Baba Yaga tests people who find her cottage—but really, she often makes sure she is found. Her visitors are most always royalty of some sort, often children. Actually, many tend to be female. They are challenged to do things like, say, keep watch of horses that always run away or clean an entire household in an impossibly short span of time. Kindness and wit are what enables a person to survive."

"That sounds like a lot of the extraordinary beings and tales out of Europe," said Fayette.

Art guffawed. "The entities of Russia are much darker to match our winters. If people fail in their tasks for Baba Yaga, well . . . she eats them, cooks them up in her oven."

Fayette blanched. "Oh. You were right, Rex. The oven *is* big enough to fit someone inside."

Rex looked vaguely ill as well. "This is the point when I remind you of what you told me, Fayette. The house keeps everything clean."

"It sounds to me as if the house has taken you in during the absence of Baba Yaga," Art said.

"She's not simply absent. She's dead," Fayette muttered. "I bet that's her body we saw in the hidden room."

Rex nodded with pursed lips. "And that invading door *was* an attack by another witch. Another house, just like our cliff house, was trying to make a bridge."

"And our house felt the need to fend it off for some reason. What does that mean?" asked Fayette.

"It means not every Baba Yaga is dead," said Art with a forcefully perky tone. "And you're blessed that your house kept you safe as it did. Now, bring me what the house wrote. I need paper and pencil, too. I'm not a translator by trade, but I'll do my best to rephrase sentences in ways that you will understand."

Fayette and Rex idled in the small parlor to give him space to work.

"I still don't understand why the house chose me as it did," murmured Fayette. "I hope it's not wanting me as its next witch. I mean, I know I'm in need of a new job, but that's not the kind of billet I intend to fill."

Rex cocked his head. "I haven't seen anything that would indicate it has those kinds of designs on you. I can't help but think of what Silas first observed about you during the séance—that you are steeped in Mother's essence. The house might have recognized that same thing."

"That makes sense, I suppose."

"Maybe the letter will confirm that," said Rex as they both watched Art.

His head rose. "I'm done. Rex, can you please read? Your voice is like no other. If your audiences could hear you speak, the studios would never let you out of contract!"

"That sounds rather Faustian," said Fayette.

Art shrugged. "I never said it'd be a good or fair contract."

"Shall I begin?" Rex looked between them with an arched brow. "'I was the home of a Baba Yaga. I have been left bereft for years. I welcome the friendship of the woman, man, and mother—'"

"Wait, it says *mother*?" Fayette broke in. "That's my nickname for my sourdough starter," she said as an aside to Art.

Rex's gaze told her he understood the momentous weight of the single word. "Yes."

The house was not only friends with her but also with *Mother*. Surely that meant the cottage and the starter could communicate on some level. No wonder Mother had been so vigorous since going there—no, really since Fayette had first gone to the house.

Rex continued reading, "'I have been a certain kind of house in the past, but I do not wish to scare you away. I am sorry that I have scared you already. I want to continue to be your friend. I keep things clean. I keep the fire going. Please be my friend. Please bring my new witch here soon, or the cliff will collapse beneath me. Also, another Baba Yaga is on the way here and will arrive very soon. She has recognized my weakness, and she will kill me and use my parts to fix her own house. I do not want that. I need my new witch right away. Thank you.'"

"Oh," said Fayette, the single word summing up her dizzied reaction.

Art raised a hand as if he were a student. "This is not good, that another witch is on the way here. Baba Yaga is terrible and powerful." His golden tan had taken on a sickly sheen.

"Her direct door failed. Now she's coming here herself," muttered Fayette. "The one thing that's clear is that the house needs its new witch, lickety-split." Which meant Fayette was *not* the witch candidate. She couldn't help but be relieved.

"That must be Heidi. Right?" Rex asked.

"Heidi's terrified of the house for some reason," Fayette said. "If we had more time, I'd say we should help the house write more letters and we could play mediator, but this situation is too urgent. We need to convince Heidi to come with us to the cliff before that other Baba Yaga arrives."

"A cliff that could collapse into the ocean at any time," said Art. "You do recall that part, yes?"

Fayette began to put on her coat. Rex and Art followed her example. "I do indeed. It stood out like a neon sign on a dark night. Even so, I won't—"

Someone began pounding on the door.

Fayette turned to open it. To her shock, Heidi stood there, her face distraught. She beckoned wildly to Fayette, then pulled out her notepad.

"What happened?" asked Fayette. "Is Mr. Fitz sick or—"

Heidi thrust the paper in Fayette's face.

Where are they?

The ferocity of her pencil had gouged holes in the page.

Fayette heard Rex and Art come up behind her. "What? They aren't home? But . . . Mr. Fitz never leaves, does he?"

Heidi gave that a thumbs-up and then wrote more.

Rarely. His wheeled chair is gone.

She looked ready to cry or scream, or both at once.

"Oh no. *Silas.*" She whirled around to face Rex. "What he last said to us, about the house—"

"He wasn't going to give up on his investigation. He wanted to help Mr. Fitz." Rex gasped. "But surely the house won't let Silas inside. They should be stuck in the road, right?"

"What's going on?" Art asked.

"Mr. Fitz was left catatonic from a severe war injury. His wife is determined to find a way to heal him through spiritualism. That medium we told you about? We met him at a séance at their house."

Fayette spun around to face Heidi. "Are you the cliff house's new witch? Is that why you're so scared of the place? You must understand that the house is pleading for you to come because—"

FAYETTE FAYETTE FAYETTE.

Her screamed name reverberated through her head as though her skull had become a mighty gong, her name the drumstick—but no, that wasn't right, either. She hadn't heard her name through her ears. This was more like someone had hooked her soul and given it a hard tug.

She sat on the floor. She had no memory of her descent. Rex's arms were looped underneath her armpits.

"Oh," she managed to gasp.

"What happened?" Rex asked as he released her.

"The house. I think it—"

Art caught Rex as he went down next. Fayette scrambled to her feet, but just as she reached to help, Rex gained his own feet again.

"You heard your name?" Fayette asked as Rex pressed the heel of his hand to his forehead.

The house had taken care to not use their names in its letter, but it clearly knew them—and reserved the use for special circumstances. Like when a mother belted out a child's full name.

"Yes," Rex croaked. "We need to get there. Now."

They dashed outside. "Silas must've found a way to access the house," said Fayette. "If he's trying more magic inside—"

"No." Heidi backed away from them, arms up. Rose branches clawed at her skirt. "You cannot go *there*. I will not go there! That house, it has too much power. You do not know what it can do, what it has done."

Fayette gaped. "Heidi? You can talk?"

"You do not know what it can do!" Heidi screamed, then turned and ran.

Fayette stared after her, torn. Should they chase Heidi down, physically drag her to the house? But no—no, they couldn't go after her. Heidi would be running the opposite way from the house, as ever, and they had to get to the cliff.

They had a friend there in desperate need of help.

Chapter 38

I shouldn't have named Stinky, no, no, no. I gave him too much power, I made him too *real*, and now he's back and reeks even more than before.

He is at the threshold of my roost with a man in a moving chair and a woman. The woman, I am glad to see, is mad at Stinky as well.

She tells him I'm a terrible, nightmarish thing—but I'm not, really! Not anymore! She's mad that Stinky brought her to the cliff, saying that she wouldn't have gone with him if she'd known where they were going, that this trip has upset her husband.

The man in the chair is not upset. I have no eyes, yet I can see that.

Stinky isn't upset, either. He's excited. He tells her he hid their destination for that reason, that this is a place where he can work a ritual that makes her husband whole.

They go back and forth, talking about waylines and convergence points. The woman is less mad now, more thoughtful. Stinky says he thinks I'm sitting on a well of power.

I hate that he is right. Hate, hate, hate. I wish my miasma could fog his senses and make him forget about me, but he is too *aware*. At least I can wall myself from his approach. He has been here before, but that doesn't mean he can enter again!

He asks if she's ever gone inside me, and she gets somewhat angry again, telling him no, of course not, that she's been close to hell in her life already and she's not going to enter it again willingly.

She *has* had a long, hard quest—she really has.

Stinky goes on to say that I'm the house of a Russian witch—wait, how did he learn that? The woman starts to leave, but Stinky blocks the wheeled chair from moving, so she has to stay and listen to him more. He says Americans always think of witches as bad things, but it's just a word, and words change, and what mediums do these days is really a lot like what witches have done for years.

The woman nods and stops trying to push away the chair.

Stinky argues that he can use me to help the quiet man in the chair, that he can do that right now, and I comprehend how their quests might start to change in really bad ways.

Three of my feathers fall out.

Stinky keeps talking, and the woman is getting more excited, and I know they are going to try to enter me, and I have to stop that from happening, I absolutely must. They've come this far, but will get no farther! I will not open myself to him, nope, not even if my woman-friend and man-friend arrive. My friends will understand why I need to refuse them passage, because they *are* friends.

But then Stinky raises his arms. In that instant, I know what he's going to say, and I feel powerless in a worse way than I did back when my old witch was freshly dead and my new witch had run away.

"Little house, little house!" he shouts, and my feet go cold with dread deep within the rocks. "Turn your back to the sea, your front to me."

I have never heard my invocation in English, but the meaning, the intent, is what matters, not the spoken language. I must heed him. I must. The witches trained my entire brood to do so.

In the old days, I quite literally would turn, as I always prefer to face toward a nearby point of power, and people on quests naturally come from places of powerlessness. Even though I cannot move my legs, I feel my wall lift away. The path is clear to him.

I cannot evict him, I cannot evict him! He has invited himself inside! Oh, my witch, how could you abandon me to endure such an offense?

They work together to bring the wheeled chair through the bushes and carry the quiet man up the rocky slope. Slowly, they come closer, closer, Stinky's reek growing, billowing. So much magic! It swirls around him like a cloud, stains him through the marrow.

They reach my door. I do not open it for them, but neither can I block the way. They enter, panting from their effort.

The quiet man is laid down in the middle of my floor. Stinky announces he'll create a circle around him—a *circle*? My old witch never worked with *circles*! More foreign magic! More awfulness! Stinky tells the woman that her husband will soon rise up on his own, and even through the terribleness, her hope and yearning glow like a miniature sun.

Stinky pulls supplies from his pack. He draws a chalk circle on my floor. I cannot siphon the chalk away. The magic he is employing is not like mine, but magic knows magic. I cannot undo his work. It's as if he is like my witch, but he's not, not at all. No witch of Rus would be so impure.

He etches words next. I feel each line like a knife that sinks deeper, deeper, deeper with each passing second. I want to fly away! I cannot help it! I strain against my nest. I know I can't fly, but breaking this cliff and smashing on the rocks, oh, that may be preferable to this torture!

The woman squeals that she just felt an earthquake, but Stinky is so focused on what he's doing, he doesn't even respond.

He creates another ring of chalk, followed by runes. He is melding magics that shouldn't be melded, binding them into me, my beautiful floor, the floor I've worked so hard to keep dust-free and clean! Oh, it hurts, it hurts; he is violating me, he is *ruining me*. I quiver, I quiver, and I cry, I scream, but these humans cannot hear me. I scare the birds, though—my cousin birds—I can feel every winged being for miles around screech in alarm and fly up and away. I'm sorry, birds, I'm sorry. I didn't mean to scare you. I don't want to scare anyone anymore— except for Stinky—but I'm hurting, and I'm scared. I'm scared of how his runes are sinking deeper, deeper, deeper than my boards to find my legs and shanks. Cutting, dripping through me like acid.

Stinky says he can feel power building up, and he isn't even scared when my oven fire flares outward. I'm not trying to reach him this time! I'm hurting so much, I can't control myself anymore. Stinky announces he's going to begin the ritual and the woman cannot cross the lines to be near her husband, no, that such an act would be quite dangerous, like breaking a dam. She stands just beyond the outer ring, hands clasped.

Stinky's eyes are closed. He moves his hands through the air, making more symbols—using another kind of magic. I can barely sense the outer world. All I know is torture.

I shake and I shake. Why is this happening? I was a good house. Was I too good? Should I have not tried to make friends? This wouldn't have happened if I had stayed alone! Or is this punishment for scaring away my new witch? Is this what happens to bad houses, to bad homes?

I kept my roof intact through harsh sun and intense storms, my fire steady and bright once it was lit anew. Was this not enough?

Was I ever enough?

Make it stop. Make it stop.

Fayette! Rex! My friends! Help me. Please. Help me.

Save me.

Chapter 39

Fayette felt the earth quaking as they ran along the street. From Art's shout of surprise, she knew he'd felt it as well—and that meant anyone around them could. That had to be what set off the birds, too; all around, she saw flocks taking to the sky. Gulls, pelicans, songbirds, all sizes, all kinds, the clouds freckled dark. Rex said nothing, his expression grim as he led the pack toward the cliff. Where Heidi had gone, she didn't know.

They came to a stop at the wax myrtles that formed the property boundary. Fayette pushed her way through—and was pushed back. "What the— The house called us; it wants us to come. House!" she yelled.

She felt a charge to the air, palpable pressure. This was different from the humidity-like thickness in the house when Silas had gone inside before. This had an edge to it. A spark. Like the tornado weather she remembered from her earliest years.

"The house must be fighting him," Rex said. "Maybe it doesn't even know we're here."

"What are we going to do?" asked Fayette.

"If I may?" Art offered a small bow and then stepped forward. He barked out a line in Russian, then stuck an arm through the bushes. He wasn't pushed back. He could get through! He gestured for Fayette to lead the way. "In most of the old stories, there's a phrase that makes Baba Yaga's house face the adventurer."

"I knew you'd come in handy," Rex said.

"I'm more than a deft hand with a needle," he said, then gasped as he stared up the rocky slope. "That— It looks exactly as it does in the illustrations! I would've known it even without the chicken legs."

The house towered over them, heaving and quivering. Fayette had to catch herself with a hand to the rocks as she lost her footing on the still-slick knobby surface. "Be careful," she said, feeling the need to state the obvious. Together, they climbed.

The front door remained open, as did the interior passage.

The main room swirled in chaos that had no sound but was a riot of color, as if all the blooms in Carmel had been distilled to their purest, brightest colors and set loose to spin through the air like a broad tornado or whirlpool. Silas had Mrs. Fitz by both arms as she strained forward, trying to enter the maelstrom.

"You can't!" Silas was shouting at her. "You can't break the circle!"

"But he's in there, alone!" Mrs. Fitz screamed back.

"What's happening?" Rex snapped.

Silas's face was ghastly pale. "I don't know. I started the ritual but it— I can't get it to *listen!*" For a second, she thought he meant the house, and then she realized he was still speaking about the ritual. He'd lost control.

"What's happening to Mr. Fitz in there?" Fayette asked. She could see the prone lump of his body as the rainbow swirled around him.

"I don't know!" Tears streaked down Silas's face. "This working was supposed to cure him, to bind his soul to his body again! But this, but I can't—"

"Stop the ritual," said Rex.

"I can't! I've tried!"

Magic. There was so much magic here. Fayette couldn't even sense Mother's presence, but she could see the jar in its nook. The way the house was quivering, though, Mother may not be safe for much longer. Fayette had the urge to rush her elsewhere, but there was no time—not now.

Fayette's one comfort, amid her flare of terror, was the surety that Mother would want her to help Mr. Fitz foremost.

Mother always did what she could to help people. Fayette needed to get better at that herself.

"If this shaking doesn't stop, the cliff could come down," Fayette said. Art had approached Mrs. Fitz and was murmuring something to her, prying her away from Silas.

"It's my fault, it's my fault," Mrs. Fitz kept repeating as she sobbed.

"Is this . . . rainbow . . . the house's energy?" Rex stood so close to Fayette, their shoulders brushed.

He regarded her as if she knew a damn thing. She tried to laugh, and it came out as a hysterical wheeze. "That's my guess. If this power somehow gains access to Mr. Fitz's soul, to his mind . . . I don't know what might happen. In that circle, I could end up in a memory of no-man's-land, far as I know." Terror pounded through her heart.

"You?" Rex said sharply. "Why do you have to be the one who goes in there?"

"Whatever you do, don't smear the chalk lines on the ground!" Silas screeched. "That's one of the most important things in spellcasting!"

Fayette registered Silas's words but focused on Rex's intense blue eyes. "Why am I the one who goes? Because you have someone who loves you. I'm a total orphan." Her grin was broad and bitter as she gave Rex a violent, full-force shove toward Art as she leaped into the maelstrom.

The chalk ring was drawn broadly, the runes underfoot spaced out enough that her large feet had space to stand. Runes! Silas had drawn actual runes like out of some Norse tale. That wasn't the only language present, though. A few feet away, flashing in blue, green, and yellow as colors swirled, were words in Latin.

"Fayette! Are you okay?" Rex sounded like he was a hundred feet away, but he wasn't even a foot.

She nodded and gave him a thumbs-up, and that's when she began to feel pain. An ache, agonizing, body wide, as if some giant had used her to roll out bread dough. She groaned and pressed both hands to her head. But this—this wasn't her pain. She felt oddly detached from the awfulness, and that's how she comprehended that she was feeling a sample of what the house was enduring. The circle was a torment. Every line, every dot had been carved into the house as if with an axe. The house, being inherently magical, exuded not blood but sheer preternatural power. The circle contained most of it, but more seeped outward by the second. The house was losing the very essence that made it *alive*.

Outside the circle, she felt Silas's presence like a pulsing ulcer. His defensive magic had annoyed her before, but now, through the house, she recognized how it sensed him: Silas was saturated with magic of all origins and kinds, creating a fragrant, foul mix. A cesspool of the most intolerable kind.

No wonder the house had ejected him before!

"I'm sorry we hurt you by bringing him here. We had no idea," she called to the house.

From this close, she could see Mr. Fitz within the inner circle. He looked immobile and peaceful, as he ever was. But if she was feeling the house's pain in this ring—what awaited her in the middle? Would she be more immersed in what the house experienced—or in what Mr. Fitz experienced? God help her! But Fayette had to keep going. She couldn't abandon Mr. Fitz—she couldn't let Rex or Art sacrifice themselves in her stead.

If this was a sacrifice. She sure hoped it wasn't. Life was just getting interesting again.

Rex yelled her name once more. She turned to give him another thumbs-up as she motioned for him to stay away.

She then stepped across the next line, into the thickest, brightest whirls of color.

Her awareness of pain was gone. All was quiet. None of the screams or cries of the outer room could penetrate this level. The pressure akin to humidity was present, like a childhood summer day without the insects or sweat, but she felt no movement of air as magic flowed around her.

"Mr. Fitz?" Fayette crouched down, careful not to wiggle her feet even a half inch to either side. More runes and words etched the floor around him. Her voice echoed as if she were in a small bubble.

She gripped Mr. Fitz's left hand.

Sensations flooded her mind. *Hand held, warmth, comfort,* followed by disappointment. *Not her hand. Just a hand.*

"Mr. Fitz?" she called again, her voice increasingly distant to her own ears as her sense of self was tugged away, away, away, as if it swirled down a drain.

Her awareness rested within Mr. Fitz.

His heart beat steadily. He digested food. He was warm. He was . . . content. There was a pulse within him that wasn't his heart.

It was . . . it was his soul.

To her consciousness, his soul was vivacious jazz, a thick blanket on a cold winter's night. She innately understood his soul was intact. Whole. As solid as a soul could be. Silas's photograph of Mr. Fitz and his hovering soul had undoubtedly been manipulated with double exposure, just as she and Rex had suspected.

But for all its thriving life, the soul was still. Dormant. Like a sleeping kitten, all energy constrained. The reason for that, she could also detect. His brain held what could only be considered dead spots. It was a mass of healed scars and gaps, but the very damage that constrained his soul also deadened pain. Many sensations simply couldn't be conveyed. His brain contained deep canyons and no bridges. She comprehended that this damage could be a terrible thing—Mr. Fitz could break a limb and not even know—but it also freed him in a major way. Mr. Fitz had only a vague awareness of his placement on the floor and that he was cold.

Over that awareness, over everything else, was a quiet, calm question. *Where is she?*

She. Mrs. Fitz.

Fayette felt her own distant body hitch a breath as she sobbed. He still knew his wife. He loved her—more than that, he was in love with her. His craving for her presence, his intense memory of the comfort she created for him, radiated through him like heat. He couldn't move on his own, but his hearing awaited her voice. His nose, her familiar soap and perfume. The skin of his cheeks yearned for the silken texture of the fine black hairs of her head as she nuzzled close. He could see her, when she was right before him, and she was *beautiful*. His lips couldn't curve in a smile, but his soul could smile. Oh, how it could smile.

Mrs. Fitz had drained her family's coffers to find the means to cure him, to make him whole again, but he was as intact as he could ever be. Gerald Fitz had been here all along, loving her, but he could never fully wake up. All the magic in this wayline couldn't rebuild his brain, nor could Mother's blessed bread cure him.

And yet Mr. Fitz's continued existence was a miracle. The love of Mr. and Mrs. Fitz was a miracle.

Fayette slipped her hand from the limp curve of Mr. Fitz's fingers, and full awareness of her own body and where she was returned to her. The house was bleeding out for no purpose.

Silas's uncontrolled magical assault needed to stop, but how? He said his efforts to end the ritual had been in vain—but what did Silas really know, anyway? He'd believed his own manipulated photography. He didn't know how to conduct a legitimate magical ritual. He sure didn't know how to end one.

Fayette pivoted while still in a crouch and, with the full width of her hand, smeared the broad chalk lines that separated Mr. Fitz from the worst of the house's wounds. Whatever happened, she knew he wouldn't endure the house's pain as she had.

With an audible pop, the concentrated magic swirled outward, orange-pink-yellow-blue flashing, and butted against the outermost ring. As she watched, the magic lifted up and then funneled downward into the outermost chalk writing. In two seconds, three, four, the colors were gone.

The house shuddered and sighed.

"Gerald!" Mrs. Fitz pushed away from Art and flung herself into the circle. Now-harmless chalk smeared and puffed up in a brief, low fog as she skidded on her knees to join her husband. She wrapped her arms around him, their faces together. "I'm here, Gerald, I'm here. Are you well? Are you *there*?" The weight of hope in that last word about broke Fayette's heart.

She stood, cringing as she straightened her legs after so long in a crouch. "Mrs. Fitz, he's been there all along."

Mrs. Fitz craned her neck to look up at her without letting go of her husband. "What do you mean?"

"His whole soul is there, intact. It's not wandering elsewhere. His brain, though . . . it healed as much as it could, but he can't interact with the world—"

"He's imprisoned, you're saying?" she rasped out.

Fayette felt Rex step up beside her. Funny how she knew the weight of his steps so well after a week of acquaintance. "I wouldn't call him 'imprisoned' at all. He's not in torment. He can't fully feel physical pain, and he's not in mental agony, either. It's more like his soul is dozing along with his body. The important thing, though, is that he recognizes when you're with him. He still knows you through all of his senses. When I grabbed his hand, he wanted it to be yours. He knows your smell. Your everything. *You're* his everything."

Mrs. Fitz's gaunt face flashed myriad emotions in quick sequence. Joy. Sorrow. Elation. Despair. "You mean, I can . . . I can never— He can never—"

"He's as well as he'll ever be, Mrs. Fitz. He's with you. He's home. He's probably happier than most people in this world."

Fayette's words shattered the last fragile pane of hope. Mrs. Fitz collapsed over her husband, sobbing.

Fayette released a rattling breath as she trailed a hand down her face. Good grief, but she was tired. Rex gave her a slight tap, and she took that as a cue to lean on him. Art stood on her other side, ready to act as a support if she tipped the other way.

"You're dead wrong," Rex quietly said.

Fayette frowned at him. "What about? When I described how Mr. Fitz—"

"No, what you said as you entered that circle, ever so ready to nobly sacrifice yourself because you're an unloved orphan. The latter point is unfortunately true, as you are an orphan, but you have someone who loves you, right here." He tapped his chest. "I imagine I'm not the only one, either."

She gave a small nod of acknowledgment. He was right. She had friends and neighbors who'd mourn her. Luis. April. Many others. Her grief had distorted her view, like bright lights over a full stage of people narrowing to a single, selfish spotlight. Rex, of all people, understood how that worked.

Fayette looked past him and saw the wall of the house.

"Oh no," she wailed. "Oh no."

The house seemed to have aged fifty years in mere minutes. The log walls were cracked and dry. There were holes in the floor, whole missing boards. The window shutters dangled, some gone completely. The floor was *dirty*, covered with a film of filth from the degrading structure—and there were large feathers, too. Looking up confirmed that there were gaps in the roof, gray sky visible above.

Panic spiked through her. "I poured the magic back into the house, but it's not improving. House, what's going on? You're there, aren't you?"

Magic quivered against her skin. The house wasn't dead. Had Silas's magic created something akin to gangrene?

Silas. He was still here, and had the audacity to gaze around with blatant fascination.

Fayette pointed at him. "This man's presence tortures this house. He needs to be evicted from the property."

Silas looked stunned. "I torture the house? How?"

"You're stained by magic of all kinds. You've dabbled like a toddler throwing oil paints, acrylics, water colors, gesso—and made yourself into a repulsive mess. You need to go."

"But I-I wasn't trying to—"

Art advanced toward Silas with a bright smile that radiated menace. "Might I have the honor of escorting you outside?"

Silas backed toward the door, hands up. "Fine, fine, I'll go." He tripped over his satchel, smacking the floor, then scrambled to his feet with the bag in his hands. "No need to play Jack Dempsey, now. I didn't mean to harm this house. I didn't know!"

"That's the problem," said Fayette. "For all the books you own, you don't know much at all, but what you do know is enough to cause people devastating harm—and this house is a person, sure as anyone is."

"But I didn't—" Silas began, the protest ending in an alarmed squeak as Art rushed him. Out the door they went.

"Hustle him all the way to the street!" yelled Rex.

"I will!" Art's voice was faint. "Sorry, there!"

Sorry? Surely he wasn't apologizing to Silas? Just as Fayette began to turn away, a short figure slipped through the doorway.

Heidi.

Chapter 40

I hurt, I hurt so much. I'm broken, I'm *dirty*, I almost died, the other witch is a growing speck at the horizon, and *this* is the moment when my new witch steps inside my walls for the first time since she fled years ago, her exit so panicked that she fell off the cliff and into the sea and almost died, and I could do nothing to help her.

When that happened, I was depleted from carrying us over the ocean, freshly bereft without my witch. And angry. I admit it, Mother, I was angry that my new witch rejected me. My witch had given everything to save her, everything, and my new witch was so ungrateful for this gift that she then forsook me.

I realize the truth now. She didn't mean to abandon me. She was scared. So very scared. She's still scared, but she's here, she's here, she's here.

Hello, my new witch. Hello! Can you hear me? Please, please say you can hear me! I'm so happy to welcome you inside my walls!

Chapter 41

"I can hear you," Heidi whispered, glancing up at the ceiling. "Mrs. Fitz, how are you? How is your husband? Is he unharmed?" Her accent added huskiness to her words. She inched forward as if across thick ice, her focus on the Fitzes.

They were why she'd braved her fear. Why she'd stopped running.

Mrs. Fitz sat up, her lips slack. "Heidi? You can talk? Did the magic—"

"I could always talk. I chose not to." She stepped to one side as the clatter of footsteps on wood announced Art's return. He was brushing off his hands with an air of satisfaction.

"Oh. You chose not to. I see." Mrs. Fitz's voice was hollow with shock. "Mr. Fitz is well. As well as he can be, according to Miss Wynne. He . . . he cannot be healed, but his soul is intact, she says. He knows me." Fresh tears streamed down her cheeks.

"I'm glad. Now you no longer need to call upon mediums! You have your answer."

Art looked at her with sudden interest. "You! Your accent. You're definitely Russian!"

Heidi's eyes fluttered shut, pained. "This is why I dared not speak to anyone, but I knew I couldn't hold back forever. I've practiced my languages in private for years so that I would not lose my abilities, and now, now . . ."

Rex turned to Fayette. "That's our confirmation. She *is* Russian, to match a Russian house."

Fayette took a step closer to Heidi, who made no effort to run this time, but she did tremble, as the house had minutes before. "Heidi, this place has terrified you. It still does. Why didn't you leave Carmel, go elsewhere?"

"For the same reason why I entered the house today. Mrs. Fitz needs me. And her husband, too. I had to come in to help them. I had to." She knotted her fingers at her waist.

"Art," Fayette said, "you mentioned that stories about Baba Yaga usually featured royalty, right?" Heidi stood a little taller, a little braver. Bracing herself for the words that Fayette was about to say.

"Yes?" Art looked between Heidi and Fayette, bewildered.

"This house and Heidi arrived here in late July 1918."

Art covered his gasp with a trembling hand. "You cannot be saying that she—that she is—"

"I am Grand Duchess Anastasia Nikolaevna." Heidi—Anastasia—no longer looked the part of the meek maid. She stood, short and defiant, life radiant in her flushed cheeks and bright eyes.

Heidi was a true Russian royal. One of the most famous people in the entire world. All along, she'd been a better actor than Rex or any person out of Hollywood, but her fear had been real. The fear had made her persona real.

"The person the papers call Princess Anastasia," Fayette said, still in shock even though the various hints and letters were a perfect fit in this crossword puzzle.

"No!" said Art as he took a step back, scrutinizing her. "Your whole family—"

"Was executed, yes. I died as well. My true body is with my family even now, but I had already met Baba Yaga."

"You made a deal," Fayette murmured.

"After I passed her tests, yes. She was tired. She could see enough of the future to know the horrors that the Bolsheviks were likely to create. She knew her old world was no more. She said she'd save me if I assumed her role." Her brows drew together in agony. "I pleaded with her to save my family. She wouldn't. She couldn't. I had passed her tests, and I alone would be saved. I didn't understand how she would go about that. I didn't know that I would feel my own death, that she'd steal away my soul, use her own flesh to form me a new body that looked like the old." Her fist pressed against her chest as if to hold her heart inside.

"Baba Yaga's last magic propelled her hut from Russia, to where I might be safe," Anastasia said. "We landed here." She looked upward again. "I'm glad you understand why I ran, and I'm sorry. I'm sorry you had to wait."

"Do you hear the house?" Rex asked. She nodded.

Fayette felt sick with horror at what Anastasia had endured. She had survived, but at such a cost. "You went through all of that, to almost die in the ocean here."

"Yes." Her grin was sardonic. "My recovery was long. I had many broken bones. I couldn't walk. I told myself I would return here soon, when I was ready, and yet . . ." Anastasia's voice faltered as she looked around the house. "That medium, he did this damage? Or was this . . . me?"

She obviously hadn't stepped in the house since she'd fled in 1918. "No. The house was in wonderful condition an hour ago. Immaculate. Silas bled the house's magic away in his uncontrolled effort to help Mr. Fitz."

"There's more magic yet," Anastasia murmured. "A vast deposit beneath us. You can't pull it in fast enough on your own, can you, house?" Her head tilted to one side. "I see. You need to work with your witch? I have no training. I know nothing. I am more ignorant than Silas Pennington. But you—you can teach me? And, what? Another Baba Yaga is nearly here, and she intends to—"

The wide-eyed terror on her face sent a chill through Fayette. For an instant, she was afraid that Anastasia would run again, but then her eyes clenched shut as if she were in physical pain.

"I didn't mean to be ungrateful," she murmured, apparently speaking to the house. "I didn't mean for you to suffer. I will not allow you to suffer more. I will not!" Her eyes opened again with a flash of determination.

Anastasia began to walk around the walls, her hand trailing over the logs. As she passed, chunks of wood flew up from the floor and back into place. A window shutter righted itself and became whole, then promptly opened to reveal sky. Feathers flew up through holes in the ceiling, wood coming together to patch the gap. On and on she went. The eroded bricks of the oven gained fullness again as the fire blazed. Candles blossomed, brilliant as peonies.

"She is the grand duchess. The dead grand duchess," Art murmured.

"Does she look familiar?" Fayette asked.

His laugh verged on hysterical. "Familiar? I saw the czar and his family in grainy pictures in the paper, as most everyone did, and she was a child back then." He shook his head. "I was in the army, but I cannot say I had any devotion to her family. Nor did I ever expect the Revolution to take the turns that it did."

"Do you think—" Fayette began.

Heidi whirled around on a foot to face them. "You must get out of the house right away. *She's here!*"

No clarification was needed. Fayette dashed for Mrs. Fitz, while the men went to Mr. Fitz and began to haul him out. "What about you?" Fayette called as she reached the door.

"I'm not leaving the house," she said. "Not again."

"Heidi, we can't leave Heidi—" Mrs. Fitz stepped outside, only to whirl around again.

"No." Fayette hooked an arm around her. "She and the house will take care of each other. Don't distract her, not now."

"Remember how to fly, house!" Fayette yelled as she helped Mrs. Fitz down the rocks.

They reached the dirt and grass. Fayette used her free hand to grab Mr. Fitz's wheeled chair. She dragged it behind her up to the tree line, where Rex met her and helped Mrs. Fitz into the road.

"Is this far enough?" he asked, looking around. Silas, fortunately, had demonstrated enough wisdom to hightail it away.

A revelation struck Fayette with icy-cold horror. "No!" she yelled, spinning around. "Mother!"

It would be horrible for Anastasia and the house to be lost in this battle, but Mother— Oh, Mother! If the house succumbed to the witch, if the witch got hold of Mother . . .

Another member of Fayette's family, gone.

"She's survived much," said Rex. "Have faith."

Faith, faith. Fayette didn't know what to believe anymore, what to pray, what to hope.

"Heidi. My Heidi." Mrs. Fitz wept, leaning over the chair handles. Art had set up Mr. Fitz in the chair again, and he slumped there, his shirt absorbing his wife's tears.

"There!" Art yelled, pointing upward. They gasped in a chorus, their view apparently unobscured by a fog of enchantment.

The other house was crystalline white, sunlight sparkling upon its icy shell. Fayette had read that airplane pilots struggled with cold at higher altitudes, but no human pilot could have survived in such a frozen contraption. Its windows could only be recognized as sunken divots, like a mummy's skin pulled taut over a skull, its door like a tunnel leading into a black maw. The ice had to be feet thick. Even so, smoke billowed from a tall chimney, and the long black-and-white-streaked wings were free of frost, as were the massive chicken feet tucked beneath.

A screechy roar emerged from the icy house. An undeniable crow of triumph.

A strange wrenching sound emerged from the cliff house. Black-and-white-speckled wings suddenly stretched from the two windowless sides of the little izba. With a soft, defiant bleat, the house rose upward. The cliff was left eerily empty.

The two houses began to circle each other in the air, each one screeching at a different pitch. The icy coating on the other witch's house made it look twice as big, but as Fayette studied them both, she realized the other house was larger to begin with. It had to be two stories, the wings stretched out ten, fifteen feet wide.

The icy house dived at the little izba, clawed feet outstretched—an attack. The house dodged, barely, the beating of its wings uneven. It hadn't flown in years, and it showed.

"Our little house is going to be crushed," cried Rex. "It's like a chick in comparison."

"How can Heidi, my girl, know what to do?" wailed Mrs. Fitz. "She doesn't know how to be a witch."

"No, she doesn't," Fayette said. "But she knows how to run and survive. Fly away!" she screamed to the heavens. "This isn't a fair fight! Go! Run, house, run! I love you! Don't die!"

Chapter 42

I am pretty certain I am about to die, and I don't want to—not at all. Especially now that I have my new witch!

I dodged my sister's first attack. I am lucky that she is slow because she is exhausted from the long flight, but I am slow because I haven't flown in years.

Down below, the woman yells for me to fly away. She loves me. She doesn't want me to die.

I know she is thinking of the other people she has loved who have died, and of Mother, too. Mother is safely encased in my oven bricks at the moment, too—not that this will keep her well if I am defeated.

Thank you for your strong faith in me, Mother! I need that support so much right now. I appreciate your healing miasma, too, as I am still not fully recovered from Stinky's assault. I don't know if I could have flown without your help.

I can read the other witch's intent right now. She is mad that she left Rus and came all this way, and now she can't readily walk inside me and do as she pleases.

If she cannot have me, she will destroy me. But she would still much rather have me.

My new witch sits harnessed to a chair I created near a window so she can see outside. She asks me how we can fight back.

How can we possibly survive this? That is what she is really asking but cannot put into her hoarse words.

My sister's massive feet kick at me again, the claws flashing like the shashkas carried by Cossacks. My wings beat hard to carry me away.

I don't know, I don't know! My sister is bigger than me, and she went up really high and is covered in thick ice and I don't want to hurt her anyway! She didn't choose to do this!

My new witch wonders if she can bargain with the other one.

This witch is crueler and harsher than my own old witch.

She nods, unsurprised. My new witch showed unusual discernment in how she researched and chose which witch she approached to make her deal. She is clever, but she is also terrified.

My new witch doesn't know what to do. She doesn't know how to wield magic, truly—she only healed me because I was still upon the wayline and I knew what needed to be done. I don't know what to do now! I am a house; I am not a witch!

What do I do, what do I do, what do I do?!

I see the town below and the cliff where I was stuck for so many years, and I think of how when I first came to this place, I sensed the power available here but not the precariousness of the ledge, and I realize that I can attempt something that may fail terribly and result in my lumber being grafted to my sister and my feathers used for witch's hats, but I must try because I cannot win a physical fight.

If we're going to survive, I must use my wits because that's the only way to survive a witch of Rus.

I'm going to try a feint! I don't know if it will work, but—

My new witch cheers me on as she holds tight to her chair as it heaves her side to side. I am bobbing around a lot and she is feeling sick. I hope she doesn't vomit, because I can't clean it up right away, and oh, I hate vomit on my floor! But I hate the idea of dying even more.

Mother, thank you for your encouragement! I'm going to do this, I am. I'm going to try!

I spread out my wings and glide back down to the cliff.

My toes clutch the mound of rocks, but I do so lightly, straddling the hole where I roosted for years. The contact allows me to draw power to keep me buoyant, which is essential because I cannot flap my wings now. I am posing as if I am trying to reenergize myself in a vain effort to keep up the fight. I am now an actor, like my friend the man. Ha!

My posturing succeeds, because I can sense the other witch's triumph and my sister's relief that the fight is at an end. The peers of my brood were never as sensitive as I was when it came to the ways of quests. They were brawnier, less inclined to introspection. More obedient. That is why I was the last adopted from my nest, why my witch was mocked for being stuck with me.

But I'm a good house—I am. The woman and man said so, and I will prove it to my new witch now.

Or I will soon be dead.

The other house glides down, claws straining for the rocks. She will land mere feet away. The land is at a steep slope there, but she has no intention to nest, only to be close enough for the witch to open the door and bid me to face her.

My sister does not know the fragility of the cliff beneath us. She does not know to lighten her weight, nor could she effectively do so if she tried, for she is large and incredibly weary.

The cliff was further weakened during my struggle against Stinky. It can barely support me now, as light as I am. It definitely cannot hold us both.

As soon as her weight presses down, there is a magnificent *crack* beneath us that shudders all the way through the spine of my roof. As the cliff drops away, I fling out my wings and fly.

My sister is not ready for the ground to fall from beneath her. She is not ready to fly again.

There is a horrible thud and a crack of lumber.

I am so focused on flight that my witch is the one who tells me what has happened as she peers out the window.

The other house struck the rocks, she says! And then it took to the air again, its icy shell partially broken and one broken leg dangling. There's also a hole near the foundation!

I can hardly believe my idea worked!

But I am still a little sad that the promontory is no more, because although I was stuck there against my will, it was a beautiful place.

My new witch laughs, high-pitched, as she recounts that the other house is flying away, back over the ocean.

As I know the shifts in the wind, I comprehend the alterations in quests.

My sister should land here in order to heal, but the witch deems the energy here to be inferior and will not corrupt her personal residence so. And yet she thought harvesting my parts would've been fine, though I'd been here for years. Human logic is a strange thing. The biggest motivation for their departure, however, is that the other witch will not deign to set foot on land that is not Rus.

They are leaving. They . . . are actually leaving.

In the depths of the heart of my oven, I understand that this is no feint. My sister is hurt, but even more, the other witch is also badly injured, for she did not anticipate the impact. They will both know great suffering on their flight back across the world's biggest sea.

I am sorry that my sister is hurt, as she did not want this battle, and I am also sorry that the witch is hurt, as there are few of her kind left in this world. But I am glad, so very glad, that I will not be murdered and plundered.

I am a clever house!

I feel my witch's profound gratitude and it makes me want to swirl and dance in the air, and so I do, gently so as to not make her ill, and she laughs.

Down below, I hear the woman and man and the others are cheering and clapping!

And Mother! I am honored to earn the accolades of an ancient and holy sourdough starter! Such clamor and praise, for me!

I almost like this attention as much as a hug and a kiss. But not quite.

Chapter 43

"You did it, house!" Fayette yelled and bounced on her feet, a fist pumping in the air. She hadn't cheered like this since she used to watch Thayer's baseball games ages ago.

The flying house tottered as it drifted downward to land in the road.

"Hollywood's tricks will seem like nothing after a sight such as this," Art murmured, shaking his head.

The house's front door opened, but seconds ticked by, and no one appeared. Rex stepped forward, his expression worried.

"I'm coming!" rang out Anastasia's voice, even raspier than before. "I am sorry. The movement . . . It is hard to walk."

"She's probably feeling as sick as if she's been on a sailboat in a hurricane, the way the house was lurching about," said Mrs. Fitz as she laid a hand on her husband's shoulder. "I'm sure she's fine, dear. Don't worry."

Anastasia finally staggered into the doorway and leaned there. She had been of a pale complexion before, but her skin was now imbued with the sickly sheen of an egg white.

A short staircase made of wood flowed out from the stoop to reach the pavement, five steps total. She hesitated a moment before slowly treading down. The house's wings tucked close to its log walls and then vanished.

"Heidi!" Mrs. Fitz pushed past Fayette. "Oh! I suppose I shouldn't even call you that now—"

"No. You *must* call me that name," Heidi said, clutching Mrs. Fitz's hands. "I will always be Heidi to you—to all of you. Especially you." She looked at Art with particular concern.

"Don't worry about me." Art regarded her with fists on his hips, his words blunt. "Did you see me bow down in obeisance? No. Did you see me scream at you because of the sins of your father? No. We are both refugees here in America. We are equals."

Heidi regarded him with a stony face and then nodded, relaxing. "Equals. Yes."

"How did you manage to survive that battle?" asked Rex.

"I don't fully know." Heidi shakily laughed as she pivoted to regard the house. "The house came up with the plan to use the cliff. I was useless. Yes, I was," she said, seemingly in response to the house.

"I say give yourself more credit. You've had a pretty rough first half hour as a witch," Fayette said.

Mrs. Fitz pulled Heidi close to stroke her hair. "What are you going to do now? You're— This house. Oh, this is all such a shock!"

"I don't have to leave Carmel right away, but the house will need to land elsewhere soon." Heidi cleared her throat. "I am sorry. I haven't talked this much in many years. Fayette. The house wants me to thank you for your kindness, today and through the past week."

"The house was kind to us in turn. It gave us shelter and it brought us women from around the world who needed help. We fed them bread."

Heidi looked thoughtful. "I'm being told about this—but, house, save more details for later, please! The bread you used to help others . . . oh. Now I am sorry for what happened with the dough earlier today."

"You were right to be concerned about it," Fayette said. "My starter's still inside the house. Is it . . . is it fine if I fetch the jar right now? Mother's all right, isn't she?"

Heidi's smile comforted her. "She is, yes. The house encased her in oven bricks during the fight. She is back on her shelf now."

"Oh." Fayette blinked fast and then guffawed. "Well, then. Here I was, imagining that jar falling and slip-sliding and breaking. Of course the house took care of things."

Fayette had entered the house many times now, but she felt strange doing so with it facing a different way. The mood inside felt different, too. Brighter, lit by something other than candles, fire, and fading sunlight.

Mother was where she had been last set. Fayette cupped the jar with both hands.

"I'm so glad that you're all right," Fayette murmured, tears in her eyes.

Mother's magic stayed at an even thrum. Not one bubble popped across her top, but then, she had just been agitated for a while. She'd perk right up after being divided and fed.

Fayette gathered her bread supplies into her canvas bag, but she wouldn't tuck Mother amid everything else. She held the jar against her breast as she approached the first door. It wavered as if it might close in her face.

"House?" she asked, surprised. "Oh. Of course. You became good friends with Mother, didn't you? I'm glad for that."

The door wavered a few seconds before opening wide. The front door remained open.

"You don't need to stay in Carmel, not because of me," Mrs. Fitz was saying as she squeezed Heidi's arm. "I've kept you here for almost ten years. You . . . you should see the world. Well, more of it. I can't believe you scrubbed my floors."

"Mrs. Fitz. To you, I am always Heidi, the girl you saved from the sea. I think I would like to help more people in such a way. Even more—yes, house would like that, too." Heidi smiled at the building.

Fayette looked down at Mother in her hands, then back at the house.

"Fayette?" Rex murmured as he stepped close. "You seem like you're about to make a serious decision."

"Are you reading my mind?" she asked him. "If so, stop it. That's creepy."

He quietly laughed. "I can't read your brain any better than I can read Cyrillic, but I saw the sadness and determination on your face just now. Whatever you're preparing to do, just know you're not alone."

Fayette smiled at him, then turned to face Heidi. "Here." She thrust the jar toward her.

"You—you're giving Mother to me?" Heidi asked, astonishment on her face.

"I think it's what Mother wants," Fayette said. There was no fluctuation of power to verify this, not outside the house, but Fayette didn't need that sensation to know that this was the right choice. "Her discard approved of you earlier, and I reckon Mother understands why you couldn't reciprocate. She knows more than any of us, I think. My granny used to wonder if Mother came down from heaven at some point to grace humanity, and I look back now and see that my family hasn't shared that blessing as we ought have. We hoarded her. Why Mother tolerated that, I don't know, but . . . that needs to stop. If you're going to set out with the house and help people, as you've already helped people in town, me included . . . well. That's good work."

Heidi had a reverent expression, as if she'd been handed a crown. "I'd be honored to take care of Mother." A smile teased her lips. "House is ecstatic."

"I'm glad." She resisted the urge to list how best to care for a magical starter. Heidi was a baker; she'd figure things out. Besides, the house could act as mediator when it came to Mother's needs. She passed her canvas bag of supplies to Heidi as well.

The shrill beep of a car horn caused Fayette to jump. A black Model T, its top down, rolled up to the group. "Why're you lot standing in the road like a bunch of geese?" The driver scowled at them. "You all oughta . . ." His expression went slack. "We'll go to the beach up in town, after all. There's gotta be parking somewhere. We just need to keep trying."

He backed up the car, giving Fayette a view of three blank-eyed children in the back seat. The vehicle rumbled back toward Carmel.

"You could see the moment the enchantment sank into him," Rex murmured. "I expected it, and yet that was still bizarre."

"We should move," Heidi said, nodding. "Some people may be trapped to the south. They can't be kept circling there."

"Heidi . . ." Mrs. Fitz rushed to give her another hug.

"I will see you soon, very soon. There is a spot above Carmel that is cleared because houses will be built there. We will land there, for now." Heidi looked from Mrs. Fitz to Fayette. "We are still having cock-a-leekie and bannocks, yes?"

"I hope so," said Fayette with a smile. "I'm famished."

Today, she was hungry. Today, she would eat. Tomorrow, well, she'd work through that as it happened.

"Oh, yes, Heidi. There's enough food for everyone," said Mrs. Fitz. As she took a step back, she regarded the house with pursed lips. "I think, perhaps, this isn't Satan's henhouse after all." She gave it a brisk nod of approval and, with that, returned to the chair. "You must be very hungry after this excitement today, Gerald," she said to her husband, her voice growing fainter as she pushed the rolling chair away.

Heidi reentered the house. The stairs withdrew in her wake.

"We'll be there soon to help you get him inside, Mrs. Fitz," Fayette called. "She's going to need support to get by if Heidi's not there all the time," she added to Rex and Art.

Rex smiled. "I'm thinking that an anonymous old friend from the army can send a windfall their way."

Art laughed. "You sly fox."

Fayette's mind had reached its new-things-I-can-handle capacity for the day, and it took her a moment to understand. "You're going to help them out?"

A blush tinged his cheeks as he shrugged. "That seems like a good use for the money I've stacked away in the bank. Mrs. Fitz can't ever know it comes from me, of course. She'd refuse, quite indignant. But if it comes from someone who holds her husband in fondness and respect, and there's no clear way to return the funds, well."

Oh, but she adored this man. He had a good heart. He wanted to help people.

She realized, with a sudden surge of affection, she wanted to help him, too.

Fayette blinked back tears. "You meant what you said in the house a while ago, about me being loved?"

"Rex isn't one to lie," said Art.

"No, he's not." Fayette took a steadying breath. "I'm pondering that proposal of yours some more. I'm not saying yes, mind. Just pondering. This can't be a conversation for just the two of us." She nodded toward Art, who looked between them, bewildered.

"A proposal? I can guess what that's about, but that seems like a big topic to address right now. This has been a very long day for me, I'll have you know."

"Yes, a very long day for me, too," said Fayette. "A long month, and we're all of four days in. Things are complex in my life right now. I have a lot to figure out."

"There's no rush," Rex added quickly.

"Besides, if you rush, people will think Fayette is pregnant," Art said. "What?" He affected shocked innocence as they burst out laughing. "I saw the papers before I left, about how Rex Hallstrom broke sweet Margaret Proudlock's heart because of this new woman. Fayette is not too old for such a thing to happen, and the reporters will say so."

"Oh, Art," Rex groaned. "You're not selling the idea to her."

"I will try to do that later, because if this proposal is along the lines that I think it is, the idea carries merit. As Fayette said, however, things are complex, especially for people like us."

People like us. A wind smarted Fayette's eyes as wings sprouted again from the house's walls; with one beat, two, three, the house was aloft, turning this way and that. What a strange yet beautiful sight! What would it be like to fly in such a house—to gaze out the windows and see the full spread of the ocean? She shook her head in awe. She'd never even been in an airplane.

"Let's mosey on," Fayette said, facing north. "Mrs. Fitz will need a hand about now, and I'm getting hungry. Soup and bread sound heavenly."

Chapter 44

My new witch is here, here, here, and she's not scared anymore. Well, maybe a tiny bit, but that only seems right. It feels good to fly again after such a long time! If I'd given things a lot of thought a short while ago, I would've doubted that I could still fly at all. I certainly wouldn't have thought that I could've made it through an aerial battle, but then the moment came and I *had* to fly and fight, I had to, and I did!

Sometimes, I suppose, you don't think, you just spread your wings and take to the air, like when first leaving the nest.

The woman and the man are good friends to me, and I like the man's man, too. My old witch would've liked him, his blood smelling of Rus, but I like him because his presence helps the first man to feel at home.

I now realize that people can be home. That when I lost my old witch, I lost my own sense of home, even though I am a house.

My new witch is by an open window, the wind blowing her hair loose from its braid. She is enjoying the view, which she didn't have the chance to do the last time we were in the air. She is still holding Mother.

Mother, Mother, do you like the view?

Oh. Well, that's good that you like being held because you *are* being held!

I think I would like to have the woman, man, and other man here again so that I can show them how the world looks from up high, how the horizon curves, how the air tastes different. That seems like the kind of thing a friend would share, and I'm their friend.

I'm a good house, a good home, a good friend. I really am.

Author's Note

Fayette Wynne is in many ways a tribute to my own maternal ancestors of a century ago, which included a great-grandmother from Sturkie, Arkansas, and a great-grandfather who worked in the oil fields of both Coalinga and Los Angeles. Fayette's family, however, came over in the 1890s, while my lines didn't come west until the 1920s.

While much of the cast is fictional, a few real-life people are featured. Swedish-born August "Gus" Englund, also known as the Marshal, was indeed Carmel's lone cop and general helper through the 1920s. He and his horse, Beauty, made regular rounds through town. Perry Newberry was mayor and city trustee of Carmel in the 1920s and also edited the *Carmel Pine Cone*, one of two local newspapers from the decade that can be found in digital form at Archive.org. Many American towns through this era had "boosterism" efforts to draw in people and jobs; in stark contrast, Carmel resisted modernization and tourism, seeking to preserve the beauty and size of their unique town.

A note of apology to the Carmel Library, too, for making a fictitious librarian into an antagonist. Librarians are figures of immense power, especially in these days, when lifesaving books are being threatened by censorship. Please, support your local libraries, including the Friends of the Library.

Mrs. Neele is, of course, Agatha Christie. I have long been fascinated by the eleven-day period of 1926 in which she went missing, and I'm not alone: Her disappearance made international headlines at the time and created an uproar when she was found physically unharmed at the Swan Hydropathic Hotel in Harrogate, North Yorkshire. When she booked her room there, she provided the name "Mrs. Neele," which was actually the surname of her husband's mistress. Some people believe, to this day, that Christie contrived the entire episode for publicity; I am inclined to believe that she suffered a catastrophic mental breakdown as a result of her beloved mother's death, her husband's callous extramarital affair, and the immense pressures of an accelerating career.

The studio pressure that Rex endures is, unfortunately, based in reality. William Haines is probably the most famous "out" star of the era, openly living with his male partner beginning in 1926. He repeatedly resisted demands from boss Louis B. Mayer that he pretend to have a girlfriend or to marry, and in 1933, when the full Hollywood Code was enacted, he lost his acting career. Billy Haines cultivated a new successful career, however, as one of the most in-demand Hollywood interior designers for decades.

Considerable research went into this book. These works, among others, were valuable resources:

- Beauchamp, Cari. *Without Lying Down: Frances Marion and the Powerful Women of Early Hollywood.*
- Benedict, Marie. *The Mystery of Mrs. Christie: A Novel.*
- Bertsch, Marguerite. *How to Write for Moving Pictures: A Manual of Instruction and Information.* (1917)
- Brownlow, Kevin. *The Parade's Gone By.*
- Cary, Diana Serra. *The Hollywood Posse: The Story of a Gallant Band of Horsemen Who Made Movie History.*
- Christie, Agatha. *The Last Séance: Tales of the Supernatural.*
- Christie, Agatha. *The Secret Adversary.*
- Christie, Agatha, and Matthew Prichard. *The Grand Tour: Letters and Photographs from the British Empire Expedition 1922.*
- Emerson, John, and Anita Loos. *Breaking Into the Movies.* (1921)

- Emerson, John, and Anita Loos. *How to Write Photoplays.* (1920)
- Forrester, Sibelan, Helena Goscilo, and Martin Skoro, editors. *Baba Yaga: The Wild Witch of the East in Russian Fairy Tales.*
- Houdini, Harry. *A Magician Among the Spirits.* (This is the work referenced by Fayette, wherein Houdini analyzes and dissects how spiritualists operate.)
- London, Jack. *Valley of the Moon.* (Insightful in its depiction of Bohemian-era Carmel. Also, emphatically racist.)
- Mann, William J. *Wisecracker: The Life and Times of William Haines, Hollywood's First Openly Gay Star.*
- Matich, Olga. "The White Emigration Goes Hollywood." *The Russian Review*, Apr. 2005, Vol. 64, No. 2, pp. 187–210.
- Robinson, Harlow. *Russians in Hollywood, Hollywood's Russians: Biography of an Image.*
- Worsley, Lucy. *Agatha Christie: An Elusive Woman.* (The three-part TV series based on the book, shown on American PBS, is also wonderful.)
- *100 Delicious Walnut Recipes*, California Walnut Growers Association. (Circa 1920s) (Mrs. Fitz makes the toasted walnut sandwiches. Bought from an antiques mall in Rogers, Arkansas.)

I'm grateful for thorough early draft–critique reads from Rebecca Roland and Yaroslav Barsukov. As ever, my agent, Rebecca Strauss at DeFiore & Co., provided daunting yet incredibly useful feedback that resulted in a better book. The team at 47North has been wonderfully supportive. I've been honored to work with editor Marilyn Brigham on this book. Clarence A. Haynes's developmental edits helped me to coax out more of the novel's soul; I'm grateful that we've been able to work together on three books thus far.

My husband, Jason Cato, is my stalwart support. None of my books would exist without him. I'm glad he didn't mind that I had to develop and maintain a sourdough starter (which, of course, is named Mother) as part of my research for the book. The baking experiments ranged from basic boules to chocolate sourdough-loaf cakes. Look for the recipes on my long-running food blog, *Bready or Not*, found at BethCato.com. There, one may peruse hundreds of recipes, many of which are cookies and bars, all of them available for free and without ads. Follow me on social media to see pictures of my bakes and my latest cheese acquisitions.

Lastly, thank you for reading this book. All too many of us are familiar with the view from the edge of the cliff. You may be a stranger to me, but I'm glad you're here.

Book Club Questions

1. Have you ever visited or lived in an area like Carmel-by-the-Sea, a place that touches the soul through its intense peace and beauty? If you have visited Carmel, what was your own experience like?

2. Fayette and Rex both work in the silent-film industry. Were you familiar with any of the films and actors mentioned in the novel? Would you be interested in watching 1920s films now that you know more about the creative process?

3. "Hope could be like bread, and difficult to ingest and digest at times." Do you agree that hope can be a difficult thing to grasp? What has helped you to better "ingest and digest" hope in your life?

4. Mother, as a sourdough starter, has no voice. How do you think that Mother's love for the Wynne family comes across? If you were in Fayette's position, do you think you would have become resentful of Mother as well?

5. Fayette's family "broke bread" using Mother's leaven for over a century. What food traditions are shared within your family? If you could choose a food item and imbue it with magical power, what would it be and what would the magic do?

6. Spiritualism was popular in the 1920s as people coped with losses from the Great War and the Influenza Epidemic of 1918, but some elements of its practice can still be found a

century later. Have you ever attended a séance or conferred with a medium? What were those experiences like?

7. The house has taken part in terrible things in the past. How did you feel about the house at first? Did your feelings change as you came to know the house more?

8. "Sometimes a person is so terrible that they must be named so that they can be dealt with." Have you encountered your own version of "Stinky," a person or problem so terrible that a proper name helps you to cope? Did that action help in the end?

9. How would you react if a door to a mysterious place appeared before you? What might induce you to cross through? What food would need to be offered to entice you to eat in this other place?

10. How do you feel about the ending? How do you think this found family will adapt after Fayette and Rex return to Hollywood?

About the Author

Beth Cato is the Nebula Award–nominated author of the Clockwork Dagger series, the Blood of Earth trilogy, and the Chefs of the Five Gods series. Her short stories and poetry can be found in hundreds of publications, including *Fantasy Magazine*, *Escape Pod*, *Uncanny Magazine*, and the *Magazine of Fantasy & Science Fiction*. Beth hails from Hanford, California, but currently writes and bakes cookies in a Minnesota home that she shares with her husband, son, and two feline overlords. For more information, visit www.bethcato.com.

Printed in Dunstable, United Kingdom

68333321R00173